Other books by Cathy Cash Spellman

FICTION

So Many Partings

An Excess of Love

Paint the Wind

Bless the Child

The Playground of the Gods

NON-FICTION

Notes to my Daughters

PROSE, PRAYER AND POETRY

Snowflake from the Hand of God

The Message

A MURDER
ON JANE STREET

by

CATHY CASH
SPELLMAN

This is a work of fiction. A number of actual historical people appear in these pages and others are discussed along with the fictional characters, but all the actions, incidents and dialogue in this story are products of the author's imagination or are used fictitiously.

A Murder on Jane Street

by Cathy Cash Spellman

For information:

The Wild Harp & Company, Inc.

www.CathyCashSpellman.com

ISBN: 978-0-578-46139-7

Dedication

This book is for my dear and remarkable friend Carol Allen Storey, without whose continuing belief in me and my work, this book would never have come to be.

Prologue

"The past is prologue."
— Shakespeare, *The Tempest*

Prologue

East Berlin, 1990

The elegant woman with the grim expression was nearly seventy, but looked fifty-five. She was deep into the age of invisibility for women. Men no longer made note of her entering or leaving a place, and much as that rankled a once-beautiful woman's psyche, she was counting on it now.

She steeled herself and crossed the entrance of the huge complex that had been the East Berlin headquarters of the dreaded STASI secret police for three decades. The hair rose on her forearms and a chill stiffened her spine, despite her determination and the fact that the beasts had been put down.

The Wall had fallen. The outraged East German people would now ransack the files that had held them hostage. Thirty years of terror didn't die easy. Recordings, photographs, dossiers, collected from frightened neighbors and children coerced into betraying their own parents. STASI files were impeccable. Body swabs and blood samples had been kept in sealed containers so dogs could hunt humans.

Thousands would storm the hated headquarters now, desperate to destroy the data that had kept them powerless. She was only precious hours ahead of the hordes because of all the money that had changed hands so swiftly; the predators so ready to pounce, the oppressed so ready for vengeance. Without makeup, in nondescript jeans and an ancient black turtleneck, her memorable bosom flattened by a sports bra, her once-glorious hair now more pewter than gold, wound tight around her head like an aged Heidi—she would not be recognized. She intended to destroy what memories remained in this godforsaken place, not make new ones.

Her benefactor had paid unscrupulous people an outrageous sum so she could get these files. Everything in East Berlin was now for sale. Including her own past. The squirrel-faced quisling who'd been bribed handed over the file containing the names of her betrayers without comment. She opened the folder to see the face of the torturer. Bile rose in her throat as she fought to breathe. To remember. To forget.

She slipped the grim documents into the bag slung over her shoulder, next to the small Beretta.

Then she disappeared.

Almost completely.

PART I

The Past Is Never Over

"Not the glittering weapon fights the fight, but rather, the hero's heart."

— Proverb

1

New York City, now

The freezing wind whistled down Jane Street. Unusually biting for Greenwich Village, but winter was a bitch this year. FitzHugh Donovan pulled his red wool newsboy cap down tightly on his seventy-three-year-old head and tugged up the collar of his tweed overcoat against the chill as he fumbled for the latchkey to the brownstone he'd owned for fifty mostly good years. But the door flew open from the inside before he could turn the key, and a five-foot-ten explosion of exuberance threw her arms around him and hugged hard.

"You're home early, Grand!" the girl bubbled after disentangling herself. Frost clouds misted from her pretty young mouth as she puffed out the words, then pulled up her muffler higher over her chin.

"And where are you off to in such a mad rush, Finn darlin'?" He smiled back at the child he loved so much; no longer a child, he reminded himself, but a nearly grown-up woman. Where fly the years, he thought as he stepped aside to let the girl hurry down the steps to the street. Turn again, turn again time in thy flight…

"Late for a shoot!" she tossed back over her shoulder, as she hefted her heavy camera bag to a better perch on her strong back and slammed the little wrought iron gate that protected the tiny front garden from the street traffic. "No time for dawdling."

"Will you be home for dinner, luv?" he called after her, marveling as always at the lithe young strength of her as she waved a happy goodbye.

She had the elegant height of her mother's clan, the dark hair of his own Black Irish ancestors, now flying heedless in the icy wind. She looked like a ship in full sail.

"No time for that, either," she shouted merrily against the wintry blast.

"But I love you!" And then she was gone around the corner.

Fitz shook his head with amusement and moved into the warmth of the familiar ground-floor apartment that was his daughter Maeve's part of their shared brownstone home. The huge white dog that greeted him with happy *roo* sounds and muted howls had the body of a wolf, the great black head of a bear, and a jaw that could take down an elk, or so he'd been told about the breed. The curly Akita tail wagged with welcome as a hundred twenty pounds of muscle and fur leaped up for a nuzzle. Fitz ruffled the dog's velvet ears and pushed him back down to the floor. It was fun to be welcomed, not to be bowled over.

"You silly great beast," he chuckled as he backed away enough to shrug out of his coat. "Give me a minute, will you? It's cold as a witch's tit out there and a man needs a cup of tea to warm him."

They all talked to the dog as if he understood every word, and perhaps he did. "Play your cards right," Fitz continued, hanging the coat on a mirrored rack near the door, "and you might get a gingersnap."

"Did I hear mention of a cup of tea?" a female voice called out from somewhere beyond the kitchen. "I'd welcome that. Dinner is still in the oven."

Maeve Donovan wasn't as tall as her daughter, but there was a slender wiriness and dignity to her movements that made people think she was taller than her five feet seven. An aureole of auburn curls ringed her head, catching the last rays of the late afternoon sun and looking like an unruly halo, as she hugged her father and felt the frost of the day on his cheek.

"What brings you home at this hour?" she asked as she filled the teakettle. It was their custom to check in with each other about their comings and goings—unlike twenty-two-year-old Finn, who thought it an absurd adult convention to always account for her whereabouts.

"That's a bit of a story," Fitz replied thoughtfully, seating himself on a cushioned kitchen chair. "I got this strange call at the shop from the Old Lady a while ago. Not a bit like her imperious self, mind you. She sounded frightened, agitated … said she needed to talk to me *urgently*."

Maeve looked up from ladling tea leaves into the Belleek teapot. "The old lady?" she asked, surprised. "I assume we're talking about Mrs. Wallenberg?" It tickled her that at seventy-three, her father did not think of himself as aging, but thought their neighbor at ninety-something was elderly and needed considerable help. The mysterious old woman who lived next door had been a customer of his bookstore for years, and Maeve knew that since she was mostly housebound now, he often stopped by with books for her—not to make a sale, just to stay for a cup of tea, so the frail, lonely old autocrat could have a bit of company. No one in the woman's family ever visited, and Maeve imagined the old girl's friends, if she'd ever had any, were long dead. She smiled at her father, thinking such random acts of kindness were his hallmark. Although his family had brought him to America from Ireland when he was a boy, he retained as much of his Irish belief in generosity as his brogue.

"Anyway," he continued, "I stopped by her place just now and I'm glad I did. She was all in a kerfuffle about a letter she'd received. She said it meant she was going to be murdered and she wanted someone to know why … not to save her, mind you. She said *that* wasn't possible because they'd found her after all these years of hiding and she had no more strength to run. She said she had an important secret she needed to consign to somebody trustworthy." He shrugged, but looked quite serious. "I believe I'm the somebody."

Maeve handed her father the steaming cup, poured one for herself, and sat down at the table.

"Did she say what the secret was or who she was hiding it from?"

He took a sip and shook his head.

"She was really agitated, luv. You might say elegantly incoherent. As if she'd stored up so much to say she couldn't quite get it all out in order or even in one tongue. She kept lapsing into German and some other guttural language—maybe Russian or Polish or something else middle European—as if her English and whatever language it was were suddenly overlapping and she couldn't contain the spill. She seemed frustrated that there was too much to explain and everything was coming out in fragments."

He shook his head, obviously more disturbed by his visit than he wanted to let on. He took a tattered old book out of his jacket pocket and handed it to Maeve. She opened it and saw that the cramped European handwriting would be a killer to decipher, assuming it was even in English. She handed it back, frowning.

"'You vill read zis, Mr. Donovan, und you vill understand!'" He mimicked the old woman's high-pitched, highly educated German accent for emphasis. "I tried to calm her down, but she'd have none of it. She said there was no time left for being calm. She said she'd get all the evidence out of hiding and give it to me for safekeeping. Once I'd read it all, I would understand everything. She said she knew I was law enforcement and I had friends in high places who could protect me. From what? I asked, of course, and she said, 'You have no idea how powerful they are. They have spies everywhere, and they're above every law but God's, and maybe even that.' She said she knew she could trust me to know what to do."

Maeve looked at her dad with concern. "And do you? Know what to do, I mean. Do you think the threat is credible? Should you call the boys at the precinct?" Her father still had plenty of friends on the job, and the 6th Precinct was nearby on West 10th.

"She's definitely scared to death of something, and maybe with reason, luv. She showed me a note, but wouldn't give it to me. Old-fashioned, very expensive stationery … elegant old-world script that read *Now you die.* Nothing else, mind you! She said she knows who it's from but has to tell the whole story in context or I'll never believe any of it. 'In two hours,' she said. 'Once I've gotten the evidence out of hiding. Without the books, you cannot understand the danger,' is how she put it. I could see she'd thought it all out and was steeling herself to be brave, so I didn't push … just said I'd come back after dinner and she could show me whatever she chose to." He smiled a bit to put her mind at ease. "You know the adage 'forgive your enemy but never forget the bastard's name'? I think she means to give me his name."

Maeve's worried frown reminded him she knew him too well to be pacified by an Irish aphorism.

"If whatever it is looks dangerous to me when I go back, luv, I'll get a couple of the boys at the 6th to keep an eye on the house tonight until we figure out what this is all about and what we can do to help her. How's that?"

"Okay," Maeve said hesitantly, "but it all sounds pretty sketchy to me, Dad. Could it just be some form of dementia? She's pretty ancient."

Fitz made a dismissive, not-a-chance-of-that face. "She's sharp as a new blade, just frightened. Really, really frightened."

"I'll go over with you after dinner," Maeve offered. "We'll sort it out."

"No," Fitz said definitively. "I'll go. If it's dangerous, I don't want you involved."

"Come on, Dad. I'm a cop's kid and a pretty good shot. This is weird, and you shouldn't go alone." They both had licenses to carry, an almost unheard-of privilege in Manhattan these days. He, because of his law enforcement career; she because he'd gotten it for her thirty years ago, when she'd been just a kid with a natural's gift of hand-eye coordination, training for a competitive sport that made her father proud.

He reached over again and patted her hand.

"I'll take my cell and call you the minute I know what's what. How's that, macushla?" The old Irish endearment made her smile, but the smile was uneasy.

2

Finn unwrapped the six-foot woolen scarf from her neck, shrugged out of the down coat she called the igloo, and tugged off her snow boots with an involuntary *ugh!* She hated these clunky accoutrements of an icy winter, but she'd learned the hard way that looking chic on a photo shoot was both impractical and stupid.

Tonight should be relatively easy, except for the nervous, high-strung energy she felt zinging all around her. She was doing a favor for Brace and Orlando, her two best pals from Parsons School of Art and Design. The Harvard of art schools, her favorite professor had called it, because pretty much every designer, artist or photographer of note in Manhattan had graduated from there. Both boys had worked their asses off to put this small collection together on a shoestring; now it needed to be photographed on the cheap for a press kit, and the clock was ticking. She was here to do test shots of the gowns so they could pick the right venue to showcase them. Pennies counted, and locations were expensive; they couldn't afford to choose the wrong one.

Orlando had interned in the sample room at Ralph Lauren after graduating, and Brace as assistant to the assistant to the head of a big-volume couture house that made a fortune knocking off the best of the Paris runway offerings each season. But after two relentless years of near-slave labor in return for priceless experience and all the Starbucks they could drink, they'd made a pact to make it on their own talent or die in the attempt.

The boys had made a jewel box out of a tiny, overpriced apartment they called the Two-Bedroom Teacup on the Lower East Side, furnishing it with hand-me-downs and objects discarded on the streets of Lower Manhattan while squirreling away every spare cent to buy fabric for the twenty-four pieces Finn now saw hanging on the metal rack in the corner. She mentally crossed her fingers as she started looking through the garments, wondering what she'd say if they turned out to be awful, but the first few pieces took her breath away.

"Oh. My. God. These are fucking amazing!!" she blurted with genuine admiration and relief. She'd seen them as works-in-progress for months, but now they were real. And exquisite. Just avant-garde enough. Just new enough. Just sexy enough, in an elegant, uptown, rich-kid-sexy kind of way. She'd been afraid they'd be over-the-top, because Orlando was a genius but hard to contain. *Brace must have stepped up,* she thought. The aptly named Brace had a steadying personality that could usually drag his flamboyant boyfriend back from whatever ledge he was perched on, but when Orlando escaped and really flew, he made Alexander McQueen look straitlaced.

"Okay, boys," Finn said, seeing that both were awaiting her approbation without wanting it to be obvious. "These are too good for any of the locations you've been talking about."

"They *are* seriously *soign*é!" Orlando intoned, as if broadcasting for the BBC.

"Just the word I was groping for," Brace said with an eye roll at Finn. "Maybe we could see if Beyoncé and Jay-Z's house is available."

"No need," Finn interjected, to avoid the verbal one-upmanship that was about to begin. "We're going to Mimi's." She whipped her cell phone from her pocket and dialed.

"Are you sure?" Orlando fretted the words out. "The work really needs room to breathe."

"You know as well as I do her house has a ballroom *and* a pool," Finn answered with a smirk. "The work can breathe either in the air or under water." She thought the boys had probably hoped to do the shoot at Mimi's, but had waited for Finn to make the offer. Mimi was her best friend, after all, not theirs. She'd inherited the mansion on 64th and Park Avenue and the fortune to maintain it from the grandparents who'd raised her after her parents' deaths. But unlike most of the rich kids Finn knew, Mimi had a heart the size of Montana, and she'd chosen to be a doctor so she could use her money to do good in the world.

She heard the line being picked up and motioned them to be quiet.

"Mim? It's me with a favor to ask," she blurted. "I need a place to shoot the boys."

She smiled at the expected witty reply, which the boys could surely guess but couldn't hear. "The gowns are too spectacular for any place but yours … and more to the point, they have no money for a location fee."

She was nodding her head "yes" and smiling broadly to let the two designers know they were in. "I'll do some test shots so we can get a feel for the best locations in your house, and I'll stop by with the digitals on my way home, okay?

"You're my hero, Mim. The boys want to say thanks," she said while motioning them to shout *thank you* in unison so Mimi could hear. Then she stuffed the phone back into her jeans.

Finn turned her gaze toward Orlando. "So, did you book Kendall and Gigi to model for the shoot, or maybe Eva?" The tall brunette had been in Finn's History of Film Noir class.

"She's in already," Brace offered, "and Kenzie, Marika, and YeJin."

Finn nodded. All good choices, except maybe for Marika, who was beautiful as a goddess but moved with all the grace of Gumby.

"And who's our 'fit model'?"

The boys smirked. "Ha! Honey, *you* are!" they answered in unison.

"And who's taking the photos?" Finn went along with the joke.

"You are!" they chorused together, delighted by their harmony.

Finn considered the logistics. It was doable. The boys had a giant rococo mirror, and these shots were just to show off the dresses, not to make viable images …. She just hoped she'd fit into the clothes. She was slender, but nowhere near model-anorexic, and these slinky wisps needed a drop-dead bod to do them justice.

"Come on, darling girl," Orlando nudged, pulling her toward the makeshift dressing area. "Drop trou and get on with the selfies. You'll be dee-vine!"

"And what if they don't fit?" she murmured as he propelled her along.

"Why do you think God invented scissors and straight pins?" he said as he unceremoniously yanked her sweater up over her head.

"Hands off!" Finn yelped as the sweater caught on a chain around her neck. "I'm not wearing a bra."

"Oh, for fuck's sake, Sister Mary Immaculata, it's not like we've never seen your tits. How many times, exactly, did you pose for life class?"

"You've got a point," she said amiably, unzipping her jeans as Brace came toward her cradling the most beautiful, beaded-silk something in his arms as if it were a newborn.

The whisper-weight layers of silk fluttered down over Finn's bare skin like fairy wings, and when she looked at herself in the immense mirror, the image made her catch her breath.

"Okay," she said when she could speak again. "For the first time in my life, I want to be seriously rich when I grow up."

"Well, you're not going to get rich just standing there, sweetie," Brace said. "And neither are we. So move your ass." He shooed her toward her camera bag and made a thumbs-up sign to Orlando behind her back.

An hour later she was on her way to Mimi's, bundled up in her igloo and mukluks, feeling like Cinderella just after the coach turned into a pumpkin again.

3

Maeve Donovan snatched up the phone on the first ring. Her nerves had been ratcheting up unreasonably since her father left the house twenty minutes before. *No need to be so on edge,* she chided herself, but that was the problem with being semi-psychic—you often got hints of trouble in advance, but they were never explicit enough to know what the hell to do.

Her father's voice was deep, serious. His "cop" voice, but husky with controlled emotion.

"She's dead, sweetheart," he said without preamble. "I've called the precinct, but didn't want you alarmed when the black-and-whites roar up outside. The place has been ransacked. It's a ruin of trashed books, papers, and all that fine old bric-a-brac she lived amidst. She was stabbed, tortured. It's ugly."

"I'll be right there!"

"No, luv. It's a crime scene now. The Crime Scene Unit will be here any minute. I'll get home as soon as I can, but that might not be for a while, considering I was probably the last one to see her alive, other than the bastard who did this. They'll need my statement." He took a breath. "And, Maeve, luv, do me a favor. Call Finn and tell her to take a cab home—tell her I'll pay for it, since she worries about money. And lock the doors and windows until we find out what this is all about, will you, darlin'?"

"Okay," she said, unconvinced. Now she knew why her hackles had been doing a jig. This was going to suck them all in, sure as God made little green apples. She didn't know how exactly, but it would suck them all in.

4

The crime-scene techs have an all-nighter on their hands, Fitz thought, surveying the shambles around him. There were three of them left in the house now. The medical examiner had wheeled out the poor, crumpled old body, and the detectives had left two uniforms to guard the house while the crime techs did their work.

Fitz was antiquarian dealer enough to know the former value of the porcelain shards and shredded artwork that now littered the destroyed room's landscape along with a fortune in trashed rare books. The old woman had owned many treasures. "From the old days," she'd said dismissively when he'd asked about her unusual collections. "I had a larger life once." She'd gracefully swept an aristocratic, long-fingered hand at the room packed with the artifacts of a grander age, her skin nearly see-through with age. Veined, spotted, delicate as an exotic orchid, long-boned as the wing of a great bird. "Once," she'd said wistfully, "long ago … all that I wanted was mine." Her smile was rueful, bitter, resigned. "These few trinkets are the leftovers. As am I."

What could be said to that particular truth? he'd thought with some rue of his own. Only the old know the sorrow of the losses wrought by age. The friends gone. The power faded. Your own relevance to the world a question mark at best. "Now your wars on God begin," as Yeats had pointed out. "At stroke of midnight God shall win." He'd shaken off the morbid thoughts and changed the subject.

He wondered if whatever it was she'd wanted him to know had died with her, and felt angry on her behalf. She'd died hard because of it.

He'd given his preliminary statement to Joe Cochrane, an aggressive up-and-comer at the 6th, and was now free to go, having promised to meet the brusque, unlovely Detective Lieutenant at the precinct in the morning. Most of the older men in the department still called FitzHugh Donovan Chief and treated him with respectful deference when their paths crossed, but some of the young turks like Cochrane considered him a pain-in-the-arse dinosaur and worthy of no special courtesy.

When Fitz had made no move to leave after giving his statement, Cochrane had dismissed him with a peremptory, "No need for you to hang around any longer, Mr. Donovan," pointedly not addressing him by his old rank or title. He'd been Chief for two decades, but out of the department for eleven years. "We'll take it from here."

Fitz had eyed the younger man from under his formidable brows with a combination of amusement and Irish stubbornness. He was too old a cat to be fucked by a kitten and had never, at any age, been won over by discourtesy of any kind.

"I'll stay for a bit," he'd replied, clearly not asking permission. "I don't have far to go to get home as it happens, and I'd like to see if anything here jogs loose a useful tidbit or two."

"This is a crime scene—" the younger man began importantly, then stopped in midsentence. Maybe it was the expression in the old man's steady gaze that said *I was examining crime scenes when you were just a gleam in your father's eye, boyo.* Or maybe it was the disgusted intake of breath from the senior crime-scene tech on the floor a few feet away, who was now staring at the detective with undisguised contempt. Cochrane hadn't made many friends among the old-timers.

"Let me know if you think of any *tidbits,*" Cochrane finished, disdainful emphasis on the "tidbits." "I'll see you at the House tomorrow."

"Aye, laddiebuck," Fitz replied amiably. "That you will."

"Asshole," murmured the CSI on the floor, rising with an evidence bag in each hand, after Cochrane was out of earshot. He'd been a kid new to the job when Fitz was already a legend on the force. He'd seen plenty of assholes come and go since then, but not too many old pros like Fitz Donovan had crossed his path.

"I was hoping you'd hang around after Lieutenant Cockring departed," he said. He wasn't the only one at the station who'd latched onto the nickname for Cochrane. "I heard you were a friend of the deceased, Chief. My condolences."

Fitz nodded acknowledgment. "I knew her long but not all that well, Jake. You know how it is with neighbors in this city. "Hello" over the garden fence or on the front stoop and not much beyond. She was too old to get about, but she'd been a customer at The Mysterious for years and I used to stop by with a book or two when I could."

The tech nodded sympathetically. He knew all about the chief's antiquarian mystery bookstore, the one he'd bought after taking early retirement because of his wife's illness. "The ME says she didn't go easy, Chief. Her fingers were snapped like twigs, burns on her old arms and face. Vicious stab wound to the abdomen. Whoever did this to her was a sadist as well as a murderer. I wonder if she gave up whatever it was he wanted. Hard to believe such a frail old bird could hold out long enough to have that much damage done to her."

Fitz grimaced at the idea of anyone capable of inflicting such suffering on an old woman, thinking maybe frail didn't do her justice. Whatever the hell her secret was, she'd put up a valiant fight to defend it.

"Did you find the letter with the death threat?" Fitz asked suddenly, and the CSI looked quizzical.

"What? No," he said, startled, "should I have?"

Fitz nodded. "She showed it to me this afternoon. An elegant piece of work it was. Fine paper and penmanship. It read *Now you die.*"

The tech's eyes widened. "If it's here, I'll find it," he said. "And Chief, if you're staying awhile, would you mind taking a look at the books for me? I know you're an expert. Let me know if you see anything I should pay special attention to. There are about a million of them, so any direction you can point me in would be a big help."

He held out a pair of vinyl gloves and Fitz took them with a small grin. "I thought you'd never ask," he said.

The room was full of books, piles of them yanked from shelves and left in tangled heaps. Most with pages ripped out or bindings shredded. Hundreds lying willy-nilly on the beautiful rosewood shelves, torn or mutilated. Elegant old-world bindings with gilded spines and magnificent art books, all tortured and trashed like their owner by some Philistine thug. *Sic transit gloria mundi,* he thought, staring at the destruction. *Thus passeth the glory of the world.*

It was the library of an erudite, or at least very sophisticated, bibliophile. Classics in several languages and a few genuine surprises he'd noted over the years of his visits. High-level math and physics texts in more abundance than a dabbler would ever own. Books in four or five languages, all obviously well read, many annotated in the margins. He wished now she'd been more informative about them when he'd asked. Musical scores, classical and operatic. Memoirs, many of which were biographies of obscure names, names that only scholars, aficionados, and old-book dealers would recognize. The collection was a throwback to a world before the Kindle.

"Say, Chief," the tech said, holding out an opened envelope with three books in it. "Looks like these were meant for you. I found it stuffed in a bush outside the front door between her house and yours, but on your side of the fence, so it looks like the guy who trashed the place may have missed it by hightailing out the back when you rang the bell. It's addressed to you."

Stuffed under a bush just in case her time ran out, or in desperation when she heard her assassin coming? Fitz frowned as he lifted out the books with a practiced hand. *You will know what to do!* the note inside the front cover read. She'd said those words, just that way, this very afternoon. *But would he?* he wondered as he fingered the books.

"Maybe she wanted you to sell them for her?" the CSI queried, taking the books back one at a time and riffling the pages to make sure nothing fell out.

One was an old, exquisitely illustrated coffee-table book about obscure Polish castles, one a well-worn German textbook of some kind, the third a notebook with a soft leather binding and lettering that spelled a word unknown to him on its spine. It was a beautiful old journal, handmade paper and binding, but it was empty except for a hastily scribbled grocery list and some notes about household matters. An oddly random selection for so lovely a book. And written in cheap ballpoint. Fitz had never seen Mrs. W. write with other than a Montblanc fountain pen worthy of a treaty at Versailles.

He fanned the interior just as Jake had done to make certain nothing else was secreted in the journal, and an odd aroma, so faint it was nearly unnoticeable, rose from the pages. Lavender, lemons, and maybe wine, he guessed, and something else that stirred a memory. *L'Heure Bleue*, his subconscious offered up from some forgotten synapse. L'Heure Bleue. A fragrance from another time and place. Vaguely sensual. An old-fashioned scent. The Old Lady had smelled like this sometimes. Like a fading flower in a forgotten garden.

He held the book up to his nose and sniffed again. It seemed more lemony now that he was consciously sniffing for that particular scent, and an idea surfaced. Lemon juice could be used as invisible ink. So could wine or perfume. Would a paranoid old woman with something real to fear and something precious to hide know about such things? And would she have the presence of mind to hide a secret in plain sight for him? And why the hell hadn't she just given it to him this afternoon along with the book she'd put into his hand? He stuffed the three books back into the envelope.

"You can take them if you want, Chief," Jake offered. "They don't look like evidence of anything relevant to me. Cochrane told me to go through the books to see if anything useful shakes out, then just leave them for her heirs if she has any. He said, no point in hauling a thousand broken books to the evidence locker."

Fitz nodded, weighing his options. Fifty years of training said you don't take anything from a crime scene. Fifty years as a detective said these books were important and would surely be overlooked if he didn't take them with him. And technically, the envelope hadn't been found *inside* the crime scene … and it had been addressed to him ….

"Thanks, Jake," he said, finally. "Tell you what; I'll help you vet the book collection so we can both get out of here before morning. I hate to see some of these old beauties lying here in ruins. If everything's been photographed in situ, I'll help you put them back on the shelves as we vet them."

He glanced at his watch. "Just let me call my girls to see they're all right and let them know I'll be a while."

"Thanks, Chief," Jake said. "That'd be a big help to me." *And maybe to the chief as well,* he thought, turning back to his work with a small, satisfied smile. And perhaps to that poor, tortured old woman. Jake, too, had caught the faint scent of lemons.

5

Maeve Donovan turned the corner the next morning and looked up 6th Avenue before deciding whether it was just too damned cold to walk, as she'd intended. But maybe the chill wind would clear her head, so she turned resolutely toward West 4th, wishing once again that the Bagel Café was still on Cornelia Street, with its perfect breakfasts served in a decrepit space the size of a postage stamp. A counter and five tables that had kept Village regulars like herself in great food at a great price for umpteen years, was now gone, like so many other Village mainstays.

So many changes in Manhattan in the past ten or fifteen years that were not for the better, she thought as she headed into the wind. She silently cursed the succession of mayors who had tipped the balance. His determination to turn the city into a haven for billionaires, a place of steel-and-glass behemoths blocking the sun from the rivers, the obscenely rich—Russian oligarchs' spoiled brats, Arab sheiks and Eurotrash—the only ones who could really afford to buy here now. Mostly to launder money, not to live.

To Maeve's mind, New York was meant to be a melting pot of neighborhoods, Greenwich Village the sweetest of them. Human-size houses, mom-and-pop shops, egalitarian attitudes that didn't just tolerate differences of ethnicities, ideas, social stations, sexual persuasions, and artfully eccentric modes of living, but welcomed them. As if to underscore the thought, she passed the Pink PussyCat Boutique with its ridiculously exuberant display of dildos, and laughed out loud at her own train of thought. The Village was meant for bohemians, outcasts, free thinkers, and just plain open-minded families like her own, who loved brownstone living on tree-lined streets and cobblestone mews, and loved cherishing the eccentricities that made the place and its people unique.

Her dad had come home in the middle of last night. He'd been too tired to tell her more than the bare bones of what had happened. They'd both gone to bed with the promise that she'd hear more details over breakfast, but, oddly for him, he'd headed out before breakfast to give his statement at the precinct, leaving her a note to say he'd tell all when he got home.

Maeve had a publishing meeting this morning for her new book, but she was dying to hear more of the strange occurrences next door and hoped her meeting wouldn't last long. *Man doth not live by publishing contracts alone,* she thought, although they certainly made earning her living a pleasure instead of a chore. Astrology, metaphysics, and her Irish mother's style of alchemical healing that she practiced at her increasingly popular tea shop on Bleecker Street were her specialties, and all three were hot at the moment.

Maeve ducked into the subway, grateful to be out of the bitter wind and determined to get the rest of the story out of her father when she got home.

6

Cochrane looked over the paperwork about the old lady's death and shook his head in annoyance. What lousy luck that she'd lived next door to that old pain-in-the-ass Donovan. He'd made short shrift of him when he'd come in to give his statement this morning, but that probably wouldn't stop the old fart from trying to horn in. What the fuck it was about him so many of the guys on the squad admired was incomprehensible. Just another old-school tight-ass who probably couldn't manage a Facebook account, never mind a case. Over the hill and pissed off about it. Probably missed the action and the media attention.

He glanced again at the medical examiner's preliminary report. Whoever had killed the old bat had probably gotten what he came for, if it wasn't just a random sadist nutjob who'd killed her. No old lady could withstand that kind of torture without spilling her guts, no pun intended.

Cochrane shoved the reports back in the folder and headed for the coffee machine. It was going to be a long day.

7

The subway car Maeve sat in on her way uptown was cold, crowded and ugly. She was old enough now to be past most illusions, she thought idly, as she willed herself into that amorphous reverie that New Yorkers reserve for subway rides. A kind of psychic suspended animation that let you isolate yourself from the ugliness of the great, ill-smelling mass of humanity surrounding you as you hurtle semiconsciously through a dingy hole in the ground. Subways were a kind of weird bilocation zone in which you switched off normal thought, pushed the immediate dank reality out of the way, lapsed into a theta state not unlike meditation, yet stayed alert enough to know if stranger-danger or what the cops quaintly called a dickie-waver might be seated next to you or hanging on the pole just inches from your nose.

Subway rides were perfect meditative times for self-inventory, she thought as stations whirled by in a blur.

Old enough now to know that diets don't work, love is not forever, good seldom triumphs, there are no poor tyrants, and world peace is highly unlikely. But aside from those few bitter disappointments, she was luckier than most. Maeve smiled at the passing theta thought. She pretty much liked her life.

She lived with her father and daughter in the family brownstone her dad had purchased decades ago, when the yuppies hadn't yet discovered the delights of downtown and such houses sold for a song to anyone willing to rescue them from decrepitude. Her sister lived near enough so they could all stay thick as thieves, as the Irish say, able to spend real time together and enjoy each other's quirks.

Her daughter Finn had been ten when the unexpected revelations about Maeve's husband's multiple infidelities had brought her world crashing down around her. While she was still reeling from the ugly gut punch of betrayal, her newly widowed father had suggested she and Finn come home to the house she'd grown up in, and she'd gratefully headed back from Connecticut, where she'd never really fit in with the soccer moms anyway. They'd rearranged the house to suit their collective needs—the bottom two floors for her and Finn, the next floor her dad's, the top floor her sister Rory's. And life had begun again. A really good life, despite the bumps in the road and the effort to piece together a life that had come undone.

Determined to work at home to make sure Finn made it safely through the sad fragmentation of divorce, Maeve had shifted gears in her professional life and started writing books about the esoteric lore she'd learned from her psychic mother and grandmother. Alchemical Irish healing recipes to be used in food and baths… mystic Irish stories trailing their magical way through the lore of the faeries, saints and minstrels who dealt easily with the Unseen world on an emerald island that was synonymous with magic … and the watercolors she'd been painting on every trip back to Ireland since childhood had added another sweet dimension to her books.

Her mom's healing recipes had eventually led to a partnership with her college roommate in a small tea shop on Bleecker Street they'd named The Philosopher's Teacup. To her amazement, the place had been embraced by Village people, tourists from uptown, and *New York Magazine* with equal enthusiasm. She probably wouldn't ever get rich from it all, especially now that the city was growing more expensive by the day, but she was doing okay, and her work gave her both creative satisfaction and pleasure.

The 59th Street subway stop jolted Maeve out of her reverie and she lurched to her feet, steadying herself as the crowd pushed her out beneath the bustle of Bloomingdale's. Just as she emerged onto Lexington, a woman in an expensive chinchilla coat pushed past her, nearly knocking her down. Maeve was about to protest when a sickening flash of vision hit her with an icy wave. The chinchilla-clad woman's husband was dying at Sloane Kettering and she was trying to hail a cab to get there, oblivious to all else. Maeve saw the hospital scene flash into her second sight as clearly as if she was standing at the foot of the old man's bed. He was going to die today, and his wife had to get there to be with him when he passed. Maeve said a silent prayer for the old couple, then shook her head to clear the remnants of the psychic vision and regain her bearings. The family gift of clairvoyance was one she cherished, but not when it showed her somebody's death.

It had always been like that for her. The female line of her family was intensely psychic, each with different gifts. Some could foretell death, the most unpopular of all talents; some could heal or dowse or talk to the deceased. Her sister Rory, who'd been a successful corporate lawyer before making enough money to follow her own dream of buying brownstones, then rehabbing and flipping them, joked about the psychic gifts she'd been stuck with, which she insisted on calling intuition, not psychism. She said that working at a prestigious white-shoe law firm on Wall Street meant that most of the people she talked to all day were half dead anyway, so the last thing she wanted after hours was to talk to the departed.

Being Celts, they all took their gifts for granted one way or another. The veil between worlds, as her mother would say, was thinner in Ireland than anywhere else on earth, so what point was there in denying the frequent intrusions of what others didn't even know existed?

Maeve's own visions were annoyingly random; flashes like the one she'd just had from the woman brushing by, or glimpses of the future she didn't always know how to interpret. On September 9, 2001, she'd been blasted awake by a vision of Lower Manhattan in a cloud of smoke and flames, the words September 11 scrawled across the skyline, but it was so incomprehensible a vision she'd dismissed it as psychic spam—until the first plane hit the Twin Towers.

Shaking her head, she realized she was far more excited about getting home to hear what Fitz had found out about Mrs. W. than she was about discussing her new book with her editor.

8

Fitz settled his large frame into the comfortable old rocker in the corner of the big kitchen and began to read the Old Lady's journal. He'd been right about the lemon juice and wine, but it was the devil's own job to reconstitute the writing so it was clear enough to decipher. Pages were filled with inscrutable scribbles that appeared to go back decades and were pretty much all utterly incomprehensible. As he'd suspected, the grocery list was an overwrite to throw people off the track. Written hastily in ballpoint, because anyone who knew about invisible ink knew using regular ink on top of an encryption could destroy the hidden text beneath, but ballpoint wouldn't. *Good spy craft,* he thought, wondering where the hell the Old Lady had learned it.

It was evidence, of course, and should have been turned in to the police lab for deciphering. But it had been addressed to him, and he had no doubt whatsoever that once it went to Cochrane he'd have not a snowball's chance in hell of getting hold of it again. And Cochrane had been such a pointedly dismissive ass when he'd gone to the House earlier to give his statement. Christ, but that man had the disposition of a wet fortnight. Fitz had almost risen to the bait and engaged in a small verbal donnybrook with Cochrane, until a line from George Bernard Shaw popped into his head to restrain him. Never wrestle with a pig, said the poet. You both get dirty and the pig likes it. So he'd decided to figure out what was going on here, first, then choose what to do about it. *He could always burn the Cochrane bridge when he came to it,* he thought with a wry smile. And from what he'd seen so far, it could take a while to even get to the bridge.

This invisible-inked journal wasn't going to be decipherable by ordinary means, that was certain. It was in some kind of code. Sigils, equations, numbers, drawings that looked like spidery blueprints. He'd need a cryptographer's help with this for sure, or maybe an engineer's or a physicist's. It was at times like these he missed having the resources of the department to help unravel things, especially the computer power. But he well remembered solving cases before computers came along, and there were other resources he could call on. Finn's pal T-square, or maybe even his old friend Annie and her oddball crew of hacktivist women who called themselves the Babushkas. Plenty of resources, he thought with satisfaction. One step at a time ...

Very deliberately, Fitz put his everyday glasses into his shirt pocket, took out his readers, and settled back into the soft chintz cushions of the chair his wife Cara had loved to sit in. Her given name had been Catherine, but Fitz had never called her anything but Cara, a shortened version of *Anam Cara,* Gaelic for beloved heart friend.

Fitz put the coded book from the envelope aside, and turned his attention instead to the well-worn journal the Old Lady had pressed into his hand "so he would understand and know what to do." At least this book was somewhat legible.

9

The Journal of Mrs. W.

They are gone now. All those I've loved. Sacrificed to injustice and the greed of evil men who revel in their triumph. But I am still alive, and the bastards will never be safe while I hold the secret. No one is truly dead until the last person who loved or hated him dies and carries all truths to the grave ...

Fitz deciphered the words with some difficulty, wishing the writing were bigger, the light better, his glasses stronger and his eyes younger.

I shall write in English, although it is my fifth language and not the one of my heart, because I will surely die in this country waiting for the moment when I can emerge from the tall grass and fire the shot that brings the curs down. If I should die before that moment comes, I must leave my story to one who will not dismiss or discard it. If I cannot seek justice in life, perhaps death will free the genie from the bottle, but only if the tale can be told in all its terrible truth. I will bear witness; the rest is up to God, who surely owes at least this much to those I've loved and lost, and perhaps even to me whom He seems to have abandoned long ago.

I was born in 1921 into extreme wealth and privilege. My father was both a baron and a brilliant physicist from a long line of the mathematically gifted. My mother was a concert pianist of great personal beauty and grace. Although she was rather cold of heart, she was a paragon in other ways. Their marriage was a perfect one for its time and place. Each understood the other's lineage, talents and social obligations, and because both families had large fortunes and considerable land holdings in Poland and Germany, they were sought-after and admired. Their dinner parties were legendary; their guest lists included the intellectual elite of Europe and the wider world ...

Fitz put down the book thoughtfully. Bells were going off in his brain. One of his strengths on the force had been his prodigious memory. Facts, figures, faces, crimes, complex legal issues all would tuck themselves away in his brain's filing cabinet quite effortlessly. It was a natural skill that added to his pleasure as an antiquarian book dealer when that became his second vocation. He seldom forgot what he read or where on a given page he'd seen it, and while his card catalog at The Mysterious was extensive, it was nothing compared to the index of his mind.

What he was reading was a story he had seen before, somewhere. A WWII family of polymaths and physicists who were supporters of the Reich. Baron von something or other … the story would surface when he got back to the shop to jog things loose. He picked up the book again, thinking the strange squiggles in the other journal might make more sense in the light of this new information.

He wondered when the Old Lady had begun this journal in preparation for her own death.

I was married at barely 18 to a man of 50 who was deemed a fine and appropriate catch by my socially conscious parents. He had a purchased title, a grand castle, a prosperous munitions and chemical business and no sons to carry on the family name. I was young, presumably fertile, and of the superior bloodline so beloved by der Führer and his ilk. This arranged marriage was not cruelty on the part of my parents, you must understand. To my father I was a beloved princess; to my mother, a tedious project nearing completion. In our social class, such an arranged marriage was expected, and something of a triumph. To be wed at 18 to such a man as Manfred Gruber was a coup. To be a spinster at 20 would have been a disaster. The fact that I was rebellious and did not like the look of this coldly ambitious toad of a man was considered no more than the jitters of a high-strung girl used to being coddled and to getting her own way—one who would now be forced to grow up. My recalcitrance would change once I bore an heir to Manfred's fortune and vast holdings. For such a man to be without an heir at 50 was unthinkable.

As it happened, his childlessness was soon explained. While I was hardly expert in matters of the boudoir, it quickly became apparent he had no interest in women, and little in me except under certain aberrant circumstances.

To all observers, our life was brilliant. Manfred bought a townhouse in Berlin, filled with the decorative treasures of a palace. Every artifact was priceless and perfectly chosen. By him. We owned four other homes and hunting lodges, including one outside Vienna, a yacht, several aircraft and endless automobiles. Servants were everywhere and jewels, furs, and designer gowns were the expected trappings for the young showpiece wife of a man of such means. I was an enviable doll in a magical dollhouse. A useless, mute toy, guarded and followed, a prisoner in my own gilded jewel case.

I was allowed no life of my own. My rebellions were quelled with punishments that were perverse and grew more and more severe. Indeed, the only sexual efforts my husband ever made at getting me with the required child was in the aftermath of brutality that seemed to arouse him. Fortunately, none of these sexual encounters took permanent hold in my reluctant and terrified womb. I conceived and miscarried twice. Sometimes God relents. To bear a child to such as Manfred would have doomed me.

I was simply another of his treasured objects. Imprisoned, spied upon, expected to perform at dinners and at hunting parties, a favorite entertainment. My shooting skills were considerable and this amused him and his friends. But I was instructed never to engage in serious conversation. Not politics, science, business, the war when it came, or any other subject of intellectual stimulation was permitted me. I was to smile at guests, or beat them in shooting competitions in which large sums were wagered, make the idle chitchat expected of vapid women, and look beautiful and desirable, so other men would envy him. My mathematical prowess and knowledge of physics, which my indulgent father had nurtured since my childhood, were to remain as hidden as my heart and soul, which week by week grew hungrier and more desperate.

That's interesting, Fitz said to himself. *Could she have been a physicist, too?*

Thus, in my seething quietude, I listened and I learned. Of the war. Of munitions. Of chemicals. Of my husband's factories and their vile capabilities. Of Hitler's plans to murder the world's undesirables. Of extraordinary scientific inquiries that were being pursued by der Führer in the quest for exotic weapons of war—both atomic and biologic—that would bring the whole world to a halt or to annihilation, it seemed.

I also knew of the medical horrors that accompanied Hitler's insane quest for immortality, for Manfred's partner, Johann Gruss, specialized in the uses of the chemicals manufactured by their company for both biological weaponry and physiological enhancement experiments. The men spoke freely of such things in my presence because I was a woman, and not even Manfred understood the scope of my intellect, my education, and my growing hatred for the men who planned to imprison the world, as I had been imprisoned.

My beloved father knew of my intellectual abilities, so like his own, as he had mentored them, practically from the cradle. But as it would have been considered unseemly for a young woman to display such gifts, he would never have made mention of them. Had I been a man, he often proudly assured me, I would have been a physicist or mathematician of note, but as a woman such talents as mine were wasted. And he had made it clear on the day of my wedding that my husband was now in charge of my destiny. Perhaps, had I told him the depth of my despair, he would have helped me, but I was too ashamed of my endless humiliation at Manfred's hands to beg his intervention, and by the time my desperation would have forced me to do so, my dear father could no longer be my savior.

It became increasingly clear to me that only I could plot my escape from this gilded cage. Only I must suffer the consequences if I did not succeed.

Fritz laid the book aside when he heard Maeve's key in the lock. What a story was here. He would tell this tale to his girls tonight and enlist their help. This was not part of an official inquiry, after all. At least not yet. And they'd been deciphering puzzles together for a long, long time. He picked up the phone to call the one Donovan who didn't live with them anymore. Rory had an analytical brain like his and would want to be party to this astounding mystery.

PART II

The Game Is Afoot

"Wealth lost, something lost,
Honor lost, something lost:
Courage lost, all lost."

— Johann Wolfgang von Goethe

10

Rory Donovan stood on West 119th Street and gazed across happily at the four-story brownstone she'd just purchased. It had lovely bones. Even great bones, she decided, assessing the elegant old façade with an expert's satisfied eye. The tall, rangy young woman smiled with utter satisfaction at the graceful bowed windows, the intricate stonework from another age, the romantic Victorian wrought iron fencing around the small patch of garden that housed an ancient, gnarled wisteria vine that had, over decades, snaked its way up nearly to the once-elegant roofline.

Rory absently brushed her short, wavy brown hair back from where the chill wind had whipped it across her strong, pretty face, shifted her briefcase to her other hand, and crossed the street. She had the purposeful gait of a long-boned yearling and her face was flushed with high color from the biting wind.

The prospect of resurrecting this one hundred-thirty-four-year-old treasure from the neglect of time and the changing vicissitudes of the neighborhood thrilled her as her law career seldom had. This was history and mystery and architecture and art and construction combined in one gorgeous package that would give her considerable pleasure, along with inevitable conundrums and headaches, for two years at a minimum. She couldn't wait to get started.

There was plenty to do to rehab this old beauty. So much had been lost that would need meticulous replacing, but so much was still there, hidden in the grime and neglect of the years.

What a glorious game of detection lay ahead of her. *Detecting was in their family DNA,* she thought with a smile, and unlike the law, when you ferreted out the secrets of a house like this and bent your efforts toward restoring its integrity, you could be absolutely certain justice would be done.

Rory took a deep breath, thinking once again how happy she was to have made the leap from law to real estate. It wasn't that the law had been unkind to her. Far from it. She'd had plenty of early successes, which had given her the wherewithal to buy the first house she'd rehabbed and flipped. Had given her the chance at age thirty-two to switch the trajectory of her career to what she'd always dreamed of doing, and here she was, successful enough at this newish game, to be the proud owner of this amazing old gem with all its promise.

She smiled happily as she mounted the wide granite steps to the heavy oak door. Her cell phone chirped as she turned the key in the lock. The text was from her sister Maeve. *Dinner at 7:30. The game is afoot. Gang's all here. XX, Me. How like her sister,* she thought with a grin. They'd both been crazy about Sherlock as kids. Their dad had read them every one of the Baker Street tales over and over. Detective and story-lover, he'd wanted them to learn the ratiocination that was beneath the surface of everything … wanted them to love the convoluted old Victorian prose and the delights of a good story well told. "Detecting isn't just about crime," he would say in a serious tone that made them know it was important. "It's about seeing the details in life that others miss. It's a mental discipline that will serve you. And an intellectual curiosity that will entertain you forever." He'd been right.

Rory peeled off her gloves and texted back. She'd already returned her father's call about the planned family confab to talk about the murder next door, to let him know she'd be there tonight. Guess the jungle drums hadn't passed the message on to the rest of their crowd yet. Before she could put her phone back in her pocket, another text dinged in, this time from Finn. *7:30 story time, AR!* it read. Aunt Rory had long ago become AR. *Mrs. W. got murdered. We have to figure it out. XX, Me.* Rory burst out laughing. How like Finn to cut to the chase. This promised to be quite an evening on top of quite a day.

Rory pushed open the door and stood still for a moment in the ancient air of the entry, just breathing it all in. Light flooded through the stained-glass fanlight, making multihued puddles on the age-pitted marble floor.

She felt as if she might just have come home.

11

The office in the new Frank Gehry tower in Manhattan would have been obscene in its opulence except that the disciplined taste was so exquisite, the quality of the furnishings, art, and objects so impeccable.

The Power Broker, seated behind a desk large enough for an emperor, was dressed in a tux and late for dinner with the Iranian ambassador, but that would have to wait until he'd handled the current debacle and filled in his brother on the unsavory details.

He stared out the wall of floor-to-ceiling windows that displayed Manhattan Island from Battery to Bridge as he listened to the disappointing report of the old woman's last hours with the sangfroid he was known for in financial circles. Inside he seethed. So many years it had taken them to track down the old bitch, it was inconceivable there were still loose ends. At least this was the last time she'd outwit them. He almost admired her decades of strategic maneuvering. A woman alone, without allies … really rather remarkable, if dangerous.

"So, she's dead, but the critical evidence she possessed is still missing?" he said, his voice neutral, but the energy that flickered behind his eyes and the carefully controlled voice making the hairs on the subordinate's arms prickle. "Is that what you would like me to understand?"

The man called Odeon, who had failed to deliver the desired results, had begun his explanation robustly, relieved to report the successful assassination. Now the ground moved under him. He'd hired a known operative for the wet work. Ex–Special Forces, highly skilled. It just hadn't gone as planned. Such things occasionally happened in fieldwork—they just hadn't happened in any op he'd planned for the brothers.

"Our agent searched her house thoroughly, sir. The safe held only a few old jewels and assorted personal papers. He ripped apart her books to be certain nothing was secreted in the bindings, left no artifact unexamined.

He found no plans, no secret cubbyholes, no diary, no Stasi dossier, no list of names …" he paused because of the ferocity he saw banked behind the eyes of the man behind the desk.

"Find me her friends." The Power Broker's voice was unnervingly soft. "Her visitors, her relatives, her neighbors, her grocer, if she had a relationship with him. It is inconceivable that your operative could not make her reveal the whereabouts of what we seek. The woman was more than ninety years old …" he left the thought unfinished.

The subordinate's hands trembled a fraction, so he locked them behind his back. Showing weakness would be blood in the water. Thank God he'd been smart enough to have his asset retrieve the letter he'd sent to soften her up.

"Is it possible the documents never really existed, sir?" he offered. "If she'd possessed anything important, surely she would have given it up under such extreme interrogation …"

The formidable eyebrows of the man behind the desk came together in a frown. "There is a file," he said simply. "You were told to retrieve it."

"Our man reported she was … unusual, sir. He's known for his uncommon skills. He broke her fingers, burned her with a fireplace poker. My God, he damn near disemboweled her …" he blurted the last of it, then regained control. He thought the look of revulsion that had momentarily flashed across the Power Broker's face was not because of a sudden distaste for torture, but because of the failure it implied.

"What does it matter *how* your man failed?" his employer asked quietly. "The point is that he failed, and you failed with him. Please know that." His voice had not risen a decibel, only the eyes said the danger had escalated. Odeon's mouth was too dry to respond so he nodded.

The man behind the desk dismissed the lesser man with a flick of his hand, swiveled his chair, and returned his gaze to the Manhattan skyline. How best to explain the news to his volatile brother, who would be here any minute? He'd begin by saying that without the old woman alive to bear witness, whatever evidence she'd gathered was meaningless. That wasn't entirely true, of course. Not now, when so much was at stake and all of it so publicly visible. All the schemes, all the decades had gone precisely as planned. The Protocol had been kept. They were a dynasty now. Above the law while appearing to serve it. Above reproach by men of lesser appetites and rewards. A dynasty with the same monumental ambitions that had caused their father to begin this journey where power begat more power and money bought the world's acceptance and obeisance. A pity that the secret the old bitch had known could keep the biggest prize of all out of their reach.

His brother would know that. It was his son, after all, whom they'd chosen to be the next president of the United States.

The man turned from the windows and stared at the family photo on his desk, and his frown relaxed a little. After all, his brother wasn't the only one in the family who had an appropriate son for the task.

12

The flames leaped and fluttered playful sparks up the chimney as three generations of Donovans perched in their favorite places in the circle of warmth that opened out from the large hearth in Maeve's living room. Fitz's scotch beamed amber over the ice cubes in the heavy Waterford tumbler, and he could see the faces he loved best in the flickering firelight, all riveted by the tale he'd just recounted.

Finn was poring over the handwritten journal; only very young eyes could read those pages in firelight. She felt her grandfather's gaze on her and looked up. "I'm thinking we need T-square to figure out what the invisible-ink book is all about, Grand. It's hard enough to make out the chicken scratch in this one where you can at least *see* the writing!" She stuck her finger in the old book to hold her place. Her long-time pal T had a scholarship to Columbia Graduate School because of his gift for some kind of rarefied theoretical numbers that the rest of the world didn't know existed, but he could only go part-time because money was scarce and his mother needed help caring for his severely handicapped younger brother.

Rory made a sound of agreement, but leaned forward the way she always did when she was wearing her lawyer hat. "We have to be *really* careful who we embroil in this enterprise, guys," she admonished. "It's evidence in an ongoing murder investigation and it may be dangerous to boot."

"But we don't really *know* it's evidence, yet, do we?" Maeve countered. "I mean, all we *really* know is that she wanted Dad to have the books so he could help her, and they may be full of secrets we haven't unraveled yet."

"Said with the delightful equivocation of a Philadelphia lawyer," Fitz said with an appreciative chuckle, "but Rory's right—first and foremost, we have to keep everybody safe. But we're definitely going to have to pull in some big science guns to figure out what these books are all about."

All heads nodded.

"I vote with Finn. We start with T-square," Maeve said. "He's pretty much family, geeky as hell, and maybe he could at least tell us who exactly we'll need to help decipher whatever it is we've got here."

"And maybe the Babushkas," Finn added eagerly. "That'd be one-stop shopping." The covey of brilliant computer-genius women who'd named their tiny conspiracy-hunting squad after the still-unidentified woman who'd been seen taking photos on the grassy knoll when Kennedy was assassinated were good pals of T's, and Annie, the formidable quant who ran their covert taskforce, was an old friend of Fitz's.

"At least we know *they* won't spill the beans to anybody," Rory said with a wry laugh. "You'd have to waterboard that crowd to pry a grocery list out of them."

Finn grinned. "Our very own Lone Gunman. Extremely chill."

"How much danger do you think we're talking about here, Dad?" Rory reverted to the question on everybody's mind.

"I've been pondering that question all day, luv. There's no reason for anyone to know we're anything more than curious neighbors at this point. But once we start poking around ..." he left the thought hanging.

"Or until whoever did it figures out *you,* an ex-chief of police, were the last person she spoke to," Maeve reminded him. "How hard can that be when we're all surveilled 24-7?"

Rory, usually the most cautious among them, weighed in. "I'm as anxious as you all are to follow up on this, so I'm not going to be the party pooper here, but whoever killed the old girl was a pro, and we don't have a clue why, yet. Did he have his own agenda, or did somebody hire him for the hit? If we get involved, do we become loose ends to be tidied up? Is that what poor old Mrs. W. was?"

"Mrs. W. said the bad guys are powerful, right?" Finn piped up, "above the law and all that? I mean, it isn't like she wasn't expecting trouble after that note Grand read, and she obviously fought like a banshee to protect whatever her secret was. That all sounds pretty dangerous to me." She looked around the room for corroboration, then added, "I'm just saying … maybe we need Liam Neeson for backup …"

Fitz chuckled. "I intend to call in a favor or two of my own tomorrow; I'll add Liam to the list. I need to see what I can find out about the old girl. The fact that she was young and aristocratic in Germany just before the war might make her traceable."

Fitz turned his gaze toward Finn, who still had the two journals in her lap. "Let's start by getting T's opinion on whether the invisible ink is up Annie's alley, luv. Between them, they can probably identify what we've got here.

"I'd like to sleep on what I've read so far to see what surfaces," he said, scanning the well-loved faces. "Meantime, anybody with younger eyes than mine who'd like to volunteer to read the Old Lady's squiggles is gratefully welcomed."

All hands went up so fast everybody laughed. Fitz loved the sound of his family's laughter. "*Oh, I have slipped the surly bonds of earth, / And danced the skies on laughter-silvered wings*," he remembered a snippet of the old poem, wishing Cara could be here to share their enthusiasm. If there was one thing the Donovans could be sure of, it was their love for one another. If there was a second thing, it was how much they adored a really good mystery.

13

Fitz had wrestled back a small pang of conscience about withholding evidence—not that he really had anything definitive yet to withhold, and a case could surely be made for the books in the bushes having been given to him, but still …

He'd gone to the precinct half intending to tell Cochrane about the find, but the young lieutenant had brushed him off with such pointed rudeness, making it clear his help was unwelcome, that it had cleared Fitz's conscience about proceeding on his own. *Or maybe it had just gotten his Irish up,* he thought with a self-aware sigh. He'd never aspired to be a saint, after all. *It's not that the Irish are cynical,* Brendan Behan had said*, it's rather that they have a wonderful lack of respect for everything and everybody.* Fitz chuckled at the accurate appraisal, but would have made an addendum to it. The Irish prized justice far more than they prized the letter of the law.

Fitz hummed to himself as he turned the key in the lock of The Mysterious and let himself in, pushing back the memories of Cara that always surfaced when he entered his small, private sanctuary. He'd purchased the shop just after his wife's death, but in his heart and mind Cara was always there with him. Gone now more than a decade, but always there in the solitude of the place. Ireland-born, from a long line of mystically gifted women, each of whom had unique psychic abilities, there'd always been a fey quality about his wife, an ethereal essence that he'd adored from the first moment he laid eyes on her. "It's as if she's always listening to fairy music only she can hear," he'd often said of her with prideful wonder. He'd cherished every day and year they'd been together, but had always felt she didn't entirely belong in this world and might early be called back to the "other" place where she was really meant to be. When it became clear she wouldn't recover from her last illness, Fitz had taken early retirement from the department so he could be with her till the end, a sacrifice he'd never regretted.

After that came The Mysterious Library, the bookshop in which he now stood. Fitz breathed in the bookish mustiness, the sense of being in the right place comforting him as it always did—this graveyard of books, his second home. Row upon row of ideas and semiforgotten wisdom and conundrums moldering in the dust of time. All his life he'd loved libraries and old bookstores, and had practically lived in the Strand on 13th Street while he worked his way through school, so it had seemed inevitable after leaving the police force behind that he'd follow his boyhood dream of owning one. That it specialized in mysteries, ancient and modern, seemed inevitable, too.

Absently, Fitz patted the pocket in which he kept his ID. He still carried the poem with which he'd proposed to Cara in the battered old leather wallet she'd given him umpteen years ago. It was his touchstone.

He sighed once and headed for the stacks where the books he had in mind resided. The Old Lady would get her day in court if he had anything to say about it. *I won't let that omedthan, Cochrane, screw this up,* he told Cara as he switched on lights. *Omedthan* had been one of her favorite words, an all-inclusive Irish indictment for stupidity, idiocy and bad manners.

He reached the stacks where the books relating to WWII resided, pulled two off the shelf, then picked up the phone to call Itzak.

14

Odeon drummed his fingers on the metal desk he'd occupied for so many years in an office as nondescript as the desk. It was a clerk's desk, scarred, gray, aesthetically unappealing enough to be utterly anonymous. *Perhaps you could say the same of himself,* he thought absently, rather pleased by the idea. Anonymity was an excellent quality in his line of work. Like a cloak of invisibility.

He'd actually been a clerk once, a very long time ago. A clerk with a talent for numbers, expediency and following orders to the letter, all of which had brought him to the attention of the Brothers. Not that he didn't have other talents they'd found significantly useful over the years—lack of conscience or scruples high on the list. He was a superb lieutenant. He did what was wanted expeditiously and with minimal mess or emotion. He did it well and consistently and with perfect loyalty to his employers, who rewarded him, not so much lavishly, as consistently.

He liked his job and was a bit puzzled as to why this latest task he'd been assigned hadn't gone as well as it should have. The operative he'd assigned to the wet work was a consummate professional, tested, talented and well vetted in the field. The man had insisted that under his extreme interrogation, the old woman could not have withheld anything from him due to the continuing agony he'd inflicted on her person. So there was always the chance that there really hadn't been a dossier after all.

Had she been in possession of anything to give up—a journal, incriminating diagrams, formulas or documents of the kind they had described to him—she surely would have relinquished them to save herself excruciating pain, or at least to die easier. There had been no safety-deposit box key to find, she'd given up the combination to the safe halfway through the man's thorough ministrations, she'd begged and pleaded for him to kill her toward the end, as was to be expected, but she'd steadfastly maintained that she had no knowledge of what he sought. She just kept saying over and over that he'd made a terrible mistake ... that she was just an old woman who'd been mistaken for someone else.

The operative said he'd believed her in the end and therefore dispatched her, then had ransacked the place thoroughly, which took more than an hour because of the volume of tchotchkes and books she'd possessed. He'd already finished his search when a persistently ringing doorbell, followed by the sound of a key in the lock, had convinced him he should exit through the back garden.

But Odeon knew something the operative didn't. His employers seldom made mistakes about information, and whatever she'd had or known was of immense importance to them. This is what puzzled him now. Could it be whatever info they sought had been kept only in her head, and age had taken it from her? After all, his employers hadn't known exactly what form the material might be kept in. Or—the sudden thought struck him—was it possible they *did* know but had withheld that specific knowledge from him to test his own ingenuity? He wouldn't put it past them. But it was far more likely, under the circumstances, that they really did not know precisely the form of the dossier.

This last, annoying possibility had made him too cranky to continue the useless interrogation of the failed assassin, so he had dispatched the man with a garrote. Less noisy than a gun and more hands-on. Easier to clean up. He was actually sorry to lose this particular operative; up to now the man had been most useful. But his employers hated loose ends.

He turned his attention back to the desk. Perhaps the old woman's phone records would prove enlightening. Muds and luds, the phone company called them, and they weren't all that easy to get hold of even with pull like his. But he had managed it, and now he opened the computer file and began to scroll down the list of outgoing and incoming messages to the old woman's number, knowing that this kind of methodical investigation would bear fruit in the end.

15

Maeve hastily finished copying the recipe from her mother's book of magic-laden Celtic recipes and remedies. She'd promised her tea shop partner, Georgia, new mystical goodies for the coming Valentine's Day menu.

No one knew when the great leather-bound recipe ledger she held in her hands had been started, or who'd been the first of their line with the Sight who had assured the presence of some kind of healing power on every page. A dozen names were inscribed on the flyleaf, her own among them. She wondered if Finn's would ever find its way there.

"Shelter from the Storm Love Biscuits" sounded nice enough for Valentine's Day, Maeve thought, closing the book.

Love, she thought wistfully, remembering suddenly how sweet and safe it had felt to be loved. Or at least to think you were … the thought trailed off. The last thing she wanted with Valentine's Day around the corner was to think of her ex-husband.

She put the great book back on its shelf. Georgia said it had been a stroke of genius to make these quirky, mystical Irish recipes the bill of fare at the Philosopher's Teacup, then put them together into a book, adding bits and pieces of Irish magical lore to each one.

Maeve wasn't sure if her mother's recipes or Georgia's genius at promotion and social media was the more probable reason her book had earned a spot on the *New York Times* Best Seller list. Whatever the magic, the money had cleaned up the last of Finn's college debt, and that was a huge relief.

Maeve tucked the new recipes into her folder and checked the list of possible new products and menu items she wanted to run by Georgia.

Last month's big winner had been the Gardenia and Rose Love Bath for Couples. In fact, couples aphrodisiac bath kits were selling even faster than the Erotic Hotcakes that were their biggest Sunday brunch item. *And why not,* Maeve thought a little ruefully. *Who doesn't want to be loved?*

The armload of jars and bottles Maeve carried clattered to the counter in The Philosopher's Teacup a half hour later with a resounding thud; she'd nearly dropped two on her way in.

"What would you think of raspberry-hawthorn jam to top off the Valentine biscuits?" she called across the shop to her business partner and good friend Georgia, as she shrugged off her coat.

"I don't know, darlin' …" the smart, cheery Texan with Dolly Parton's body said, looking up with amusement. "What's it good for besides tastin' yummy?"

"According to Mama's book, it provides 'rainy day heart comfort,' which works perfectly with the lightning protection you get from the biscuits. And as a bonus, it 'makes men fall madly in love.'" Maeve deadpanned the last part and Georgia exploded with laughter.

"Hell, honey, we can charge double for that!" Georgia's full-throated laugh was always so genuine it made others laugh, too, which was something Maeve got a big kick out of. Georgia had a wicked sense of humor and blurted outrageous thoughts nonstop, like asserting that Southern gals were just like Yankees, only prettier and a lot smarter about men.

"Shelter from the storm sounds just right for this rotten weather y'all are so good at dishin' out," Georgia shot back. "Do the men fall in love with you or the biscuits? Oh, never mind! I suppose either one'll do. But on Valentine's Day we don't want anybody protected from gettin' struck by Cupid's lightning, that's for damned sure."

"In Ireland I'm afraid you're more likely to get struck by a thunderbolt than by Cupid," she answered with a short laugh. "That's probably why we had to invent magic biscuits."

Georgia knew Maeve still smarted over her husband's infidelity, which had blindsided her and ended their marriage unexpectedly when it turned out the fling she'd discovered hadn't been an isolated event, but a long-standing pattern of deceit. Northern gals just didn't seem able to understand men's philandering nature like Southern gals did. Everybody south of the Mason-Dixon line knew most men would stick it in a watermelon if there was nothing else readily available.

"Are you sure about that, honey?" she asked. "What about all that romantic poetry your crowd's so famous for?"

"Not my crowd!" Maeve laughed, shaking her head so hard her curls bounced. "We Irish are too priest-ridden for romance. Our poets write love poems about God or fairies."

Georgia chuckled, glanced at the clock, poured two cups of hibiscus jasmine tea, and sat down.

"I got the news flash about your neighbor from Finn," she said conspiratorially, "but she didn't have time for all the details when she ran in for her latte." Georgia lifted the cup to just under her nose to take in the delicately exotic scent with obvious appreciation. "What's the scoop?"

"It was all pretty grim," Maeve answered. "Tortured and murdered is not a good way to go at any age, and Mrs. Wallenberg was well into her nineties."

"Whoa, Nellie!" Georgia said, eyes widening at the new details. "Tortured, you say? I thought it was just a robbery. Was she hiding somethin' real valuable the robbers knew about?"

"Dad thinks there's more to it, but nobody knows anything concrete yet."

"Is that why I heard him scurrying around next door at an ungodly hour? Is he scroungin' for clues in those old books of his?" The Mysterious Library and The Philosopher's Teacup shared a wall and a fireplace in the old building that had been split into two shops by some enterprising owner at the turn of the last century.

Maeve smiled. "You know Fitz. He's a dog with a bone when there's a crime afoot, and he seems to be taking this one personally because she'd asked him for help the same day she got murdered."

Georgia's eyes widened again.

"He really misses being on the job, doesn't he, darlin'?" she said. "I mean, he was so good at it and he retired early for such a sad reason."

Maeve's eyes retreated for an instant to that terrible time a decade ago … her mother dying by inches, her father at her bedside every hour of the final months.

Maeve saw the compassionate understanding in Georgia's eyes.

"He's never regretted the choice he made so he could be with her at the end," she said quickly. "I'd stake my life on that. And yes, I know he misses the job. How could he not miss it? But he loves his books, too." She nodded her head emphatically as if to corroborate her own testimony. "Unraveling their secrets, tracking them to their source. He says the game's the same, it's just that the stakes are lower." She smiled.

"Well, maybe not this time, darlin'," Georgia mused. "It looks to me like the good Lord just delivered a bona fide murder mystery right to your Daddy's doorstep. Talk about the Lord providin' …"

16

Marika, the pencil-thin, five-foot-eleven Swedish sylph from Finn's senior year at Parsons made the exquisite twilight-gray satin gown radiate sensuality and rich-bitch in equal measure. She was draped across one of the many white sofas in Mimi's vast living room, head thrown back onto an armrest, one foot positioned on the other arm to expose a half mile of leg, the strappy extravaganza of Blahnik sandal dangling languidly from her big toe. She was the embodiment of sexual satiety.

"Have we got this one?" Brace asked hopefully, taking in the tableau from the doorway. "I think it's a wrap after this."

"You betcha!" Finn said in a perfect Sarah Palin imitation, lowering her camera. She straightened up and looked around, deep in thought for a minute.

"Now that it's covered for the New York *Vogue*-y people and *Women's Wear,* what do you say we do something that'll knock the socks off the guys at Italian *Vogue* and *Numéro*?" She ticked off edgy mags in her head as she considered the next shot. Maybe she should add *The Last Magazine* to that list, too.

"I'm all for that," Orlando piped up. "Like what do you have in mind?"

"Like, let's shoot her hanging from the fire escape that's outside the bedroom wing, or in the panic room," Finn replied, starting to gather her gear to move it. "Have her splayed against the wall in there wearing combat boots with the gown instead of Manolos, with an Uzi or an AK in her hand, ready to defend herself against the world."

"OMG! Yes!" breathed Orlando.

"WTF. No!" Brace countered, with noticeably less enthusiasm.

"Hold on a minute," Mimi interjected nervously. "You know how I feel about guns. And I don't know about photographing inside the panic room. I mean, the whole idea of having a panic room is not to let anybody know you've got one!"

"Really?" Brace gave her a look. "I thought the whole idea of having a Panic Room was to show everybody how filthy rich you are."

Finn grinned, already planning the shot, then turned to Mimi. "Not to worry, Mim, we won't show *where* in the house it is, and we're not even identifying whose house it is anyway, unless you want a credit."

"Dear God, no!" Mimi said hastily. "A credit won't be necessary."

"Okay, then. We can use that gorgeous samurai sword your grandpa brought back from the war. We just need something that looks lethal."

Finn hung her light meter around her neck and picked up her tripod. "Let's do something crazy good and wrap this sucker, so we can order a pizza. We've got great pictures—you'll see—and I'm starving."

Mimi smiled, relieved. "No need for pizza. Glendine has a gorgeous meal waiting for us downstairs. We filthy rich types have cooks, remember?"

"And thank you, Jesus, for that!" Orlando breathed in his best Betty Davis stage whisper.

"On to the panic room, ladies," Brace nudged, picking up props as he went. He could see Mimi was terrified he'd break something precious, but was far too gracious to tell him to be careful.

"Don't worry, darling," he said casually as he breezed past her out of the living room. "I grew up filthy, too. I know how not to manhandle the Meissen. Now, where exactly have you hidden your palace of refuge?"

"I'll show you," Finn called over her shoulder. "It's really cool. You'll love it. Head upstairs toward the master bedroom."

They trooped up the marble staircase and into the huge dressing room that was attached to Mimi's room. Finn reached for a hat rack on an upper shelf, twisted something unseen, and the entire wall slid away to reveal a steel door that looked like a vault at JP Morgan Chase.

"Holy fuck!" Orlando breathed, awestruck and envious.

"We weren't *this* filthy!" Brace amended his earlier statement.

Mimi placed her hand on an electronic pad and the vault door opened to a surprisingly comfortable inner sanctum.

"Welcome," she said, "to a place I hope never to get any use out of."

Mimi and Finn had been BFFs ever since first grade at Sacred Heart 91st Street. After Mimi's parents had been killed in a tragic accident, Mimi had gone to live with her maternal grandparents, and the warm, riotous and love-filled Donovan household had become her refuge and second home. Neither girl gave much thought to the difference in their social standings, but every once in a while, like now, it crossed Finn's mind that Mimi's wealth was a lot to handle, even for Mimi.

17

Itzak Levy gave his old chess partner Fitz a quizzical look as he shrugged out of his heavy woolen coat and scarf with a small grunt that was comment enough on the bitter, cold wind howling outside The Mysterious.

"I take it from what you hinted at on the phone, this is not entirely a social visit, my friend?" His old eyes were bright with interest. He was ten years older than Fitz, but a lively intellect and eager curiosity kept him young, as did his work at the Wiesenthal Center. "I'm all ears, as the children say."

Fitz hung up Itzak's coat and led him toward the small inner office that was mounded with books on every surface. He called to Charlie, the young man who helped him out at the register part-time, to say he and his guest were not to be disturbed except by Georgia.

"I'm in need of your expertise, Itzak," he began, "and as incentive, Georgia said she'd send over tea and biscuits from next door."

Itzak leaned back contentedly in his chair. "In that case, I'll work for food," he said, his voice merry. "It will not be the first time, I assure you." His face crinkled pleasantly when he smiled. "I take it you have a new case for us to ponder?"

"Excellent deduction, but I'm not at all sure yet what the hell I've got. Other than lots of questions I think you could shed some light on for me. I know I can trust your discretion about what I do know…"

Itzak folded his gnarled fingers on the table and waited. "So … a top-secret non-case, then?"

Fitz nodded. "My neighbor was murdered two nights ago. The police are on it, but in a half-arsed way. An old lady in her middle nineties, no family pressing for answers, it could be a burglary gone sideways … you know how it goes. It's too easy to dismiss this kind of event. It appears we all reach the age when the world can live without us." He chuckled ruefully and Iztak nodded.

"She was your friend?"

"More a friendly acquaintance and a customer. But I think there's nothing simple about the way she died, so I'm nosing around."

"The police want your help?"

"Not one jot or tittle of it, truth be told! They find me a consummate pain in the arse. Even worse, an *old* pain in the arse. Which is why the discretion is needed."

It was Itzak's turn to chuckle. "The young do not comprehend how much we *alte kakers* know," he said.

"Nor how much we care," Fitz finished the thought. "But this time, I have to stay unofficial unless I can find something important enough that they can't dismiss it—and me—out of hand."

"Ah," said Itzak, the small sound filled with understanding. "Clearly a job for *two* old pains in the arse, then."

There was a knock on the door, then Georgia's cheerful face peered around the corner, and without waiting for an invitation she sailed into the tiny space carrying a tea tray.

"Well, butter my butt and call me a biscuit, boys. What on earth are you two sweetie pies doin' crowded into this overstuffed closet when there's a whole tea shop right next door that would just love to give you the attention you deserve?"

Itzak turned an imaginary key in his lips in an exaggerated gesture of secrecy. "We have state secrets to discuss, my dear Georgia. No one must overhear us."

"Cloak and dagger," she responded with conspiratorial gusto. "My absolute favorite! You'll definitely need sustenance if it's a secret mission. Good thing I brought pastries." She set the tray on the edge of Fitz's old desk, edging back books as he hastily tried to clear a space. Itzak eyed the tray with unfeigned delight. He had tasted her pastries before.

"Like Old Vienna!" he breathed.

"More like old Dallas by way of Dublin, darlin'," she said, tickled by his enthusiasm.

"International cooperation! What could be better?" Itzak mumbled through his first mouthful of pastry.

"Call me if you want more anything," she said with a wink, turned, and let herself out.

The woman could coax a laugh from a crumpet, Fitz thought as he watched her go.

Itzak took another blissful bite and a sip of tea, then got down to business. "So what exactly is it you need to know, my friend?"

"What can you tell me about a German baron who was also a physicist, and may have worked on Hitler's exotic weapons program?" Fitz asked.

Itzak raised an interested eyebrow. "There were two, actually," he answered. "Both brilliant, both Nazis. One turned on Hitler, so the story goes, and was killed along with his whole family in the camps in the last days of the war. Von Ardenne and von Zechandorff. It was the latter who ran afoul of der Führer.

"I searched for von Ardenne after Operation Paperclip, actually," Itzak mused. "He was most likely one of those who got a new identity from Odessa and your own OSS. The Zechandorffs perished in the camps, but there were rumors that von Zechandorff's elder daughter escaped and surfaced later under arrest in East Germany. They said she had an encounter with the Stasi, but again, I'm not certain of the details. That was never proven either, and to the best of my knowledge, she was never found. If she really was sent to the Hohenschönhausen, she most likely died there. Those Stasi bastards were old KGB, and their torture skills were legendary."

Fitz pursed his lips and nodded. "I think someone found her two nights ago on Jane Street and tortured her to death."

"Mein Gott!" Itzak murmured. "She must have been older than I by a decade, ya? How terrible to be pursued by such evil for a lifetime! How can you know for certain it was she?"

"I can't. Or at least I can't, yet. But she left me something that suggests it's possible."

"Can you show me this something?"

"I have it here," Fitz tapped the worn journal. "Or at least, this is part of what she left with me. But I must caution you first, Itzak. We must handle this very carefully, not only because of its unofficial status, but because my hackles are up about just how dangerous it might be for anyone who pokes the bear. It may not be safe to involve you until I know more."

Itzak shook his nearly bald head with its fringe of fuzzy Einstein hair. "Just remember if you will, Fitz my friend, that I'm a very old man, and thus I no longer fear death as I did when I was young and had everything to live for. If you have need of my help, you shall have it. Remember, I have resources that can be formidable when set in motion searching the Nazi past …" he let the thought linger. He knew Fitz understood the reach of the Wiesenthal Center in the US, Europe and the Middle East. Itzak had been hunting and documenting Nazis for a lifetime.

Fitz hesitated, then decided. "If you can get me any information on the two physicists' families without triggering anyone's suspicion about why you're asking, I'd be grateful.

"And one more question, Itzak." He again hesitated. "Were the exotic weapons real? She speaks of her father's involvement in their design and of her husband's fortune somehow tied to them. Do you have any way of knowing if anything beyond the V-2 rockets ever was produced, or if the rest of the stories were all part of the superman mythos Hitler constructed? I know the conspiracy theorist crowd talks about foo fighters, antigravity devices, flying saucers and time machines, but everyone in our government laughs off the idea that any of these projects ever got off the ground."

"Nonsense!" The old man made a dismissive sound. "The Wunderwaffe was unquestionably real and deadly. And most likely all their avant garde weaponry landed in the hands of your own military, to be cloaked in secrecy like so many other truths about the war. Greed for these weapons was the reason so many Nazi scientists were saved and given new identities and jobs in the US by Operation Paperclip. But the trail to finding the truth about these creations is circuitous and bloody. So much disinformation. So many cover-ups in high places. So many scientists and their weapons escaping Nuremberg with the help of your government. Deals were already in the works more than a year before the war ended! Himmler, Kammler, Bormann, who were the fathers of the exotic weapons program, as well as countless high-level scientists, were already negotiating with the powers on the Allied side in '43 and '44, or stockpiling their research and data on the secret projects to use as leverage when the end came. Money was being sent out of Germany by the carload to assure their futures."

"Why was this not made public at the Nuremberg War Crimes Tribunal?" Fitz asked.

Itzak shook his head in disdain. "Nuremberg was merely a smokescreen to placate the media and the public," he said. "Did you know, for example, that despite the immensity of the atrocities and nearly eleven million dead, only twenty-two of the leading Nazis were indicted at the Trial of Major War Criminals at Nuremberg? Tokens for show-and-tell. Only twelve were sentenced to death, the rest to prison terms. There were subsequent trials yet more than three thousand of the worst of the Nazi war criminals were helped to escape by Odessa, the Vatican, the Russians and your own government under that clever bastard Gehlen. Indeed, your OSS/CIA saved the bulk of them—the crème de la crème, so to speak, of the scientists. Operation Paperclip gave them all new identities, and those identities reinvented the past so completely it was made to appear that *none* of these men and women had been Nazis during the war, only poor scientists forced to do terrible things against their will. The lies were outrageous. An unspeakable insult to the dead."

"We Irish say a man sleeps easy on another man's wound," Fitz said, and Itzak nodded agreement.

"Your aerospace program was littered with these scientists. They are the ones who put you on the moon ahead of the Russians because the US gobbled up the best among them and Russia got only the midlevel minds. NASA got

Werner Von Braun and his thoroughly whitewashed dossier. And, of course, your pharmaceutical and agricultural giants gobbled up the geneticists. Your current glut of GMO foods and unscrupulous pharmaceutical practices are a tribute to their mindset as well as their genetic research. And universities in the US and Canada were used to explore covert mind-control programs under the aegis of what became your CIA after the war. Some of these experiments were quite horrifying, and most were tested on unwitting subjects."

Fitz's jaw was rigid as he listened. Some of this he knew, but not all.

"What you say makes sense of Eisenhower's farewell address, when he warned us to beware of a takeover of our country by the military-industrial complex …" Fitz said, letting the thought hang. "He must have feared where these Paperclipped bastards would lead us."

"Indeed, my friend. So many terrible things he must have known … so many cover-ups. All this is just the tip of the iceberg, I assure you." Itzak breathed in deeply, then exhaled, as if to forcibly expunge the sordid memories.

"But let us not try to solve all the problems of the known world today over tea and pastries, Fitz. Let us begin with what may be one injustice we can actually affect, eh? I'll find out what I can for you about the von Zechandorffs and the Wunderwaffe and be in touch."

Fitz, from the shop window, watched Itzak make his way carefully down Bleecker amidst snow drifts, his ancient frame hunched and facing into the wind. A metaphor, he thought, for his friend's life. Family lost to the concentration camps, he had somehow survived and lived to bear witness. Pushing forward, seeking truths. How must he feel about the magnitude of such soul-scarring injustice? he wondered. How does any man survive seeing the beasts prosper, when he knows how many of their innocent prey were slaughtered and consigned to unmarked graves?

18

Maeve pushed her rolling chair back from her drawing board to get a better perspective on the illustration she was working on for the new book. She had a hard time concentrating with Mrs. W's death niggling at her so persistently.

The spirit of the page felt right to her—the lush Sligo countryside in the watercolor had captured the ineffable soft-silver shimmering light she'd only ever seen in Ireland. It was an otherworldly radiance, fey and fragile, one part mist, one part sunlight filtered through fairy wings, she thought with a smile. She always missed that light when she wasn't there. She always felt she was in heaven when she awoke to it on the first day of every trip back.

Her publisher had been bubbling over with good news at their meeting, so she needed to get to work in earnest. The books were selling, and so was the ancillary merch, the calendars, greeting cards, kitchen gizmos Georgia had insisted could piggyback on the book sales. Now they wanted another book in the pipeline as soon as she could finish one. Part Irish travelogue to mystic sites, part recipes, part whatever else she'd like to add into the mix, they'd said.

Should it be a love story or a fairy tale? she wondered, trying both on for size. Come to think of it, maybe love stories and fairy tales were one and the same. And if a love story, should it be one of the tragic ones that populated all the old Irish myths? Deirdre, or Bronwyn of the Sorrows? Tristan and Isolde? *Why were Irish love stories always doomed to a sad ending,* she thought with some annoyance, trying to remember a happy one. Chesterton had called Ireland the land of happy wars and sad love songs. Probably the influence of Catholicism on the race consciousness, she thought, the legacy of the great oppressors of anything sexual in a people who'd been markedly robust and randy in the days before Christianity. The Scots, despite their Presbyterian leanings, had managed to remain lusty and they, too, were Celts.

She laughed a little at her own goofy train of thought, remembering how as a child she'd had a recurring dream of her own great love story to come. How she and the handsome man who would sweep her off her feet would live in a great Georgian manse near the sea or maybe a castle, and how they'd write their own great love story by living happily ever after.

"So much for my plans versus God's," she said aloud to the empty room.

She'd been so mind-fucked by her husband's unfaithfulness. It was no wonder Dante had reserved a whole circle of Hell for betrayers, just below the one for murderers. It was so visceral a wound when one who held your heart and your trust in his grasp used that vulnerability and love against you. More than a decade hadn't yet been enough to expunge the damage. And maybe once a romantic, always a romantic, no matter how hard fate tries to disabuse you of the handicap.

She might be able to trust some man again, at some indeterminate time in the far future—maybe—but how could she ever trust herself? Her judgment about her husband's love, his character, his integrity had been so very, very wrong. "He was a just a great con man, luv," her father had said sympathetically, "and con men are very good at their task; it's how they survive. Honorable people are easy marks for them," he'd said. But that was an argument for the intellect, not the heart.

She'd dated since the divorce, of course. There was even one man in her life she felt close to. But the closer they got, the more she withdrew on the levels that counted. He was, however, the one she wanted to talk to about the murder next door. Maybe it was knowing the victim that made this case feel different and disturbingly dangerous for some reason she couldn't grab. Maybe it was just knowing the gruesome details of a crime so close to home that had spooked her. But for some reason she couldn't explain, she felt an urge to bring Declan in on it as a sounding board.

Maeve got up from the drawing board, stretched, and walked to the window that faced her winter-barren garden, hugging herself against the suddenly awakened memories of the day she'd found out the impossible truth about her ex-husband. The love letters she'd found written to another woman—love letters identical to the ones he'd sent to her. Word for word. If they'd worked once to seduce, why not again? She pushed away the image of the duplicate words that had been such a knife to the heart.

"Stop it, Maeve Donovan!" she admonished herself suddenly, glad she was alone in the house. "Just stop feeling sorry for yourself and count your damn blessings." Loving family. Great daughter. Sweet home. Useful career. Good friends. Excellent dog. What the hell more could you ask of life? It was so much more than what most people got from the capricious gods.

But none of that meant she'd ever be able to trust her own judgment again where men were concerned. None of that meant she didn't wish she didn't know now what she hadn't known then.

Still ... she'd feel better if she could talk to Declan Fairchild about the old lady's death and the strange story that was growing around it like some exotic flowering vine.

19

One of the best things about Finn's gallery gig on Rivington was that the owners were so loosey-goosey about the hours she worked. Professor Simonelli at Parsons had recommended her to the gallery owner, who had been looking for a flexible part-time employee with a solid art background. One who could walk the talk, look downtown-chic enough for the well-heeled gallery hoppers, yet was knowledgeable enough to talk the walk with the actual shoppers, the ones who knew the good from the not-so-good and who were building their art and photography collections as astutely as their financial portfolios. Lower East Side galleries were getting all the action now, and business was plentiful.

Downtown savvy looking, with a mane of glossy brown hair, gray-green eyes that tended to see through to the heart of things, and a good-natured disposition zinged with a wicked wit, Finn was well schooled in her art forms and had the benefit of Mimi's tutelage about whatever it was that rich, young New Yorkers were lusting after on any given day. Willing to work all night and beyond at openings, or to be called on a last-minute whim when business suddenly boomed or a client requested her, she was available when needed, 24-7. In return, the gallery's unorthodox schedule allowed her time to build her own portfolio, take on whatever freelance work she could find, and make enough money to support herself.

Living rent-free at the family compound meant most of her money could go for equipment, photographic paper, and printing, all of which were stupidly expensive. When it troubled her conscience that she didn't pay rent for what she thought of as the best living space in New York, Fitz assured her it gave him the greatest pleasure in the world to be a patron of the arts. When freelancing bar mitzvahs and Greek weddings got her down, she reminded herself of how good her life was compared to most of the artist kids she knew.

Finn tried to pay her good fortune forward by helping out her friends whenever she could, T-square being the one with the least money and the biggest heart. Like now, when he was taking time out from classwork and all the chores he did for his mom because of his little brother's handicap, to take her to see the Babushkas, even though he'd probably been up since before dawn and it was nearly evening. It had been a long day for her, too, but she was anxious to do something to help solve Grand's murder mystery, so she'd asked him to pick her up at work and take her to the Babushkas.

Finn had to trot fast to keep up with his monumental strides. "What did you tell them?" she puffed as frost clouds billowed around the words, "and if you don't slow down, I swear to God you'll have to carry me!"

T slowed to a canter. "Bare bones," he answered, as economic with words as everything else. "Just wanted to make them drool." He was six feet six or seven, lean as a knife blade, with an Afro the likes of which hadn't been seen since Selma. Finn thought it made him look a bit like a long-handled bottle brush and wondered what African tribe had generated such a lovely and unlikely masterpiece of brain and body. He had a handsome baby face, just like when they'd met in the playground in Washington Square Park all those years ago. She'd been crying because somebody'd pushed her off the swing, and T had put his six-year-old arm around her and offered to punch the offender. They'd been friends ever since. Some kind of karmic connection, she imagined, unquestioning but grateful.

The laundry on Mott Street near the Ten Ren Tea shop looked like every other one south of Canal. Chinese lettering on the fogged-up windows, freshly starched shirts on hangers filling every nano-inch, billows of steam coming from somewhere behind a curtain, accompanied by the thumping sounds of pressing machines clamping down on their prey.

A bell tinkled as T opened the door and waved a cheerful hi to Auntie Ling, the owner, who was getting ready to close for the day. Finn reached out to hug the little Chinese woman who, being an acknowledged kung fu master, wife of a martial arts master, and mother of Lulu, a math genius, was so much more than she appeared with her slate-gray hair plastered to her face by sweat in the heat from the steamers. Then she hurried after T through the curtain and the door behind that to a staircase that led to the lair of the Babushkas. Another door. The sound of many locks unlocking, and they were in.

Computer screens normal, large and jumbo lit the room. Also enough electronics and unrecognizable technology for the deck of a starship. Multiple eyes looked up over computer screens around the room, blinking at the intrusion like small animals peering out from the woods. Several sets of fingers stopped tapping keyboards as both new arrivals shrugged out of their coats, scarves, and boots and looked around.

"Hi guys," T said, waving a long-fingered hand to encompass all collectively. "Annie here?"

"She's here!" a gravelly voice much older than the others in the room called out from somewhere. "Hold your water."

Annie Shearman, seventy-eight, strong as a bull elephant and twice as feisty, made her entrance. The professor emeritus of this oddball group of counterculture patriots, conspiracy theorists, hackers and government watchdogs, whom she had assiduously culled from the grad students she taught at Cambridge and Columbia, greeted the visitors with a nod. She was small but sturdy, with slate-gray, short-cropped hair and eyes that saw everything and disapproved of most of it. Finn knew she'd once been listed as a candidate for a Nobel Prize in some mathematical discipline too complicated for mere mortals to even know its name.

"So what part of the TAE can I help you with today, cherubs?" she demanded. "Chop chop. Time is money."

"That's Truth About Everything, right?" Finn whispered to T. The Babushkas used so many acronyms instead of words, it was hard to keep up.

"Specialty of the house," Annie clarified. "T says you need some."

Finn had been with them all before, both in the company of T and Lulu Ling, with whom she practiced her Wing Chun kung fu, but she wasn't part of their inner circle by any stretch. An astronomical IQ and a degree in something rarefied like the string theory that Annie taught was needed for entry to that level of play. The Babushkas tolerated her, maybe even liked her, although it was never easy to know exactly what they thought about anything when you were dealing with such mega-nerdiness or Asperger's, or whatever it was that fueled the people in this room besides Red Bull. But Finn knew her friendship with T gave her entry to a world most people never even glimpsed, so as a photographer and keen observer of the human condition, she was grateful. She sometimes thought theirs was a little like the psychic world her mother and their female antecedents had inhabited. A secret and mysterious subculture that really ran the world but nobody knew was there.

"Go ahead, child," Annie prompted. "Spit it out."

"I know I don't have to tell you guys this has to stay top secret—" she began.

"You're joking, right?" Matrix interrupted, closing her laptop with a snap and giving Finn the stink-eye. Finn took in the spiky black hair with the dark purple stripe, the one electric-blue eyebrow that undulated across a brow shorn of ordinary eyebrows, the Aztec glyph on one cheek and large red triangle on the other, the full sleeve of computer code tats on one gym-toned arm and runes on the other and couldn't help herself.

"You look fucking amazing!" she blurted. "I'd kill to photograph you!"

"Take out a camera and die where you stand," Matrix replied matter-of-factly, unfolding herself out from behind the desk like a cat stretching into wakefulness. "Wazzup, girl?" She high-fived Finn, then sat back down to watch the proceedings. She knew Finn had always admired her look, was gratified by that, but wouldn't have admitted it under torture.

"Do you guys know anything about Nazi exotic science?" Finn began earnestly.

A burst of derisive snorts and stifled laughter rose from behind screens all around the room.

"Does the Pope shit in the woods?" Matrix answered.

"Only *everything*!" Bridget Monahan, the oddly prim enigma with the drop-dead body, Greenwich-Palm Beach creds, awesome skills, and a weird religious bent, piped up. Finn knew from T that Bridget claimed she talked to both God and ETs from Alpha Centauri on a regular basis.

Suddenly serious, Annie asked, "What exactly do you need to know? Exotic weapons, genetics, poison gas for the death camps, V-3s, Die Glocke, antigravity, foo fighters …" She paused expectantly.

T and Finn looked at each other and grinned.

"Probably all of that," Finn said drily. Grand would be so thrilled. "I may have to get back to you on specifics."

"And priorities, please," Bridget interjected.

"… and priorities," Finn continued. "And if you know all that, you know we'll probably have to get a few more people into the room before you spill it all."

"Not *this* room," Matrix stated bluntly. "*You* only get in because of T. No one else does."

"And Fitz," Annie added in a way that brooked no dissent. "This is for Fitz, I take it?" Annie pursued.

"Yes, ma'am," Finn replied. "Fitz gave T a book he needs you to look at."

"Wait till you give this an eyeball, Annie," T said, handing over the encrypted book and a notebook into which he'd been decanting preliminary sketches. "There's some real cool stuff I could grok and a lot more I couldn't. It's a real mother …. Fitz says it's all connected to the murder of the Donovan's next-door neighbor, but it's written in invisible ink, so we need a little techno-magic to speed things up."

All eyes were on him now.

Even Annie looked intrigued. "Hmm," she grunted, first flipping the pages, then holding the book to her nose. "Shouldn't be hard to raise the invisible images with the new software Bridget's been working on. Most invisible ink has a short shelf life, but there's been some, made by savvy chemists, that has lasted decades—so it's possible we'll be able to decipher most of it. Can you leave this with me for a few hours or have you got time to stay and help?"

He shook his head ruefully. "Fitz said you can keep it to figure out what you need to do. He'll hit you about a meet-up PDQ. I've got to pick up my brother from daycare right now, but I can be back right after that to help out."

"Tell Fitz he's got my attention. I'll see what I can make of this and be in touch."

"Thanks, Annie," Finn said, then turned to the others. "Thanks, all of you, in advance! Grand will really appreciate any help you can give him on this one. He cares about this case more than he's letting on."

All heads were already back to their screens, ignoring the leave-taking, but as if on cue several hands shot up, fingers splayed in the Vulcan salute. Finn saw T give the countersign.

"Live long and prosper!" she called back over her shoulder and managed to make it down the stairs to the laundry before collapsing into T in a fit of uncontrollable giggles. The Babushkas always left her totally awestruck and with an irresistible urge to laugh.

PART III

Coming Events Cast Their Shadows before Them

"Revenge is a kind of wild justice."

— Francis Bacon

20

From Mrs. W.'s Journal

My mother's ancestral home was the Milewicz castle in Lower Silesia. It was an astonishing medieval fortress with a history burdened by centuries of the fortunes of war. Begun in 1247 and perched on a rocky peninsula hovering above the River Kwisa (the Germans called it Queis), it commanded a vast border between countries that had changed rulers and names a dozen times in a millennium, but in my fairy tale childhood it stood sentinel between Poland and Germany.

Lower Silesia was a magical kingdom of vast primeval forests and villages so picturesque they could be illustrations in a child's book. Snowcapped peaks and fertile valleys, lavish landscapes and healing springs had made this lush part of Poland, on the cusp of Germany, a favorite destination for many of the ruling families. Only 90 miles from Berlin, castles dotted the landscape in such abundance that in my childhood innocence I believed it was quite normal to live in such splendor.

The area around the Jelenia Góra valley in particular had played host to kings, popes and princes for the better part of a thousand years, and it was there I learned to ski, to ride, to hunt with gun and bow, to dance and frolic, and to expect that life would provide me always with only that which is best. The world of privilege I inhabited defies conscience now—in my times of terrible hardship I have remembered such beauty and safety with both gratitude and anguish.

My mother was famed for her musicianship—in her own way, she was as multigifted as my father, but as her gifts were not shared by me, they seemed less important than his. She had played piano by invitation in some of the great concert halls of Europe and been sought after by many men, I was told, because of her heritage, beauty and virtuosity, but my father, it seemed, had been the only one to see beyond her cold and imperious nature to a depth of soul that called to him. Or perhaps, as with most marriages between rarefied families, she was simply the perfect choice of consort. They were happy together, as far as I could tell. While Maman lacked most of what I longed for in a warm and loving mother, to me my father seemed the most perfect Papa who had ever lived. From my earliest days, he recognized in me the mathematical gifts I had inherited from him, and so he tutored me in math and physics as if I had been born a boy.

Although we lived in Berlin, all summers and many school holidays were spent at the castle. I knew the valleys and mountains of Lower Silesia like the back of my hand—well enough to believe, in my desperate flight from my husband Manfred, that I could find refuge in the vastness of the terrain that surrounded the old fortress. Nowhere in Germany would be safe for me if Manfred pursued me, so I chose to run toward Poland and the remembered safety of childhood. When one flees in terror for one's life, young, alone and terribly afraid, decisions are more visceral than prudent. I, more than most, knew the reach and power of the Reich and the truth of the camps to which I would be sent if found—in such danger, one runs on instinct more than acumen.

Why did I choose to go in the direction I did? Childish memories of safety? Fear of heading into the totally unknown? Some relenting god who meant me to survive and bear witness? I do not know. I never knew.

It was winter. Snow covered the world, but I was immortal as only the young can be, and so on that night in 1944 when I escaped Manfred and rode off into a world of carnage I could barely comprehend, although terrified and in debilitating pain, I felt freer than I had since childhood. Little did I know that freedom requires a plan, friends, safe haven and preferably a world in which opposing armies are not marching toward each other and leaving scorched earth behind.

I thought I'd suffered before, but compared to this journey it had been child's play.

The reality of my escape was a litany of horrors. Stabbing pain from my fractured ribs made riding hard and breathing harder still. The weather made movement slow, and quickly exhausted my horse, who was malnourished within days. There was devastation all around us ... food for humans, never mind an animal, could not be had for love nor money. The war had left nothing untouched, and the roads I'd intended to travel were blocked at every turn by police or soldiers. A journey that should have taken days stretched into weeks of pure, unadulterated horror. Terror ate at my gut as relentlessly as starvation.

Fitz laid the book on the table and pulled out his handkerchief to wipe his eyes. The Old Lady had been the age Finn was now. Alone, terrified, injured, hunted. *What precisely had made this young woman race headlong into such terrible trauma,* he wondered? Was it her husband's cruelties or growing knowledge of the truth of the Holocaust? Why did her story touch him so viscerally? Was she a metaphor for the injustices of the world that had always made him want to fix as many as he could find? Was it because she'd left him custodian of the last precious fragments of a life for which she'd fought so hard? Or was it that she had asked his help and he had failed her? Did it really matter why? She had touched him and awakened in him the quest he knew so well. The quest for answers … for truth … for what semblance of justice could be wrung from an imperfect world.

The great white dog, sensing his master's emotion, rose, concerned, stretching the sleep from his long limbs. He moved in close to the rocker Fitz sat in and laid his head on the man's knee protectively. Akitas didn't care to bark and did so only at intruders or danger; instead they roo'd their meaning in eerie, almost human cadences that all owners soon came to understand. *What's wrong?* his soft rooing seemed to say now. *Don't be sad. I'm here.*

Understanding that the dog was offering comfort, Fitz ruffled his velvet ears then rose from the rocker, suddenly reminded of his age by the creaking of his knees and stiffness in his back. Age wasn't something he let himself ponder very often; there wasn't a damned thing to be done about it, so why bellyache? But there was no denying the seventies were different from all ages before them.

"Self-pity'll get you naught but an early grave," he admonished himself sternly. "You're alive and the poor Old Lady isn't, and if you don't get a move on, she'll never see justice!" Feeling better for this little self-directed homily, Fitz took his red parka from the hook by the door and pulled it on, then followed it with the red newsboy cap that was his hallmark. He snapped the leash onto the collar of the dog, who was now prancing with excitement at the prospect of a walk in the freezing snow and wind. Akitas had a double coat meant for the frigid mountains of Japan, where they'd been bred to guard the emperor and hunt boar, bear and elk in subzero temperatures. Of all the dogs called wolf-breeds, they were believed closest to their vulpine ancestors in instinct and sheer power.

Fitz opened the door and the icy wind blew a gust of wet snow into the foyer. The dog leaped at the sheer joy of it, then remembering he was expected to be a good boy and behave well on his leash, he wagged his tail furiously for forgiveness. Kuma looked up at Fitz in appeal as he roo'd an urgent request to get a move on.

"I understand, boy," Fitz responded, meaning it, a snippet of O'Flaherty's words blown into his memory by the biting wind. *"I was born on a storm-swept rock,'"* he recited aloud, "'*and hate the soft growth of sun-baked lands where there is no frost in men's bones.'* Sure and we're two of a kind, aren't we, Kuma?" he told the dog, who roo'd his agreement and Fitz laughed again.

"You're a great silly beast, but a faithful and understanding friend." Fitz chuckled as he shut the door behind them and made sure it locked. The dog's name meant "great wolf," and standing at attention on the stoop, ears forward, muzzle lifted into the wind, anyone seeing him would have thought he belonged at the summit of Mount Fujiyama, not on Jane Street.

21

Declan Fairchild tossed his briefcase onto the priceless Louis Quinze sideboard that graced the entrance to his New York home and kicked off his shoes. He was tired. Too tired for the dinner he'd planned with Maeve Donovan, if the truth be told, but she'd said she wanted to ask his help about something rather delicate and he wouldn't have said no to her for the world.

Of all the women on his speed dial, she was without question the oddest, and arguably the one he'd be most likely to call friend rather than girlfriend, colleague or arm candy. She was neither very young, nor very available, as were most of the women who threw themselves at his money, power and connections. But there was something about her, a mystical charm he couldn't quite define, that always delighted him. She was smart, funny as hell, and pretty in that womanly way the Celts had of captivating a man's heart as well as his loins, but that didn't really explain the pull he'd always felt around her. She'd intrigued him longer than most, and seemingly with very little effort on her part.

He waved a hand at Dougal, the small brawny Scot who ran his life like a precision instrument and made him laugh with his dry, canny take on life's vicissitudes. The man was as old as the Giant's Causeway and had served Dec's father.

"A wee dram to warm your bones, sir?" The word sounded more like *sorr* in the old man's thick Highland brogue. Three fingers of thirty-year-old scotch had already been poured into a heavy crystal tumbler that had once graced the table of a long-gone laird, or so the story went. Dougal held out the small silver tray and Dec smiled appreciatively as he lifted the drink.

"Ms. Donovan's coming for dinner, Dougal," he said after taking a sip.

"Oh aye, sir," the little man replied, "as if I didn't already know that and more. Tis a pity you look as if you've not got the strength of a limpet to enjoy the fact."

The cheeky response made Dec chuckle. "I've been known to rally in her company," he replied.

"Aye, sir, see that you do. I'll have cook set out oysters to see you on your way."

Declan couldn't help but laugh. "'He was a brave man that first ate an oyster,' " he quoted Swift.

"Aye," said the Scot, "but he was rewarded for his courage, now wasn't he?"

The old man had always had a warm spot in his heart for Maeve. *It was the wild red hair,* he thought with a grin. And the "bonny bosom" that Dougal had remarked on in more than one conversation over the years. "Not like the toothpicks you go out with, sir, with the man-made titties with nary a jiggle left in them."

Dec downed the rest of the icy scotch, enjoying the restoration it supplied, then headed for a place where he could shed the bespoke business suit and put on something that made him feel like himself again. *That was another good thing about Maeve,* he thought. She liked him best when he was just himself.

He wasn't denigrating the perks, sexual and otherwise, that came with his wealth and position. It was just that, after his much-loved wife and child had died, he'd known he'd probably never choose to marry again, and being head of a conglomerate with offices in Dublin, New York and Tokyo had assured his popularity with women, some of them quite interesting. Of course, the perks tended to leave a man wondering if money and power were the only things about him any woman valued, but he didn't think that true of Maeve.

He'd been her client—he supposed you'd call it that—and friend ever since their paths had crossed more than a decade ago, soon after her divorce. Her esoteric knowledge had surfaced at a dinner party, where she'd suddenly leaned across the table and warned him not to sign a seemingly perfect deal that was scheduled to close the following day. On a whim, he'd followed her unasked-for advice, profited greatly by it, and sought her out for more.

Over the years of their friendship, he'd used to his advantage Maeve's astrological services for investments, her healing remedies for various ills and injuries, and her occasional psychic hits about his life. She'd made it clear from the get-go she wasn't all knowing, that her psychism was sporadic, and he liked that honesty—but she definitely did know *some* things he didn't, and he liked that, too.

Dec's convoluted train of thought went with him into the shower. He wasn't a true believer in anything but hard facts and good business choices, but underneath the practical, intellectual exterior that served him so well, there was an Irishman's understanding of the land, its fairy folklore and its uncanny, inexplicable magic. Just as there was the touch of an Irish brogue in his well-educated, Oxford-trained voice. It wasn't such a stretch to know that just as he had a gift for making money, she had a gift for the Old Wisdom.

He stepped out of the now steamy marble bathroom into his dressing room naked, and feeling very much better than he had an hour before. An evening with Maeve might be just what he fancied tonight, after all. It couldn't be called a date and that was a relief in itself. He'd wined and dined her sometimes over the years, even flown her to his castle in Ireland when she was researching her most recent book. But more often than not, they'd just wander into Donohue's Irish Pub on Lexington and 64th in jeans and tee shirts to spend an anonymous evening over a couple of pints and grilled-cheese-and-bacon sandwiches.

Their lifestyles were so different, neither expected the relationship to be anything more than a cherished friendship. *Perhaps that was the fun of it,* he thought, pulling on a pair of chinos and a well-worn cashmere sweater he wouldn't have worn in other company. When she'd called today he'd asked if casual was good enough for tonight, and the pleasure in her voice at the suggestion had reassured him. No agenda, just friendship and perhaps the hope for a bit more.

Maybe *that* was the part that intrigued him about her. Other women threw themselves at him, or tried to seduce him into some kind of commitment, but Maeve just seemed to get a kick out of the time they spent together and didn't appear to want more. In fact, she might want less. That thought made him laugh out loud. Dec shook the whole weird line of reasoning away and ran his fingers through his wet hair.

Dammit! he said to his dripping reflection as he took a last look in the mirror. *Never mind figuring out what* she *wants from me. Why can't I ever put my finger on what I want from her?*

22

Fitz settled back to finish reading the chapters he'd just scanned into PDFs for those who needed to know the next chapter in this extraordinary tale before they next gathered. He especially needed to get it to Annie, who was not only wise but had a knack for putting obscure pieces together to form a clearer picture.

Who had enough to lose that it was worth pursuing a woman for seventy-five years and then killing her? And what prize was being protected here? Mrs. W's or someone else's? He wondered as he took up the journal.

This wasn't an easy read, as the story hadn't been told in order. It had obviously been written at different times, with memories added willy-nilly as they occurred. This was an all-too-human document, not a scholarly treatise, and all the better for it, he thought as he opened the book to where he'd left off.

Mrs. W's Journal

But I must tell you now of the terrible truth that precipitated my flight into the unknown.

By mid-1943, the war was a frenzy of contradictions. Hitler was growing fiercer and more unstable by the day, but was still certain his exotic weaponry could turn the tide of war in the Reich's favor. Yet a number of his highest-ranking henchmen were far less certain of a happy outcome. They were already making plans to escape and facilitate a Fourth Reich outside Germany.

Should the war be lost, a new Reich would rise from the ashes of the old one. A number of Hitler's most trusted subordinates had begun funneling vast sums of money and post-war power positions to favored men in many countries; this was meant to fund a standing army for the new Reich.

My husband Manfred boasted to me that more than 750 corporations worldwide, which had affiliations with giant German conglomerates serving the war, had already agreed to help create this nearly invisible Fourth Reich-in-waiting.

He spoke quite contemptuously of the complicity of the American OSS, which was so anxious to gain access to German military and scientific secrets, they planned to save the most prominent scientists from prosecution should there be a post-war tribunal. Secret deals were already in progress, he said, with the US, Russia, Spain, Argentina, and others in a bidding war to gain the technology and the scientists who had created it. A plan called Eagle Flight was already in place for Hitler's death to be brilliantly faked should the need arise.

Whoever you are, dear reader of this journal, I do not think you can conceive of the arrogance of men like those who controlled the Reich, for they truly believed they were Aryan supermen and that either military victory or Eagle Flight or the superiority of their science would ensure the continuing power the Reich and the Nazi philosophy deserved.

To facilitate all this, many of the Nazis' most important secrets were being vouchsafed to trusted men. My husband and his partner, Johann Gruss, were chosen to help implement the plans of the High Command. The Wunderwaffe program of exotic science and weaponry was being wildly accelerated in several secret locations as a last-ditch effort to win the war militarily. Yet at the same time, the godfathers of these exotic science programs, Kammler, Bormann, Himmler and their trusted henchmen, were making their own deals and feathering their own post-war nests with astronomical amounts of stolen money, plus documents and blueprints of the top-secret science they oversaw! Both Manfred and Johann Gruss were in the thick of this top-secret conspiracy.

Nazi science was light-years ahead of the Allies in vision and technology, Manfred assured me, and for good reason. They'd had thousands of unwilling test subjects and no foolish constraints of conscience, ethics or morality to hinder them in their research. The Jews, gypsies, homosexuals and all the other non-Aryans in the camps had supplied an endless stream of expendable labor and helpless guinea pigs.

Thus the scientific breakthroughs that had already been made were extraordinary enough to either destroy the Allied armies in battle, or to be used as bargaining chips for escape at the war's end to lives of unimaginable wealth and power, using new identities. Manfred said powerful secret factions within the US, Britain and Russia had been making covert overtures to purchase at any cost the brilliant exotic science and medical knowledge that had been dangled in front of them by intermediaries since 1943. These three powers also lusted after the scientists who had created such wonders, so the safety of the majority of the perpetrators of terrible crimes against humanity would be assured after the war.

No matter how the war ended, Manfred told me gleefully, Hitler intended to survive and to make sure the new Reich survived with him. Throughout his rise to power he had used five body doubles, men who had been groomed, dressed and tutored to be perfect mimics of der Führer. One of these men would become his dead doppelganger, if need be. Hitler's suicide would be faked, his bunker abandoned and burned so the Allies would accept this disinformation as reality.

Der Führer would be long gone by that time, flown out of Berlin by Hannah Reitsch, who was his private pilot, and then spirited out of the country via a circuitous route through Denmark, Spain and the Canary Islands, before being taken to safety on one of the high-powered U-boats Germany had already perfected.

According to Manfred, Hitler and his chosen inner circle would go to a lavish German enclave being prepared in Argentina. Juan Perón, president of Argentina, had personally invited Hitler and his High Command to hide there in Bariloche Province. This would place the leadership of the Fourth Reich close to the secret military base called Neuschwabenland, which the Third Reich had already created in Antarctica.

Fitz made a mental note to ask Itzak and Annie if any of this could be verified.

23

The old Wallenberg bitch used the phone less than any woman Odeon had ever encountered. Was it truly possible she had only called tradespeople, and even those quite sparingly? Perhaps all her friends were long dead, and she didn't appear to have any family at all, although he wasn't sure of that as he couldn't be certain of her real identity. She seemed not to have existed at all before coming to the US. Of course, so many records in Europe had been lost in the bombings and the Russian takeover of East Germany; that might explain the missing paperwork, but it complicated his task. The Nazis had kept meticulous records, and the Stasi, too—if they could be found, perhaps that was the next thread to unravel. This time he'd do the work himself, so there would be no further mistakes.

The list was sparse. Balducci's, a small handful of local restaurants who delivered, a plumber, an electrician, a dentist, a dry cleaner, a doctor, a bookseller, a lawyer, the fuel oil company. She'd made four calls the day she died, he noted. A grocery delivery service in the morning, her lawyer, the cleaners, and a bookstore later in the day. Late enough, he wondered, that she might have received the letter he'd sent and reached out for help? But if so, why call a bookstore and not the police? Of course, the call might have had nothing whatsoever to do with the letter, he mused thoughtfully, and she might have made the calls before it had even arrived.

He circled all the tradespeople he intended to visit. He'd start at the top of the list.

24

Fitz had been interrupted in his reading of the journal by a complicated request from a very good customer, a request that on any other day would have excited him. Now it was a distraction from the journal that had become his obsession.

Ghisella—he'd begun to think of her by her first name—had promised to reveal the heart of her secret, and he was riveted.

Mrs. W's Journal

Manfred's partner, Dr. Johann Gruss, was an expert in the exotic medical and pharmaceutical programs that promised genetic formulas to create the perfect soldier, as well as the mind-control techniques needed to brainwash the rest of the military into mindlessly following orders; Manfred's factories were churning out the munitions the war relied on, so both men had grown not only obscenely rich but very close to Hitler. Manfred's ego and cruelty expanded with this closeness, so I lived on the knife's edge. The more I learned of the truth, the more frightened I became, for I was now leading a dangerous double life.

My father had refused to work the laborers to death in the factories he oversaw just to meet increasingly insane delivery dates for the secret weapons. He feared his arrest was imminent, so he begged me to consign certain secret data to a journal to be written in invisible ink of his own devising. He insisted whatever secrets he possessed must not be lost, as humanity would someday need to know the truth of the depravity the Reich planned to perpetrate. He gave me scraps of cloth and paper covered in scientific drawings to be sewn into my clothing. He would whisper terrible secrets about what was planned, as he knew my memory for facts and figures was unusually keen, and for the better part of a year he tutored me in the astonishing new physics he was engaged in helping to create. Every time I visited him, I was instructed. Each time my terror ratcheted higher, for surely this knowledge would be a death sentence for us both if it were discovered.

More frightened by the day, I continued to play the role of perfect wife to Manfred. I told myself all this intelligence could be used as a bulwark against whatever precarious fate awaited me and those I loved—the more I knew, the more bargaining chips I would possess. Yet, at any moment my duplicity could be unmasked, so I lived in a constant state of heart-pounding hell. Had I not been young and strong, I doubt my heart could have withstood the ever-escalating terror I lived with.

Finally, I learned that orders had been signed for my family's arrest and transport. My father had been arrested for insubordination, Manfred told me, and my Mutti, sister and brother were suspected of having Jewish sympathies. I begged Manfred to intercede for those I loved, but he would not. My family ran to me for sanctuary, but the Gestapo agents literally ripped my nine-year-old sister, Magdalena, from my arms as they beat my brother, Max, into a coma from which he never awakened. I pleaded on my knees for their lives, but Manfred stood watching as they were dragged away, an arrogant, satisfied smirk on his lips, and I saw quite clearly then the depths of his hatred for me.

I took an oath of vengeance on that day, lying in the dirt at my husband's feet, which binds me still. <u>I will never forget</u>! I vowed to whatever gods might listen. <u>I will never cease to seek justice for those I love</u>.

Heartsick and terrified, I believed I would quickly follow my family to the grave, but I found out soon enough why Manfred had issued the orders for their arrest and not mine. It was to cut off my last possible means of escaping his nefarious plan for me.

Three days later, he appeared in our bedroom with a document he said I had to sign.

———•———

Fitz turned up the light and switched to his reading glasses.

Mrs. W's Journal

Der Führer had assured both Manfred and Gruss that a deal was being brokered with the American OSS to save their lives and to assure their inconceivable fortunes, whatever the outcome of the war. But Hitler wanted something extraordinary in return.

A child must be conceived using Hitler's sperm, he told me. A child who would be raised to establish a Nazi dynasty and bloodline that could fly under the radar as long as necessary—none but the highest ranking would even know of its existence until the ultimate victory was in sight. Hitler believed that in this way, his bloodline would continue and his genetic "immortality" would be assured. Then, because of his progeny's superior genetics and the unlimited money that would be supplied to support the education and preparation of this dynasty, someday one of Hitler's lineage would be groomed to become president of the United States. Thus, no matter what happened in the war, he would win in the end.

This mad plan he called Endsieg. The Final Victory.

When Manfred told me of this lunacy, he was jubilant, seemingly nearly as unhinged as Hitler himself at this preposterous prospect. For the very first time in our life together, Manfred said he was happy I was not currently pregnant, and to assure that I remained that way, he would no longer share my bed. For I had been chosen to become the carrier of Hitler's seed.

"Jesus, Mary and St. Patrick!" Fitz breathed softly. "That poor woman …" He put the book down for a moment to imagine her state of mind and heart at that news, shook his head, and went back to the page.

Mrs. W's Journal

I was young, Aryan, aristocratic and married, so no questions would be raised about my pregnancy. I was also beautiful, he said, and perfect breeding stock. None but the most trusted of Hitler's inner circle would even be aware of this covert dynasty in the making—it would be the biggest and most dangerous secret of them all!

Fitz adjusted his glasses, took a deep, thoughtful breath, and forced himself to read on.

Manfred had proved both his loyalty and discretion. Hitler's own very sophisticated genetic science team would perform the insemination, so there would be no chance of error.

I was rendered mute by the magnitude of the horror he was describing with such delight. I tried to breathe, to comprehend, to imagine the future, but all I could think was that the only thing worse than a child of Manfred's would be a child of the maniac who intended to rule the world by bathing it in blood.

Manfred showed me a document signed by Hitler himself that would seal the agreement they were calling the Endsieg Protocol. He said I must sign it to make the bargain legal.

Of course, I knew I had no choice but to comply, but I bought a bit of time by saying I must read it in its entirety so I would fully understand the details of all I was to do to be worthy of such an honor.

Manfred left the room triumphant, and I sat stunned, silent, powerless and doomed. But in my anguish an idea surfaced. If I could somehow gain access to this damnable document, perhaps I could somehow find a way to use it to destroy them all.

25

Maeve and Rory both stared at their father as the family sat in the glow of the firelight. No wonder Fitz had been so agitated by what he'd found in the journal today. He'd asked Rory to read it aloud to them before sharing the info with anyone else. What Rory'd already read to them had made the hair on Maeve's arms stand straight up.

Rory, once a history major, turned her eyes wonderingly back to the book in her hands. They'd opened a wormhole into history—*real* history that was visceral and rending, not the sterile stuff of history books written by experts, years after the suffering was over. This was what human beings felt in the grip of terrible forces beyond their control. Her voice became huskier as she read.

Over the next months, physical humiliation after humiliation was perpetrated on my unwilling body as I was probed and primed with drugs they said would ensure fertility, but which made me violently ill instead. In the end my body won.

After three attempts at insemination failed to make me pregnant, Hitler's geneticists rejected me as useless and probably in danger of dying if the hormonal injections continued. Manfred begged them to try again, but Hitler was impatient and determined, and the war news was growing dire. He turned to Gruss to fulfill the demands of the Protocol. Gruss was unmarried, but more than willing to wed whomever Hitler chose to fulfill this astounding destiny. A woman had, in fact, already been vetted as his bride-to-be—she came from an extremely wealthy Nazi sympathizer family in the Midwestern region of the US.

Arrangements had already been made to give Gruss a new name, dossier and an outrageously wealthy and compliant American wife. He would also be given a vast fortune and a place on the board of an American OSS-controlled company with deep ties to Germany. As a consolation prize for this devastating news, Manfred would be financially rewarded, but because of my failure he would not reap the ultimate prize.

My husband's rage could have felled mountains.

I had seen Manfred's fury before, but never like what this news provoked. I believed he would kill me outright or send me to the camps to die with my family.

In our bedchamber, he waved the now useless Endsieg Protocol at me as he made his sepulchral announcement: the once-in-a-lifetime opportunity to fulfill Hitler's dynastic dream and to reap the rewards in perpetuity had been wrenched from his grasp because of my inadequacy. He fondled a leather belt with an immense gold SS buckle as he spoke. I saw what was to come and steeled myself to survive. The first blow threw me to the floor. The ones after that are a blur in my memory. Manfred beat me so viciously that as I drifted in and out of consciousness, I remember hearing my own screams and knowing they were of rage as well as pain. A kind of mad triumph at having thwarted his plan kept me alive.

I felt my ribs crack and my face turn to a bloodied, unrecognizable pulp, but I clung to the absurd hope that if I could stay alive and steal the Endsieg Protocol, I could perhaps escape with the most fearsome secret of the Reich in my hands. What I would do with it I did not know.

Desperate need for revenge can drive one to desperate acts of courage. I would stay alive. I would make them pay. I would somehow, someday bring the beasts down. I repeated it like a litany as my bones broke and my flesh bled onto the antique carpet.

My stomach emptied itself and I lay in a mass of blood and vomit on the floor of our gilded bedroom, a wounded animal. Manfred realized I could not be seen in this pitiful condition at the dinner party he'd planned for that evening and it was too late to cancel, so, still seething, he left me; the Protocol, already signed by der Führer but now useless, lay under the desk where it had landed during the assault.

Once he was gone, I dragged myself upright, stuffed the document into my bloodied bosom, along with the book of my father's formulas and what small jewels I could carry in my pockets.

Night had fallen and I dared not wait. In indescribable pain and panic, I struggled from our terrace to the ground below, fighting for breath and consciousness with every foothold. I had a small handgun and my hunting knife. I made it to the stables and managed, with the kindness of a groom who shared my love of horses, to steal a mount, a rifle and a pair of cross-country skis before I bolted for the countryside, praying I could disappear into the chaos of war.

"The Russian army was approaching from the east and the Americans were bombing in the west, but knowing I would be killed if apprehended, this was all I could think to do. My family was incarcerated or dead, I could not trust friends or relatives not to turn me over to Manfred or the Gestapo; my only hope was to disappear. The only place I could think to go and disappear was my childhood castle of dreams and the forest surrounding it.

This was the first of three escapes God has allowed me in this lifetime. There will be no more for me.

"Blessed God!" Maeve murmured, trying to take it all in. "How can you live next door to such a woman and not realize who or what she was? Some psychic I am!" She sounded genuinely shocked.

"So the secret she was keeping isn't just about the science in the book T and Annie are copying?" Rory began.

Fitz shook his head. "At least part of it must be about the science, or she wouldn't have hidden it as she did ..." Then he felt Maeve's hand on his arm.

"She stole the signed Protocol and kept it," she said quietly. "That *has* to be it."

"But if that's the case, Mom," Finn put in, "does that mean the Protocol has been fulfilled already? Is somebody out there actually Hitler's spawn? And maybe Mrs. W knew who that somebody is?"

"And if so, how in God's name could we ever prove it?" Rory finished the disturbing logic. "And why *wouldn't* they kill us, too, if they find out we *know*?"

26

Fitz and Annie Shearman spotted each other in Washington Square Park the next day, acknowledging each other with the slight pleasant nod that frequent park walkers sometimes offered. Neither would have discussed more than the weather on an unsecured phone line, so her call to him at The Mysterious asking for an obscure first edition of *Allan Quatermain* had been the signal for a meeting in a code they'd established when he'd opened the bookstore. There were other titles that meant other locations and times of day or night, but this was a favorite for both.

Each had come equipped with a bag of pigeon food, and the bench they sat on was a familiar one. The pigeons who flocked around the circle of largesse Fitz had established before sitting down formed a perimeter meant to discourage other bench sitters from coming close. But the day was icy, the park near empty, and the hungry pigeons plentiful. In these days of electronic distance-surveillance, such a minimal security measure was hardly a guarantee of privacy, but *old habits die hard,* Fitz thought with a wry smile, and he got a kick out of Annie's practical paranoia. After all, just because you're paranoid doesn't mean nobody's watching you.

Fitz offered his bag of birdseed to Annie in a casual way and she did the same with hers, the exchange of bags seamless, as if an affection for pigeons was all they shared. She knew his brief for her about whatever he'd learned so far would be inside the bag, along with the list of proposed attendees at their planned gathering. She'd tucked a similar thumb drive into her own little brown bag assuring him she had the technical means to suss out what was written in invisible ink, and was already working on an assessment of what it all meant.

Annie scattered the seed, clucking and cooing at the birds, then stuffed the bag into her jacket pocket. He knew she'd vet the group he wanted at the meeting, digest the brief, destroy the communication, and let him know when and if they'd be proceeding. This was not their first rodeo.

"There's a story that might intrigue you," he said, and she looked mildly interested. "I've scanned a few pages for you so you'll have the gist. We could talk about it on Thursday, if you'd like. At the Book Club …." He smiled and rose to leave.

"I think I'm free Thursday," she responded, with a smile he thought hadn't changed all that much since the sixties when they'd first become friends. The face around it had, but not the smile. Annie Shearman was a perfect example of the kind of folk the Village had once abounded in—brilliant, eccentric, with a high regard for conscience and little for authority. Fitz both liked and admired her.

He watched her walk away, back straight as a new blade despite her accumulating years, thinking about old times. He'd known her through thick and thin, his career on the force, her academic ascension into the ionosphere of computer sciences with its segue into intelligence, conspiracy, and, finally, whatever the hell she did now. Whatever it was, hacktivism or other high-level cyber-snooping, he knew she did it brilliantly. They could trust each other with their lives and on two occasions, had actually done so. But long ago.

He'd outlined the bare bones of what she needed to know on the thumb drive in the birdseed bag and added the most relevant pages from the journal. They explained enough that the rest of the specifics could wait until Thursday night. He knew she wouldn't come empty-handed or alone. Some one of her team would bring a jamming device, even though he'd sweep for bugs before they arrived at the shop. He didn't like the way the world was going, but Annie made him remember there were still good people fighting the good fight.

Fitz turned toward Washington Square North, the stiff wind whistling through the bare brown branches all around him. Thursday would give him twenty-four hours to see what he could add to the intel for the gathering. He had a feeling time was important here, although he wasn't exactly sure why.

* * *

Annie plugged in the thumb drive from the birdseed bag and smiled at the paradox of old and new spy craft, just as Fitz had.

She began to read and didn't stop until she'd read every word twice.

"Fucking bastards!" she said to the empty room. "Filthy, fucking bastards!"

Then she sat back in her chair, moved both by the woman's anguish and by the fact that she now understood how Fitz had become so embroiled in all this. It wasn't merely the mystery around the crime that had hooked him, it was the woman's cry against injustice. *How like him,* she thought with a thin-lipped smile. He doesn't want to let the bastards win.

Well, neither did she.

27

"Hitler's death was a well-thought-out forensic fraud." Annie made the statement without preamble. It was Thursday night at The Mysterious and all eyes in the room were on hers: old, wise, cynical, bright as a newborn's.

The shades were all drawn. A sign on the door read, "Sorry to close early. Book Club tonight."

Fitz had already briefed the assemblage on what he knew of the death of Ghisella Wallenberg and all he'd gleaned from the journal, and Itzak had provided what little he knew of her probable family before the war and after.

"Whatever you think you know of the last days of the Third Reich is bullshit, concocted by the Funny Fellows, as the Brits called their disinformation specialists, and their American counterparts at OSS, which later became the CIA," Annie continued.

All four Donovans, Itzak Levy, T-square, Matrix and Bridget—both fiddling with laptops as if they were extra appendages—and tiny, quiet Lulu Ling, all sat on the old overstuffed chairs and sofas that helped lure booklovers to The Mysterious. Declan Fairchild leaned his six-foot-three frame against the book stacks, managing somehow to look casual and commanding simultaneously. *They must teach that in CEO school,* Fitz thought, scanning the group with slightly amused satisfaction.

Georgia came and went with tea and nibbles, occasionally stopping to listen intently.

Finn wished she could snap a few shots of this unlikely gaggle. She felt like she was on the Island of Misfit Toys and had to suppress a smile.

"For that matter, much of what you think of the entire Second World War is bullshit, but we'll leave that for another time. More relevant to your current inquiry is the fact that Hitler did not die on April 30 in that Berlin bunker, and the Third Reich was subsequently followed rather smoothly by the Fourth Reich, which still pulls the strings of the world's money markets and a helluva lot else."

Murmurs of surprise punctuated the room's previously respectful quiet. Declan frowned and moved without consciously intending to, to perch on the arm of the overstuffed chair that Maeve was sitting in.

"You're certain of this?" he said, sounding intrigued.

Annie cocked a speculative eyebrow at him before answering. "I don't make statements I can't document. Should you need corroboration—"

"No need," he said definitively. "Please continue."

"Hitler and his associates played the long game," she went on. "Their intent to control and manipulate the world was genuine. They fully understood that money is power, and power works best in secrecy and obfuscation. They believed they would win in the end.

"As early as 1943, it was apparent to those in control that the war might not be won on the battlefield, despite Hitler's exotic weapons program—which might take too long to come to fruition—so it must therefore be won on an alternate playing field, as a fallback position. As you perhaps know, most of the great European banking fortunes had been built over the previous two centuries by certain banks like the Rothschilds backing both sides of any conflict, so the ultimate winners were *always* the bankers. Hitler's cabal knew this well enough, as several members of his elite team of cronies *were* the bankers, thus, measures were assiduously put into place to seed money and men of the Third Reich into businesses and positions of power worldwide, so that whatever happened with the death camps and the weapons and the war, the philosophical and financial Nazi agenda would still be achieved."

"Are you saying the deals we're aware of, like Operation Paperclip, started much earlier than we think?" The question on everyone's mind was voiced by Rory, whose lawyer brain was suddenly sorting endless possibilities, thoughts clicking into place like pennies in a coin sorter. "I know Operation Paperclip seeded all kinds of Nazi scientists into corporations and aerospace here with bogus non-Nazi creds, but I always assumed that was just rats deserting the sinking ship."

"I'm saying vast German conglomerates with hundreds of corporate affiliates worldwide, many of which were funded by and full of Nazis and Nazi sympathizers, were used to funnel war criminals out of Germany and into many countries, including our own. Do you really think the current ruthless philosophies of big pharma, big agriculture, genetic engineering of food and the like, which are crippling our current world, all happened because of spontaneous combustion? A good part of it was a pragmatic, arrogant Nazi eugenics agenda put into place decades ago that has borne bitter fruit. The military and industrial complex was also infiltrated, and became the recipients of untold Nazi technologies that were further along than ours." Annie studied the room's faces for signs of naivete.

"If all *that's* true," T-square said quietly, "then maybe our never-ending wars and all those militarized cops who look like Darth Vader's storm troopers, and the war-surplus tanks that are drivin' around our cities—maybe it's all part of this long con you're talkin' about, too?"

"And how about a banking establishment that's too big to fail?" Maeve mused.

"And don't forget the crazy money gap between the one percent and the ninety-nine percent that's tanking my generation's future," Finn chimed in. "You're saying maybe none of these things is just an accident?"

"It's a good bet the fallout is all around us," Annie said. "Nazi philosophy said the best way to enslave a people is not to let them know they're becoming slaves. That way they never fight back. Goebbels, Hitler's Minister of Propaganda, said it succinctly enough: 'Propaganda works best when those who are being manipulated are confident they are acting of their own free will.' Disinformation, control of the media, control of truth, the choice of some random group to become the hated minority—dictators all follow the same agenda."

Itzak leaned forward in his chair. "I, of all in this room, have not the slightest issue with ascribing inconceivable evils to the Nazis," he said, old emotion charging the statement. "Much of it, I myself witnessed and was brutalized by. But this monstrous worldwide conspiracy you suggest is so huge, I fear if it is true, we are quite powerless to affect it, much less stop it! They have a seventy-five-year head start!" There was something so eloquent in his frustration that Finn wished she could have captured the old man's image at that moment. *The evidence of past suffering was too profound for a digital age,* she thought, *it needed the starkness and depth of field of black and white film.* The intensity in the room was thick as peanut butter.

"If Annie's right about the scope of what we're blundering into," Dec interjected, "and I have no reason to believe she isn't—then we must be very certain of just what part of this beast we're choosing to poke, mustn't we? We're not going to dismantle a seventy-five-year-old conspiracy that you say already rules the world with only the Frodo-army in this room, surely."

He returned his gaze to Annie inquiringly. "I'm curious, Annie," he asked. "Why did you begin where you did? Surely you wouldn't be here if you didn't think we could unravel *something* useful about what happened to Mrs. W?"

"I simply wanted you all to fully understand that her secret evidence—whatever the hell it was or is—could have far-reaching, very dangerous tendrils in the now. It appears *somebody* pursued a seemingly harmless old woman for seven decades, then brutally murdered her to keep *something* secret. We don't yet know exactly what that secret was, but if we understand the enormity of the kinds of things it *might* be, we can be forewarned and very, very cautious. Because of her age and the Nazi connection, it's too easy to make the mistake of thinking we're poking at a beast from ancient history. This beast may be very much alive. If we plan to release the kraken, we'd damn well better know how krakens operate."

"Excellent point," Dec said, taking in the faces around the room. He could see they were concerned by Annie's intel, but not deterred.

Fitz cleared his throat. "You're right, Annie, my girl," he said. "This is a plateful of mortal sins we've got here, and obviously we need to know a helluva lot more than we do now before we poke any beast at all. Nobody in this room should go one step farther if he or she wants out, and so far, this is just a fact-finding mission. I brought us all together in order to pool the skills of any willing to offer their expertise in hopes of unraveling an intriguing mystery, not to trigger Armageddon. We may never know what happened to the Old Lady, or why.

"We may never gain one ounce of justice for her. We most certainly will *not* bring down any evil empires. But I, for one, would like to know what they wanted from her, so I'm game to investigate at least a little further. What I'm *not* game to do is to endanger a hair on the head of anyone in this room."

Maeve felt a ripple of anticipation energize the room. "Okay, maybe we could take this one step at a time, Dad," she offered. "Anyone who wants out, this is the perfect moment to say so, no questions asked about why, no harm done."

"In or out," Rory interjected, "we should all pledge our absolute silence about what we've heard here tonight so that nothing about it leaves this room; we owe each other a sense of safety." All heads nodded yes to that.

"One more thing," Maeve added. "We should pledge that if any further information is gathered by those who choose to stay in the game, and Fitz or Annie feel the danger has seriously escalated because of that, they'll pull the plug instantly and get us whatever help is needed."

"The danger level has already escalated!" Matrix snapped. "Just being here tonight loops everybody in. Do you seriously think nobody is watching us?"

"There's a 37.658 percent chance we're being watched and a 68.936 percent chance somebody in this room will trigger a trip wire without meaning to," Bridget piped up with her usual digital sangfroid. "You people are not trained in covert—"

"Hang on, everybody!" Rory interrupted again. "Let's be cautious, not totally paranoid. Even if somebody gave a rat's patootie about the fact that we're all together here tonight—which I highly doubt—we're just gathering intel and sharing cookies. We could be researching a book project for The

Mysterious for all anybody knows. As a matter of fact, that's a perfectly plausible cover story for the moment. But let's poll the panel anyway. Does anybody want out right now, before we tiptoe into trip wire territory?"

No one stirred.

"OK, then," she said in her sensible lawyer voice. "Let's just think of this as a video game with multiple levels where you can opt out. But it might help if we find out exactly what each of us thinks we can bring to the game if we choose to stay in until the next level." She looked pointedly around the group. "I'm in because Fitz is in and I can gather intel pretty discreetly because of my legal connections and friends. Nobody would question it if I suddenly decided to research a book on the legal implications of Nazi history, or banking for that matter."

"I believe I'm in a superb position to ferret out facts about Ghisella's life that are not easily accessible in this country," Itzak added judiciously, and everyone noted that he, too, had begun to call the old woman by her given name. "I very much wish to know more about where she disappeared to after the war. From what I've found thus far, she deserves our respectful attention, and perhaps even our admiration. Thus, my friends, I am most definitely still *in* our little investigative conspiracy."

"The drawings and formulas in the book you're having Annie and me vet are fucking brilliant," T interjected, making no apology for the expletive. "Way cool and way deep into quantum physics and quantum mechanics—like the kind nobody was even supposed to know about seventy years ago, except maybe Tesla. You'll have to pry that book out of my cold dead hands if you want me to stop now. I am hooked, big-time!"

Dec cleared his throat, looking so somber everyone expected him to opt out. Instead he said, "My grandfather, like a great many members of the Irish and British aristocracy, was a Nazi sympathizer." That startled everyone but Itzak and Annie, who knew more about the fabric of lies woven around WWII than any of them. "The expedient explanation was 'the enemy of my enemy is my friend,' but I think it went far deeper, and had more to do with money and lucrative alliances than loyalty, so I'd like to know more. And my family gives me access to high places. I'm not prepared to opt out just yet."

Lulu Ling had not said a word until now. "You must increase your physical skills," she pronounced suddenly in her practical dojo voice that brooked no argument, despite the fact that her diminutive china-doll beauty made her look about thirteen. "I will speak with Master Ling about your schedules. There is much you will need to learn now if you are to be safe. I will offer my guidance with your workouts."

All who knew Lulu understood the generosity of this offer. Between grad school, the laundry, the dojo and the Babushkas, Lulu's life was nothing but obligations, every one of them demanding. The girl had no leisure time whatsoever and a schedule that would have felled Muhammad Ali.

Annie waved a hand dismissively to say she wouldn't be here if she weren't in.

"We go where Annie goes," Bridget chirped brightly and Matrix said, "Fuckin' A."

Maeve looked around at the faces of her family and made a gesture encompassing all Donovans. "We go where Fitz goes," she said.

"Thank you," Fitz said quietly. "All of you. What say we divide up chores, see what a week buys us, then reassess options at our next meet to see if we take this any further, eh?"

Finn stood up and stretched her long limbs. "Slingshots at the ready, boys and girls," she said with enthusiasm. "Goliath awaits."

Fitz smiled at his granddaughter.

"Excellent rallying cry," he said approvingly. "After all … Goliath didn't win."

28

The cups and dishes had been cleared, and the group dispersed one by one or two by two. Only Maeve and Georgia lagged behind, having refused all offers of help with the cleanup so they'd have a chance to talk privately.

"You were uncharacteristically quiet while all that was happening," Maeve said. "So what's up?"

Georgia nodded, her usually smiling lips pursed and thoughtful. "Mm." She made a noncommittal sound. "Truth is I was decidin' whether or not I wanted into this thing at all, whatever *this thing* is." Maeve's eyebrows rose and she waited for more.

Georgia put the last dish in the dishwasher, closed its door and clicked the "On" light. "You know I'm a Texan," she began and Maeve laughed out loud.

"Hard to miss," she said.

"Most Yankees figure I'm from Georgia because of my name, but I'm Texas through and through. My granddaddy made his money in oil like a lot of other tough old birds, but I don't generally trade on that. Leastways not up here in Yankee territory."

Maeve looked quizzically at her friend. "And this is relevant why?"

"Because I got me a good life here, Maeve," Georgia said, hanging her apron on the hook and sitting down on a kitchen stool. "I got more'n enough money for freedom, I love this business we've got going and I'm real good at it. I've left my crackpot family in the dust and only have to see the last dysfunctional member of it when I feel like it …" she paused. "So I'm not real sure I want to get mixed up in a clusterfuck that's big *and* dangerous. I'm not sure you should either, by the way, but I know you Donovans, and this thing was dropped on your plate by fate's fickle finger, so sure as shootin' you guys won't walk away."

"And …" Maeve prompted, sensing more.

"And I might be able to find out some things that could help … family things. We got more skeletons in the closet than the Smithsonian bone room." She looked up at Maeve, who was surprised by the intensity behind her sky-blue eyes.

"There's a lot of muck to be raked here, honey, if this murder is hooked into any old Reich at all."

Maeve's auburn curls bounced as she shook her head vehemently. "Then you're out, Georgia. Fitz will understand your reticence, no questions asked."

"That's just it, Maeve. I love your daddy like he's my family, too. He'd never abandon me if I needed help, and if this thing escalates into a brouhaha where you guys *all* need help, I'll be goddamned if I'll leave you in the mud by the side of the road. I just needed to think it through and kitchen work always helps me do that, you know? But I was listenin' real good all the way."

Maeve reached across the table and patted Georgia's hand. "Why don't you sleep on it," she said quietly. "You'll know what to do, in the morning."

Georgia shook her head and stood up. "No," she said definitively. "My head's made up right now. I'm in. And I might be able to supply some ammo, once I get my mind wrapped around what's really going on here. Looks like I'm gonna have to start payin' attention in class!"

"As if you ever let anything get by you, girlfriend," Maeve responded with a laugh. "Isn't that a steel trap under your Stetson?"

"Damned straight it is!" Georgia replied, and smiled for the first time all evening.

29

T and Finn left the meeting together and turned toward Jane Street. They needed time to talk, and the frigid air was better than an energy drink after the warmth of The Mysterious and the squishy comfort of the overstuffed chairs.

"How much time have you got to work on this, T?" she asked, concerned, wrapping her scarf tighter against the brisk wind. "You've got school, work, your mama, your brother … it's a lot."

"I got all the time in the world for Donovan Central, baby girl," he said good-naturedly. "I don't need all that much sleep and I'm really jazzed by what's in that book. Annie is, too. Wunderwaffe, antigravity machines—I mean, the world thinks all this stuff never existed at all, but it looks like it did and was maybe used by some really bad dudes to continually gain and consolidate power. If all that's true, we've been lied to a lot. These encryptions are a major mind-fuck."

"Wunderwaffe!" Finn mimicked the German. "Makes you wonder how the hell anybody ever took these people seriously. It sounds like a German breakfast cereal. And let's not forget Hitler's toothbrush mustache. Any other country would have laughed him off the podium."

T smiled indulgently at her. Finn was always irreverent and funny, but he hoped that didn't mean she wasn't taking Annie's warning seriously. The kinds of things in the Old Lady's book meant millions, maybe billions, to the military and aerospace. And those weapons, if they really existed, they'd gone *somewhere* to make somebody a fucking fortune. And that kind of money had trouble written all over it.

"You're right, babe, but Annie's got her finger on the pulse, and if she says this shit is dangerous, we gotta listen up."

"I got that," she agreed. "Even discounting some of her monumental paranoia, she's usually right. As it happens, I'm up to my fanny in work this week. Three days at the gallery, two late-night events, I've got darkroom time booked and some big prints to deliver, but I want to stay in the loop enough to have something to contribute by next week's meet."

"You looking for marchin' orders, or do I detect a plan bein' hatched?" he asked speculatively.

"Possibly," she answered. "It occurs to me we have a whole lot of words but no pictures of the original players. Yet the Germans were fanatics about documenting every frigging thing they did, down to how many gold teeth they extracted from each victim at the camps. And Hitler had Leni Riefenstahl, his personal propagandist filmmaker, at his side 24-7. Leni used to bop around Poland in a Nazi uniform, but then got whitewashed by the PTB after the war so she wasn't a Nazi anymore, just a war correspondent."

"You seem to know a lot already." T smirked at her shorthand for the Powers That Be. Very Buffy and Angel.

"I only know enough to know there's got to be a lot more, if we can just track it," she said, her breath coming out in frost clouds. "Those heartless creeps documented all their crimes. So maybe there's photographic evidence we could dig up. You know, stuff we could use in our investigation. I mentioned it to Itzak and he seemed to like the idea."

They stopped in front of the steps of her house. "Shouldn't you stay over, T?" she asked him earnestly. "I mean, it's late and it's freezing out here."

T-square smiled at her concern. "Thanks for the invite, baby girl, but I promised my mama I'd take KayZee to school in the morning. Mom's got stuff to do real early." Seeing the worry on her face he added, "I'll be fine. You know I'm part owl and I work real good at night. Plus, I'm jonesing to get back to that book ASAP. Annie's squad got the invisible ink knocked to where they can photocopy the text. She slipped me a bunch of pages tonight."

"Okay," she said reluctantly. "Just take care of yourself. You don't live in the best neighborhood, you know."

"And who's fault is that, white girl?"' he jibed. "I's an oppressed minority." They both laughed and she reached up to kiss his cheek and hug him. T-square was one of a kind, she thought, watching his easy lope down Jane Street before she turned to go inside. If anybody should make it in this sorry world, it should be T.

30

Mimi whizzed down the hospital corridor, her hands full of files. She'd promised to meet Finn at home early to help finalize the caterer's choices for the boys' launch party. With two days to go, there wasn't much time, but escaping the hospital tonight was looking dicey. She glanced at her watch, opened the file room door with her elbow and thought about little newborn life in the NICU that she'd helped save today. Those tiny fingers and toes turning from blue to pink, the look of sheer gratitude and relief in the eyes of the new parents, had more than made up for every extra hour this day had asked of her.

She'd never known her own parents because they'd been killed in a ski-lift accident in Gstaad when she was two. Raised by her wealthy, stern but doting grandparents in great luxury, she'd never wanted for a thing. Except for the kind of utter devotion and unconditional love she'd seen in those parents' eyes today.

It wasn't that her grandparents hadn't loved her, she quickly amended her own ungrateful thoughts, but they were from a different class and a different era. Of a primly Protestant bent, they'd dutifully fulfilled every single obligation of raising a granddaughter with good will and purposeful intent. But there was no great joy in them and no frivolity whatsoever.

She knew the tragedy of their daughter's death was a blight that had never quite healed and that propriety was the code of their class, so they could never really talk about their loss or grieve with the child left behind so she could grieve, too. Why on earth was she letting herself go down that stupid old path, she chided herself? She'd had a privileged childhood, so this old abandonment nonsense was ridiculous! And she'd had the Donovans.

Going to Sacred Heart 91st Street had brought her to Finn; best friends always recognized each other from the get-go, so that part was easy enough. And Finn came equipped with a rollicking Irish family, as warm and merry as her grandparents were cool and austere. The Donovans had embraced her with love and magic … stories of fairies and kings … stories of heroes and angels and love that conquered all. They'd laughed with her and held her when she cried over the hole in her heart that came from losing parents. And they'd understood that all the money and luxury on earth couldn't compensate for the loneliness of a little girl raised in a marble mausoleum and expected to be perfect in everything she ever said or did.

Mimi shook her head to clear it of such unwanted thoughts and quickly filed what she'd carried in. It was just that seeing the solidarity of the Donovans as they rallied around the new mystery that had dropped into their laps had reminded her of how different her childhood had been from Finn's. And how very much the Donovans' closeness and love for each other touched her heart and, truth be told, had taught her most of what she knew of love and generosity of spirit.

Planning the showcase party for the introduction of Brace and Orlando's new line with Finn was all about love, too. And true friendship and sharing. In pretty much all areas of young, merry, in-the-know New York-y adventures, Finn was the perfect wingman. Maybe because she'd been born to a family that ranked happiness above money and loving friendship above pretty much everything else.

Mimi scooted out of the file room in search of her attending, grateful she'd had time to get a better perspective on things. Truth was, she was luckier than most of the whole world, and it didn't do to ever forget that fact.

She turned a corner of the corridor, stopped and headed toward the NICU. Maybe she had time to take one more look at that newborn miracle who was loved so very much.

31

"Uncle Hutch?" Georgia hoped this late-night phone call wouldn't backfire. "It's me."

"I'd gleaned that much, darlin'," he drawled back at her in what he called his "whiskey and wild women-lovin' " voice, deep and gravelly. "What can I do for you, sugar? It's been a while."

She ignored the jibe. It was, after all, only the truth and she wasn't proud of it.

"What do ya'll know about the crooks in the family, Uncle Hutch? And how much truth are you willin' to tell me?"

She could hear his low chuckle and the movement of his chair being pushed back from the Texas-size desk in his office. She'd seen both often enough to know she had his attention. It was two hours earlier in Texas and Hutch was still in his office.

"I s'pose it all depends on how much you'd care to know about how many nooses we got in the family tree, and why you want to know it, honey pie." She wondered how many more confections he would conjure in his endearments. No wonder she baked for a living.

"Somethin's come up that makes me curious about Granddaddy's doin's in the Great War, is all," she said, her Texas accent suddenly thick as molasses. It was the accent she could only use within the borders of the Lone Star state if she expected to be understood by anybody.

"And whyever would such doin's interest your pretty little head?" he asked with some curiosity of his own.

Hutch was the only one left in her immediate family from her mama and daddy's generation, and the only one she loved in the whole crowd of leftovers, as she thought of the gaggle of cousins and other assorted kin she had strategically not seen in a hog's age. But loving him didn't mean entirely trusting him. B.H. Hutchinson Walker—or Big Hutch as he was called by the locals—was a wily old buzzard, a hard drinking, hardheaded oilman with the same gambler's lucky streak that ran in her family sure as other people's families passed on buckteeth or freckles. He'd practiced law from his ranch, punched cattle, and taught her how to hunt, so she knew he had a warm spot in his heart for her, too. Hunting in Texas was damned near sacred. You didn't share your hunting secrets with any relatives likely to shoot you.

The conversation had gone as well as it could with neither side giving up any information beyond hello, so far. Georgia thought, drumming her long manicured nails on the desk while deciding her next move. If she wanted Hutch to give up any family secrets it would have to be face-to-face.

"Uncle Hutch," she said in a honey-coated tone that could give a man diabetes on the spot, "I don't suppose you got room for a boarder for a couple of days, do ya?"

She knew that'd tickle him. There were so many bedrooms in the old homestead they'd lost count.

"Well now," Hutch said with a genuine smile in his deep voice. "That'd be right nice, darlin', wouldn't it? Lemme just see if I can get Luz to find a spare nook or cranny for you to put your sweet lil butt in."

It was Georgia's turn to smile. Luz had been her uncle's housekeeper damn near since the Alamo.

"Give her a hug for me, Unc," she said. "I'll be there soon as I can catch a plane."

"Want me to send one up for you, darlin'?" he asked. "Flyin' commercial's for peons."

"Now you're just wantin' to show off your toys, Uncle Hutch," she teased, remembering how very rich he was. "No need for crankin' up your air force, but thanks anyway. I kinda like peons."

"Suit yourself, darlin'," he said amiably. "Just call when you know your flight number, and I'll send Juan to fetch you." He called all the

Mexican help Juan or Juanita so he didn't have to remember their names.

Georgia said her goodbyes, then picked up the phone again, this time to make a reservation.

32

Fitz settled in with the book that had wormed its way into his detective's heart, adjusted the light over his shoulder, and continued reading Ghisella's tale of her flight from her husband.

Mrs. W's Journal

My journey was a litany of horrors. The weather was ferocious, my exhausted horse was malnourished within days. Once, I traded an emerald brooch for a loaf of stale bread and a handful of oats for my mount, feeling grateful for the bargain.

"Wolves tracked us by night, howling, hungry. I understood their need for I, too, was starving and weakening because of it. I was struck dumb by the suffering. Everywhere one's eyes alighted there was anguish and ugliness. Where there had once been lush, bucolic landscape, now there were charred ruins, slaughtered animals, bodies unburied at roadside or work gangs of skeletal prisoners trying to dig the frozen earth to inter them. When you came upon a living human, you were appalled by what you saw in his feral eyes. Rage, sorrow, horror and the terrible cunning that comes with the will to survive at any cost, had been distilled into atavistic madness in those terrible eyes. Most, you knew at a glance, would sell you to the enemy for a crust of bread.

I had learned from bitter experience to stay clear of humans if I could, but finally I knew that soon I would be able to go no farther. I had eaten only scraps of rotting garbage for three days. My horse had been stolen by a man who had begged aid at the roadside, then smashed my head with a rock when I stooped to help him. He'd left me to die in his place, robbing me of what warm clothing I wore, the horse, and all my meager possessions.

I awakened in a fugue state, near dusk. Injured and freezing, I dragged myself upright, uncertain if I could walk at all; my vision was blurred and my last strength had ebbed as I'd lain on the frozen earth. Dazed, depleted, despairing, I trudged for a time on blocks of ice that had once been feet, how long I do not know. Night fell and I knew I would not see morning.

But then, in my semiconscious state, I saw a structure materialize through the falling snow, to the far left of the road. It was not a mirage as I'd feared, but a ramshackle barn with a hand-lettered sign by the door that read "Gerhardt Steiner." Praise God the door was unlatched, for I hadn't the strength to force it.

I dragged my frozen body to the farthest interior corner, and burrowing as best I could into a stack of vermin-infested hay for warmth, I lay my throbbing, bloodied head down and consigned my soul to God.

Sometime later I woke from a sleep so deep I had no idea where I was or why, to find a large, shabbily clad man bending over me. His weathered face showed consternation and something more complex—concern, compassion, fear? Perhaps all three. What it did not show was the feral ferocity I had encountered on the road. There was gentleness in his middle-aged countenance and his tired eyes were kind.

I tried to rise, but a wave of vertigo and the dizzying nausea that comes with starvation forced me down again as a fierce pain speared my head and sent me backward, gasping.

"Stay down! You must not yet move, fraulein!" he whispered in an urgent, educated voice. "You are injured, starving. I must fetch you water. And blankets, ya?" he added as an afterthought. "Later, when it is full dark, we must hide you within the house—you will be safer there."

Fitz laid the book over his knee and took a sip of the strong honey-laced tea that sat on the table beside him. This was a turn in the story he had not been expecting. *Could this be a tale of love as well as war,* he wondered, heartened by the thought. Now, wouldn't that be grand, entirely?

He'd call Itzak with one more piece to add to the puzzle.

PART IV

An Enigma Wrapped In a Mystery

"Number rules the universe."

— Pythagoras

33

T-square, Annie and the girls were working on the whiteboard and glass wall that flanked the big computer screen, as well as on a tableful of diagrams culled from the encoded book. Complicated by first having to decipher the invisible ink, then to redraw the blueprints and copy the accompanying text, it had taken all four of them, plus the only two hours of Lulu's time she'd been able to eke out from the dojo, schoolwork and helping her mother in the laundry below, to get even this far. But the excitement in the room was palpable, and escalating with each new mind-blowing page that emerged.

There were specific plans, formulas, schematics for machines he'd never seen the likes of. Flying-saucerlike aircraft that could take off vertically. Antigravity devices. Some that seemed to suggest time and space themselves could be manipulated or altered permanently. "This is fucking amazing!" T kept saying, to Annie's amused agreement. She couldn't have said it better.

"Don't you know any other adjective?" Bridget snarked once, primly.

"Sure do," T answered amiably. "I know swive means exactly the same shit as fuck in the original Anglo-Saxon, but swive sounds too fucking lame to describe what we've got here, babe."

"He's got a point, Bridge," Matrix set the question to rest by raising her one eyebrow. "This stuff is dope."

Bridget rolled her eyes in defeat and Annie smiled indulgently. "Now, now children, play nice," she said. "We're in the presence of greatness. From what I've seen so far, this book is a scientific Rosetta stone and we've just begun to translate it. Whoever is responsible for this work was an inspired genius, or perhaps he was just the scribe for the work of many other such geniuses, but we don't yet have a clue about the full scope of what this book may contain. I'm dividing up responsibilities and putting a timeline on it."

"T," she said in her handing-out-class-assignments voice. "You're on diagrams. Every one of them has to be reproduced and identified as fast as accuracy allows." She turned to Bridget.

"You're on the math, B. We need every equation copied, worked on and worked out. Do you understand?" Bridget beamed her assent.

"Matrix, I'm giving you strategy and logic. Tell us what exactly we're looking at and tell us who would consider it worth killing for.

"I'm taking the encrypted text, and I'll get Lulu to pitch in when she can. Forty-eight hours from now I want to know what we're looking at so we can begin to figure out what the hell to do with it."

"And *who else* wants to do something with it, don't forget!" Bridget interjected brightly. "And how to stay under the radar and alive while we do it." Her irritatingly PC, cheery voice always seemed annoyingly at odds with the gravity of her words, but everyone in the room knew she had a dynamite brain in that Barbie body. That dichotomy had worked well for them on more than one occasion, as she could pass for "normal" better than the rest of them, so they all just grunted agreement and got on with the work. Forty-eight hours would probably be sufficient if you didn't sleep through any of it. And who could sleep when you were in the presence of greatness?

34

Itzak was more excited than Fitz had ever seen him. When they'd spoken on the phone, he'd been so elated by Fitz's revelation of the Steiner name that he'd asked Fitz to hurry over to his apartment. Now he barely waited for his visitor to shrug off his coat before pulling him toward a table overflowing with books and papers.

"Come! Come, my friend!" the older man said, pointing excitedly as he propelled him toward the table.

"I think I have found our girl *after* the war! And if so, what a girl she was!" He said all this in the same voice others might use after winning the lottery. "Fitz, my dear friend," he breathed as if announcing world peace, "I believe she was Magdalena! *The* Magdalena!"

He reared back to enjoy the expression of matching delight he fully expected on Fitz's face, but saw only puzzlement, and realized this was not Fitz's area of expertise. He opened his mouth to explain, then saw the penny drop.

"Magdalena, the Polish spy who might be only a legend?" Fitz asked slowly, trying to remember what he knew of the obscure story.

"Precisely!" Itzak beamed, his joy restored. "The Magdalena who skied past the Russian army patrols with coded secrets for the Polish resistance scribbled into the pattern of her head scarf! The one they called the Phantom, or the Magdalena, about whose exploits so much was written, yet no one knew what became of her after the partitioning of Germany. Everyone just assumed she'd been killed or captured and sent to the gulags, as so many had been. But what if she was not? What if she was somehow living next door to you!"

"Tell me exactly what you know." Fitz, now seated, had caught the excitement of the discovery.

"Know? I know nothing for certain! But I *think* there are possibilities here that are mind-boggling. What do you know of the Polish resistance toward the end of the war and after?"

Fitz shook his head. "Very little, I'm afraid."

"No matter!" Itzak dismissed this ignorance with a flick of his hand. "So few remember now, it might never have happened. But the *courage* of these people … the stupendous bravery …" he made a gesture that said no words could be adequate.

"They called themselves the Cursed Soldiers, didn't they?" Fitz asked, tentatively plucking the words from some long-ago-read tome about the doomed anticommunist movement in Poland that had followed the war and preceded the Berlin Wall by a decade. "Or something like that … ?

Itzak's eyes lit up with delight at the recognition. "With good reason, my friend! You see, the men and women of the Polish Home Army tried to prevent the total Russian takeover of Poland after the war. They knew the Soviets were little better than the Nazis. The Russians promised the Polish patriots amnesty if they surrendered, but instead, those who surrendered were turned over to torturers who would have made Mengele look like a dilettante. But the ones who *hadn't* been tricked into surrender were then left to save their captured comrades, so they formed the Freedom and Independence Union to liberate the hundreds of political prisoners held by the ruthless Russians. They became known as the Cursed Soldiers because they were without a country, without supplies or help or even acknowledgment by any of the world's governments, who simply turned a blind eye to their existence and their heroic suffering. But despite all this they did manage to liberate hundreds of captives before they themselves were hunted down, tortured, and either killed outright or sent to the gulag."

"And this Magdalena?" Fitz prompted. "What do you know of her?"

"Ah … our Phantom, yes. Sometimes she was called that, too," Itzak mused. "She was said to be exquisitely beautiful and an aristocrat whose family had died in the camps. She and her husband had become stars of the Resistance in the last days of the war, then helped lead the Cursed Soldiers afterward. She was said to be a woman skilled in hunting, shooting, riding, skiing—all the pleasures of the aristocracy—but more than that, she was brave and resourceful.

"She knew the Polish and German border terrain well enough to be able to slither through both the Nazi and the Russian lines before *and* after the war. Somehow crossing on foot, skis or horseback, carrying messages to the Polish government in exile in London and to the British intelligence service that was, as usual, up to its aristocratic nose in espionage of every sort, playing every side against the other for their own agenda. You know the old joke that says if you closed the British Foreign Office for a month you'd have peace in the world for a hundred years, yes?"

Fitz nodded. "You don't have to tell an Irishman how the MI6 boys like to keep the kettle boiling. But what exactly makes you think our Old Lady was this Magdalena?"

"The timing, Fitz! Her astute knowledge of the border between Poland and Germany, the references I have found to rumors about the Phantom that match the stories you've shown me in her journal. And, the names, Fitz … the names! Magdalena was the name of Ghisella's little sister who was murdered—I believe she took that name as an act of remembrance! And her husband during the Resistance was Gerhardt Steiner! The Steiner name you called with jogged it all into place, don't you see?" he looked beseechingly into Fitz's face for capitulation.

"And there's more … Your granddaughter approached me at our meeting with an idea, so I went searching and found what might be a useful clue …" he handed Fitz a faded, cracked and wrinkled photo.

"This is purportedly the only photo ever taken of the Phantom. As you can see, it is badly damaged. But I believe it resembles an early photo of the von Zechandorff girl I have found in the Wiesenthal archive. My intention is to take this to a friend to pursue it further. His parents died in the war, one in Auschwitz, one in Buchenwald. Mannheim himself was a small child when the Gestapo came to take his family, and rather than take such a small boy with them, a soldier crushed the child's body with rifle blows in front of his father and mother and then left him for dead. But he was not dead, only horribly maimed. A neighbor somehow kept him alive and saved him from the Gestapo. God alone knows how. He has spent his life in a wheelchair, but he is acknowledged to be our greatest living archivist of the war.

"My intention was to see if he could restore this image in his darkroom. But then, on seeing your granddaughter so grown up and so skilled in photography, it occurred to me that with your permission, perhaps I would ask her to work with Mannheim. To find other images of the von Zechandorffs and the others who populate Ghisella's story. If we could put together a photographic dossier ..." he left the thought hanging. "It is what you would call a long shot, ya? A hunch. But perhaps a young woman of Finn's talents would find this an intriguing piece of photographic history to pursue?"

"Is this Mannheim here in the city?" Fitz asked, calculating how much risk to Finn this might entail and knowing, even as he calculated, that she'd leap at the opportunity.

"He lives and works in the bowels of the old docks around Catherine Street. A warehouse he inherited from the one uncle who'd had the good sense to emigrate to America before it was too late to get out of Germany."

"I'll have to meet him first, Itzak."

"Ya. Ya, of course. I would expect this. Shall we go? We could leave right now, could we not?"

Fitz nodded, reached for his coat, and waited for his friend to bundle himself into a long black overcoat from another era and an obviously hand-knitted woolen scarf that had seen better days.

The two men headed out into the icy wind, one looking determined, the other hoping that whatever the mystery was they were pursuing would not make him regret that he'd entangled those he loved best in its snare.

35

Rory unwrapped her muffler, pulled off the wooly hat that had kept her ears warm in the freezing wind and shrugged out of her down jacket. The wind was bitter outside and the sky dark enough for a mother of a storm, but so far only slowly drifting flakes of snow had begun to waft into the streets.

She spotted her sister at a tiny table in the corner of the Teacup, smiled and waved as she made her way through the growing lunch crowd. The two women hugged, and Rory sat down as Maeve put her cell phone down on the table beside her cup of tea. They made a habit of having lunch every Friday so they could share some private sister time, which they both cherished.

"Checking out the stars for our mission?" she asked, glancing at the horoscope on Maeve's phone screen before it blinked out. She knew enough to pay attention to Maeve's starry predictions. "How are we doing?"

Her sister grimaced. "It looks to me as if this little adventure of ours has bigger potential than we know yet; that's the good news, *maybe*? But also real danger attached to it. That's what's making me twitchy."

"Got any more intel on what and why?" Rory asked. "That's not much to work with."

Maeve shook her head. "Nothing specific yet, but my nerves are on high E and it clearly engulfs us all in some kind of emotional terrorism."

"Should we try to convince Dad to abort his crusade? He wouldn't willingly put us in danger."

"Not sure we could or even should," Maeve answered, thoughtfully. "There's some kind of karmic attachment here that's sucking us all in, and some kind of enlightenment we're meant to receive if we follow it through." She hesitated. "But it's not simple and the danger is the real flesh and blood kind, so I'm thinking it might exact more of us than we'll be willing to give.

"Anyway, I don't think Fitz will let go of this—he feels obligated because she asked for help and he never got a chance to give it, and besides, both his cop radar and his historical book obsession have been engaged—a heady combo platter—so it would be tough to get him to let go on either count."

"Hmm," Rory murmured noncommittally, opening the menu to change the subject. "It's a soupy day," she said, glancing out the window at the increasing flurries. "Got any magic on the menu that provides clarity as well as warmth?"

Maeve smiled. They took each other's gifts for granted and had always been super close in spirit, despite distinct differences in personality and inclinations. Rory hated healthy food and Maeve knew it, but she played along perusing the menu.

"Here we go!" she said with satisfaction. "Here's a biscuit with Gotu kola in it, and there's rosemary and basil in a hearty, cold-weather soup to go with it. No magic maybe, but stick-to-your-ribs nourishment along with your clarity, right? We call it Brains and Brawn Winter Wondersoup."

Rory looked suspicious. "Sounds like one of those meals that tastes like you're eating a lawn somewhere in Asia."

Maeve laughed out loud. "Ah …" she mused. "I know you all too well, my dear sister!"

Rory plunked down the menu. "I'm going for chicken noodle. Good-for-what-ails-you soup."

"Never a wrong choice," Maeve grinned, "and far more Rory-like."

"To tell the truth, I'm kind of psyched about this case myself," Rory said, shrugging out of her jacket. "Not as much as Dad, maybe, but this is a wormhole into history and that's a big turn-on. And I'm getting a huge kick out of assembling our little cabal of conspirators. I mean, the brainpower in that crowd is off the charts."

"To say nothing of the heart-power of a bunch of people willing to go out on a limb to get justice for somebody they don't even know!" Maeve agreed. "I'm turned on, too. But then there's transiting Mars, Uranus and Pluto to consider … they can be real pains in the ass. Flak coming at you out of left field with unwanted surprises."

Rory sat back. "Usually I'm the prudent one about things like this, Maeve, you know that, but I really want to do this! Weird, right? But it's history, mystery and a shot at justice—three of my very favorite things—and I'm also afraid that even if we back out, Fitz won't. It's not just that he feels obligated, I think he feels an old-fashioned call to duty—to be a warrior again. You know what I mean? He's got a chance to be what he's great at: a crusading detective who serves the cause of justice."

She stopped for breath. "I guess I don't want him left to do it without us."

Maeve reached over and patted her sister's hand where it lay on the table. "Me too," she said, squeezing it once. "In for a penny …"

Georgia, on her way out of the kitchen, spotted them and whipped out her order pad. "You two look cozy in your corner. What can I get you to warm the cockles?" She listened, put the order in, and came back to chat between customers. She also told them she'd booked a flight for the next morning to Dallas if the weather didn't interfere.

Rory's newly purchased house, Maeve's new book and the new show at Finn's gallery all took center stage in their conversation, but underneath it all was a buzz of excitement with a weirdly dangerous tinge. Both Donovan sisters loved detecting, and both would follow their father wherever he led, but murder was murder, and that put a different spin on this particular mystery. And it was very close to home.

36

Mannheim's loft was on a cobblestone street in a grungy waterfront part of the East Village, but once inside, Finn was astounded by the obvious efficiency of all the gadgetry, ramps and appurtenances that had been installed to make the place livable and workable for a disabled man in a wheelchair.

She felt exhilarated by the possibilities. The call had come from Grand before she'd even had a chance to tell him about her own, similar photo search. Obviously, the universe simply meant this to happen.

Grand had admonished her six ways from Sunday about taking care to visit this decaying area of the waterfront only in daylight, and he'd been right about that. Seeing the derelict buildings, warehouses and piers she'd passed on her way to Mannheim's warehouse was like a trip through forgotten New York history. With their cobblestones and decay, these streets had barely changed since the first longshoremen worked the Manhattan docks and impoverished immigrants had filled the tenements with misery and desperate hope. It would be beyond spooky at night and god-awful dangerous.

Not that Finn wasn't confident about her own ability to take care of herself. She was strong, trained, and at five feet ten, she didn't look like a pushover. She was competent in Wing Chun and kickboxing, so she wouldn't go down easy if assaulted, but she knew enough not to be overconfident, either. You could always be badly injured or worse by a larger, better trained or more ruthless assailant, or by one who took you by surprise or had a gun in his belt, so she'd taken stock of her surroundings on her way from the subway and kept a wary eye out even though it was still daylight. Now, standing in this amazing space, she was glad she'd made the trek.

She felt psyched but a little nervous about meeting Mannheim. This was the kind of photographic project a photographer lucked into *maybe* once in a lifetime. Images nobody else possessed? Images from a time frame that had shaken the world to its foundations and chronicled monstrous crimes against humanity? Besides, like many millennials, she was fascinated by WWII history—especially now that so many similarities to that time were cropping up. Vilifying the press, the idea that the bigger the lie the easier to bamboozle the people: it was too similar to the Hitler playbook not to be scary as hell.

If Itzak was right, it would all be mirrored here in faces and street scenes, concentration camp images and god knew what else she'd be privileged to see. Enough to show the depravity to which man can stoop, she imagined, and the courage of those who somehow managed to endure or even prevail. She wanted, needed to see these faces.

She'd always thought of photography as almost a sacred calling, although she'd never say such a hokey thing out loud to anybody but T. A calling that let you bear irrefutable witness to the truth of life on earth. And that's what Itzak said was archived within these walls.

Psyched didn't begin to cover it.

The gnomelike man with the shockingly disfigured face who had answered the door in a wheelchair reminded her of a Picasso painting, all features askew but riveting. His pain and courage were written so clearly in his face, she thought as she watched him fussing over a tea tray in his kitchen. His facial bones had been fractured by the soldiers, Itzak had said, as well as his left arm, back, leg and pelvis. The family who had saved his life had nursed him as best they could, but they'd had few medical skills and no means of setting such fractures except in the crudest manner, so both body and face had healed in a misshapen way, as if stitched together from mismatched, mangled spare parts, a living indictment of man's inhumanity to man.

He'd left her in order to put on the tea kettle and was now heading back to where she stood transfixed. He was pulling a small wheeled cart behind him. She offered to help, but he said he could manage.

"So you are the famous Finn," he began, a kindly smile lighting his oddly off-center mouth and eyes. His obvious cheer in the greeting made her laugh a little as she answered.

"I'm the *non*-famous Finn!" she said, holding out a hand to him. "And to tell you the truth, I'm a little awestruck at being in the presence of the man who has assembled the most brilliant collection of World War II images in the world." She really meant it and he could tell.

"Ah, so you are charming as well as lovely," said Mannheim, his accent more mellifluous than she'd thought German could ever be. "Then we must both be honored in our meeting, for I've been told by both my friend Itzak and by your grandfather that you make extraordinarily beautiful images and are a genius at portraiture! I should like to see your work one day. Perhaps the beauty of your photographic vision will serve as a counterweight to the horrific images that populate my archive. Although, to be honest, I've always thought the eloquence of the faces in my collection a most beautiful tribute to humanity's courage in the face of impossible odds."

Finn had no idea what to say to that and felt moisture fill her eyes and color rise in her cheeks. Her fair skin blushed easily and it flustered her when it happened. There was so much she wanted to say ….

"Sit, my dear child," he said, seeing her sudden embarrassment. "Let us speak for a moment over tea. I will tell you what I've assembled here and you can tell me precisely what would help you most in our current quest. Then together we shall see what can be accomplished to give a voice to those who were denied one, ya?" He smiled again, and she was once more startled by how the generosity of his smile transformed the ugliness of what had been done to him.

"That would be perfect!" she agreed, on firmer ground talking about the work. "We need to find out if Mrs. W was some famous spy I've never heard of who might not even be real," she said, suddenly animated, “and we need to find a bunch of creepy old Nazis who got new identities from the CIA and who might be the ones who wanted her dead after seventy-five years.”

Mannheim suppressed a chuckle. “Excellent!” he said. “Finding creepy old Nazis is what I live for. Let us drink tea and then begin, yes?”

37

The dimpled and ginger-haired young man named Charlie, who helped Fitz at The Mysterious whenever his grad school hours permitted, tilted his head up from the desk behind the counter and looked with curiosity at the medium-size gray man who had just entered the shop, wondering why the guy made him feel uneasy. There wasn't anything out of the ordinary about him. Maybe that was it. He was too ordinary, not like the Village characters or erudite bibliophiles who tended to shop at The Mysterious. He was stocky for his height, as if he'd worked too hard at the gym on his upper body and neglected the rest. But in every other way he was medium everything. Medium height, medium clothing, medium gray salt-and-pepper hair peeking out from under a fedora.

"May I help you?" Charlie asked, shaking off the odd feeling.

The visitor smiled. At least Charlie thought that was what the peculiar rictus of the mouth was meant to be. He'd seen smiles that didn't make it to the eyes, but this one didn't even include both lips. Like he'd been novocained at the dentist.

"Just browsing, really," the man replied in a soft, gravelly voice. "Are you the proprietor?"

Charlie chuckled good-naturedly. "No way," he said. "That'd be Mr. Fitz. I just help out. Feel free to browse and let me know if you need anything."

"I do have a fondness for books about World War II," the man amended. "You don't by any chance specialize in those, do you?"

Charlie shook his head no but said, "Not our specialty, but we do have a few …"

"If you could point me toward them?" the man said pleasantly, but his eyes were sharp and feral as they took in the interior of the shop, like a shark scouting for his next meal.

"Sure thing," Charlie responded, coming out from behind the high desk and walking toward the stacks. "How'd you find us?" he asked over his shoulder, making conversation.

"My friend, Mrs. Wallenberg, may have mentioned your shop to me. She and I had some interests in common."

Charlie looked suddenly stricken. "Mrs. Wallenberg—" he started, then stopped. "She was a customer for a long while," he stammered, not certain if he should mention her death. "I think she was a friend of Mr. Fitz…"

"Really? A friend, you say?" The man turned and moved in a new direction, picked a random book off a shelf, held it a moment, then put it back unexplored. "Tell your Mr. Fitz I'll be back to chat about our mutual friend, won't you?" He again took in the details of the shop, as if committing them to memory, before heading for the door.

"Do you want to leave your card, sir?" Charlie asked, hackles rising again. "I'll pass it on to him when he comes in."

"Thank you, no. Just let your boss know I'll be back for a visit one day soon." The bell on the door tinkled behind the man as he exited. A double-parked black SUV with darkened windows waited outside. Charlie saw him get in the back and say something to the driver before the door closed.

That's one spooky dude, Charlie thought as the car wove its way into Bleecker Street traffic. He'd tell Mr. Fitz about the visitor when he got in.

As if the thought itself had conjured him, Fitz walked out from behind one of the stacks and nodded at the young clerk. He had obviously let himself in by the back door and chosen not to make himself known to the visitor.

"An odd one, wouldn't you say, Charlie?" Fitz said thoughtfully. "You handled him well."

"Yes sir. He gave me the willies."

"I could say the same, laddie. I'd put good money on the fact he's never laid eyes on Old Lady Wallenberg."

Charlie nodded agreement as Fitz turned back toward his office.

So they've seen the phone logs, Fitz said to himself. *They're fast and professional, and now they'll be back to see what I know.*

38

The gray man had been wearing gloves, so no fingerprints. Fitz allowed himself to feel brief annoyance at that. The slouched fedora he'd worn and the way he'd held his head turtled down into his muffler had kept the surveillance camera behind the desk from getting a clear shot of his face. He made a mental note to install another camera inside that would provide a different angle. Ditto the one outside the door, as the visitor had donned large sunglasses immediately on exiting and had kept his back to the camera even as he'd slouched into his car—but it would have been good to get the license plate.

But he'd be back for sure. Fitz picked up the phone to call Frank, the handyman who'd handled all the odd jobs for the business, the brownstone, and a heavy helping of Rory's house-rehab work, seemingly forever. Frank would set up more surveillance cams so they'd be ready for the man's next visit.

Fitz drummed his fingers on his desk and took inventory of his options, just as he'd always done when he was on the job. Detecting was 80 percent perspiration, 20 percent inspiration, 100 percent imagination. Always had been. The perspiration collected the puzzle pieces—evidence and suspects. The imagination let you play out the *what ifs* of the crime as each new piece fell into place. And the inspiration? Well, that was the part for which you needed the grace of God and a fast outfield. And experience didn't hurt … he had plenty of that.

The little gray man was the only clue they had to who was behind all this, and he'd be back. It wasn't often you got handed a cold case that had been in deep freeze for seventy-plus years.

Fitz leaned back in his swivel chair, hands behind his head, and mulled over what they knew so far, meager though it was. All their clues were from the past, not the present. The only things they knew for sure had been cold for three quarters of a century. But the murder was now, the little gray man was now … that was a start. Like any cold case, you had to lay it out end to end and start picking at the bones of it, one by one.

He lifted a pen off his desk and started to make a list:

- Was Mrs. W really the Magdalena?
- If so, who were her friends and enemies?
- Who might still be alive?
- Where had she been during the missing years?
- What was the significance of each of the books she'd left him?
- How valuable was the secret they now held at least part of, and to whom, after so long?
- Who would profit most by her death and how?
- Would this one death be enough to satisfy them, or were there more to come?

The journal and notebook were the keys to it all. He'd have to read faster. And he'd have to pursue whatever else he could find swiftly because it was hard to assess the level of danger for those he cared about until he knew more.

He laid down the book and smiled to himself. He was exhilarated despite his fatigue. He could feel the pieces cooking in his mind. The legwork. The canvassing. Talking to neighbors. The way police work was done in the old days, before computers and databases. Somebody knew something, and ferreting out whatever people knew was the gift he'd been born with and honed over half a century.

39

The hour was late as Fitz sat reading long after Maeve and Finn had said goodnight. The fire in the hearth was on its last legs, but the lateness of the hour and the quietude was perfect for immersing himself in the memoir.

Mrs. W's Journal

Gerhardt Steiner was a large man in mind and heart as well as body. Although I had no way to know any of this when I nearly died in his barn. All the men I had ever known—with the exception of my father—had been arrogant, autocratic and, other than when sexually aroused, utterly disdainful of women. I was unprepared for Gerhardt's decency. While those I had known were of the gentleman class, this man's gentlemanliness was intrinsic—it emanated from the core of his being.

I can see all this now with 20-20 hindsight, of course, but on that night in the frigid, ramshackle barn, my life ebbing with every labored breath, I saw in him nothing but the faint hope of warmth and survival.

He carried my half-delirious body from barn to farmhouse in the middle of the night, covered by a dirty horse blanket in case eyes were watching despite the hour, and he laid me in his own bed. He had only veterinary skills to see to my injuries, but he believed those skills could be enough. And I lived.

I cannot remember the days that followed, but flashes of the nights and the fever dreams come back to haunt me even now. Gerhardt slept on the floor for days after relinquishing his bed to me, but soon knew the only way to still the screams that could alert the authorities was to hold me in his arms. Thus, reluctantly, he emigrated back to the bed beside me, fully clothed for proprietary's sake (as he assured me later). He held me through the long nights, soothing my sobs as if I were a child and holding me close, hoping I would find a semblance of safety in that.

All I know of the first weeks in Gerhardt's world has been gleaned from his memories, not my own. Gradually, as I strengthened, we concocted a story to satisfy the neighbors or the soldiers if they would come, as we knew they inevitably would. I would be the wife Gerhardt had left behind when he'd fled Berlin to help his parents on their farm. Fearing the escalating dangers in the cities, I had chosen to find him now and resume our marriage.

Flimsy as it was, this story might be enough in wartime, we reasoned. Soldiers paid little attention to women other than to evaluate their potential for being raped, and a great many Germans were pouring into the rural areas because they were being given the homes and goods stolen from the conquered Poles. The Steiner farm had not suffered this fate because it was isolated and barely profitable, so it was not of immense interest to the Nazis other than as an occasional source of provisions.

I had no idea then that Gerhardt was a partisan and a respected voice in the Resistance. That knowledge would only come with time.

Fitz straightened in his chair. "By God!" he said aloud to the still room. "She *was* the Magdalena. Itzak was right." He headed for the kitchen to make tea and stretch his legs, all vestiges of fatigue banished by what he'd just learned. They'd have to find hard evidence to support it, of course, but he knew in his bones this was the truth.

Steaming mug in hand, Fitz pattered back to the living room on slippered feet. He was really too tired to read more, but too intensely involved in the story to stop now. What if there was more here about Ghisella's role with the partisans? Itzak would be so elated. He adjusted the reading lamp to its highest wattage and began to read again.

Mrs. W's Journal

All I write of in this book is ancient history now—and how strange it is to think of the anguish and ecstasies of one's own life as history—but to fully understand, you must know something of the political situation on the Polish-German border as the war flourished, foundered and finally went down in flames, only to leave us with new terrors to endure at the hands of the Soviets.

Silesia, rich in mineral wealth and natural resources, had been a juicy plum ripe for the picking when Hitler decided to rule the world, beginning with Poland. With usual German efficiency and ruthlessness the Nazis had soon turned this fairy tale kingdom into a reconstruction of Hell, as concentration camps like Auschwitz-Birkenau and more than 400 other, smaller hells were built and populated with suffering humanity destined for extermination.

Gerhardt's mother had been Polish, his father German—he had a gift for language and accent—so he had managed to remain on his parents' farm after their deaths, because its produce had been commandeered to feed the German soldiers who were pouring in on every side. The Germans considered him German, the Poles considered him a Pole. No one considered him important.

As the war escalated in chaos, greed and terror, life became increasingly unbearable. The Russians were advancing from the East, raping and murdering as they came; the Germans were eradicating the native Poles, the Allies were bombing and inching ever closer with their ground troops. Evil, death and destruction ruled. Concentration camps littered the landscape with burial pits and crematoria belching the stench of hurried death and despair so even the air was poisoned. What had once seemed an earthly extension of Paradise had become a killing ground.

Yet, if you can imagine such, in the midst of this madness, Gerhardt and I tried to create a semblance of a life on the knife's edge of annihilation.

We began to tell each other our stories. If we were to survive together, we must learn to trust each other. And in truth, to be able to trust anyone in so perilous a world, in which dangers threatened at every turn, was a miracle in itself. One's nervous system lived on such hyper-alertness that it was nearly impossible to find rest of any kind, so such trust was a respite like no other. Except, of course, for love, which was, I see now, the inevitable result of our mutual need and, perhaps, of a Divine Providence that had for once relented. Without Gerhardt I would not have survived. Without the love that grew between us, perhaps survival wouldn't have mattered.

He was 28 years older than I, and rather than being put off by that, I took comfort in his wisdom and stalwart courage. Tentative step by tentative step, we took each other's measure and told each other the kinds of truths that ordinary courtship would never have allowed. This was not a flirtation, but a laying-bare of souls on the brink of death. Sex, when it came for us, was a blessed release from the terrors that consumed us. Stolen moments of feeling our bodies, not simply being trapped in our terrorized and horrified minds, gave us the only respite we had—an inconceivable comfort snatched from fate's unwilling hand. In Gerhardt's generous care I learned the exquisite pleasure of being loved, in ways I had not dreamed possible with Manfred's twisted rutting.

When he spoke with the German or Russian invaders or the few local Poles who still lived in our area, Gerhardt's voice was gruff as theirs. When he sat by my bedside reading Goethe, Brecht and Rilke to me into the long sleepless nights, his voice was educated, his ideas lofty, his depth of soul a balm to my own. The touch of his hands brought both pleasure and safety as passion and the ecstasies of sex allowed us moments when the world around us faded and only our love remained. It saved us.

He had been a professor of history at the University of Berlin in 1933 when the persecution of Jews began with the burning of books by Jewish authors, followed by the expulsion of Jewish professors. He had seen the handwriting on the wall and a wealthy student of his—a youth named Dieter Streger—had admired Gerhardt enough to understand his plight. Dieter helped him get the needed papers to flee the city in '35, to take refuge on the tiny farm of his parents, where he hoped to wait out the gathering madness. His father was dying and his mother followed a year later, so the fiction of his coming to help them was enough to allow him entry to an isolated peasant world, which was soon to turn to flame and then to ashes.

A farmer by day, Gerhardt became a partisan by night. There were others in this beleaguered part of Poland, who, after the country was ravaged by Hitler's forces, were determined to fight back in whatever way they could. Sabotaging shipments, disrupting radio transmissions, stealing food supplies—every single act of rebellion counted in such desperate times. He found these others and joined the Resistance.

There was really never a decision to be made about whether I would join Gerhardt in this dangerous work with the Underground ... it was as inevitable that I lend whatever skills I had to his, as it had been inevitable that we fall in love.

Fitz let the journal drop to his lap and sat staring for a long time into the dying hearth fire, lost in thought. *Where do you find the courage to fight against such odds?* he asked himself. *Knowing you could be turned over to the Gestapo's torturers for a single wrong move or sent to the Siberian gulag, never to return.*

He said a silent prayer to St. Michael, patron saint of warriors, for the souls of all who sacrificed themselves to resist tyranny in every war since the dawn of time. Maybe he'd stop by the 6:00 mass at Saint Joseph's in the morning to make the prayer more official.

Fitz finally laid the book aside and stood up to stretch his stiff limbs. He was too tired to stay awake another hour and yet he owed Ghisella that, he thought, suddenly realizing how profoundly his relationship to this dead woman had changed. She was no longer the Old Lady next door… she had become something else to him now. He wasn't sure quite what that *something* was, but the change was real.

What must she and Gerhardt have suffered before it was done? he wondered as he climbed the stairs to his bedroom. What was the full extent of the secrets she had managed to protect through the years, that had caused evil men to follow her for seven decades, yet not quite defeat her? And why had destiny placed in his hands the only clues to a possible way to save whatever it was she'd lived and died to protect?

The dooms of men are in God's hidden place, Yeats had written. With Ghisella's doom, God had certainly outdone Himself.

PART V

Piecing the Puzzle

"The oldest, shortest words—yes and no—are those which require the most thought."

— Pythagoras

40

Georgia fluffed her hair, straightened her skirt and took a good deep breath of hot-as-hell Texas air. Even if it was just Texas airport air, it smelled like home. Not that she'd want to live here anymore, she reminded herself, but there was something about Texas that called to you like no other place on earth.

She'd had a great flight—flying first class pretty much assured that. She never flaunted her Texas money with her New York friends, who had no idea the kind of fortune her daddy had left her, but every once in a while it was nice to just be plain old rich. She might like flying with peons, she thought with a chuckle, but she sure as shootin' didn't like those squishy little peon seats they squoze you into in coach.

She put on her big Chanel sunglasses and looked around for the car she knew would be waiting for her outside the luggage area. Sure enough, there was Juan #1, as she used to call him when she was a kid. But Juan #1 was special—and his name was Diego. She'd be sure to make a point of using his name when she hugged him hello. She took another happy breath of Texas, waved her hand wildly to let him know how glad she was to see him, and braced herself for the barrage of welcomes she knew was coming. Texas might be complicated as hell, but Texas was home.

"There are ex-wives and ex-husbands and ex-Baptists," somebody once said. "But there's no such thing as an ex-Texan." He'd been right about that.

41

B.H. Hutchinson Walker, all bull-like six feet five of him, was standing in the driveway along with a flock of his employees, who knew Georgia from the old days when she'd been everybody's favorite.

He was still just as broad and imposing as she remembered, but he'd grown old in the time since she'd seen him last and that gave her a pang. She didn't want him to be other than indestructible. His hair was sun-bleached white, not the salt-and-pepper she remembered, his belly bulged a little over the big Lone Star belt buckle he always wore and his back wasn't straight as a Texas pine tree anymore. But there was still the unmitigated power. The power of pride and smarts and money. The power to take what he wanted when he wanted it radiated off the man like he was made of plutonium.

Hutch's sun-craggy face was dark and lined as tooled leather, his eyes under shaggy brows were squinting into the sun as she ran toward him—because that's what she'd always done: run to Uncle Hutch with a skinned knee or a broken heart.

"How're you doin', darlin'?" he drawled in the controlled-thunder voice she knew so well. After the near-fatal bear hug she'd expected and thoroughly enjoyed, he held her out at arm's length so his laser-smart eyes could examine her head to toe. "You're lookin' just as ornamental as ever, sweet girl," he said approvingly.

"I'm still bootin' ass and takin' names, Unc," she answered, amused at how easy it was to fall into the old comfort zone of "talkin' Texan."

"That's my girl," he said with satisfaction. "I'd expect nothin' less of a Walker filly."

Georgia smiled, hugged each of the well-remembered servants in turn and followed Hutch into the mega-ranch monstrosity that was the family fortress, memories crowding her as they always did when she got here. Good ones, bad ones, everything in between. Too many and too suffocating to live with on a daily basis. But maybe not so bad to visit every once in a while. She'd try to do better about visits now that she knew Hutch was actually growing old—an idea that seemed unthinkable when applied to her indestructible uncle.

She now knew a damn sight more about how her family and the other oil-rich robber barons they knew had made their fortunes, and a damn sight less than she'd need to know before returning to New York, so she'd have to keep her eye on the ball and think about the changes in Hutch later.

She'd made her plan on the plane. Now all she had to do was outfox the smartest poker player she'd ever seen in action to find out the truth.

Should be fun, Georgia thought suddenly. After all, she was no less a Walker than he, and she, too, played a mean hand of poker.

42

Finn rummaged in the closet, tossing long-ignored boxes right and left until she got to the one she wanted. Yes! Her old Parsons memorabilia box that held the school projects she'd been proudest of and kept tucked away to show her children someday was still there. She yanked the box to the front and dug to the bottom of it.

The ancient photo album she held up triumphantly was decades older than Finn's time at Parsons, but it was exactly what she'd wanted to find. That, and the pile of old photos in an envelope marked Mrs. W.

The idea had come to her in a dream. The kind of dream her mother told her was important because it was a way for your subconscious to push important insights to the surface so you couldn't overlook them.

She stuffed both album and envelope into her backpack and headed out to Mannheim's.

"Manny!" Finn called out even before he opened the door. She'd started calling him that a few days ago, and he seemed to get a big kick out of the informality. "I have a gorgeous idea and maybe the means to make it work!"

He motioned her forward and she whooshed into the space as if jet-propelled.

"And what might this great idea be that brings you here so early?" he asked, amused by the exuberant entrance.

"When I was a kid, I used to visit Mrs. W," she answered in breathless non sequitur. "She told me amazing stories about castles and ballrooms … you know, girly stuff. Anyway, we got to be friends, so I have lots of images of her I took after I got my first camera and used it on anything that stood still long enough—even used some of her pix for school projects at Parsons.

She was so Old World, you know … from some fairy-tale wonderland that will never exist again—" She realized as she said it that Mrs. W's dream world had been a nightmare for Mannheim and stopped short.

"I'm so sorry, Manny!" she blurted with real contrition. "I didn't mean to be insensitive …" He waved his hand to dismiss the idea.

"Anyway, I remembered she had a family photo album that got saved from the war in a vault in Switzerland and was given back to her after the armistice by a friend who'd protected it. It always made her sad to look at it, but I could see it was precious. You know, saved from before she lost her whole family and everything else, but the point is I've still got it! She let me borrow it once for a school project and I confess I never gave it back." She looked suitably chagrined for a nanosecond.

"So here's my idea! What if we could age-regress the Old Lady pix and age-progress the childhood shots in the album to meet in the middle? Not only would we have proof that your Phantom is Ghisella, but maybe we could even find horrible Manfred."

He looked impressed. "Perhaps we could do that—" he began but she cut him off.

"Wait! There's more," she blurted. "What if we could use the same tech on the Nazis? What if we could use it on images of all the people near and dear to Hitler—the Inner Circle—and the people like Ghisella's husband and his nasty partner—you know, the ones close to the Iron Throne? Then maybe Grand could track them down and find out what's really going on here.

"You've got tons of stills and movie footage in your archive and there's probably more out there if we hunt. What if we could build a photo library of the likeliest players, then use the really sophisticated facial and body rec AI that maps familial features and body language to nail disguised suspects—it's really cool, but also pretty terrifying. Maybe we could figure out who became somebody new under Paperclip? They couldn't *all* have gotten new faces and bodies, could they? At least it might *out* the ones who *didn't* get new faces from plastic surgeons in Costa Rica. Maybe?" She looked at him expectantly.

"A definite maybe!" he answered, touched by her ingenuity and earnestness. "And well worth a try."

"Great! Now let's call Annie. She'll know how to get that kind of tech for us. T says the kind of cutting-edge software we'll need for this is only at the FBI or NSA—even Interpol doesn't have it all yet. But Annie has lots of friends all over cyberspace she can crib from, or she'll know how to hack into it. *Whatever* ..." Her cell phone was already in her hand.

Mannheim shook his head at how easily she spoke of technology, and of stealing it, for that matter. She'd brought one or two others of her small troop to visit him and he'd been astounded by their knowledge and diversity, both in skills and personalities.

The girl named Matrix was an extraordinary creature and her meshuga friend who talked to angels and Alpha Centauri was equally so—and yet both girls were brilliant. Oy! who would believe such a troop of oddballs on an almost biblical quest in the name of justice? Who but Manny? he said to himself, relishing the awful nickname—the first he'd ever had.

"We're on the move, Manny," Finn said, grabbing the handles of his wheelchair and propelling him toward the door. "Where's your coat? I'm calling us an Uber. I can't push you to Annie's."

"No need for either," he said through his crooked grin. "I have a specially equipped car in the warehouse. I shall drive us there."

"Cool!" she said. "Point us toward your chariot, then—Annie's only a few blocks away on Canal. You are going to absolutely love her. If she'll let you in without T in tow, that is ..." She frowned, then brightened. "No worries! With me and Matrix to vouch for you, you'll be a shoo-in."

43

Rory put down the fat folder of information she'd culled from the internet, the investigator she'd used and trusted when she was practicing law, and the data she'd picked up from the research librarian at the 42nd Street branch of the New York City Library after Bridget had given her a quickie rundown on cutting-edge biometrics, whetting her appetite for more.

She'd spent the entire morning digesting a lot of more disturbing data than she'd bargained for, probably because it was so morally and ethically complex and ambiguous an issue, and much of it raised her lawyer hackles, to say nothing of her emotional Irish ones.

The same surveillance that empowered law enforcement, endangered most of the privacy rights that were assured by the Fourth Amendment. And both the technology used and the cavalier approach to collecting the data that was being sanctioned because of security fears, were far more invasive than she'd realized. It was damned disturbing to see how insidiously it was inching us closer and closer to Big Brother and the Under His Eye total control of our movements, freedoms, rights and ability to function as free people.

She reprised in her head the notes she'd made, frown lines deepening as she remembered. Fingerprints were old hat. Facial recognition now could pick out and ID a single face in a crowd of a hundred thousand, from a satellite hovering thirty thousand miles above the earth. The FBI databases now contained facial rec for nearly 60 percent of the citizens in the US, despite the fact that 95 percent of them had no criminal background whatsoever.

Now scars, tattoos, birthmarks and skin textures were being logged, as well as eye distance, eye socket depth, ear configuration, and other physical characteristics. Iris scans, voice recognition, hand geometry, and gait were all identifiers, and thermograms of body temps were being collected.

People were willingly offering up their DNA by the millions in a search for ancestry info that wasn't all that accurate, but was being passed on to both corporate and governmental sources for future reference. Whole industries were being spawned that had never been dreamed of before: finger vein recognition tech could ID blood vessel patterns beneath your skin, and a company in Canada was offering a wearable wristband that used a person's electrocardiograph reading to authenticate identity. Behavioral traits, too, were being monitored and followed.

Holy fucking shit! Had nobody read *1984* or *Animal Farm*? At least a vast number of millennial women were watching *The Handmaid's Tale* on TV.

Why were the sheeple lining up to be the first to try the RFID chips being tested all over the country? Did they not realize that a totally surveilled society could have all rights rescinded at the whim of a government or military who wished to rule? What if your RFID chip status denied you food, water, or access to medical care if you didn't play ball with the right political party? Absolute control wasn't such a stretch of the imagination, when you realized how easily people could be swayed by the kind of disinformation Hitler had excelled at and, more recently, others right here in the US.

Mind-boggling. Utterly mind-boggling, that people were marching happily toward the potential for being enslaved and not even knowing it. Talk about a bloodless coup!

Rory shook her head to clear it and to calm herself down.

Okay, she admonished herself. So much for the bad news! Now for the good news. All this available data might make their search for the Hitler bloodline easier, provided Bridget and her cohort could gather the right relevant data and use it to help ferret out which families were most likely to fit the criteria. *More a Hobson's choice than Sophie's,* she thought. After all, at the moment, there was no way to avoid all the people, governments, and corporations who were surveilling your data, but at least in this instance, something good might come of it. *Uh-oh*, she reminded herself. *Slippery slope if you let the end justify the means, girl.*

She laughed a little at her own internal debate and decided to tell the group what she'd learned—maybe they could all wrestle it to the ground together.

Which reminded her that she wanted to talk with Annie about the moral and ethical dilemmas she must face in her strange world of hacktivism. How, at the end of the day, does someone with as highly developed a moral compass as Annie justify the laws she breaks in the pursuit of truth? Or does the moral imperative of finding the T.A.E. and knowing how to do that give you absolution of some kind? A good question to bat around with Maeve, Fitz and Finn one of these cold winter nights. But not until this case got solved, of course. One mighty conundrum at a time was enough to handle.

44

Texas

Hutch looked up from the *Financial Times* and smiled at his niece. She was one fine lookin' woman, he thought, so much like her mama. He sat at the head of an immense mahogany table on which were the remnants of the gargantuan Tex-Mex breakfast he'd just consumed.

"Looks like you've been fortifyin' yourself for a big day, Unc," Georgia said as she kissed him on the cheek, then helped herself to eggs and toast from the silver salvers on the sideboard.

"You know me, sugar," he said with satisfaction. "A steak or two a day keeps the economy up and blood pressure down."

She laughed at his absolute confidence that whatever he was doing, he was doing it right. "I'm not sure the medical establishment would agree with you on that one, Uncle Hutch."

"What do those peckerwoods know about us Hutchinsons and Walkers, darlin'? We got big appetites. Gotta feed the flame."

"Matter of fact," she said over a bite of toast, "that thought might be just what I've come to talk to you about."

Hutch cocked an eyebrow at her and chuckled. He'd been waiting for her first shot over his bow.

"I was fixin' to do a little huntin' today, myself," he said in non sequitur. "I don't suppose livin' in that big ol' city of yours has screwed up your aim any? Why don't you put on your ridin' britches, sugar, grab yourself a shootin' iron or two from Juan and we'll make us a day of it. Luz'll pack us a lunch and we'll shake some of that New York soot off your boots."

It was a ritual, she knew. You ride, you hunt a little, you sit on a rock and stare at the vast Texas landscape and you talk. Far from prying eyes and ears, it reminded you of who you are and where you come from, so you could say things you'd never say indoors.

"Cain't think of a thing I'd like better'n that, Unc," she said, and as the words left her mouth, she realized she pretty much meant them.

"We lookin' for birds or whitetails, B.H.?" Georgia asked as they saddled up. For a long-ago reason she always called him Big Hutch or some variation of it when they hunted together. She thought it was probably a last vestige of baby-bravado she'd cooked up when he'd taken her hunting younger than her daddy said was allowed. Hutch had made her feel grown-up and empowered, so she'd switched to his Big Hutch initials to claim her grown-up status, and it had pleased him no end. Just as all her milestones had.

"Deer season's near over," he said, "but we still got a few days left. Birds are plentiful, and if you want some real fun we can do a night hog shoot. I just got me a bunch of them newfangled night vision goggles Seal Team Six used to put down that sumbitch bin Laden."

Georgia wrinkled her nose and shook her head. "I hate those things like the devil hates holy water, BH. An hour after I take 'em off I've still got a headache and too much green makes me nauseous."

"Suit yourself, darlin'," he said, maneuvering his big horse out onto a prairie trail that seemed to stretch to infinity. "What're you packin'?"

She patted her saddle mounted .30-06. "I got old Bessie, a .45 and a crossbow," she said. "Think that'll do it?"

He chuckled appreciatively, like he used to do when she was a precocious kid with the promise of big steel balls. "Unless we cross paths with a pack of pissed-off Apaches, I'd say you're loaded for bear, sweet child."

They rode in silence for a while and Georgia relaxed into the saddle like she'd been born there, which was pretty near the truth, she thought absently. Riding, roping, barrel racing, learning to track and hunt; these were the pursuits of her childhood that took her far enough from her parents' endless battles so she could be happy for a little while, just as they'd sustained her after her mother died.

She knew there'd be no discussion of why she was here until after lunch or after their first kill, so she pulled herself out of the deep reverie the landscape had provoked and began to look for sign. Much as they loved each other, she'd have to earn Hutch's respect before she asked him for anything. It was the way it had always worked. You earn what you think you have rights to—she'd heard her daddy say that a thousand times. And you don't earn nothin' forever. Just for a while at a time.

45

"Bingo!" Fitz thought as he took the measure of the man who had just come into The Mysterious. The one he'd been waiting for. *Was he the perpetrator,* Fitz wondered, assessing him, *or merely the messenger?* More than just the messenger, he guessed. The confidence the man exuded didn't usually come in square gray packages. Fitz was alone in the shop as Charlie had classes today, but he had a lovely old Colt 1911 under the counter, so he wasn't concerned for his own safety. He'd always thought if this particular model .45 had been good enough for Old Blood and Guts Patton to rely on, it was good enough for him.

Fitz was as eager to learn what he could from this man's visit as the other man was to learn something from him. The thought turned up one corner of his mouth just a little.

"May I help you find something?" he asked genially. "Or are you just here to browse?"

The man, fairly unremarkable physically except for his disproportionately large upper body and his dead-ferret eyes, smiled a bit, too.

"Are you the proprietor?" he asked, looking around him, taking in details then returning his eyes to Fitz. "I hear you specialize in mysteries."

Fitz nodded. "We do that. Old ones and new. And we have a large antiquarian selection. Do you have a particular author in mind?"

"Not an author, just the recommendation of a friend."

"I see. And who might that be?"

"Ghisella Wallenberg shopped here, I believe?"

"She did, God rest her."

"And did you know her well?"

"Sadly, no. Long, you might say. But not well. She'd been housebound for some time, you see, and unable to shop much."

The man's eyebrows went up quizzically, as if questioning the veracity of the response. "She had borrowed several books and documents from me shortly before her death," he explained. "And unfortunately, she never returned them. I was hoping they might have been given to you in error. I understand the police gave you a number of her books after she passed?" He was watching Fitz's face intently.

"And where might you have heard such a tale, Mr. …?"

"Grey," the man supplied, and Fitz nearly laughed out loud.

"Well then, Mr. Grey … where did you hear that, I'm wondering?"

"From the police," the man said matter-of-factly. "They said you sometimes consult with them about books."

Fitz nodded. "I do that, indeed. But in this case, I consulted at the crime scene, you might say, but the police gave me none of Mrs. Wallenberg's books. I'm afraid your informant was ill-informed. I expect if anyone has your books, they'll be in the police evidence room. That would surely be the most likely place for them, wouldn't it now?"

The man smiled his mirthless smile, but didn't respond.

"What titles are you after, if you don't mind me asking?" Fitz added in a mildly curious tone. "Just in case I can duplicate them for you."

Mr. Grey pursed his lips. "Not titles really. Just family journals, diaries, papers. Most in German or Polish. Did you see anything like that, Mr. Donovan? They wouldn't mean anything to anyone else, of course, but to my family … you understand."

"I do understand," Fitz said, drawing out the word as if thinking carefully about it. "But I'm afraid I didn't see anything at all like what you describe, Mr. Grey. There were bound books in several languages, but no journals that I can recall. And any loose documents such as you describe wouldn't have been in my purview anyway. I'm not a document dealer, only books. I'd suggest you try speaking with Lieutenant Cochrane at the 6th Precinct. I believe he's in charge of the case. Perhaps he can help you find what you're looking for."

The stocky gray man leaned forward and rested his arms on the chest-high counter in front of Fitz. The gesture was subtly threatening.

"Perhaps I haven't made myself clear," Grey said, all cordiality gone now. "These books are of great value to my family. We *intend* to retrieve them."

Fitz tilted his head in a gesture of mild reproof at the man's odd behavior. "Be that as it may," he answered him, "as I've already told you, you won't be getting them from me, as I haven't got them."

"Make no mistake," Grey snapped. "We will go to any lengths to secure these books and papers, Mr. Donovan. I want you to understand that quite viscerally, you see. We intend to retrieve what is ours, and we will take whatever measures are necessary to achieve that end."

"Will you now?" Fitz answered, holding the man's gaze, his eyebrows lowered into a decided frown. "And just who might this almighty *we* be?"

The man didn't answer for a moment, then said, "You can just call us The Family." Fitz could hear the capitalization in the man's voice.

"Whoever your family may be, Mr. Grey," Fitz said evenly, "I have already told you I do not have what you're looking for, so I'm afraid you'll have to do your ferreting elsewhere." His voice was just as cold as Grey's.

Grey nodded. "But *you* have a lovely family of your own, haven't you, Mr. Donovan?" he said. Turning, he moved toward the door, then stopped abruptly.

"That young granddaughter of yours is something of a beauty, isn't she?" he said genially over his shoulder. "There are men who would consider her quite a valuable prize." Not waiting for an answer, he opened the door and left the shop, the little silver bell on the door still tinkling after he was gone.

"Jaysus, Mary and Joseph," Fitz whispered into the empty shop, "now that's a threat if ever I've heard one."

He hoped the new cameras had caught the smarmy son of a bitch this time, but he'd put everyone on high alert, for the game was now surely afoot, and this game was dangerous indeed.

46

Georgia settled into the shade of the hunting blind and uncovered the big thermos of coffee Luz had packed for them. She didn't really mind field-dressing a catch, she'd been doing it since she was four, but she was grateful Uncle Hutch had had the foresight to have two of the ranch hands with a Land Rover within cell phone distance to do the dressing, cleanup and transport. She'd taken down the deer with one spectacular shot to the buck's heart, and that was enough to open the door to conversation, just as she'd known it would be.

She handed the steaming mug to Hutch and said, "I need to know some things, BH. I suspect there's family secrets involved."

"And I need to know just what *things* and why you're pokin' around secrets. Same as always. Are you in some kind of trouble, sugar pie?"

He gave her the probative stare that had turned many a defendant into Jell-O on the stand and waited.

"I'm not sure yet, BH. I could tell you this is intel for friends who are in trouble and that'd be true enough, I think. But I suspect this of being the kind of trouble that could spread out and suck in anybody who pokes a finger in."

"Hmm," he grumbled. "So why poke?"

"Because I love my New York family and I can't leave them to fend for themselves if there's a way I can help."

"I see. And exactly how does our family tree of reprobates figure into this trouble in New York City?"

"I'm not sure it does. It's just that I'm starting to learn things about the oil business around the 30s and 40s—things I never knew. That maybe things were a lot crookeder, a lot darker than I'd ever realized. And if that's so, some of what *you* know could maybe help my friends with what they need to know."

Hutch leaned back and sipped his coffee. It was strong enough to raise a blister on a boot.

"There's a whole pile of darkness that's best left right there in the dark, darlin'. Things your daddy and I did, and before us, your granddaddy—no worse than every other rancher who ever got rich from oil, mind you—but things that might not make you sleep any better at night, if you follow me?" He looked at her quizzically as if to assess if she knew what she was getting into.

When she didn't answer, he spoke again. "Just tell me them fancy-pants New York friends of yours haven't turned you into one of them lily-livered liberals who want to give everything back to the people we rich kids stole it from in the first place, because if that's the story I'd have to tell you right up front, I'm real happy with my ill-gotten gains."

Georgia laughed out loud. "No, BH," she assured him, "what I need to know isn't going to put you anywhere near the poorhouse. I give you my word."

"Well then," he said after another gulp of coffee. "Why don't we just go shoot us a few more varmints while we're out here in God's country. Then tonight after dinner, we'll start us a conversation and see how it goes."

He poured the dregs of his coffee cup out on the ground, stood up, and reached out a hand to help her to her feet, and Georgia relaxed a little. It was clear enough Uncle Hutch still had plenty of snap in his garters. Also clear that she'd passed the first gate with the deer. She wondered what the price of tonight's conversation would be.

Maybe just a few, more frequent visits home, and having seen the age on him for the first time, maybe that wasn't such a bad idea. He'd always been too indestructible for mere mortality, but now she just wasn't so sure that was true.

47

Mannheim was now an official member of the conspirators, so after everyone but Georgia, who was still in Texas, had assembled at The Mysterious, Finn booted up her laptop and set it on a desk for all to see.

"We've got her nailed," she said triumphantly, flashing a photo of Mrs. W on the screen. "Our own superhero spy! And there's much more we're onto now, but Manny and Annie will tell all. It's a really cool story, and it'll give us a chance to crow about our photographic detective work!" She took an elaborate mock bow and waved her hand at Manny so he could take over.

"In all my years of assembling photos of the Holocaust," he began, "I had unearthed only one possibly bona fide image of a woman rumored to be the Magdalena. To be sure, I had a number of photos of the von Zechandorff family, several generations of them in fact, but I had no reason to connect the dots to Magdalena until Itzak brought me the names from the journal ..." He beamed a smile up at Finn, who towered above his wheelchair. "And also brought me the tall angel who stands here beside me. It was she who provided the photos of Mrs. W's childhood holidays in Poland and the idea of how we could use them in our quest."

Finn interrupted. "I used to visit her a lot when I was little," she explained, "and she would serve these exotic teas and pastries she got from that Viennese bakery on 86th in Germantown, and she'd tell me stories of her fairy tale childhood in a great castle by a beautiful river and a magical forest, yada yada yada, you know?

"She had this old photo book she said had been saved in a Swiss vault before the family lost everything in the war. She'd get all teary-eyed and her voice would get sad or angry when she ran her hands over the images—it kind of touched my heart and got me thinking about how photography documents things that should never be lost and it's really the only way to the truth because you can't trust paintings and words can be changed, but photos nailed reality.

"I mean, victors write the history books, right? They skew the story their way. But images didn't lie in the old days." She frowned. "Since digital, it's a different story, but back then you could rely on them. Anyway, it seemed like a big deal to me and made me want to be a photographer when I grew up." She looked around to see if people understood.

"She also showed me pictures of the Polish castle her grandma owned. It's in that coffee-table book she left for Grand, so I knew it was all real, then there were images of her father in some German textbooks. She was so proud of his academic achievements. 'Not merely noble blood,' she would say, 'but a noble brain and heart!'"

"Ah," said Mannheim, obviously delighted by his young protégé, "but my dear Finn, you must tell them of your inspiration about *how* we could use these photos for our quest."

Finn looked excited by what they'd done, but obviously too modest to take full credit for it. She shook off the compliment and pointed to T and Annie's crowd seated to her right. "The Babushkas did all the heavy lifting on the high-tech face and body recognition software we needed to tell us things," she said, "I just had the idea that it could erase time and help us ID people long dead and gone … and maybe even their descendants."

Annie cut in, direct as always. "Finn thought we could age-regress the pix of Mrs. W in old age, and age-*progress* the childhood snaps she'd saved, and maybe we could get a definitive ID that way. And she was right. Ghisella Wallenberg was Magdalena, all right. And she was one hell of a lot of woman! Beautiful, smart, brave as hell, athletic and resourceful as Wonder Woman." She looked around the room at the rapt faces.

"Some of you in this room know history, but maybe not enough to make Ghisella/Magdalena seem worth fighting for, so I'd like to digress for a moment so you can hear some of what the world has conveniently forgotten. Like the fact that the Polish Resistance Movement was the largest underground antifascist resistance in all of Nazi-occupied Europe." She looked around for dissenters, and finding none, continued.

"The Polish resistance disrupted German supply lines to the Eastern Front and saved more Jewish lives in the Holocaust than any other Allied organization or government. But who now even remembers that they existed? They provided critical military intelligence to the Brits, without which the Allies might not have won the war!

"The largest Polish resistance organization was Armia Krajowa, or AK as it was known then. This group remained loyal to the Polish government-in-exile in London and it had strong ties to the Allies and to British intelligence. Gerhardt and Ghisella were integral parts of AK's resistance."

She could see this was new information for most in the room.

"The courage and daring of these Polish partisans were staggering. They harassed, ambushed, sabotaged, delayed or attacked every single fighting group the Nazis sent against them, from the SS to the Wehrmacht to the Panzers!

"Every single act of these partisans mattered," Annie added. "Every derailment and delay, every broadcast intercepted or interfered with, every act of sabotage and diversionary tactic helped to win a seemingly unwinnable war. Every message about the atrocities in the camps made the Allies more determined to beat the sons of bitches."

"A comrade of Gerhardt and Ghisella's, Witold Pilecki, actually allowed himself to be captured and sent to Auschwitz so the truth of the atrocities there could be exposed to the world," Mannheim put in. "Can you even conceive of such mad courage? It was tantamount to consigning one's own soul not only to death but to hell.

"His reports had to be smuggled out of the camps and sent across enemy lines to the Brits and other Allies—an almost impossible task. But it was the Allies' prime source of intelligence on the death camps of Auschwitz and Birkenau and their forty subsidiary camps. An underground cadre of couriers undertook the mission to get these hard-won messages through the enemy lines. Which is where our Ghisella comes into the story. She was the star courier who became the legend that inspired others to believe in the impossible!"

Annie retook control of the narrative. "She was a brilliant horsewoman and skier, which helped her cover vast stretches of difficult terrain. And she turned out to be as fearless as she was beautiful. She seduced guards to get through checkpoints, inscribed coded messages into the patterns of her headscarf to get them through border checks, passed as a young soldier by donning the uniform of one she'd just killed. She was a seductive chameleon and she could shoot the ace out of a playing card! Many of her more astonishing deeds are in the history books, but the top-secret ones are not. Her legend remains, however, and she became all the more mysterious after the war when she simply vanished and was assumed martyred."

"Hold it there for a second, Annie, please," Rory interjected, admiration and excitement in her voice. "I just finished reading a passage in her journal that's so relevant to what you're saying, everybody really should hear it in her own words." She picked up the journal and flipped to a page she'd marked.

Mrs. W's Journal

Once I was well enough, I saw that the skills I had been taught in my privileged aristocratic life could now be valuable to this life-and-death struggle. I became both spy and long-distance courier. Liaison with both the Polish government-in-exile and the Brits, who had their fingers in every covert pie.

My lineage assured me acceptance—the Brits love nothing so much as an aristocratic pedigree—my languages and my ability to traverse long distances on skis or horseback made me a valuable asset. And, of course, the fact that I was a woman—thus considered less dangerous and less important than a man, made me a good choice for courier. I mention these details not to give myself airs, but to explain how in such desperate times, every talent is useful if you are willing to put your life on the line. We trained each other, and those who had been at this longer trained the newcomers. One is not born a partisan: one is made so by dire circumstance.

My greatest danger would be rapists, the leaders told me—and that was true. Women were spoils of war. It has been estimated that the Russians raped more than one hundred thirty thousand women on their way to Berlin. Thus, the fact that I was adept with guns and longbow, trained in competitive fencing, etc., was an asset. All this made them believe I could protect myself if attacked, although it was my impression that other than Gerhardt, the leaders gave my safety little thought at all. And in their defense, no one engaged in the resistance had any rational expectation of safety.

Some of my narrow escapes from death or capture have been chronicled by others; the most secret and significant ones, of course, could never be spoken of without reprisal, and thus were never recorded at all except in the limbo of my own mind and heart. In truth, there was so much selflessness and bravery shown by so many of my comrades that I would be embarrassed to call myself a hero, as others have named me. This was simply a time of heroes and self-sacrifice.

If in order to document the truth of my existence, you need to learn more to corroborate my testimony, information exists about my exploits in history books—which I have never read, as the pain was too great and they were probably wrong about most of it anyway. What is not in any book about the war's end is the betrayal that I suffered at the hands of my former allies.

Here is the terrible truth:

At the war's end, when we were no longer needed, we were dismissed and consigned to history's trash bin. The Brits and the Polish government-in-exile—who had used us so relentlessly and relied on us for intelligence, no matter what danger that demanded of us, neither acknowledged our contribution to victory nor helped us to save our brave comrades who'd been stranded at war's end. As God is my witness, I tell you that without us, the war would have taken a different turn. The perfidy of these Allied leaders is a blot on the escutcheon of the Empire on which they pride themselves.

Gerhardt, the kind and generous intellectual to whom I had long since given my heart, was a true hero of those terrible times. Without his unwavering conviction that we could win against impossible odds as long as we kept fighting with all our strength and cunning, I and many others would not have survived the war, nor the treachery of those in high places who, when it was over, left us to fend for ourselves in a nightmare Soviet world that was little better than Nazi rule.

Our time with the Cursed Soldiers, trying to save as many as we could with no weapons, no food, no help from our former friends, was as bleak and terrifying as anything we had yet suffered. We were exhausted nearly to death by all we had endured and shocked by the perfidious betrayal of the governments we had helped to save.

Gerhardt and I survived only because we loved each other, and because we learned from the betrayal of those in high places to expect little reward for great achievement. And, perhaps, by the grace of God.

But do not make the mistake of thinking me saintly because I could bear with such suffering. A saint I surely was not!

I did not forgive. I hungered for revenge.

I railed at God and demanded the chance to bring the curs down. Not all of them, of course, that kind of justice never happens in this imperfect world. But the deaths of one or two of these evil bastards at some critical moment, for the destruction of their dream, that is what I demanded of God. For if I had learned anything in the resistance, it was this: Sometimes, the removal of one critical stone from a mighty dam can cause a flood that cannot be contained.

Rory laid down the book, reached for a Kleenex from her handbag and looked around the room through tear-blurred eyes to see moisture on nearly every cheek.

"But my dear friends and comrades on this journey," Manny piped up, "this is just the beginning of where Finn's idea and the Babushka's technical prowess have led us. Now we will use our knowledge to find Gruss and his progeny!"

The little group disbanded, both sobered and elated by what they'd heard about the technology now in play and the mysterious woman who had set all this in motion.

48

Texas

Dinner was done. Bourbon was poured. A fire blazed in a hearth big enough to roast an ox.

Georgia sat in the smaller of the two big leather wingbacks that flanked the fire and tried not to look as impatient as she felt. She watched her uncle slowly flipping the pages of a long document. By the concentration he was lavishing on it, she felt certain it was about money. She tried to sort out exactly what she was feeling besides annoyance, and realized every nerve ending was on high alert—a little anxious, a little excited, a little champing at the bit—just like she always felt when she was on a hunt. The thought made her smile inwardly and she consciously cooled her jets. This was, after all, a hunt of sorts, one that could have real consequences for her friends, so she'd better get it right. And maybe for herself, come to think of it—who the hell knew what she'd learn about her family in the course of the next few hours that she didn't really want to know. Judging by Hutch's current tactic for delaying the conversation, it would probably be pretty unsavory.

Georgia saw him glance up to gauge how much longer her patience would hold out against his strategy, and she aimed a dazzling smile at him.

"I serve at the pleasure of the king," she said sweetly and he guffawed, put down his papers and lifted his glass to her. She returned the salute.

"Let's get to it then, sugar pie. What exactly do you want to know and why?"

"Can I trust you, Uncle Hutch, to keep whatever we say here in strict confidence? You have my word I'll only let as much out of the bag as you give me leave to share."

He pursed his lips, lowered his formidable eyebrows and gave her "the stare."

"You shouldn't have to ask me that, sweet girl. You should know it in your bones."

She nodded understanding of the rebuke, then said quietly, "My friends are counting on me and I gotta keep them safe, but I respect the family, too, so it's best if we're straight with each other about all that from the get-go."

He acknowledged what she'd said with a nod of his own, then as succinctly as she could, she told him the story of what had happened in New York.

"I know it's a long shot, Unc. But I also know you *know* things that're never gonna make it into the history books. Oil is in your veins and oil is what kept the Second World War going, oil has the power to put people on thrones or topple dynasties. Soooo … I need you to tell me if our family had ties to Hitler because of the oil and the war, and if so, were they intimate enough so you could help me help my friends to ID Mrs. W and maybe put some of the puzzle pieces in place before anybody I care about gets hurt?"

Hutch puffed out his cheeks then let the air out slowly, deciding how to proceed.

"I know a lot, darlin'," he said, thoughtful in his delivery of the words. "Some of which could be damned dangerous for you to know. The people our family was dealin' with back then were real bad apples—the kind that hold grudges. I'll tell you a little history and some relevant facts and then I'll let you know what has to stay between us. Agreed?"

She raised her expressive eyes to his, saw the unmistakable love, grief, and, to her surprise, guilt in them and nodded agreement.

"The history you need to know to understand the rest, is this: whatever you *think* you know about history is fifty percent horsepucky. Disinformation is how governments, including ours, manipulate politics, and politics is just another name for money. And every war since time began is about money."

He waited for that to be absorbed, then continued.

"Before World War II actually had us by the balls, there were plenty of ties to Germany among the rich and powerful in this country. Including us. Hell, most of our big industrialist fortunes had links to at least a dozen German conglomerates that were in the forefront of big business worldwide. Besides which, German industry and the German army needed a helluva lot of our oil, just like everybody else.

"I'm assumin' you already know that the super-rich all over this planet know each other, marry each other, conspire with each other, and above all, keep their pesos in each other's banks! Warburg, Rockefeller, Rothschild—you know the names. Great fortunes beget great banking empires and great banking empires beget everything else that isn't tied down.

"When WWII happened, oil became a real hot ticket and that made it top priority for US foreign policy. Rest assured, pretty much *anything* the US has ever had a hand in in the Middle East was to protect its oil interests there, never mind all the highfalutin horse manure they cover it up with, like patriotism, duty, and flag flyin'. The buildup of Israel and Iran, aid to so-called moderate Arab regimes like Saudi, Kuwait and Jordan—that was all just Washington doublespeak for keeping the region under our thumb. And for keepin' out the Brits and the Soviets, who were also greedy bastards who wanted the self-same thing we did.

"And believe you me, there was one helluva lot of manipulatin' goin' on, and skullduggery at the highest levels to win the spoils and to keep the general population ignorant of the truth." He thought a minute, then amended that. "Which is not to say there weren't moral and human issues at stake in that old war, as well as great acts of bravery and self-sacrifice. But individual humans are a damned sight different than governments when it comes to the heroics and the livin' and dyin'.

"I've lived through a whole bunch of wars now and I can say with real conviction, WWII was a noble war. One where most everybody really believed they could make the world a better place and bring lasting peace by their sacrifice. Of course, in most every war since, the boys dyin' on the firing line and the old men makin' deals in the conference rooms are cut from real different bolts of cloth." He looked hard at her to see if she was following. "The old men mostly profit and the young ones mostly die and it's a damned shame."

"Now, throughout all this manipulation and skullduggery, your granddaddy and even my granddaddy had their fingers deep in the pie.

"Standard Oil and Texaco were suckin' up oil right and left here in Texas and in California. And we Texas oil folks were lobbyin' and advisin' up a storm, both bein' patriots and protecting our own interests, playin' with the really big kids 'cause we had the money, the oil rights and the balls to do it. But darlin', we are talkin' hardball here! No quarter given.

"When they say behind every great fortune is a great crime, they ain't just whistlin' Dixie, child. Whatever it took to win is what our kinfolk and their cronies did back then.

"We knew Germans. Hell, we knew Hitler! We even sold him oil in the '30s and '40s. So did the Brits. And yes, I see your next question in those big, bright, idealistic eyes of yours. We felt just fine about supplyin' his army with both oil and oil technology as it got up a full head of steam. Course, we didn't know then about the atrocities and such …" he paused.

"You know bankers like the Rothschilds, they make a habit of funding both sides of every war, in every century. Both the North and the Confederacy in the Civil War, the Germans, Japs *and* us in WWII—they got no compunction about putting their money wherever it's gonna make the most money back. So I'm not proud of it, but we did the same damn thing with Hitler. For a while at least …" He paused and took a long breath.

"Truth is, we only stopped because it would have looked unpatriotic to keep it up. Course, we pretended it was real altruistic and all, but it wasn't. Good business is what it was. Just like selling to the Nazis had been good business for a time."

He was leaning toward her, elbows on his knees, big hands clasped between them.

"Did our granddaddies know about the concentration camps?" she asked, her voice uncharacteristically lacking its usual gusto. "About the Jews, the gypsies, the torture, the gas chambers …"

"Dunno, darlin'," he said, "and that's the damned truth. But I can make an educated guess that it wouldn't have mattered to either one of them all that much if they did."

She looked into his face, her own more serious than he had seen her since her mama died. "Would it have mattered to *you*, Unc?" she asked.

He returned her earnest, questioning gaze. "Now that's another one of them answers you should know in your bones," he said simply.

BH Hutchinson Walker stood up and turned his body toward the blazing fire, hands extended toward the grate as if warming them, his broad back to his niece.

"I'm sorry, Unc," she said softly behind him. "It's just sometimes it's hard for me to know where the power player ends and my beloved uncle begins …"

He nodded without turning.

"Sometimes that's hard for me to know, too, child. We were raised to be hard men, your daddy and me. Only way for us to survive your granddaddy's hardness." He paused, then added, "He was a cruel bastard, and we bore the brunt."

She got up too, and, moved by the old pain in the man's voice, came up behind him, then reached out to hug him hard, laying her head against his broad back as she had done a thousand times as a child.

"You paid a big price for the money and the power, didn't you, Unc?"

He didn't answer directly, but said, "I'll help you with this, sugar, and I believe I may know a useful thing or two, now that I know what it is you're after." He paused and she felt him take in a long, deep breath.

"Your mama," he said, "she had a heart like yours. Your daddy thought it made her weak, but he was dead wrong. She was stronger than all of us."

Georgia remembered all the terrible fights she wasn't supposed to hear when she was growing up in this house.

"You loved her, didn't you, Unc?" she asked, knowing the truth of it even as her words touched the air. "I mean, really *loved* her."

Hutch turned from the fire and drew his niece into his arms, kissing her gently on top of her head, just as if she were a lonely eight-year-old again.

"It doesn't do to love your brother's wife," he said, "not if you mean to be an honorable man … but Lord Jesus, there wasn't any way on earth not to love your mama." He sighed a little. "I thought she hung the moon."

She heard the crack in his voice, then felt him pull himself together, and they both sat back down in the big armchairs self-consciously, neither speaking. Hutch reached for his half-full glass.

"Let me ponder all this tonight, darlin'," he said, changing the subject, his voice a little deeper than usual. "Tomorrow I'll tell you whatever I can come up with that I think you might need to know."

It was true, then, she thought as she let herself out of the library, tears trickling down her cheeks. Great fortunes weren't just built on hard work, smarts and good luck, as those who made them liked to tell their grateful progeny. They were built on guile and lies and terrible dark secrets that could break your heart.

PART VI

Stranger Danger

"To live in hearts we leave behind is not to die."

— Thomas Campbell

49

There was so much to know in a neighborhood, Fitz mused cheerily as he battled the cold wind tunnel that was Bleecker Street. He knew the Village streets like the back of his hand, knew the likeliest places for Mrs. W to have traveled when she was still able to walk well enough, and she had walked well into her early nineties, convinced by her European mind-set that exercise would keep her young. Maybe she'd been right about that, all things considered.

Mom-and-pop shops lined the big street and the little winding ones that were its offshoots. Plenty of shop people to talk to, plenty of cameras to canvas, perhaps with potential data about who had been in the neighborhood the day Mrs. W. died.

Fitz had already done all the preliminaries he could by phone. He'd tagged his friend at Immigration to help Rory trace info on Mrs. W's arrival in New York, whenever the hell that had been, he'd put the arm on friends still on the job to get him her phone logs, and he'd asked Annie to figure out a way to winkle out banking information, as following the money usually paid big dividends.

Old-fashioned police work, the way it had been done in the early days, pre-computers and cell phones, when there were phone booths on street corners and proprietors of shops and cafes shot the breeze with their customers, getting to know them in casual yet sometimes oddly intimate ways.

He'd even checked in with Cochrane, just to do things according to Hoyle, and had been told in no uncertain terms to keep his nose out of police business, just as he'd anticipated. But Fitz had been doing police business before Cochrane was born, so it rolled off his back like water off a Muscovy duck.

So far, none of this had borne much fruit, but that didn't mean it wouldn't. Police work required patience and fortitude, and he had to admit to himself he was having a fine time doing what he used to do.

He had one more stop to make, and an unlikely one at that: the dry cleaner both he and Mrs. W had patronized. Fitz pushed open the door and walked into Spindler & Sons Dry Cleaning Establishment, grateful for the rush of moist heat that engulfed him in the confines of the shop.

Young David, Spindler's grandson, was behind the counter as usual. Spindler & Sons was a three-generation business, like so many in the Village. "I didn't expect to see you out on a day like this, sir," the young man said politely. "I could have delivered, but I didn't see any of your family's clothes on today's list."

"No worries, David," Fitz reassured, "I'm here on a different mission entirely. Mrs. Wallenberg brought her clothes here, didn't she?"

"Oh, yes, sir. And most particular about them, she was, too. And she had some beautiful things, you know? Very old-world. Very expensive and meticulously cared for. I just heard about her passing. It made my father sad."

Fitz looked closer at the boy. "Did he know her well, then?"

"David!" A gruff voice chastised the boy from behind a curtain. "Who is that asking questions? You know better than to gossip about our customers. I'm ashamed of you!"

The young man's face reddened. "I'm sorry, Grandpa," he stammered, "I didn't mean ..."

The curtain parted and an elderly man with a fierce expression pushed through them, but when he saw Fitz, his scowl softened. "I didn't know it was you, Chief," he said. "I thought that little gray man had returned."

"And what little gray man might that be?" Fitz asked, amused that everyone seemed to have the same a.k.a. for the disquieting little man.

"A day or two after Mrs. Wallenberg died he came here to ask about her. Very rude he was. Very pushy. Asking questions that were none of his business."

"Is that right? And did he give you a name or a way to contact him, by chance?"

"No. But I would not have contacted him, and he could tell it. I told him Mrs. Wallenberg was too old to come into my shop. That I hadn't seen her in years."

"But that wasn't true, was it, Simon?" he said, admiring the old man's gumption. "Good policy on your part, though, if you didn't like the cut of the man's jib. What exactly did he ask?" Fitz pressed.

"Nosy things! Like how long did I know her? Where was she from? Where was *Mr.* Wallenberg? I told him nothing. Ghisella was a great lady."

"Ghisella? You knew her well enough for first names, then?"

"I knew her since 1991. We were both from Germany. We reminisced sometimes. You, I will tell this to, Chief, because I know you are only looking for who hurt her, ya?"

"I'll do my damnedest to run the bastard to ground," Fitz replied, intrigued by this turn of events. "1991 is when she came here?"

"Ya. She said she was from East Germany, after the Wall, you know? But it wasn't true. I know a Berliner when I hear one. And an aristocrat at that. But I never troubled her about it. So many of us had so much to flee from after the war. So many had so much history to hide from."

"Will you help me find her killer?" Fitz asked pointedly.

The man winced at the word "killer." "If I can, without endangering my own family," Simon replied carefully.

"Why do you fear that?" Fitz asked.

"I did not like the little gray man. I knew too many like him in the old country. The Nazis. Then the Soviets. Cold eyes. No hearts. Blood on their hands. Ice in their souls."

Fitz nodded. He'd known many such in his time, too.

"Please do not tell the police I know anything, Chief. I will tell them nothing if they come!"

"You fear them, too, my friend?"

Simon shook his head sadly. "I'm an old man, and have seen much and trust little. I speak only to you."

Fitz nodded. "I'll tell no one. You have my word on it."

Simon continued to hold his gaze but said nothing.

"Did the great lady have friends, Simon? I ask only to find out what happened to her. To find some justice for her terrible death."

"I have seen little of justice," Simon answered coldly. "Perhaps it exists, perhaps not. I will think on what you've said, Chief."

Fitz tipped his head to the side, deciding if more could be accomplished.

"Fair enough," he said finally, and silently handed his card to the old man. "Should you need it, my mobile number is on the back," he said, then left the shop, the doorbell tinkling behind him.

Old-fashioned police work, he thought, as he bucked the wind outside and started toward home and hearth and those he loved. You just never could tell which unlikely person knew *something*. And this man definitely knew something … the question was, would he reveal it?

50

Texas

Hutch was already on the wide verandah when Georgia came down for breakfast. His boots were covered with trail dust and his jeans looked like they'd already done a day's work.

"Just how early did you get up, Unc?" she asked him, genuinely curious. "You look like you been rode hard and put away wet."

"Didn't see much point in sleepin', honey pie," he said. "Lots to think about after last night's talk and a few facts to dredge out of the past by their scrawny asses. I was followin' a hunch about what you really need to know, and that sent me sashayin' down memory lane, big time. It also sent me into files that ain't been opened since my daddy died."

"Bless your heart, Unc. I swear I didn't mean for you to lose sleep over my problems …"

He brushed the thought away with a dismissive sweep of his big hand.

"I'll be a long time dead, darlin'," he said with a wry laugh. "I'll catch up on all my sleepin' then, I expect."

She sat herself down next to him on the top step like she used to, and he reached over to pat her knee.

"So what was your hunch and how'd it pan out?" she asked quickly, not wanting to think there might ever be a time when BH wouldn't be in her world. Coming home had taken her down memory lane, too.

"It occurred to me there's a piece of this pie you ain't got a fork into yet. You got a posse of varmints that've long gone to ground and you got no way to track 'em cause whatever tracks they left have been trashed by time."

"Meaning …?" she prompted.

"Meaning you got to find out who stood to gain the most, or maybe not *lose* the most, if the Old Lady got sent to her Maker a might early. Maybe you got to know who did somethin' long ago that he or his heirs might still be keen on keepin' secret now. It occurs to me your varmint has been just as hidden as his prey was all these years, and that thought triggered possibilities. Are you aware of Operation Paperclip?"

"I am," she said. "The OSS that later became the CIA saved a whole pack of scientists and engineers and such from the War Crimes Tribunal at Nuremburg by giving them new identities and covering up their Nazi pasts with real big lies and altered biographies."

"Right you are, sweet girl, but it wasn't just scientists they saved, and that's what everybody tends to forget. It was businessmen, too—by the bushel. Serious scoundrels, the kind that run empires and look like CEOs in fine haberdashery while they do their dirty work. The kind that could keep the Reich going even without old Herr Schicklgruber at the top." She smiled at the use of Hitler's other family name.

"We dealt with a pile of 'em, or I should say our daddy did—and then your daddy and me dealt with their sons, who were real fancied up by our time and rich as Solomon. But we knew who they really were because our daddy and granddaddy had been around when they reinvented themselves. In fact, our crowd knew a lot about their crowd because oil was the bridge between worlds—oil and money and power. And keepin' them three things intact can make a man keep a lot of secrets."

"Run that one by me again, Unc?" she asked, trying to follow. "Are you saying we need to know if Mrs. W's enemy might've been saved by Paperclip, then slipped under the radar into big business, so we wouldn't know they were ever Nazis? But maybe Mrs. W knew?"

"I'm saying some of them bastards founded dynasties—real big dynasties—and the richer they got, the less anybody remembered they were ever Germans, never mind Nazis! Kinda like the British royal family. Who even remembers they're all Krauts named Saxe-Coburg, who rebaptized themselves Windsor after WWI? A pile of these—let's call them born-again

Krauts—all got to look like American success stories two generations ago, so nobody gives a damn anymore about where they hailed from because money is the best deodorant. And I can think of any number of them, who were sumbitch Nazis, who been flying under a false flag for decades and it occurs to me they could be just who you are looking for."

Georgia took a sharp breath. She'd never known her uncle's instinct to be off about underhanded deals, and this was about as underhanded as you could get.

"And if you're right, Unc ... if I'm following your trail here—we should be looking at powerful dynasties with German roots and a really big fortune or really big political power to protect? Because they might carry a grudge against somebody who could ID them and somehow impact their money or power? Ridiculous as that might sound after nearly eighty years?"

"You're followin' me just fine, darlin'," he said with a crooked smile. "If it's a genuine vendetta that could impact genuine money or power, eighty years is just an eye-blink to some."

He stared hard at the horizon, and threw the stone he'd been toying with out in an admirable arc. "Trouble is, you got too many varmints to track unless we can thin the herd a mite. So that's what I been up to all night. Weedin' out the ones close to Herr Hitler who might have something to protect that your old lady had the means to bollix up."

"Like somebody from the Hitler bloodline who could get to be president?" She said the words, realizing just how terrible they were.

"Now, you're cookin' with gas, darlin! Let's get us some coffee and start scroungin' through what I know of the nefarious past."

51

Fitz pushed open the dry cleaner's door and stepped into the welcome warmth. Simon Spindler sat behind the counter poring over a mountain of papers that looked like invoices. *A man after his own heart,* Fitz thought … one who trusted paper more than computers. Spindler looked up at Fitz and held up a hand, both to acknowledge the man's presence and to ask for a moment to complete whatever his task was.

"I've met your little gray man, Simon," Fitz said in a serious tone. Time was important now. "Stocky, too large on top, oddly short and lean below. Dangerous eyes."

Simon nodded confirmation. He said nothing, but his scowl said it all.

"He threatened my family, Simon, and I believe you know something you haven't told me. So, man to man … I've come to ask you what it is you are hiding. I need your help to keep my girls safe."

Simon looked up from the stack, held Fitz's gaze a long moment, but remained still. Finally, after a long silence on both their parts, he rose and went to the door of the shop. He called to David to watch the counter. "If anyone comes, you must call me. No one must hear what we will say." He said this with pained urgency in his tone, then turned to Fitz. "I would lock up, but you may have been followed. We must hurry so you won't be here long enough to raise suspicion about why."

"Come!" he said in a sepulchral voice, gesturing for Fitz to follow him through the curtain that divided the counter and cash register from the private interior. It was apparent someone lived in this space. Simon? David? Beyond the rows of freshly cleaned clothes that took up half the space was an area set up as a small, tidy sitting room and kitchen.

"You are correct," the old man said, obviously hard-pressed to part with even that much information. "I found something."

"After I heard Ghisella was dead—murdered in cold blood—I went to the last batch of clothing David had picked up from her. I was sorely troubled by her death; it brought back terrible memories for me of the old days. Torture, death, destruction that those who live in safety here cannot imagine. We had sometimes spoken of this to one another through the years, Ghisella and I. Not often, just sometimes ... when something triggered truth. We who have known war and fear recognize each other, you see, by the haunted eyes we share. By the always-wary glances at the door. The fear of jackboots on the pavement or the stair ..." He looked at Fitz to see if he understood.

"Some of us are branded from the camps: all of us are branded in our souls. There is no escape from the memories and no way *not* to recognize one who shares them." He paused, cleared his throat, and took in a long, deep breath, letting it out slowly, carefully, as if it were precious and shouldn't be squandered.

Fitz knew he mustn't speak, must only listen to whatever it was Simon would draw from the deep well of pain within.

"I remembered a conversation we'd had once, years ago. It wasn't as if we shared intimacies, you understand—she was a great lady and I was a tailor—but we shared history and tragedy ... and humanity that sometimes needs to be expressed. She spoke of how in the worst of times, terrified and fleeing the evil ones—how we would hide things, precious things in the seams of our clothing, hoping to save *something*, anything, of our former lives and dignity."

Spindler's voice had grown husky with unspoken emotion.

"She knew I was a tailor, and so she asked me if ever I'd found remnants of such treasure after the war and the occupation. I said ya, I found many such! Not money or jewels, like the rich had hidden to buy freedom and maybe safe passage, but photos of children or parents, notes for loved ones to read if you perished, a baby's tooth or a lock of hair ..."

His eyes were far away now, no longer staring at the shop's back room. Simon pulled a large handkerchief from his pocket, blew his nose and dabbed self-consciously at the tears on his cheeks. Fitz swiped at the moisture in his own eyes.

"She had a few exquisite dressing gowns. The kind women of high birth wore in long-ago times. How she had managed to preserve them for so many years I do not know. The day she died, she called the shop and demanded an immediate pick up. It was unlike her to do this, so David went right away to collect the laundry bag, and she told him no one must ever know of these garments. We were to hold them until she came for them herself, or until *you* did. My grandson said she seemed agitated and frightened."

Fitz looked puzzled. "But Simon, if she said this, why did you not give me the clothes when I first came here asking?"

"Because I was a coward, Chief! I wanted only to hide and to keep my family safe. When I learned of her murder I intended to dispose of these garments. The little gray man made me fear for the ones I love. I have seen eyes like his before and nothing good followed in their wake. I wanted no part of this dangerous intrigue that had brought Ghisella such suffering and harm. Do you understand? I was afraid!" His eyes pleaded for sanction.

"You're not a coward, Simon," Fitz's voice was husky. "You're just a father and a grandfather, that's all. A protector of those you love."

Simon nodded, wanting to believe.

"What did you find in these clothes, Simon?"

"Diagrams. Mathematics. German text. Some in the seams and hems, cleverly disguised by intricate sewing and by beadwork on the outside of the seams. Some written directly onto the fabric itself and then double-seamed to hide it. Some on very old paper. Diagrams of what I believe to be equations of some kind, worked into patterns on the fabric itself and then further obscured by embroidery and decorative embellishments …" He shook his head at the intricacy of it. "It was not easy to find and impossible to decipher.

"I wanted to destroy it. But she had died for this secret and I couldn't bring myself to burn it as I'd planned."

"I removed it all, cutting carefully, and I drew patterns to show where each piece had been secreted. Then I burned the scraps. After you came here, I decided I would leave it all in God's hands. If you came back, I would give this to you. If not …" he shrugged eloquently. "And here you stand."

"So it is as God wills?" Fitz asked.

"Who could know such a thing?" Simon responded with a scowl. "I am only a tailor. So, I have made a vest of these pieces in your size. If you put it on under your jacket and coat, no one will know what you carry."

Fitz looked startled but nodded. "Then you assumed I'd come back?" he asked.

"Ghisella Wallenberg trusted you, Chief, and she trusted few men. I believed you *might* return and I must be ready for you."

Fitz slipped on the vest, wondering what in God's name it signified. He'd go straight to Annie with it to find out.

"You're a brave man, Simon, braver than you think. If and when I can, I will tell you what you have contributed to our quest."

"No!" the old man said sharply. "I want only never to have to speak of it again."

Fitz exited the shop and hurried toward Ling's Laundry on Canal. If he was being followed, he hoped it would seem like just another chore to be ticked off a list. He'd off-load the vest to Annie, make a few more needless stops, then head home.

52

Dec Fairchild sat in his office staring out the window. This crazy, quixotic mission the Donovans had embarked on had gotten under his skin. Or was it really only Maeve who had taken up residence there lately? One way or another, she was on his mind pretty much all the time now. And so was some old dead woman he'd never laid eyes on, but now felt somehow responsible for seeing her get justice! Bollocks.

He leaned back in his chair, stuck his well-shod feet up on his desk, and steepled his hands in front of his chest—then realizing how much he must look like his father doing that, he knotted his fingers behind his head instead and returned his feet to the floor.

This needed sorting. Right now.

If he could figure out why it was all niggling at him so he couldn't concentrate on business, maybe he could figure out what to do about it.

It was hard not to like Fitz. There was something archetypal about the man. Something stalwart and decent. He was the kind of man other men follow instinctively. Honorable, tough-minded, good-natured. Obviously compassionate, too, or he wouldn't be leading this crazy charge. Or this oddball gaggle of would-be helpers. He'd heard about most of them from Maeve over the years of their friendship, of course, but seeing them assembled, so wildly diverse in their smarts and capabilities, and so earnestly willing to take on a mystery that the police seemed to want no part of … *that* was touching and quirky and damned formidable all at the same time.

And then there was Maeve. And the obvious bonds of love and goodwill among the Donovan family members. He'd heard about that, too, over the years, but seeing it all in action was riveting, He thought of the cool, measured calculation of his own family, who always seemed more intent on assessing each other's usefulness than on offering warmth or love around the table.

Maybe it was time to admit to himself that he fancied her as more than a good friend. It had occurred to him lately that simple friendship was a cover story that had worn out its usefulness, so maybe a bit of self-honesty was needed here. If he helped her now … helped them all with their jousting-with-windmills mission, it would change things between them. He knew it would, and had surprised himself by feeling relief at that fact. He didn't want to run away, as he usually did. He wanted to run toward possibilities he had thought long dead and buried. It was time to figure out just what his heart was trying to tell him.

So he'd better do some serious soul-searching because she wasn't one to be trifled with. He wanted her. Had for a while, in fact. But if he stepped over the line they'd both drawn in the sand, he stood the chance of hurting her badly. And of losing what they had. Besides, Dougal would kick his ass around the block if he did that, and he was just the man to do it. He smiled at the image.

It was obvious to him that he had no intention of walking away from Maeve. He'd just have to figure out how to walk toward her without scaring her away.

Dec picked up a pen, started to jot down some ideas about where he could best begin to help: Banking. War spoils. Euro and Middle East connections. Dieter Streger. He'd start poking into all of these potential threads. But he tapped the last word on the list. The man would be in his nineties if he was even still alive, but he might also have progeny to whom he'd passed on clues. He was the only name they had of someone who had actually known Ghisella and Gerhardt both during the war and after. And he was from a wealthy and prominent family that might have survived the war intact. At least it was a place to start being useful to this Quixotic mission.

53

Matrix squashed her crazy Russian fur hat down on her head, pulled the fuzzy ear flaps into place and tied them, then bundled herself into the magnificent shearling coat that had been a Christmas gift from her dad, a man with both taste and big bucks. She stuffed her laptop and a folder into her backpack and headed purposefully toward the loft door. With her furry boots and outrageously expensive but mismatched fur adornments, she looked like a chic escapee from Genghis Khan's Mongol horde.

"Where are you off to in such a rush?" Annie called after her.

"Mannheim," Matrix answered. "He and Finn need what I've got. More later!"

Cryptic as ever, Annie thought, once the door had slammed behind the girl. Not her usual MO to leave the loft, but it seemed she had formed a bond of some kind with Mannheim. They must have something big cooking.

Things were starting to fall into place, and they needed a meeting to share the latest intel. She and her team had a lot to add to the stew now, and more was clarifying every day. It was appallingly obvious how many branches of government and how many corporate entities that served them had conspired together to make millions off Nazi tech—and to keep a patriotic and self-sacrificing nation as ignorant as possible of the facts with a monumental disinformation campaign. Those dangerous comporate entities were becoming household names, long since whitewashed and reinvented. Stealth technology? Antigravity capability? Space travel? Perpetual energy sources? Weather and mind control? GMO foods? If all this was in the wrong hands, what had they done with it here and in space? Weaponized it, profited from it, pulled the noose of control tighter over the man in the street? Probably all of that and more.

Annie had no illusions about the perfidy of governments, corporations or greedy men, or about the self-serving agendas they profited from. No illusions and no respect. It was why she did what she did. Why she'd always trained the smartest students she could find to buck authority, to question everything, to peel back bullshit and media hype, to delve where they weren't supposed to dive, to find the T.A.E. To be ready for a very uncertain future.

T.A.E. Truth About Everything. Until humanity swallowed the red pill and watched the false realities crash and burn, there could be no chance of a better world, no abatement of hatred, no elevation of the human condition or safety for the very existence of the planet. And maybe no way to escape the inevitability of a dystopian nuclear future. Even with the T.A.E. there were no guarantees.

And the clock was ticking. Humanity was on a timeline to destruction as technology, bots, 24-7 surveillance, drones and AI got more efficient, and bombs got bigger and more sophisticated, in a post-truth world where there wasn't a moment to lose.

Surveillance was everywhere. Lies were so big they were believed without question. Agendas were in place that would complete humanity's path to slavery, and humanity was marching right into it thinking they were free.

Hitler had known how to enslave a whole populace while making it feel empowered. "A lie told once remains a lie but a lie told a thousand times becomes the truth." Goebbels's Nazi propaganda ministry's brand of doublespeak was alive and well in Washington, DC right now, and more and more news outlets were being compromised. She knew exactly where suppression of free press led. Especially in the atmosphere like the current one, where hatred had not only been allowed to surface, it was actually encouraged. Where tyrants were admired and befriended, as if their despotism was a show of strength, and lies were used to incite hatred, riots, threats, and acceptance of unspeakable acts that were supposedly in the national interest. Where greed for money and winning at any cost trumped conscience, truth and the rule of law.

Maybe that's why she was willing to lend her considerable resources to Fitz's little army and obsession. Because in her heart of hearts she knew it was always an army of little guys who fought back, who had a prayer of altering the odds. Magdalena had known it, too.

Or maybe it was just that the willingness to spit in the eye of a tyrant was what her life was all about. She turned back to the code she was writing, hoping T had some time on his hands tonight.

What she wanted to run by him could be the key to their Rosetta Stone, if she was right about it.

54

Rory charged down the steps of the New York Historical Society in high spirits. They'd been incredibly helpful and open to all her inquiries, God bless their erudite hearts. Unlike the Building Department, which was a mare's nest of obstruction, chaotic filings and congested red tape. It had taken all her charm and patience to wheedle out the old drawings and the history of purchase for Mrs. W's house. Truth be told, it wasn't entirely the fault of the clerks—so much of New York history was not on computer, but still sitting in boxes in dusty file rooms. Nonetheless, the day had proved fruitful and she couldn't wait to share what she'd learned.

Proof of whoever or whatever Mrs. W had been before 1991 was still eluding her, and Fitz or even Annie might be better able to ferret out that info. But she had at least learned that the Jane Street house had been purchased *for* the widow Wallenberg, not *by* her. No sign of a *Mr.* Wallenberg had she found anywhere, and a European holding company had made the deal for the property. It had also contributed money to Mrs. W's account in a sporadic but consistent flow ever since the home purchase. The funds were from a generous blind trust; Rory hadn't yet been able to follow the money trail to the source, but this she knew how to do and would get on it in the morning.

Obviously, Mrs. W had family money or well-heeled friends who had protected her interests for a long, long time.

Interesting. But where were they now? Did they even know she was dead?

Interesting, too, was the fact that two of the exasperated clerks she'd sweet-talked into helping her scrounge for intel had said she was the second person to ask for info on Mrs. Wallenberg since Tuesday.

55

Dec raised his pint of Guinness toward Maeve and smiled across the table at Donohue's.

Maureen Donohue, who'd inherited the restaurant from her father and made it a neighborhood home-away-from-home for both the anonymous and the famous, had stopped by the table to chat and laugh with them for a few minutes—always a pleasure—and they had each ordered their usual dinner and settled into the warmth and camaraderie they both cherished. They thought it was the best-kept secret in New York—a great Irish pub and steakhouse, known mostly to those who loved great food in a friendly, cozy atmosphere, where intellectuals, celebrities, cops and all sorts of others mingled contentedly without ogling each other or intruding on privacy. Originally a neighborhood staple, it now seemed to cater to a variety of happy New Yorkers, the literati and a wide swath of undercover celebrities; the well-known and the not-so-well known equally delighted to be there.

Dec was in a stellar mood. A deal he'd been working on for the better part of a year had come through today and he wanted to share the news with a friend. Or more than a friend. Definitely not with a casual flirtation or a stranger whose motives he'd have to vet. Not with a sycophant or a flatterer. There was a helluva lot to be said for being a rich bachelor in Manhattan, but the more he embroiled himself with the Donovans, the more time he wanted to spend with Maeve. She'd been his first phone call after the good news had surfaced this morning, and he'd realized after she said she'd meet him, how empty he would have felt if she'd said no to his invitation.

"I have something to celebrate, too," she said with a grin. "My publisher accepted my first draft with enthusiasm, and Finn just got one of her images accepted for a big museum show in Berlin, and they actually want her to go over for the opening—a good sign that she has a shot at getting her work into their permanent collection."

"Brilliant, on both counts," he said, meaning it and raising his glass again. "What say we fly over for her show, drop her off in Berlin to network with the art crowd there, then you and I take a little holiday in wine country. I know a small chateau with a lovely vineyard on the Mosel River—it's like a scene from a Christmas village under a tree. I'd really love to show it to you."

Maeve cocked her head a little and looked amused as she breathed it all in. The sweet evening, the celebratory good spirits, the lovely invitation. "You have a disconcerting habit of forgetting that I'm a working girl with responsibilities and family obligations, who can't just run away to play in fairyland at the drop of a hat, even if she wants to."

"I haven't forgotten a thing," he said, chuckling. "I know *just* who you are, my elusive butterfly. You can sidestep a seductive invitation so deftly I'm only slightly offended each time it happens. Truth is, I'd delightedly take your whole family with us if I thought that would do the trick. It occurred to me recently that you always make me happy, Maeve. Whenever we're together, I'm so much happier than when we're not."

"Only *recently*?" she teased.

"Indeed. Even when you're embroiling me in conspiracies and intrigue that would send any other man scurrying. Speaking of which, when's the next book club meeting?" He glanced around to see who was in nearby booths, then lowered his voice. "I've got an idea I want to run by you, Fitz and the others—"

Maeve interrupted. "Tomorrow night, I think," she responded eagerly "Rory has info about a European trust that's been supporting Mrs. W for years, and she thinks you might be able to trace it easier than she can through your family's banking clout—"

Just then, Maureen was back with their steaks, two more pints and a witty story that made them all laugh out loud, so they both took the opportunity to let the conversation run in more frivolous directions.

But later, when they parted company, neither one really wanted to leave, and both realized that when the current distractions were over, they'd probably have to fish or cut bait. There was real heat between them now as well as friendship, and they could either fan the flame or extinguish it, but they would have to deal with it soon, and whatever their choice, it would change everything.

56

Annie had photographed and x-rayed the information gleaned from the dressing gowns, then assembled the result on the big screen so she could easily move the pieces around. Some ink was faded, some indistinguishable, some vivid as the day it was drawn or written. All of it was staggering in its importance. And it was the final piece that completed the astonishing puzzle. No wonder it had been kept separate from the journal and guarded until the last protective barrier was about to be breached.

What had her gobsmacked was both the brilliance and the ingenuity—no, the *raw courage* was a better description of this act of concealment—of the woman who had sent this message from beyond the grave.

It was the final piece of the scientific puzzle, of that she was certain. But it was so astounding, if she was right about it—it quite simply changed everything.

"Am I looking at what I think I'm looking at?" T-square's eyes were wide and uncertain as he stared at Annie's equations.

"I believe so," she answered, her voice tight. "It's why I called you, T. For corroboration and strategy. The fallout from making this data public could be catastrophic."

"Like maybe we-be-outing-the-greatest-fraud-in-history catastrophic?" he prompted with a grim smile.

"Like maybe assuring us both a Nobel Prize or a bullet in the brain," she went on briskly, all business. "I'm calling it "new physics" for lack of a better inclusive term, but feel free to rechristen it if you've got a better name. It's an entirely new take on how the universe works."

"Holy shit!"

"Well said. The real trouble is that it isn't new at all! It's been right here on planet Earth, in *somebody's* hands for seventy-five years."

T shook his head. The implications were mind-numbing.

Not only had this alternate science existed, it must have been sold to the highest bidder decades ago, a bidder who had doubtless used it to be light-years ahead of ordinary science and all the competition. It could have already opened doors to the cosmos that even the most brilliant scientists were still butting their heads against.

"How close are your women with the calculations?" he asked. He'd called the Babushkas 'girls' once and gotten his head handed to him. Even though he'd meant it to be affectionate, not demeaning, he'd realized that to them it was the equivalent of some white guy with half his IQ calling him "boy."

"Close enough to know we're right. But not so close on figuring out where it went and who used it to what end ..."

"Aerospace, military, governments," he ticked off probabilities. "Probably passing it all off as breakthroughs from DARPA labs, maybe deploying things in space we all don't know about ... maybe places like Groom Lake-Area 51 are real good cover for such secret doings. A conspiracy this big has to include the highest echelons of the powers that be! Like maybe even the president?"

Annie nodded. "Or maybe whoever it is who pulls the strings of the president?"

T took a minute to digest what she'd just said. "And maybe we all be dead meat if we ever let this particular cat out of the bag."

She snorted her reply. "Fuckin' A," as Matrix would say, T-square. Fuckin' A!"

57

The two powerful brothers locked eyes over their cognac. It had been a long day and each was feeling the weight of it, but for differing reasons.

The presidential primary race was going better than planned. Zachary Reese had charisma to spare, his uncle Werner mused, as he watched his brother Heinrich, now called H by all but family, bask in the glow of yet another coup for his senator son. It appeared Senator Reese had a fairly clear shot at the presidential nomination now, and Werner covertly both admired and envied his brother and his brother's son, their Teflon ability to walk between the raindrops. The golden glow of money and success seemed to mark their passage through the world.

It was a gift their father had possessed and passed on to them. The old man's manipulations of government, Wall Street and the financial marketplace had left both Werner and his brother among the richest men in the country, or on earth for that matter. And their prosperity was well deserved. There hadn't been an hour in either of their lives when they had strayed from the course of Germanic discipline he'd taught them, or failed to protect the legacy of power he'd left in their hands. It was meant to be a bulwark for the Fourth Reich, although it could never be called that except among the Inner Circle of The 13, the power brokers who really pulled the strings of the world. But it had also provided them money, power and the certainty of being above the law.

It was a pity Heinrich still worried so much about the old woman they'd pursued, found and dispatched. What real harm could she do them now? In Werner's view, it was a mistake to keep obsessing about the perhaps apocryphal dossier his brother thought could derail his son's presidential campaign, which was meant to place the ultimate power into their hands.

The presidency wielded both symbolic power, and actual power seldom exercised: it was men like them, invisible to public view as kingmakers, who knew how to manipulate the office of president to accomplish things yet undreamed. So much had been put in place already, and a vast amount more could be accomplished swiftly by presidential order once Zach was in office. It would be a bloodless coup— enslaving the country that thought itself the Land of the Free without having fired a shot or letting the slaves know what servitude they'd bought into.

Ghisella von Zechandorff was finally dead. The dossier, if it had ever existed, was lost and, most importantly, the world didn't give a shit about Hitler anymore. He was very old news, and the Reich had successfully morphed its identity and power beneath the cloak of the everyday crimes of greed, lies and manipulation that had become so commonplace they were hardly noticeable anymore. If the damned Protocol was ever found, without Ghisella's corroboration it could be discredited easily enough as a forgery. A soiled footnote to history, no more than that, and utterly unprovable.

Werner had decided to give his subordinate one more shot at redeeming himself after the botched retrieval mission. Odeon had served him well for thirty years and it wouldn't be easy to replace his knowledge and talents. But the man's failure was too conspicuous, pinging as it did on his brother's radar. So he'd bought the man another try for the prize. Heinrich could be a real prick about failures.

There were two ways to handle this if Odeon failed again: give the task to another asset, or simply lob it back into his brother's court. It would be important to make Heinrich feel he'd won some points in the one-upmanship game they'd played since boyhood, and that was somewhat galling; yet it might be the better choice in the long run. Henrich was always a bit careless when he was preening about winning something over his brother.

Truth was, Werner would like to be rid of the task and he'd like to keep Heinrich smug about it, so he could make some strategic moves for his own son under his brother's radar. If there was one thing their father had taught them, it was to give no quarter, especially to siblings. All's fair in love and war, and business is war. The trick was to keep your opponent feeling smugly victorious while you cut his legs out from under him.

Werner smiled at the thought of bringing his brother down a peg or two just as Heinrich rose to greet their guest, striding across the room as if he owned the world.

Well, come to think of it, Werner mused, watching his brother's confident strides, *he did own it.* They both did. Heinrich had let this matter of the Protocol distract him, while he himself was already five moves ahead of his brother on the chessboard. In the end, he would win, so Werner, too, smiled and rose to greet their guest.

58

Odeon felt a trifle rattled by this morning's conversation in Werner's office. He ticked off a mental inventory to discern if he'd been at fault in the steps he'd taken thus far—not that fault would matter. Only results. He had visited or vetted every possible connection to the von Zechandorff woman. He'd triple-checked the meticulous list of all those he'd interviewed on this vexing project. None of von Zechandorff's acquaintances had raised his hackles except the former police chief. What, after all, would be Donovan's motive for interfering? It didn't seem his relationship with the dead woman merited his involvement.

If the documents had existed … *if* she'd found a way to pass them on … *if* she'd managed to interest anyone at all in her seventy-five-year-old cause, Donovan was the only candidate who made any sense at all. But why would he bother? The man had nothing to gain by getting involved, no living witness to protect, no money to be made, no reason to bring his family to the attention of forces that might harm them. It was absurd. But human nature was sometimes difficult to fathom and the stone could not be left unturned. Not after that had been made so clear to him by his employer today.

His own job, and perhaps his own life, were now squarely on the line. Werner had made that clear. Had it not been for that fact, Odeon would simply have closed the file at this point. But that wasn't possible now that solving the riddle appeared to have become a bone of contention between the two brothers. He'd have to rattle Donovan's chains quickly, and maliciously enough to see if that changed the man's mind about disgorging the prize. From what he'd learned of Donovan, his family was his Achilles' heel. Threatening the lives of those he loved should do it. If that didn't produce results, the damned dossier probably just didn't exist, and it would be time for Odeon to disappear.

From what he'd been able to glean, Donovan's friendship with the old bitch had only been lukewarm, more a commercial bond than an emotional one. Certainly not the kind of bond that would make a man put his family's lives on the line. But perhaps he'd been too subtle with his threats up to now. Perhaps the full extent of the danger hadn't yet been made sufficiently clear to the man. Odeon would have to remedy that in some novel way that would leave no scintilla of doubt in Donovan's mind that they meant business, and no doubt in his own employers' minds that he'd moved every mountain on their behalf.

He'd need to cripple the man in his deepest vulnerability—hurt him enough to take the fight out of him. Something novel and exquisitely painful that harmed his family should do the trick.

Odeon checked his own passport and cash position just in case he found it necessary to disappear quickly. He had no illusions about what happened to those who failed the Brothers.

Odeon smiled a bit at his own foresight in never having had a family of his own. Whatever it was that appealed to people about wives and children had always eluded him anyway, but over the years, this particular flaw in the human psyche had proved a useful vulnerability for exploiting others.

Kill somebody's child or other close relative, and they usually came around before you had to kill them, too.

59

Maeve studied the tarot cards in front of her. Her mother had taught her how to read the cards and the tea leaves. Had even trained her with scrying tools like mirrors, a bowl of ink or water, or the great crystal ball that now sat under a velvet cover in her bedroom, far from prying eyes. Maeve had a gift for piercing the veil and bringing back knowledge, but people often misunderstood the use of these ancient tools, so she only used them for clients who requested such help. Those whom she knew well enough to know they'd understand the provenance of the messages received.

The uninitiated equated all this with a magic trick—and in many ways it was magic; what else could you call a means of contacting other realms and dimensions of consciousness? But for the most part, tarot and scrying were merely ways to help a person gifted with second sight to focus on a specific problem in a specific way. A focusing inward and outward to levels of consciousness most people never reach, levels where more information could often be tapped into so it could be interpreted by the gifted one.

For the most part, Maeve used astrology alone to answer her clients' questions. Most people could somehow trust the information gleaned from the stars easier than that gleaned from pure psychism, which many considered one step above hocus-pocus.

But right this minute, Maeve was looking for answers for herself and those she cared about deeply, so she was pulling out all the tools. She lit the white candles, asked protection from the great archangels who guarded the Watchtowers of North, South, East, and West, and reshuffled the cards.

She was hoping for guidance about this quest for justice they were enmeshed in. She feared it was far more dangerous than any of the participants yet realized. But she also understood the magnitude of this strangely layered puzzle they'd been drawn into. What it looked like on the surface was one thing. What it portended for each of the players who had been called to the game was quite another. She'd felt danger escalating for days and it seemed to touch them all, so she wasn't sure where it would hit first or how to deflect it. Whatever this was, it was both nebulous and potentially lethal. She needed answers and she needed a timeline.

Maeve laid out the cards, then sat back in her chair trying to calm herself. She wouldn't have been disturbed by the Death card alone. That could just mean transformation, not necessarily bodily harm. But any tarot lay that ended with the Nine of Swords was alarming, and combined with the Three of Swords, even worse than she'd feared. Clearly real death was on the table here … but whose, when, where … it seemed to encompass all of them, but how was that possible? She stood up abruptly, put on her coat, and left the house, desperately needing air.

60

Mimi knocked tentatively on Dr. Patel's office door, then stuck her head in when told to enter. The Indian geneticist was a pleasant-looking man in his early fifties, tall and rangy, with gray-tinged hair and sun-lined skin the color of light coffee. He'd told her he ran ten miles a day and he looked it; a wiry, sinewy strength emanated from the quiet man.

He had a world-class reputation because of his work on DNA gene drives, the new hot button in genetics, but he had little of the pomposity she'd come to expect from so many of the big-rep docs she'd encountered at the hospital. She'd had two good experiences with the man, when her Down syndrome research needed expert help and when he'd agreed to mentor her over a year ago. In both cases, he'd been courtly and full of willingly shared knowledge, a man who obviously loved his work so much he was happy to teach an eager student.

"Dr. Patel," she ventured, not wanting to intrude. "I'd love to ask your thoughts on a project I'm working on. I know how busy you are, so I don't want to take much of your time, I'm just hoping you might point me in the right direction to find the answers I need."

Looking a bit more absentminded than usual, he motioned her inside, and she realized she was distracting him from something that had his full attention.

"I can come back later …"

"No, no. Dr. Halberdson. I welcome the distraction, truth be told." He had a warm smile. "Has this to do with your Down's research?" he asked, and she shook her head.

"It couldn't be further from that, Dr. Patel," she began. "This time I'm pursuing a question of bloodline. Specifically, the bloodline of Adolf Hitler."

He looked startled and a little bemused. "I must say, that is a bit unexpected. What on earth has sent you off in that direction? A doctoral dissertation, perhaps?"

She laughed. "It might lead me there one day, but at the moment I have a friend in law enforcement who asked me how one would go about tracing a bloodline through several generations, if even the original DNA is in question. Hitler's story filled that bill. My friend's dilemma has to do with the validity of using traceable elements of genetics to find progeny of someone thought not to have had children."

"Ah!" he said, leaning back in his chair. "An intriguing idea, that. So you do know that the body said to be Hitler's was most probably not his at all?" He raised a questioning, dark eyebrow and she nodded. "As a geneticist, one keeps one's eye on such historical anomalies. In fact, about a year ago there was an article in one of the scientific journals that pinpointed several such DNA mysteries of history, if you will, and Hitler's was high on the list. Let me do a bit of poking about and I'll see if I can find it or any other relevant articles for you.

"And do you know that a great many of Hitler's eugenics scientists may have landed at Rockefeller University after the war?" he added. "That could be a thread for you to follow. Although, I'm not sure how transparent their answers would be to any questions along this line of inquiry. Rockefeller supported both Hitler and eugenics, you know."

"I didn't know that," she answered, interested. "So you think he might have taken in some eugenics specialists who were creating the perfect Aryan and the perfect soldier?"

"Indeed—all with nicely whitewashed dossiers after the war, I might add. But, of course, they may all have gone to the military instead."

"Operation Paperclip?" she pressed, interested.

"Paperclip and other clandestine operations, I'm afraid. These scientists had also been tasked, so the rumor goes, with making Hitler immortal, ghastly thought though that be. But if there is a bloodline to be found, that would be a kind of immortality, wouldn't it? And you can imagine how many of those with unlimited bank accounts would be willing to pay for *that* possibility."

"A terrifying thought," she murmured, wondering how much truth about history had been hidden from the world. Maybe the Babushkas weren't paranoid after all—maybe they just knew more secrets than the rest of us.

"I truly don't want this to be an imposition on you, Doctor, but any clue would be helpful …"

"Not at all an imposition, rather intriguing, actually." His eyes looked merry. "Especially if you promise to tell me where your investigations lead."

"I will when I can," she replied earnestly.

It really was kind of him to take time to help. The big guns in any medical field always knew how to ferret out info from sources no one else knew to pursue.

Mimi glanced at her watch and grimaced. She was late, and Finn would be waiting with the florist and the boys. This intro party for their line seemed to have taken on a life of its own. All the work was being done by the others, thank God, but she didn't want to look disinterested. And if the truth were told, she was having fun just watching it all take shape. Finn was so good at making events happen with panache, and this one promised to deliver.

She grabbed her coat from her locker and scurried out to find a cab.

61

Finn's automatic new-customer smile changed to puzzlement when she recognized Declan walking into the gallery. *God, he was good-looking,* was her first thought, followed by *why is he here?*

He was standing in front of a newly acquired piece as if giving it serious consideration. And wow! Wouldn't nailing him as a client put gold stars next to her name with the owner, who was now looking up from his desk with a predatory gleam in his eye, and just about to make a move in Dec's direction. She pushed the unworthy thought away and walked toward the familiar man with open arms.

"Hi Dec," she called out, tickled by the look of surprise on her boss's face. "Don't tell me you found an empty spot on a wall that could use a new painting? I thought you were full-up."

He embraced her, smiling, and acknowledged the gallery owner with a hand gesture, then took her arm proprietarily and led her in the other direction.

"Inasmuch as you know my walls so well, what would you recommend?" he asked, just loud enough to be overheard.

"Upstairs or down?" she queried, playing along. If this was a shopping expedition, it wasn't for a painting, but it was still fun to be the object of envious stares.

"Downstairs," he replied, "maybe near the solarium."

"Then I'd take a look at the Simonelli triptych. Of course, you shouldn't ignore two or three of the new artists the Times applauded on Sunday. They're all young and wildly talented, so you might want to get in on the ground floor. But I still like the Simonelli best. It's a knockout if you like encaustic."

When they got to the farthest corner of the gallery, Finn laughed and said, "Okay, out with it. What are you really here for?"

"Am I that transparent? I thought I'd handled this with superb finesse."

She grinned. "To the uninitiated perhaps, but you forget I come from a long line of Donovan detecting genes."

He laughed, and she thought he only got better looking for it. What was wrong with Mom that she resisted jumping his bones? It was obvious he was into her.

There was such a nice easiness about the man, she thought, watching him. Not like the usual demeanor of the rich, arrogant and pretentious who kept the downtown art markets hot as they tried to overwhelm you with their new knowledge and their limitless bank accounts. Finn had been watching Dec at the meetings and she hadn't found anything not to like. Mom was probably just scared of getting hurt again, so keeping her distance.

"I'm here for some advice and"—he began hesitantly, looking for the moment uncertain and younger—"perhaps your blessing."

Finn's eyes widened. "Okay, I did *not* see that coming."

"I care very much about your mother," he said, "and I'm worried about her safety. And yours, too, for that matter. Maeve and I have been friends for years, as you know, but I'm having the devil's own time getting her to think of me as anything more than that..." His breed wasn't capable of being flustered, but the perfect facade of confidence had crumbled just enough to show Finn a hint of unaccustomed vulnerability. "I'm hoping you approve of my intentions, and if so, that you'll give me a pointer or two on what I'm doing wrong. I had to get you alone to ask, so here I am."

One of the gifts Finn had been given in this lifetime was near perfect pitch when it came to judging people's character. As well as their bullshit. Which this wasn't. So she decided to be forthright.

"My father almost killed her with his con man skills," she said. "Mom never quite got over being so completely bamboozled by him. I still don't speak to him more than twice a year, when he calls for Christmas or birthdays, because he really did a number on her and I despise him for it. But he's still in her head and he definitely interferes with her love life."

"Are you saying she still loves the man, then?" Dec asked, confused.

"Far from it! She just doesn't trust men or her own judgment about them anymore because of him. She's scared and wounded. I was only a kid when it happened, but I remember how devastated she was. His lies nearly killed her."

Dec looked troubled but didn't speak, so she continued.

"She likes you, Dec," she added, trying to un-confuse him. "I think she likes you a lot. So if you really want my advice, just don't mess around with her heart if you're not seriously interested, or if you're the flit-from-flower-to-flower kind usually found in the ranks of those in your tax bracket. But if you really care … please don't give up too easily. She's a prize worth fighting for in my opinion, and I'd love to see her happy." She smiled at the serious look on his face, like he was untying the Gordian knot.

"And by the way, just for the record, I really like you, too. But if you break her heart just because you can, I'm warning you now, I won't be held accountable for my actions."

He chuckled. "Fair enough, lass," he said. "I accept your challenge."

He really did seem like a good guy, she thought, then said, "And now I'd better get back to work before they fire me."

Dec laughed. "I think it would be wise for me to build a small bridge to your employer, just in case I need to come in for more advice. Those in my tax bracket usually don't shop without purchasing something." His eyes were now merry. Irish eyes, smiling. "Choose something for me, won't you? A painting, a photo, a triptych. Something your instinct tells you is *the* piece to own. On the way out, I'll let your boss know I'm good for it."

"Oh my God, Dec!" she breathed. "You don't have to do *that*." His generous gesture startled her. "We can meet for coffee on my break next time. I mean, Starbucks is pricey, but at least it won't cost you a painting!"

"I don't *have to do it*, my dear Finn, but it would give me great pleasure to do so. You've lightened my heart today and I'm grateful."

She saw him stop for a moment to speak with the gallery owner before heading out. At the door, he turned and winked at her.

"You *know* Declan Fairchild?" her boss said incredulously after the man had left the gallery. "Have you got any idea how rich that man is?"

"Not really," she answered, trying to keep a straight face. "I think it's bad manners to ask family friends what their net worth is, don't you?"

But she stared after Dec as she saw him get into the car his driver had double-parked outside the gallery. She and Fitz had both seen the chemistry between him and her mom and knew about the comfort they'd shared for years in each other's company. He was courtly, charming and, she believed, somewhat smitten. But she also knew what a romantic her mother was at heart, a condition that as far as she and the girls of her generation could tell, was usually a ticket to heartbreak. But maybe, just maybe, if there really were any honorable family men left in New York City, there could still be a chance for her mom to find love. So she decided to give him a helping hand. She also decided to tell him he didn't have to splurge on any more paintings. He could just be good to her mom.

62

"What do you think of Dec and my mom as a couple, Mim?" Finn asked as she poured two glasses of wine and carried them to the couch in the center of her loft. The sofa faced the giant windows that looked out on the snowy roof deck and the glittery night lights of Manhattan beyond.

"Hold that thought," Mimi gasped from the doorway. "I'll have things to say after I regain my breath from tramping up the thousand steps to your apartment! I feel like I just climbed Casterly Rock!" Mimi plopped down two grocery bags, a small overnight case and her handbag, and tried to catch her breath.

Finn laughed. "You get used to the five flights, trust me. It's great exercise. Lulu says my leg muscles are so strong now I could kick through steel plate or put somebody through a wall if the need arises."

"You could probably run the four-minute mile, too, after this kind of workout on a steady basis," Mimi said, shaking the snow off her jacket as she hung it on the hook by the door.

Finn handed her a glass of pinot noir as recompense.

"Girl, it's cold out there!" Mimi said, curling up in her usual corner of the couch and taking a grateful sip of the wine. "But in answer to your question, I think he's a babe and your mom's the best, so it's a perfect match. Why?"

Finn told her about the gallery encounter and Mimi's eyebrows went up. "I think it's really quite romantic," she said judiciously. "Just like in the olden days when the handsome prince had to ask a girl's father for her hand in marriage! I mean, he's about as close to a handsome prince as you could get these days. We'll just have to keep a closer eye on him now to see if his character holds up to scrutiny. You know men with *that* kind of money and *that* kind of good looks generally don't have great creds for fidelity, and I know that counts with your mom."

Finn nodded in agreement, got up and began to unpack the takeout bag Mimi had brought. The best Chinese food around was en route from the hospital. Both girls got a kick out of cooking, but tonight wasn't the night for that.

"The boys are super excited about the party, Mim," Finn said, changing the subject. "It's really awesome for you to be doing this for them, you know."

Mimi smiled at her friend. "What's the point of having my mega-house and all that goes with it if I can't share? Besides, I totally love of the boys and I'll probably be clothed for life as a result. I just hope they get some good PR out of it."

"How could it not in that gorgeous setting? Those gowns are made for a lifestyle like yours."

Finn glanced over at Mimi's overnight bag. "Glad to see you decided to stay over in my humble abode tonight. It's too cold to head home."

"I love your abode!" Mimi answered, meaning it. "You know that. Besides, it's still a mess out there and I really don't like going home to that big empty place late at night, especially in the winter. It's different if you're there, or if Eva and Tony have the fireplaces going so it seems more welcoming. But all by my lonesome it can feel kind of forbidding."

"You really need a Kuma, Mim. He's mostly a person." Finn knew Eva and Tony, Mimi's house-managing couple, were only there part-time now, and fabulous as the house was, when you were all alone in it, it could feel big, cold and spooky.

Mimi took a quick bite of kung pao chicken and nodded. "I haven't ruled that out," she managed, "but a dog is a big responsibility and my hours at the hospital are still so cockeyed .... It's probably crazy to even keep the house going at all, but it's the only home I've ever lived in and it's my only physical connection to my memory of my parents."

She looked serious, suddenly. "Want me to put out some feelers among the rich and relaxed to see what Dec's reputation is with women? You know there's bound to be gossip about so eligible a guy."

Finn nodded her head "yes," her mouth full of dumpling. "I don't know if gossip is ever very accurate, but what the heck. I'll ask Georgia, too. She seems to have a handle on men."

Mimi grinned. "Southern women are trained from the cradle about two things, far as I can see. Men and guns. You and Fitz have the guns nailed, so I think Georgia's a good bet for the men stuff."

The girls put their heads together over the guests' seating arrangements for the show, gossiped about politics and everybody they knew, then packed it in around one o'clock because Mimi had an early shift at the hospital the next day.

PART VII

Family Matters

"No man ever wore a scarf as warm as his daughter's arm around his shoulders."

— Irish Proverb

63

"So when do we call the next meeting of our Bleecker Street Irregulars?" Finn asked through a mouthful of toast at breakfast. Mimi had scooted out an hour before and Finn was in her mother's kitchen.

Maeve, standing at the stove waiting for the kettle to boil, and Fitz sitting in Cara's rocker reading the *Times*, burst out laughing simultaneously.

"By God, why didn't I think of calling us that?" Fitz chuckled, laying down the paper.

Finn grinned at the enthusiastic response. "It's who we are, right? I'm just saying … I already told T and Mimi we needed an official designation and they approved. I think we all make a pretty good detective team—and maybe this won't be our last investigation, so we need a name, just in case. BSI has a CSI vibe but with infinitely more style, right?"

"BSI it is, then," Fitz approved with a grin, "and in answer to your question, I think we should do our next meet as soon as Georgia's back from Texas." He turned to Maeve. "Do we know when that is?"

Maeve picked up the whistling kettle and poured the bubbling water in on top of the waiting tea leaves. "She's supposed to get back the day after tomorrow," she said as she poured. "She'll be bursting at the seams with news for us by then, so she'll want to pass it on right away."

Finn looked up. "I didn't know she'd checked in, Mom. When did you speak to her?"

"I didn't. She's been under radio silence ever since she got to Texas. But the flash came over the airwaves to me last night loud and clear." Both Donovans knew it was Maeve's way of describing the psychic hits she got randomly.

"All I know is that some papers, photos and intel she's gotten from her family archives will trigger Dec to make a trip to Europe to follow through on some info that dovetails with her story. I'm not sure, but I may have to go with him."

Fitz's mouth twitched at the corner, covering a paternal smile. He knew Maeve felt much more for Declan than she cared to let on. He wanted her to find love again; he wasn't sure this man was the one to risk it on, but she'd have to start somewhere if she was ever going to let any man into her heart. Declan seemed decent enough, smart enough and friend enough, but he was a high roller and temptations were many for his sort of man. Mrs. W's murder had thrown them all together, so now Fitz could get a better look at the man in action.

Finn wasn't so circumspect. "I wouldn't fight too hard *not* to go," she said with a snort of unsuppressed approval. "I mean, Mom … the guy's a hottie and has a plane so you won't even have to get squashed into a middle seat."

Maeve laughed. "I know, sweetheart … the trappings are pretty seductive. It's just not always that simple to sort out how I feel about his high-flying lifestyle, pun intended. I mean, dipping into luxury from time to time is heaven, but having to live in a gilded fishbowl and be perfect, chic and beautiful all the time wouldn't be so much fun … or even possible, come to think of it. To say nothing of having to get my face lifted every five years as most women in Dec's world do just to keep their husbands interested."

"Well, maybe you're overthinking it, Mom. I'm just saying. He's a babe and I think he has the hots for you! Maybe you should give the guy a break. I, personally, like the way he likes you."

"A lovely way of putting it," Fitz approved. "He does seem something of a gentleman despite his net worth."

"You know what they say, Mom," Finn added. "Money doesn't give you happiness, but it's better to be unhappy in a Mercedes than on a bicycle!" They all laughed and Maeve answered, "But that's just it, luv. I have plenty of happiness right here and now, and my current lifestyle suits me just fine." It surprised her that Finn was so invested and her father not opposed.

"You could both be right, of course …" she added noncommittally, "but for now, let's just get back to the BSI. I'll let everybody know it's time for us all to catch up with each other's efforts, and I'm dying to know what everyone's so excited about." She cocked an eyebrow at Finn and continued. "Like for instance, maybe you and Mannheim would care to share what you've just put together? It's pretty significant, don't you think?"

Finn looked momentarily startled, then resigned and amused. "You know it's mildly annoying to have a mother who's psychic? I mean, how do I ever get to pull off any surprises? But yes, I think we've got something big to spill."

"Trust me. You've got more layers than an onion, and even second sight doesn't see through all of them." Maeve said it with good-natured maternal amusement. "You've managed to slip a few surprises by me over the years, kiddo."

Finn bounced up from the table and grabbed her camera bag from the counter as she sailed by. "And that's just as it should be, Mama darling. A girl needs her secrets."

"Where are you off to then with your secrets, mavourneen," Fitz asked with a low chuckle and an Irish endearment. "Gallery? Mannheim? T-square? Dojo? Mimi? Somebody's bar mitzvah?"

Finn reached over and kissed the top of his head before turning toward the door.

"Ask Mom," she called over her shoulder. "She probably knows already. Love you both!" And she was off to *wherever* in a cloud of Daisy fragrance, her happy footsteps echoing down the hall and then out the door.

"She's a rare bird, our little one," Fitz said affectionately, "much like her mother. And she seems to like this Declan man of yours." He smiled benevolently at Maeve and she knew he was wishing for her the kind of love he'd shared with her mother. She also knew how rare and unlikely such a lifelong love affair would be.

"He's not mine, Dad," she corrected gently.

"Well, maybe he should be," Fitz responded, surprising her. "I won't always be here to keep an eye on you, you know. And I'd hate to think of you alone forever … I'd like to see you safe and loved before I go." Finn had told him of the gallery visit.

Maeve felt her eyes mist up a little, so she crossed the kitchen to give him a quick hug. Fitz looked knowingly at her, understanding how empathically she sensed the feelings of those around her.

"Now, now," he said, aware of a bit of moisture in his own eyes. "Sure and your bladder's near your eye, macushla." He called the women in his family that when he was worried about them. She knew it meant "pulse of my heart."

He reached up to pat her cheek. "It goes with the gift, you know—your mother had a heart that felt every emotion in a ten-mile radius. She always said it's the payment you make for the Sight, this empathy that feels emotion so deeply, your own and everyone else's. I expect it makes the need for tears more frequent than for the rest of us, so nature complies with abundance."

"I miss her so damned much, Dad," Maeve responded. "We don't get over the loss of the ones we truly love, do we? We just get through it and learn to keep going."

"It's the tribute we pay for the privilege of sharing the world with them for a time," Fitz said softly. "We grieve for the loved and lost forever, and that's just exactly as it should be. They deserve no less from us."

Maeve leaned down and wrapped her arms around the father she loved so dearly. He hugged her back, and she wondered how she'd ever bear it when the time came for him to leave her, too.

64

Mimi's vast ballroom had been transformed by Finn, Brace, Orlando and an army of florists, decorators, caterers and assistants. The stage and runway looked like a hybrid of Chagall's chapel and the hottest after-hours club in London. The lighting, the music, the vibe was so young, chic and moneyed, Finn couldn't decide what she was feeling. Thrilled for the boys? Psyched by the buzz being generated? Disgusted by the over-the-top opulence? Just plain knocked-out by such fairy-tale magic? Probably all of that.

She shook her head, laughed at herself and decided to just opt for gratitude to Mimi for all she'd spent on making the boys' dream of a dynamite line-launch come true. Mimi, always generous and gracious, had said she was having as good a time planning this party as the boys were, but Finn knew that wasn't true.

Mimi inhabited a rarefied world other people barely glimpsed. She dated guys from that world, when she dated at all, and she went to the parties of the rich and relaxed in an effort to support their charities, have a modicum of fun and stay in the mainstream, but such things were not what made her happy.

The hospital and her work there made her happy. Saving babies and helping them thrive made her happy. Mimi was all heart, and Finn had always wondered how that could possibly have happened in the pinched conservative world she'd been born to. But Maeve said it was all obvious in Mimi's birth chart. Retrograde Pluto in the fourth house meant loss of parents in childhood. Leo moon for largesse, Cancerian sun for a need to nurture, something that meant medical karma that had pushed her into doctoring as a profession, and a trine to Chiron somewhere in the chart that Finn couldn't remember, but Maeve said it was always prominent in a true healer's chart. Whatever the ingredients in the stew, Finn knew tonight's generosity was something special.

Tyler Reese, the senator's son, had his eye on Mimi as the party warmed up. And he wasn't alone in his ogling. Finn had parceled out the photography for the show to a couple of talented Parsons classmates, so she didn't have any real obligations this evening, she told herself happily, other than to look good in the knockout gown Orlando had made specially for her and to talk up the talents of the boys she was hoping to help catapult into the fashion limelight.

But that didn't mean she wasn't seeing every detail with a photographer's eye. Spotting a mini photo op, she swooped the Canon 7D out of Enrico's hand with a whispered apology and snapped a quick batch of Tyler watching Mimi, dancing with Mimi and pretending not to watch Mimi. It amused Finn that Mimi never seemed to notice who had the hots for her, so she'd decided, in best wingman fashion, to document just how many guys had an eye on her pal tonight, and that required a lot of pictures.

And why wouldn't they? she thought. Mimi had the perfect WASP body, tall, slender, big boobed, small everything else. She looked drop-dead in the gown Orlando had given her and she was the only one who didn't seem to notice; she seemed to take all the near-perfections of her life for granted without ever being a pain in the ass about it. No arrogance, just noblesse oblige, good-natured acceptance and a fervent willingness to share.

Finn smirked as she nailed the shots, then handing the camera back to Enrico, she pointed to two other handsome dudes who looked like Versace ads or maybe Ralph or Calvin models. She told Enrico to be sure to get at least one head shot and one body shot of everyone in the room, and if he spotted any guys checking out Mimi to get a shot of that, too.

God, they were a good-looking bunch, these trust-fund babies, Finn thought, watching the tableau unfold. Perfect height, teeth, shoulder width; expensive haircuts and the perfect tailoring of bespoke tuxes didn't hurt, either. She was standing at the edge of the action on the dance floor, assessing the obvious success of the evening like a smug den mother, when some gorgeous guy she'd never met grabbed her arm and pulled her onto the dance floor with a playful flourish. He had to be six foot four, and for such a big guy he had some notable skills. Finn loved to dance and she loved really big men who towered over her own considerable height in heels, so she abandoned all assessment—except maybe a brief curiosity if he was proportional all over—and let the music and her masterful partner sweep her around the dance floor with a practiced hand.

Friends who were rich as Croesus had pals who looked like Greek gods *and* had been to the best dance classes, she thought irreverently. If only they didn't have egos bigger than their bank accounts .... She sighed. Maybe for tonight she didn't care about all that. Relaxing into the moment, she showed off some moves of her own.

Then a pompous poop of a blond guy she'd met once before but didn't really care to know further swept over and cut in. She didn't want to be impolite so she just went with it, disappointed but game. Until his banter turned to politics and he made a snarky comment about the #MeToo Movement, and she needed to escape before she acted on her immediate urge to punch his lights out.

She spotted T watching her from the outskirts of the dance floor and made a "help me!" gesture behind the back of the jerk who was so busy pontificating he didn't even notice.

T chuckled, put down whatever it was he was drinking and ambled onto the dance floor in her direction.

"I believe you have monopolized this lovely young lady long enough," he said to Finn's partner with an exaggeratedly winning smile and equally exaggerated diction. "Mind if I cut in?" He took Finn's hand and tugged her away before the guy could sputter out an answer.

"You know us poor black kids got some game, too," he said as he spun her out onto the floor in a flashy maneuver.

She giggled. "OMG! and I thought that was just a stereotype."

"Saw your Bat Signal," T grinned, "and figured you needed ex-filtration."

"You're my hero. And, I might add, you're also an awesome dancer, so this is a win-win for me." T was her go-to pal for hitting the dance clubs when they both had a night off and enough money between them to float some fun, a convergence that didn't happen nearly often enough.

In response, T spun her out in an awesome arc that made everybody step back to watch. After that, they really had no choice but to make a show of it.

65

The uneasy feeling had been niggling at Maeve all day. A "by the pricking of my thumbs" kind of amorphous worry that was ratcheting up by the hour with no clear focus. She kept catching glimpses of chaos and pain: nothing clear enough to define, but all disturbing. She'd called all family members just to check that they were okay. But there were no red flags, so she'd forced herself to dismiss the growing anxiety as psychic spam.

She stood on the subway platform, tired and frazzled, waiting for the E train along with the mini-gaggle of long-past-rush-hour stragglers, and looked around her. She kept trying to shake off the edgy discomfort that hovered, while admonishing herself to stay alert. Subways were not only ugly, they were dangerous, especially at night, and it didn't pay to let yourself get distracted in an isolated underground world.

She glanced at her watch for the umpteenth time, willing the train to come, wanting to be home in bed, wanting this long, tiring, twitchy day to just be over. Wondering how Mimi and Finn's party was going. Twelve-thirty, she read, thinking how dumb she'd been not to take an Uber home after her dinner with an old uptown friend. But when you live in Greenwich Village, cabs from uptown cost a fortune, so she'd long ago gotten out of the taxi habit and learned to rely on the subway. But she was just too tired and edgy for it tonight and should have known better.

She checked the platform nervously. There were only a few kids, a middle-aged couple, and two young soldiers in fatigues on the big platform, plus a homeless-looking guy in a gray hoodie propped up against a wall, asleep. Gratefully, she heard the rumble of the looked-for train and relaxed a little. She moved closer to the tracks to peer expectantly down the tunnel for the oncoming lights.

The punch that sent her sprawling headlong onto the tracks came out of nowhere and was so powerful it lifted her off the platform as it propelled her forward. She hit the iron rails too fast to save her face from skidding into filth and there was barely time to be terrified before her head smashed something iron, hard enough to make everything go black.

She had a momentary flash of Finn and Rory in terrible danger, then there was nothing but the roar of the oncoming train.

66

Rory stuck her phone back in her pocket and looked at the clock: 12:07? Seriously? What the hell could cause a problem like this in an empty house at this time of night? What the construction guy texted didn't make any sense at all. She'd been comfy in pj bottoms and an old tee shirt, an I.P.A. from some new microbrewery in Brooklyn, and a good book to keep her company. The absolutely last thing she needed was to take herself uptown in the bitter cold. Shit!

No. That wasn't quite right. The *really* last thing she wanted was to have anything go wrong at this jobsite. And what Carlos texted was happening could be a serious problem by morning. She didn't really know Carlos well enough to trust his assessment. He was a temp replacement while the project manager was on a family emergency flight to Florida. But she couldn't take a chance … she'd have to go see for herself.

Grumbling, she pulled on jeans and a turtleneck, boots and a down jacket. Maybe she could handle this herself, at least until morning.

What a cosmic pain in the ass! Rory bundled up, arranged for a Lyft and gave the driver the address in Harlem. They were starting to call South Harlem SOHA now, a sure sign the neighborhood the house was in was about to become a target for savvy shoppers. Her purchase of this old beauty had real financial promise and was worth losing a few hours of sleep over.

67

The white-coated waiter in Mimi's vast marble foyer, now filled with well-clad guests, smiled. The fashion editor in the enormous Tom Ford glasses lifted another glass of champagne from his tray; he smiled at her, then headed for the kitchen. Gracious old townhouses like this one could afford the space for a catering kitchen as well as an ordinary one for daily use. Glass-fronted walls of dishes for every possible occasion, gleaming copper pots and pans hung from ceiling hooks, a huge freezer-refrigerator combination, eight-burner chef's stove, extra wall ovens—all the needs of the very rich and their pampered guests could be met here, he thought, a sneer replacing the plastic smile he'd been flashing all evening.

The storage rooms he'd already sussed out beyond the catering kitchen would be a perfect hiding place. After the guests were gone. After the staff had packed up and moved out like an efficient culinary army. He was just extra help, hired on for the night. No one would miss him when he slipped away in the chaos of mop-up. No one would even know he was there until he wanted them to know.

68

That's weird, no lights. Rory navigated her phone app to confirm she'd completed the ride, then stood staring at her pitch-black house, which was more than a little ominous-looking in the snow. Or maybe it was just the idea of being alone on a deserted 119th Street at this hour in an only half-gentrified neighborhood that was spooky. Besides, Carlos was inside. He'd said he was calling from *inside* the house, hadn't he?

Rory fitted her key in the lock and pushed the heavy old door open, calling the man's name. Nothing. No sound but the wind and the creaking noises old houses excelled at. Light switch, she told herself. Flip the light switch. This is the part in the horror flick when the heroine is blithely traipsing down the darkened basement steps where the axe murderer is lying in wait and the audience is screaming "turn on the fucking lights, you idiot!" She laughed out loud at herself and fumbled for the light switch—which produced nothing at all. Shit!

Rory stood stock-still. Maybe Carlos had to turn off the electrical because of the water problem. That could make sense. She took the heavy-duty flashlight out of the tool bag she'd grabbed on her way out of her apartment and switched it on.

"Carlos!" she shouted again, as she flashed the light around the room and moved tentatively forward. "Carlos! Where the hell are you and why aren't the lights working?" There wasn't time for more than that before the world fell in on her.

Rory came to on the freezing floor, pinned beneath the debris that had crashed down on her. She tried to straighten her painfully trapped leg and to force her brain to make sense of what the hell had happened.

Her head throbbed so it was hard to think straight. When she struggled to move, she realized she was trapped by a joist and large pieces of the floor from above. She was lucky to be alive. A mountain of old plaster lay atop the pile, and the dust and the weight of the ceiling parts made breathing hard. How had she gotten here and how long ago? Her thinking was fuzzy and nothing made any sense.

The text from Carlos swam to the surface: *there was a serious water leak on the jobsite,* he'd texted. She'd better meet him at the house right away. That had been around twelve something. It was impossible to tell how long she'd been unconscious. Minutes? Hours? She managed to pull her left hand free of the mess of plaster, ragged wood shards and debris, but the glass on her watch was too cracked to read the time in the heavy dark. It felt late, but that might just be the New York winter dark that made everything from five o'clock on feel like midnight.

Phone! Where was her phone? She tried to extricate her other arm. By the feel of the weight that was crushing her, she was lucky she wasn't dead. But why had the ceiling collapsed at all? It made no sense. She'd checked it for structural soundness herself with the architect, just a few days ago … old houses had floors and ceilings collapse all the time for a thousand reasons, but that was why they'd inspected the second floor so carefully before letting workers into the space. The ceiling that now pinned her couldn't have come down by accident. Somebody had to have loosened an old joist or sabotaged a supporting beam.

Holy shit! That *somebody* could still be in the house.

Rory's brain snapped into overdrive. *Okay. So I need help and my phone is the fastest way to get it. I have to find the phone!* Her eyes were accustomed to the dark now and she could glimpse the strap of her shoulder bag just out of reach. She tried to wriggle toward it, but had to suppress a cry as a fierce, fiery pain shot up her twisted leg. It was heavily pinned and hurt like it might be broken, but if an assailant was in the house she shouldn't let him know she wasn't dead.

Danger flashed in her now fully functioning brain. *Have to pull myself together fast and make a plan. There must be something in this debris long enough to maneuver the handbag strap into reach. Breathe. Remember to breathe. Find the tool you need. Don't let the fear in. Just find the tool and get to the phone.* Her father's sensible voice spoke in her head. *"When in trouble say a prayer, then do your damnedest."* It was the Irish equivalent of "trust in Allah but tie your camel to a tree." Did cell phones have a patron saint yet, she wondered, then remembering that St. Joseph was the patron saint of carpenters she thought maybe she'd better have a word with him, too, about what could make an old but perfectly sound ceiling suddenly collapse on top of her. Both thoughts almost made her laugh out loud. Whistling past the graveyard, Fitz would have called humor like that at a moment like this. A way to stay in control of your fear.

Rory grasped a long piece of conduit lodged in the pile above her and yanked as hard as she could. If she could wriggle it free, it just might reach…

69

Rough hands were trying to yank Maeve's arms out of their sockets. Her mind logged excruciating pain as she fought her way back to consciousness. She was being dragged upward and her shoulders were being nearly dislocated. She tried to yell *Stop!* but multiple voices were screaming, the hands were relentless, and the scarf around her throat was choking her so she couldn't breathe or scream. Freezing concrete ripped at her legs and then she felt/heard the roar as the train ripped by her and people were shouting things at her in languages she didn't understand.

Her awareness blinked back on enough so she understood that the icy cold beneath her was the filthy concrete subway platform and the hands that still gripped her arms must also have saved her life.

Sweet Jesus, what had just happened? And if she'd just escaped death by inches, why was her inner terror still ratcheting up into the stratosphere? Her heart was pounding. Her head was imploding as the truth slammed home. She was safe from the train, but the people she loved most weren't safe at all.

70

The party had gone perfectly. The runway show, Brace and Orlando's snappy repartee with the press, the clothes, the glam and glitz, all just as they'd hoped. It was nearly twelve-thirty by the time the last guest had departed, the caterers had finished with cleanup and Finn and Mimi made their way up the long marble staircase feeling sated and elated.

That wouldn't last long.

71

Brace and Orlando lay in the huge bed in Mimi's grandly appointed guest room, utterly spent and grateful the girls had insisted they stay over after the party. What a night it had been! Like a dream come true. Response beyond what they'd ever hoped for. The clothes in the setting they deserved. The music, champagne and dancing after the show, like something out of a 1940s film noir.

Mimi and Finn had outdone themselves and would be clothed for life with the relentlessness of those bibbity-bobbity-boo Disney fairy godmothers, and even *that* wouldn't be enough of a thank-you!

"I'm all talked out, how about you?"

"I have only seven words left. I counted them." Brace idly trailed his fingers down Orlando's arm as he spoke.

"I'm too tired to blink!" his partner gasped, but Brace could hear the excitement beneath the fatigue. "My smile muscles gave out about forty-five minutes ago, but I'm too tired to fuck and too wired to sleep."

"I've got Ambien if you want some …"

"No way! I want to just lie here and replay it over and over in my head until I die of happiness."

"Good plan," Brace answered. Drama queen didn't even begin to cover Orlando's hyperbole. But who could blame him; tonight every bit of it was deserved.

He swung his long legs over the edge of the bed. "My stomach is flipping out from all that champagne, Lando. I'm headed to the kitchen for warm milk. Want anything?" Brace stood up, trotted to the bathroom and came back with a bath towel around his bare hips.

Orlando knew his even-tempered partner had an ulcer or close to it, because unlike himself, Brace held things in, worried, brooded and never screamed obscenities at the top of his lungs. "Want me to come with?"

he asked, hoping the answer would be no.

"Nah. Stay put. Enjoy your replay. I'll be back in a minute."

Brace ambled down the stairs doing some replay of his own. A house like this could be theirs one day. A mansion to show his father that being gay didn't make you a wimp or a loser who didn't deserve to be his son. All the doors of the future had swung open tonight and the dreams were flooding in.

He shook his head to shake out the anger and sadness that lurked so close to the surface of his mind and his heart whenever he thought of his dad. Tonight was only for triumph and happiness and a conviction that all the exhaustion hadn't been in vain.

He pulled himself out of the reverie two steps from the bottom of the staircase. That couldn't have been a movement he just saw, could it? Just some weird flicker of the lights on the street beyond that had tricked his eye.

Shee-it! The intruder, who had ditched his waiter's uniform and was now clad in cat-burglar black, stood stock-still. What the hell was this kid doing up? Takedowns were easier when everybody was asleep. Shock and disorientation plus the reality of a gun pointed at you in the dark made compliance a shoo-in. Unless you were unlucky enough to hit somebody with military training. That could be dicey. All that hero complex plus know-how complicated things. But these were just kids. Two girls and two fairies should be easy provided he followed the plan. Let them all settle down, grab the girls, use them to threaten the guys into getting tied up. Alert the driver, head out the back door, pile the girls into the van and his part was done.

He wondered who the guys paying for this would sell the girls to. They were both prime meat. Any trafficker worth his salt would have a few randy sheiks on his speed dial—they could be worth a fortune and his own fee was a percentage. Especially if they were virgins. He smirked at that stupid thought. Nobody was a virgin at their ages, not in Manhattan.

Brace warmed the milk and sipped it, the uneasy feeling still prickling between his shoulders. Just more fucking nerves, he admonished himself. *Calm down already!*

Then he headed for the staircase, saw the shadow, man-shaped, unmoving. No mistaking it this time. Somebody was in the house who shouldn't be there. He dropped the cup, hoping the sharp clatter on the marble floor would alert the others, then he ran like hell, dropping the towel, taking the marble steps two at a time. He was yelling, "Lando! Run!" at the top of his lungs. "Somebody's in the house!"

The blow that took him down was hard enough that his head bounced twice on the marble steps before he lost consciousness.

72

Inch by inch, hurting and on high alert to every creak of the old house, Rory wriggled herself out from under the debris. She thought she heard footsteps on the floor above, but it might have been the house settling, or the rest of the unsupported ceiling fixing to fall, or her nerves on high E .... Her leg hurt like hell. She couldn't let that matter now, but she couldn't go far on it, that was for sure. She managed to get to a standing position. On her feet, clutching her phone in one hand, she grabbed the sturdiest piece of ceiling stud she could find with the other, just as the sound of careful footsteps on the creaky staircase shot through her and her heart hit the stratosphere again. She shifted behind the hall coat-closet door; it was sagging and half off its hinges, but it was cover. She shoved her phone into her butt pocket and clutched her makeshift weapon in both hands.

Think baseball! she admonished herself to quell the panic. *You're a good batter. Always were. Now's your chance to prove it. You're up at bat, runners on first and third. You gotta hit it out of the park, kid. No sweat.*

The man named Carlos hunkered down over the pile of downed ceiling, obviously looking for her body. Not because he wanted to help, she could tell that by his unhurried movements and his silence. He was just checking to make sure she was down! He was part of the trap. She swung the piece of wood in her hands like a Louisville Slugger. The satisfying thunk and grunt as the man went limp made her grateful for every baseball game she'd ever played with Fitz and the kids in Washington Square Park. For every game she'd ever been to, for every sports magazine about how players psyched themselves up for the homer despite the nervous adrenaline coursing through their veins.

She grabbed her coat and purse, left Carlos in a heap on the floor, and fled the house as if her life depended on it. Cursing her crippled leg that slowed her down and hurt like h ell, she flagged a passing gypsy cab. To hell with the house, to hell with the guy in it. She was just glad to be alive. She tried Maeve and Fitz from the cab, but Maeve went to voice mail and Fitz was answering another call.

73

The voice on the phone was cold and precise and Fitz was half asleep.

"Cooperation would be so much more sensible than putting your family at further risk, Mr. Donovan," it said. "We're reasonable men. We simply want our documents back." Then it went to dial tone. The message cleared any vestige of sleep from Fitz's brain.

He slammed the phone down on the night table and lurched out of bed a little shakily when it rang a second time. Feeling for the light switch, he cursed at the dark and the fact that it took him a moment now to get his balance.

It was Rory's voice this time, ragged and coughing, as if she'd been caught in a dust storm. She was calling from a cab to tell him to call 911. Somebody had tried to kill her. She'd been trapped under debris from a falling ceiling and had clocked a guy who must have sabotaged the house and caused the collapse.

Fitz glanced at the clock, heart racing, brain struggling to make sense of what was happening. Why the hell was she at the jobsite in the middle of the night? She sounded hurt, scared, and trying to downplay her narrow escape for his sake, but how like her to have managed to escape a trap *and* coldcock an assailant while she was at it. He told her to tell the cabbie to take her to the Jane Street house. He'd call the cops and paramedics to meet her there.

"I don't need paramedics, Dad!" she interrupted. "I'm shaken but okay for now. I'll get an x-ray in the morning. Just send the cops to my new house to find that guy. Are Maeve and Finn alright?"

Ice water hit Fitz's spine. *Christ Almighty! He didn't know the answer to that.* "I'll try to raise them right now, luv, Finn's at Mimi's and Maeve should be home long since. Better get here as fast as you can."

"Don't worry, Dad," Rory said, hearing the urgency in his voice now. "I'll be home in twenty minutes. If you hear from them before then, please,

please call me! And don't go anywhere without me, okay?"

Fitz grabbed the edge of the table to steady himself as he pulled on his old woolen robe to go down to Maeve's floor to rouse her. He reached the door, then doubled back to grab the downstairs keys from the hook near his bed, just as the phone rang a third time.

"What the hell ...?" he breathed, grabbing it from the bedside table yet again.

"Chief?" a once-familiar voice said the word just like in the old days. "This is Mike Martinelli, from the 6th. I wanted you to hear this first from somebody you know ..."

Fitz's heart picked up speed. Nobody on the job prefaced good news with those words.

74

Fitz clutched the phone like a lifeline.

"It's your daughter Maeve, sir," Martinelli was saying. "She's going to be okay, but somebody pushed her in front of the E train half an hour ago. She's at Beth Israel. You'll get a call from somebody at the ER any minute. But when I heard the news and recognized the address, I figured it'd be better coming from somebody you know. Do you want me to send a car to get you there fast, Chief?"

The irregular pieces were snapping into place. "Yes, Mike, and thanks a million," Fitz replied, his tone putting the younger man on high alert. "But there's more—I'm not sure just what, yet—but I do need your help with it. My daughter Rory was attacked, too—she's in a cab on her way here . . . and I haven't yet tried to raise my granddaughter." He explained the threatening phone call that had awakened him, as grateful for the smarts on the other end of the line as he was for the help. He'd need to be in two places at the same time—here for Rory, there for Maeve—these two incidents were no coincidence. Not after the phone call. And what if the girls didn't answer their phones?

He heard Martinelli's shout to someone in the squad room. "It's the chief. He needs backup. No! Not *him* . . . the old chief, Donovan. He's on Jane Street. I'll get the details and clear it. If he says he needs backup, we give it to him, for Christ's sake!

Then Martinelli said, "Hang in there, Chief, I'm sending a car for you right now. Don't worry. We've got your back."

Fitz thanked him and grabbed his cell with one hand, and his trousers with the other. He hit the speed dial photo of his granddaughter, but the call went straight to voice mail.

"Holy fucking Jesus!" he breathed aloud as he pulled on the rest of his clothes and snapped his old S&W 3913 into an ankle holster. "What in the name of God have I gotten us into?"

75

"Mimi!" Finn's urgent whisper pierced through the fog of REM sleep instantly. "Wake up *right now*!"

Mimi struggled to sit up, slightly disoriented by sleep and the leftover haze of the party that had ended less than an hour ago. She never consumed much alcohol when she entertained, but she'd had two glasses of champagne and that, plus the exhaustion and the adrenaline-drain that always followed hosting a successful social event, meant sleep had been instantaneous; she'd been deep-dreaming since her head hit the pillow.

"What?" she started to blurt but Finn clapped a hand over her mouth peremptorily.

"There's somebody in the house! I think they've got Brace. I heard him scream." She whispered the words, fear in her voice, then added, "The phones are dead."

Mimi's fear sheared through the fog of sleep and she sat bolt upright, chilled by sudden understanding and the urgency in Finn's voice. The servants were gone for the night … she, Finn and the boys should have been alone in the house and the alarm hadn't gone off, so if somebody was here who shouldn't be, this could be bad. She saw the door from the adjoining guest room where Finn had been sleeping was ajar, just as a wide-eyed Orlando burst in.

"He went downstairs for milk," he blurted. "We have to save him!" He sounded frantic.

Scooping up her cell from the night table on autopilot, Mimi slid out of bed and, barefoot too, followed Finn noiselessly toward the panic room door, hoping they could get there before somebody else did.

Finn's mind was in overdrive. If whoever "it" was had Brace as a hostage, they were all fucked, unless they could find weapons and get help from the outside. If whoever it was had beaten the alarm system, maybe they could beat the panic room, too.

"No cell service!" Mim murmured with her usual presence of mind, as the panic room door slid open.

"Give me the samurai sword from the shoot, if it's still in there!" Finn whispered urgently. Mimi's eyes widened.

"I need a weapon, I'm going for help. If they've hacked the alarm system, we could be trapped. We need to get word out somehow."

"How?"

"The fire escape."

"That window probably hasn't been opened since the Hoover Administration! You may not be able to get out through it."

"I'll have to try. You two get into the panic room. If these guys are smart enough to hack your system and block our cell phones, one of us has to go for help." She wasn't asking permission.

"Oh, Finn …" Mimi breathed, trying to control the terror in her words as she slapped the sword into her friend's hand like it was a surgical instrument.

Seconds, Finn thought. She might have only seconds to get to the fire escape. She watched the saferoom morph swiftly into a closet again, said a prayer, and headed back into the master.

It sounded as if somebody was dragging Brace up the steps, his head smacking every step on the way.

76

Mimi and Orlando stared into the panic room as the door slid soundlessly into place behind them.

"I can't be here!" Orlando breathed the words in a frantic whisper. "I've gotta help Brace! He's out there all alone … I can't just leave him there!" Mimi knew the room was soundproof but whispering still seemed safer. Her heart was pounding in her chest and throat and her breathing was fast and shallow. Orlando was ghost-white and shaking.

She tried her cell again. Still nothing. She tried the panic room phone. Nothing there either. Finn had guessed what they were up against and made the right move, but that meant she was out there all alone.

"He wanted milk and went downstairs to get it," Lando breathed, sounding asthmatic. "Then there was a crash, like china falling, and then he was screaming for me to run …"

Mimi nodded, her own heart doing flips. She'd played this scene in her head a million times. Ever since she was a little girl and her guardians had hired a security expert to explain just how many dangers there were for the children of the super-rich and what plans had been put into place in case of kidnapping. She knew there was a ten-million-dollar insurance policy in place to pay ransom if ever needed, and a team of ex-military negotiators on call for an extraction. All too macabre to think about, so she'd practiced the drills and tucked it all into some back pocket of her mind. But practicing something and living it were two different things. When you practiced, fear wasn't lapping at your gut and making it hard to think or breathe.

"Okay." Mimi tried to force her voice calm enough to get him to focus. "So we're safe for now and Finn has a shot at getting the word out. You know how resourceful she is. When the panic room is engaged it sends a signal to the monitoring company. They'll call, and when they get no answer and no stand-down code, they'll send the police."

"But what if something goes wrong?" Orlando pressed, his words rushing out as he tried to put the pieces together. "Like if whoever these guys are, they already thought of that and somehow scammed the system? What's Plan C? I mean didn't they already get into the house, past the security system, without triggering the alarm? And they've got my boy! I have to do *something*, don't I? I just don't know what to do." His voice was ratcheting up and his eyes were flooding. She could see how close he was to hysteria and bit her lip before answering.

"Plan C?" she said finally, as cheerily as she could muster. "Damn! I guess I never got beyond relying on Plan B. But you know the Donovans—they'll come looking for us!" He wasn't buying it.

"I have to get Brace!" he said, as if she hadn't spoken at all. *He could be going into shock,* she thought as she wrapped her arms around him and felt his body trembling and his skin going clammy. The triumphant night, then this nightmare? It was a perfect storm for sending anybody as tightly wound as Orlando into shock.

"And then there's the fact that Finn's mom's a mystic and her Grand is always on the case—" she began again, but a voice on the intercom cut the next sentence short. It sounded matter-of-fact and ominous at the same time.

"We have disabled all communication systems except this one," it said.

"Who are you?" Mimi demanded as evenly as she could. "What do you want from us?"

"We'll let you know when we come for you," was the answer before the click.

Mimi stood stock-still for a moment, then, weirdly, reached into the minifridge and pulled out two bottles of water, handing one to Orlando, who looked at her as if she'd lost her mind. "Drink this *now*!" she commanded in her best doctor voice. "I'm a doctor, remember? Fear floods the system with adrenaline. Water will help flush it out. We have to think clearly, Orlando. It's the best way to help Brace and Finn. So fucking *hydrate*!"

"Okay, okay!" he managed, staring at her. Mimi *never* used swear words.

"But I want to hydrate at Starbucks."

Mimi breathed a small laugh of relief. Somebody in shock probably wouldn't be capable of humor.

"When this is over, remind me to tell T he can make his fortune by improving on state-of-the-art security systems for the rich," she said. "Mine seems to need a little work."

"And maybe an Uzi or two?" he offered, then obediently drank the whole bottle of water in a single gulp. He raised the empty bottle to her in a salute. "I'm not going hysterical on you, Mimi. I promise you I'll hold it together, on my mother's grave and she isn't even dead yet. It's just that I really love him, you know? I mean like he's *everything* to me." Orlando's voice was on the verge of tears, but steadier than before.

"I know, Lando," she soothed, as she clicked on the security monitors that should have given her visual access to all the rooms in the house. A blizzard of snowflakes was all she got, as the screens blinked on one by one in a disappointing display of nothing useful.

"And Finn is my best friend forever … so they *both* have to make it, and we have to keep our wits about us to help them do that."

They stared at each other, as Mimi tried not to imagine the odds of Finn facing the kind of men who had scammed a high-tech security system armed with only a five-hundred-year-old samurai sword to defend herself. And Orlando tried not to replay his partner's scream telling him to run.

"Okay, then …" Mimi said the words for both of them. "How does trying telepathy sound to you?" She was only half joking.

Orlando tried to smile at her but couldn't. "Is that our *only* plan?"

"So far," she said with a grim attempt at looking confident as she took two more bottles of water out of the fridge.

Thank God there was a bathroom in here. And why the hell had she been such a wuss about stocking the place with guns? At least that would have given Finn a fighting chance.

77

Finn had slipped soundlessly out from behind the sliding shoe racks that housed enough shoes for a family of centipedes. The intruder had been on his way to the master suite when Brace's moans from the staircase had turned him around and slowed him down. She heard a muffled exchange. It sounded as if Brace was badly hurt and pleading, but the guy was berating him for not being able to stand up and walk. Then he seemed to be dragging him painfully up the stairs again.

"Where are the others?" he kept shouting and Brace didn't seem to be making any sense in response. Then there was the sound of something being hit hard, a grunt of real pain and finally silence.

Barefoot, she scampered into the master, locked the door behind her just to gain time, knowing the old lock wouldn't hold for long. She tried the window.

Fuck! A hundred years of repainting had it stuck tight, but the window in the guest room had been opened a crack to let in the crisp night air. She ran to the adjoining room, used the old sword blade to pry off caked paint from the frame above the slim opening to free it. She muffled the sound of the window sliding up with a pillow and peered at the size of the ledge outside. Holy shit! It was maybe a foot deep, tops, and she got nauseous just thinking about heights. The freezing air hit her like a force field, but shocked her into movement. There really weren't any choices. Whoever had engineered this break-in was good at his job. She wouldn't have long to escape and she needed to get help now. She knew it in every bone.

Finn grabbed the lap robe from the window seat and knotted it around her shoulders like Superman's cape. The wind was frigid as the North Pole and her coat was miles away downstairs. Why the hell hadn't she grabbed a sweater or jacket, to say nothing of sneakers, from the closet? *Fuck!* No time for regrets. The afghan-thingy knotted around her neck was all there was, so she gingerly climbed out onto the ledge and tried very hard not to look down and not to throw up.

78

Rory was out of the cab so fast the driver shook his head with wonder. In his country, women did not behave like this. They didn't run around in the middle of the night and place frantic phone calls about being attacked by men.

There was a cop car parked out in front of the Jane Street house and an old man at the door as the woman hobbled up the steps, obviously in pain. He saw the relief in the old man's face as he embraced the girl and he thought of his own daughters safe at home. He started to pull away as quickly as he could, but the cop in the car flagged him to a stop. He probably would have to answer questions now and lose his next fare, but at least he'd have an interesting story to tell his wife when he got home.

79

Georgia was bone weary and looking forward to being back in her own bed, but her nerves were also ramped because of all she'd learned and hadn't yet been able to download to Maeve and the others.

She hadn't slept on the plane despite the comforts of first class; everything she'd pried out of Uncle Hutch kept circling in her brain like a runaway train.

She gave the driver the address of the shop on Bleecker and went to the Teacup rather than home. She wanted to drop off the bag of research, make sure all was copacetic and give herself time to calm down enough to sleep. She was too wired to sleep yet, so she stayed an extra hour to even out the jet lag of the two-hour time difference.

Finally, she yawned, turned off the lights and headed toward the back of the shop to get her handbag before letting herself out the front door onto Bleecker. When she glanced out the back window as she checked the lock, she saw a figure dressed in black slip stealthily out of a doorway two shops down. All vestiges of sleepiness vanished.

What the hell?

Georgia slipped off her shoes and inched back toward the counter where she kept her shotgun. The old double-barreled Beretta was locked and loaded and accessible behind the panel she'd had installed to hide it from casual view. She might be living in New York City, but she was born and bred in Texas, and all these laws about locking up your guns and keeping your ammo in a safe made no sense to her at all. What the hell good did it do you to keep a gun for protection if you couldn't get to it in time to protect yourself?

She quickly tucked herself into the best hiding spot she could find and waited, checking her watch for nearly a full two minutes before she heard the man working quietly and efficiently on the locked back door. Georgia forced her breathing to quiet just as he opened it and stepped soundlessly into the tea shop.

80

Maeve's nervous system, as well as her spidey-sense, were throbbing now as she fought the attending doctor at Beth Israel. Signing herself out of the hospital AMA—against medical advice—was the best she could do at this point because they were threatening her with a barrage of tests that would take twenty-four hours that she couldn't afford away from her endangered family.

Her head was bursting and her shoulder felt as if it had been dislocated but none of that mattered; she had to get to her family. They were all in terrible danger. As long as she could stand, she had to get to them to tell them what she'd seen in the vision. Somebody wanted to kill them all and it was all happening in real time. Happening *now*, and Finn was in the most danger of all.

She answered her cell, grateful to hear her father's voice, and blurted what she knew.

"It's alright, luv," he soothed. "I've got Rory with me. She's hurt but ambulatory and we'll pick you up in a matter of minutes. Mike Martinelli from the 6th is here with me now. He says they stand ready to help us any way they can."

"Thank God you and Rory are okay and together!" she breathed, relieved, "but we've got to get Finn. She's in terrible danger, Dad. We all are, but Finn's in the most trouble. I hear her voice calling me, *willing* me to know what's happening. She's scared to death and freezing. We have to go to her …" he could hear in her speech pattern she wasn't entirely in this world. He knew the signs well enough.

"What do you see, luv? You must tell me everything, Maeve, so I can help her. Mike will take us to her." He put the phone on speaker.

"She's high up and she's freezing. Her feet are on something ice cold—cement or stone—and she's scared to death. She's shouting to me in her mind to send help! Her cell's not working. She's sick to her stomach, afraid, determined. But mostly she's high up and scared to look down—you know how she hates heights! She's afraid she'll fall, afraid she won't get to the ladder before he catches her .... She's edging an inch at a time along an icy ledge."

"What ledge? Who's after her? What ladder, luv? Tell me what you see ..."

"Oh, sweet Jesus!" she breathed as if his urgent questions clarified the vision. "She's on a ledge outside a high window ... third floor at Mimi's."

"Shit!" Martinelli said, reaching for his radio. "I'll call dispatch. I'll have the car that's at the hospital now bring your daughter to meet us. What's the address where the girls are?"

He didn't bother to say "Don't worry, she's probably out on a date like every other kid who doesn't answer her grandfather's call on a Saturday night." With everything else that was happening, this wasn't that.

Rory rattled off Mimi's address and the driver made a fast U-turn and headed for the FDR, sirens blazing, lights flashing.

Martinelli was on his cell sending a rescue team to the Park Avenue address. If it turned out to be a false alarm, he'd deal with the flak in the morning. No Donovan was going to die on his watch if he could help it.

81

Georgia quieted her breathing, feeling the familiar weight of the shotgun in her hands, thinking the key to surviving the next few minutes was smarts and experience. She had both. She patted the weapon and played out all the ways it could go down if she kept her wits about her.

There were two night-lights on in the alley he'd come from, so she figured it would take his eyes a minute to get accustomed to the pitch-blackness of the shop, and that gave her a meager advantage. She knew every inch of the terrain and she was hidden from his direct sight line by a mirrored partition at the end of the coffee bar where she'd snugged herself in. She could see him in the antique mirror angled across the way from where she hid, so she watched him pocket the lockpicks and check for his gun in one practiced motion.

He was skilled and trained, whoever he was. The gun in the belt rig looked like a Sig or maybe an HK, she saw as he began to ease it noiselessly from his holster. No point letting a guy in Kevlar gain the advantage of a drawn sidearm, so she spoke from the darkness.

"Put it back in your pants!" she snapped, making the intruder's head jerk up.

"I've got a gun," he responded coolly. "I won't hurt you if you come out and do as I say."

"Damned straight," she answered, swinging the shotgun into view. "Sorry I can't promise you the same."

"Take it easy with that thing," he countered, evenly. She could see he still believed he was in control as he said in that voice men use when pacifying pesky women, "I'll put my gun down nice and easy …"

His coiled-spring body language said otherwise. Georgia waited, knowing he had something else in mind entirely. Then his knife was out of its sheath so fast he had to be military, so she fired the first barrel before the Ka-bar had a chance to do any damage. He flew backward, his arm and shoulder an unusable, bloody pulp as he slid toward the floor.

"You are dumb enough to squat with your spurs on, son," she pronounced as she steadied the long gun with a practiced hand and reached for her phone with the other. "I was born with this Beretta waitin' on me in my cradle. Now, while we wait on the police, why don't you just tell me who sent you here and why, because you just broke into my property armed to the teeth and anything I do to you before they get here hardly counts at all."

Georgia pointed the long gun at his crotch and smiled as she dialed 911.

82

Finn, heart racing, tears frozen on her cheeks, scared to death, grasped the frigid metal rail and sobbed her relief as she clung to it for a moment, trying to breathe. The fire escape was colder than the stone ledge, if that was even possible, but clutching it let her vertigo abate enough so she could get air into her lungs, and let her eyes drift down for the first time since she'd exited the window. Holding on for dear life, she tried to make her freezing limbs function enough so she could climb onto the rickety old apparatus. She knew how fire escapes worked and how to disengage the locking mechanism because Grand was such a fanatic about safety and she lived on the top floor of an old house, so he'd shown her the ropes years ago. Her fingers, so numb with cold, were clumsy working the catch and she wasn't at all sure she could make it down the iron rungs on the blocks of ice that used to be feet.

The damned thing creaked when it started to unfold, but she was so grateful she'd made it to the fire escape at all she didn't care as long as she could get to the ground after the ladder dropped as far as it could go. A long jump, but not impossible.

Please God let no one else be waiting in the alley below. Please God! *Please* … She breathed the prayer and jumped. "Please Mom. Come soon! I really need you."

Finn hit the ground, fell hard and painfully, rolled, picked herself up and tried to run. She stumbled, fell as far as her knees, then pulled herself up and ran again, clutching railings to stay upright. She kept calling her mother in her mind because she'd felt the psychic link between them engage while she was still on the ledge. Her mother knew she was in trouble …

Panting, stomping up and down on feet so cold they made her stumble at every step, Finn was nearly a block away when her phone finally found a signal. She got through to Grand. His voice on the line was as emotional as she'd ever heard it as she blurted the details of the night. He told her to stay right where she was, that he was on his way with her mother and Rory, then she heard the sirens heading toward her. *Mom!* she thought, tears finally spilling down her cheeks too abundantly to freeze. *Mom got my message and sent help!*

She leaned against the building for a moment to try to regain her equilibrium and her breath. Then she turned and tried to hobble back toward Mimi's house, thinking with every footstep of Ghisella walking miles barefoot in the snow after her boots were stolen. Understanding ... finally, everything.

PART VIII

Fish or Cut Bait

"The rabbit runs for his life,
the fox runs for his dinner.
Bet on the rabbit."

— Proverb

83

It had been one hell of a night for Fitz Donovan, Martinelli thought, studying the older man as he exited the house near dawn. But he'd kept his cool throughout as the detective had done his job, issuing orders, sending uniforms where needed, admiring both the old guy's stamina and how he managed to keep it together as the stories were told, statements taken and arrangements made for surveillance of the Jane Street house.

The boy with the skull fracture had been taken to the hospital and his family notified. The police surgeon he'd called said if Rory wasn't in too much pain, she could wait for X-rays until morning, because hairline fractures sometimes didn't show up well on X-rays for several hours.

Fitz had even helped him take a preliminary statement from the ballsy blonde Texan with the shotgun, who'd had the squad wrapped around her little finger after the story of the bungled break-in made the rounds, along with a description of her standing over the guy with her foot on his balls when the uniforms answered her 911 call.

Whoever had trapped the two kids in the Park Avenue panic room had fled when the cops came banging on the door, but it had obviously been a highly professional team to have scammed such a sophisticated security system, so it was impossible to assess what they'd intended to do to the girls if the cops' arrival hadn't interfered. Whatever the hell was going down, the chief knew a lot more about it than he'd let on so far, but that was something Cochrane would have to deal with in the morning. For now, Martinelli was just glad he'd been on duty tonight and able to help. He liked Donovan. Always had. And obviously so did a lot of the guys at the House who remembered him from the old days. There'd been plenty of volunteers offering to help once the word spread, even among the men who were going off duty and said they'd help out on their own time.

Martinelli said goodnight to the last of the walking-wounded Donovans and left a couple of uniforms to keep an eye on the house. Tonight's craziness had opened up new possibilities about the next-door neighbor's murder. Could be whoever had offed the neighbor was behind all this, too. Maybe he thought the Donovans had ID'd him when he killed the old woman, maybe he was just a nutcase who wanted to kill people on Jane Street. But this blitz had been methodical and high tech. Had it been meant to scare, kill or force somebody's hand? Hard to tell yet.

He wondered what Cochrane would make of it all. Rumor had it the cocky bastard couldn't stand the old guy, but then the lieutenant couldn't stand most people. He was a real jerk about a lot of things and had made few friends since arriving at the 6th, but he wasn't a bad cop. Just a hard-ass with all the people skills of a buzz saw.

Detective Martinelli took a last look at the house and the now-vacant one next door. Both looked placid enough in the early dawn light. Old, elegant brownstones from a more gracious age, rehabbed over the decades and looking peaceful enough on the quiet, tree-lined street. But this definitely was not business as usual on Jane Street. Of course, this was New York and Greenwich Village, both of which meant anything could happen here.

He signaled his partner at the wheel to drive and settled back in the seat, longing for a lot more coffee.

84

Dec looked worried when Fitz opened the door to him early the morning after the attacks. "I just heard from Finn about Maeve, about all of them …" he said. "I didn't call for fear she'd tell me there was no need to come. How is she, Fitz?"

From Finn, was it now? Fitz thought as he judged the look of concern on Dec's handsome face and pronounced it genuine, stepping aside to let the man enter.

"Come in, Declan, lad," he said. "It's cold as a tax collector's heart out there. In answer to your question, she's better than you'd think possible, all things considered …" He reached for Dec's cashmere topcoat and hung it on the entrance hall's mirrored coatrack.

"She'll be happy to see you, I think. She's in her studio." He gestured down the hall. Dec knew the way, but Fitz followed anyway to announce the visitor.

Maeve's injured face looked up from the book she wasn't really reading because her head hurt too much, as Dec moved forward to put his arms around her. "You had me scared to death, Maeve," he said, and Fitz heard the truth in the words as he closed the door behind him and left them to their privacy.

Maeve let her head rest on Dec's chest for a few beats, grateful for the solid warmth and the momentary sense of safety it provided.

"I can't believe I didn't see it coming, Dec. I mean, I knew *something* was way off all day yesterday, I *knew*, but I couldn't put a name to it."

"Perhaps there was just too much of it going on all at once to parse," he said, the touch of Ireland in his voice seeming more pronounced than usual. "All of you in danger, not just one. This is serious, Maeve. We've obviously poked a hornet's nest and we need to reassess where we go from here." He hunkered down beside her chair so they were eye to eye.

"Would you come stay with me for a bit, lass, so I can keep you safe? Dougal would be only too thrilled to have you where he could keep an eye on you." He stopped for a moment then amended, "Truth be known, *I'd* be only too thrilled to keep an eye on you."

Maeve heard more in his voice than just concern for her safety and she squeezed his hand.

"I can't leave Fitz and Finn and Rory," she said softly, "but I love you for wanting to offer safe haven. Dougal, too. Please tell him for me.

"Besides, we're all meeting tonight to share what we know and figure out what comes next. Why don't we see what everybody has to say about all this and then make whatever plans we can. After last night, I think we all need to make some big decisions."

He stood up. "I know from Finn that Rory has a torn meniscus and a hairline fracture in her leg, so she's staying with you here at Donovan HQ for the moment. With great reluctance I'll accept your turning down my perfectly sensible invitation, Maeve, because I understand your need to be with your family." He smiled, and she felt the small quickening in her chest that his eyes sometimes caused when he looked at her the way he was now. "But I'm putting my security people on the case, and the invitation to stay with me and Dougal is open-ended. And we could take you all in if that would give you comfort …"

She started to protest, but he shook his head. "No arguments about the security, at least, Maeve," he said emphatically. "Fitz will back me up on this one. You're all in danger and now you're all in the same nest. It's just too easy a target, too vulnerable to attack, and the precinct is still handling it as just a random series of events—but there's so much they don't know. Please. You must let me do this for you. I don't want anything more to happen to you …" he seemed about to say more, but stopped himself.

Wondering what the end of that sentence might have been, she nodded. "Gratefully accepted, then. Last night was quite an eye-opener."

"We're to be at The Mysterious at eight," he answered, "so I'll send my car to gather you all up at seven thirty."

"Thanks, Dec. Rory's leg is more painful than she's letting on and she'll be on crutches. Everyone is coming, and everyone has a lot to say."

He nodded. "I have more than a bit to say myself. But first, would it hurt your face if I kissed it?" She smiled at the boyishness of the words and was touched.

"As in 'kiss and make better'?" she said the words from everybody's childhood facetiously, as she turned up her face expecting a kiss on the cheek. Instead, he bent down to her and, brushing her hair gently away from her bruised cheek, he kissed her full on the lips in a way that said far more than friendship and concern.

When the kiss was finished, she looked at him questioningly. "I almost lost you, Maeve," he said simply.

Then he let himself out of the studio, said goodbye to Fitz and was gone.

85

Maeve was seated in front of the big bow window in the parlor when Cochrane arrived to take her statement. The silvery winter sunlight behind her made her mop of red-gold curls look like a burnished halo circling her bruised face. He stood for a moment in the doorway thinking he hadn't expected her to be this good-looking, then chided himself for the unprofessional thought—but hell, he was human and a guy, so .... He walked into the room as she looked up from whatever she was writing. One side of her face had a small bandage, the other was badly bruised, but she still looked damned good, considering ...

"Come in, Lieutenant," she said with a slight smile. "Detective Martinelli told me you'd be coming by to talk with me. I hope you'll forgive my not getting up to offer you a cup of tea, but promising to stay off my feet for forty-eight hours is the only reason I escaped the hospital at all."

She saw his frown of concern and spoke quickly. "I feel better than I look. Doctors tend to over-worry and we Donovans are hardy stock."

"So I've observed," he said, derision clear in his voice.

Maeve smiled, deciding to opt for civility. You catch more flies with honey than with vinegar, her mother used to say. "I'm aware, Lieutenant, that you and my father have not been great friends, so maybe we should attempt to put that aside for now—I know that's what Fitz intends to do. He wouldn't have asked for help if he didn't intend to use every possible resource to keep us all safe. If you're willing to do the same, maybe we can help each other get this right."

Cochrane started to say the Donovan family had no place in his case at all, but stopped himself. She was hurt, her sister was hurt, her daughter had been threatened, her business partner had been attacked. She had a place in it, just not the one she probably wanted.

Very succinctly, Maeve laid out the bare bones of what she and Fitz had decided to tell him. *He asked good questions,* she thought. Good cop questions, and he had those penetrating cop eyes that made you feel pinned by their insistence and their cynicism.

She told him that Mrs. W, whom they knew long but not very intimately, had told Fitz she was in danger two hours before her death, had refused to let him call the precinct, and had asked him to return after dinner when she would be more forthcoming about the nature of the danger. When he'd returned, she was already dead. Maeve made no mention of the books Mrs. W had left for him, nor had Fitz. Cochrane already knew this much of the story, so she covered this part quickly, then went on to last night, telling him of her own assault and what she now knew of her sister's, her daughter's and her business partner's experiences.

A few days after the murder, she told him, Fitz had been visited at The Mysterious by an odd little man calling himself Mr. Grey, who had thought Fitz had some papers or documents he wanted, so Fitz had suggested he contact Lieutenant Cochrane at the 6th. Then the odd little man had made a thinly veiled threat by speaking of Finn.

Close enough, she thought, once he'd left. Close enough for now.

Lieutenant Joe Cochrane stood on the sidewalk after leaving the Donovan house, letting the chill wind pummel him, letting the muffler he'd gotten for Christmas snap into the bitter wind like a flag at reveille.

It was obvious Maeve was holding back, just as her father had done with Martinelli. Both telling a nicely rehearsed percentage of the truth. Not lying, just equivocating. What the hell was it they knew? And why the hell would the old guy ask the department for help and then keep back vital information? This was getting interesting. Dollars to doughnuts he would hit the same wall with the rest of their crowd when he interviewed Rory and Finn. Well, maybe not the Texan … she sounded like one for the books, so he'd have to wait and see about her story.

He'd go around them, do some digging, find out more about the old lady and then take a run at Fitz. Instinct told him he'd need to unearth enough evidence on his own to wheedle the rest out of this canny crowd.

Could Donovan have taken something important from the crime scene, he wondered? Unlikely but possible, and at least accusing him of doing so might rattle him enough so he'd spill something useful. He'd keep that possibility in mind for the moment.

The icy wind was clearing the morning cobwebs and he was intrigued enough to want to know more. What if once Martinelli had gotten into the act because of the attacks, Fitz had decided to use that entrée so the squad would be up to speed on the danger in case whoever it was struck again? That could make sense of the partial intel. It's not that he *wanted* to tell them anything, but he suddenly had to tell them *something.*

But had these crazy incidents just been a shot fired over the old guy's bow? Had the attackers meant to kill or just terrify? The subway could have killed Maeve if those two soldiers hadn't been there to pull her to safety, the ceiling could have killed Rory if she'd been a few feet beyond where she'd stood, and who knew what the perps had intended to do to those girls if the uniforms hadn't sent them packing. Girls like that would be worth a pretty penny in the upper echelon of the sex-slave trade—plus the Halberdson girl was worth millions in ransom. Were the saves all coincidence, or was the whole night staged to scare the crap out of Fitz?

Was the family playing dumb because they were terrified but under duress of some kind not to break silence? Or were they playing dumb because they thought they had a better chance of solving it on their own? Interesting. Maybe worth his time after all.

Cochrane stepped into the waiting car idling at the curb.

"Where to next, Lieutenant?" the driver asked.

"Let's tackle the Texan," Cochrane said. "A place called The Philosopher's Teacup on Bleecker."

The young detective in the driver's seat smirked.

"My prayers are answered, Loot," he said grinning. "Those doughnuts she brought over were spectacular. I mean, not as spectacular as her bodacious ta-tas, but something to write home about."

"Just drive, Rinaldi," Cochrane said as sternly as possible while trying not to smile. He couldn't blame the kid. The whole tale of Georgia and her takedown of the intruder had been the one bright spot in everybody's last twenty-four hours.

86

The call came from higher up the food chain and had all the earmarks of having originated at City Hall, inasmuch as that made no sense whatsoever.

Cochrane had spent the day interviewing the vics, following up on what little he knew and trying to find out more about the dead old lady who seemed not to have existed at all before 1991. Was that because she'd come from behind the Iron Curtain where records were scarce to nonexistent, or because she'd been somebody else entirely, who'd brought a new identity with her to New York?

Now he put down the phone, a thoughtful expression clouding his usual resting bitch-face expression. He'd just been ordered in no uncertain terms to drop the Donovan case. It was all just a coincidence, the commander said. No connection whatsoever to the murder next door to the family. No reason to believe the attacks on the Donovans were any more than coincidental accidents. No need to waste city resources on pursuing a dead end.

Really?

Cochrane drummed his fingers on the desktop and tried to calculate the odds of four violent incidents happening to the same group of family and friends on the same night being a coincidence.

Fuck. Shit. Piss. And corruption. He thought the words individually, just like his prissy sister Maureen would. Now he'd have to push Donovan to see what he really knew, and maybe speak again to the rest of the family, who didn't really seem to be nutballs from what Martinelli had told him. Just people hiding something he wanted to know.

He'd start by rattling the toughest one of the lot. If his commander got his knickers in a twist about him ignoring orders to drop the case, he could always say the interview had been scheduled before the cease-and-desist call came in and he hadn't wanted to diss Donovan by turning him away.

The thought was so PC it made him smile, because PC was something he did not excel at.

87

Lieutenant Cochrane's desk was free of paper and pictures, other than one of him receiving a commendation of some kind from the commissioner. Fitz could see into the man's glass-walled office from where he stood at the squad room door. The old blinds were open and Cochrane was seated behind his surprisingly clean and tidy desk.

He allowed himself a moment of nostalgia, breathing in the familiar scent of the 6th. He had no choice now but to let Cochrane into the mix, no matter how unpleasant the prospect. Not after the attacks. The real question was how far in: how much info would help, and how much would just muddy the waters and keep Fitz from getting to the bottom of what was really going on here, which had taken on a new urgency. This was no time to get into a hassle about withholding evidence with a man who had a chip on both shoulders, so he'd have to tread carefully where facts were concerned.

Now that Cochrane knew something was up on Jane Street, unless he was brain-dead, he'd have connected the dots between the murder and the four attacks. It was best to get out ahead of this while it was still possible, lest the PD's well-meaning digging cause more harm than good. His family's lives were on the line now. If he needed the help of the department, he'd call in every favor he'd ever earned. If he needed to get Cochrane to cooperate, he'd find a way to do that, too.

The key was to assess what Cochrane was really made of. Martinelli had said he was a pain in the arse but a decent cop, and some kind of talent must have gotten him to a lieutenant's rank. He'd have to take the measure of the man without letting him know that's what he was up to, of course, so that was this morning's mandate. Maybe, being interrogated about the four incidents was a godsend—the perfect chance to see Cochrane in action and judge just how much he could be trusted, if at all.

Fitz made up his mind, squared his shoulders and strode forward. He'd never known a really good cop with a really clean desk, but there was a first time for everything.

Cochrane had primed himself into a piss-poor mood before Donovan entered his office, as he'd decided putting the screws to the old guy would get his Irish up. His mood was considerably worse after more than half an hour of questioning Fitz with zero success. Not that the old guy had tried to pull nonexistent rank or been uncooperative, but it was obvious he knew a helluva lot more about the murder next door and the attacks on his family than he was letting on, and no amount of questioning had rattled him enough to make a single slip.

Cochrane was good at his job, and it rankled that he'd missed the possibility of the old lady's death being more than a psycho break-in looking for loot. Rankled, too, that he now had to deal with an old fart who was giving him nothing useful despite his best efforts. But, it would piss him off even more if he had to give up on this before he had a handle on what the hell *this* was.

A half hour later, they still sat in Cochrane's office, not an interview room, and the door was mostly open, so there were plenty of listening ears in the squad room, but Cochrane didn't give a shit. He wasn't expecting to get Donovan to crack, he just wanted to unnerve the old guy enough so he'd make a mistake or two. And it wouldn't hurt to take him down a peg in front of his cop cheering-section. Besides, Cochrane needed a benchmark on how far Donovan was willing to go to protect whatever the hell it was he knew.

He figured he'd either piss him off enough so he'd let some cat out of the bag, or he'd convince Donovan that unless he came clean his family would get no more special treatment from the 6th. If he got nothing interesting from him, he'd just drop the case as he'd been told to. But that thought pissed him off, too, because his cop senses said there was more to this weird picture than he was seeing. *Shit.*

When he could see Fitz's patience was finally wearing thin, he decided to up the pressure and take one more shot at him from a different angle. Hit him with something that might make him mad enough to fight back. He was Irish, after all.

Cochrane leaned back in his chair with a nasty smirk on his face.

"You know Donovan, you're some piece of work …" he said, considerably more malice in his tone than in the rest of the interview. "If you want to know what I think, it's that you've been lying through your teeth and withholding evidence from the get-go. You're interfering with an ongoing investigation and I have reason to believe you stole important evidence from my crime scene. Truth is, you've crossed so many lines here, I could have your ancient ass thrown into Rikers. So I think you'd better can the bullshit you've been laying on with a trowel since you got here and tell me what you really know about why Jane Street is suddenly the hub of a fucking crime wave." He leaned forward, arms on his desk, and adjusted his face to menacing, then said very low, "I'm not known for my patience."

Fitz's frown could have turned Medusa to stone. "I imagine you're not known for your good manners, either," he said implacably.

Cochrane stood suddenly and slammed his big fist down on the desk so hard it made his one photo and coffee cup skitter to the floor.

"Now you listen to me, you pretentious old fart—" he began, but Fitz cut him off in a voice Cochrane hadn't heard before.

"No!" Fitz said, steel in the word. "You listen to me, you arrogant horse's arse! Much as I appreciate the exquisite totality of your ignorance, I'm here to help you with your case. You've the disposition of a banshee and a tongue that could clip a hedge, but I don't give a good goddamn about either one, so if you think you can intimidate me, you're up the wrong tree.

"Here's the long and the short of it. I came here today because I need you to help me protect the people I love, and you need me to solve your case and a helluva lot more that you don't even know is going on here! And to keep the almighty ignorance of your poking around from landing your arse back on a beat in Canarsie. I've been told by some I trust that you have a bit of talent the force can use, although as God is my witness, I've seen none of it thus far.

"You have absolutely no idea how big and how dangerous a game is in progress under the tip of your considerable nose, but in return for your keeping a civil tongue in your head and using what I've heard is a decent cop brain to do what's needed, I'll show you the way through this bog. Because as of this moment I'm so far ahead of you, you couldn't catch me if your balls were on fire. But I'm willing to give you the benefit of the doubt to keep anyone else from getting hurt or killed."

You could hear a pin drop in the squad room.

Fitz's voice got colder still.

"But I'll give you fair warning, boyo. If you fuck with me or don't do your damnedest to protect my girls, I'll chase you so far over the hills of damnation the good Lord Himself won't find you with a telescope.

"Now sit your arse down and listen up!"

Heads were bent all over the room, hiding grins. All sounds of breathing, typing and talking had ceased altogether as everyone braced for the coming explosion. But instead, Cochrane sat back down in his chair and a rare smile creased his face. "Okay, then," he said, stifling a laugh. "So now at least I can see why some of the guys like you."

Then he got up again, made a rude gesture to the listening squad, and slammed the door to his office. "You been doing nothing but sizing me up since you got here," he said to Fitz. "Am I right?"

"I was."

"And you intended to tell me what's going on all along?"

"Only if I thought you gave a damn."

Cochrane nodded, understanding. "I give a damn, but I've been told by 1 P.P. to drop this."

Fitz's eyebrows went up. "1 Police Plaza, is it? That should tell you something."

"How about if *you* tell me something. Like what the hell is going on here?"

"Why would I, if you're dropping it anyway?"

"I didn't say I was dropping it, just that I've been *told* to. And even if I do have to drop it officially, *unofficially* I may still be able to be useful if I choose to be. You've got friends around here … friends who don't want to see your family hurt. And besides, your Texas Ranger is a sight to behold. And I wouldn't want to piss her off while she's still got that cannon of hers."

Fitz was quiet for a moment. "You know, it might actually be better that you've been warned off, now that I stop to think about it. Otherwise you'd have to paint by the numbers and that'll help no one. What say you give me your word you'll do your damnedest to keep my girls and my friends safe and you'll keep in confidence the tale I'm about to tell you, inasmuch as you're off the case anyway. Then, I'll tell you enough of a bizarre story that I can enlist your brain in helping us work our way out of a dangerous conspiracy that goes back decades. Another smart cop brain on this couldn't hurt a bit. Just in case I've missed something important."

"I'm beginning to think that's not a high probability," Cochrane said with a short, wry laugh. "But let 'er rip. You never know."

88

That was quite a doozy of a tale Donovan had spun for him, Cochrane thought, sitting at his desk after most of the squad had left for the day; the night shift seemed to him quieter than usual. He drummed his fingers on his desk and thought it all through for the third time.

He still didn't have the whole story, that was clear. But he had enough to think hard about what the fuck to do with it. He had the perfect right to do absolutely nothing. In fact, he had orders to that effect. He could get a few of the uniforms and maybe a couple of the detectives to keep an eye and an ear on any activity on Jane Street without too much flack—the higher-ups would be happy and that could be that.

Of course, he could make a case against Donovan for taking evidence from the scene, but why bother? The books had been addressed to him and as much on his property as on hers. And maybe he himself would have done the same if his family was in danger from some nutjob who'd killed the woman next door in such a grisly way. If he had a family ... which he didn't anymore. But going after Fitz would be a distraction, and having seen him in action today, maybe a big mistake.

On the other hand, if Fitz was right and this mess involved heavy-hitter bad guys with political juice, why bother to get involved at all? Was it the redheaded daughter who attracted him and probably understood what dating a cop would be like? He wouldn't mind keeping an eye on her himself. Was it annoyance at being summarily warned off? Was it that the old guy had turned out to be so much more than he'd expected? He drummed his fingers on the desk one more time.

Curiosity. That's what it was. Plain and simple. You weren't a cop if you didn't have a seriously overdeveloped sense of curiosity. He'd always been a history buff, and this whole mess was like a time warp into the past and all the skullduggery he'd always sensed had surrounded the end of WWII.

Now he'd just have to decide what to do about all that.

Oddly, the first thing that occurred to him was to see if he could get a handle on one of the other members of the Donovan clan.

89

"Either they've got an employment agency full of the most inept hit men in the annals of New York City crime or they just meant to scare the crap out of us, not kill us," Rory said matter-of-factly as the Donovans and Dec sat in Maeve's kitchen an hour before they were supposed to be at The Mysterious to discuss what had happened with the entire group.

Dec had suggested it and said he'd bring takeout—or rather his driver would, but he'd called to say he was bringing dinner and wanted to talk before the big meeting. He'd said the walking wounded could not be expected to cook and so it was either sending Dougal to their kitchen or bringing Chinese. They'd opted for the latter.

"You could be right, luv," Fitz said, "Or not. The trouble with that assumption is that both accidents could just as easily have been fatal and we don't know what they intended to do with the girls once they had them. Sex trafficking is big business these days. If more of the ceiling fell on you or your leg had been broken so badly you couldn't fight back … if the soldier boys hadn't been on that subway platform with Maeve … we just can't be sure of anything. Attacking an entire family is a very bold message. It takes planning and serious money."

Dec leaned forward. "I agree we can't bank on their ineptitude. We need to make contact and try to convince them we don't have what they want."

"I've considered that, laddie, but we don't know who we're up against or why."

"So the next time you get a threatening phone call, you call their bluff and say we want to meet. I'll try to negotiate if you'll permit me."

"Once *they* know that *we* know who they are, even if you convince them we don't have the Protocol, they'll still see us as loose ends because we *know* about the Protocol. I'm not convinced we'd be any safer … maybe less so."

Dec looked dubious. He agreed in principle, but wasn't sure Fitz's strategy was the way to go. And as his feelings had grown for Maeve, he was determined to keep her and her whole family safe.

Last night had really shaken him. These people, whoever they were, were funded, smart and tapped in. There had to be a way for a man with his resources to use them to keep everybody safe. He'd talk to his head of security as soon as he got back home—maybe even talk to his father, who had connections everywhere—police, politics, banking, both legal and, he supposed, not legal.

But those connections were a loose link: not only did he not want his father to know what was going on, he couldn't be certain which side he'd be on, if he did know the whole story.

Expediency was his father's hallmark, and he followed only his own rules.

The meal was glum as no one knew what to say, so they decided to call it a day and move the meeting of the BSI to the following night. Finn sent a text to everyone to let them know that nobody was really in good enough shape to talk tonight.

90

The babble of voices as Fitz called the restive group to order the following evening was anticipatory and nervous as hell. Everybody knew about all the incidents, had conversed with the near-casualties, and was paying strict attention.

"I'd like us to begin our reprise of the last forty-eight hours with our own Annie Oakley," Fitz opened with a smile meant to lighten the gloom. "I'm told the boys at the 6th have talked about naught else since she turned over the perp to the uniforms with a heel on his privates, a shotgun in the crook of her arm and nary an eyelash out of place."

The group applauded and raised their teacups in salute. "I expect you'll have a whole new raft of cop clients at the tea shop now," Fitz added, beaming at Georgia, who took a theatrical bow.

"Just added bulletproof doughnuts to the menu to accommodate our boys in blue," she quipped.

"I think it's time we took inventory of what we've learned, so let's get the show on the road with you, Georgia," Fitz said with a chuckle. "So, what exactly did you find out in Texas, lassie, that has you smiling like the cat that ate the canary?"

Georgia sat up straight as a schoolgirl and tapped a fat envelope, then handed a thumb drive to Finn.

"My uncle Hutch, God bless his rascally heart, spilled a lot of beans about skullduggery and complicity during the big war and after. Greed was the only clear winner it seems, and oil was in the thick of everything.

"But it appears my granddaddy, who was on a first-name basis with the bottom of the deck, was up close and personal with all the players on all sides, then my daddy and Uncle Hutch knew the next generation of sons a' bitches real well, too. But here's the news I'm bustin' to tell. My granddaddy—aside from being an SOB—was also paranoid enough to keep a closetful of dirt on all the players! You know, like an insurance policy of Mutual Assured Destruction? I'll-keep-your-secrets-if-you-keep-mine kind of paranoia. Sooo …

"One of the secrets he kept in his stash was the real identities of his Nazi playmates! Hutch wasn't sure how granddaddy came by all this intel but said it probably involved greasing the palms of the guys in DC who were busy Paperclipping new IDs onto old file folders. Bribery will get you everything bein' one of his mottoes."

She smiled with a hint of triumph. "We spent the night narrowing the field. I got all the names, dates, *whatever,* on this thumb drive which I will now happily hand over to those who know what to do with it." She nodded at Annie and her troop. "But Hutch and me, we stayed up all night doin' it the old-fashioned way. We thinned the herd to six candidates. They're in this envelope. If you disagree, no harm, no foul, but there's one family in particular that has all the earmarks, as well as a current hat in the ring for the presidency." She beamed.

"All six have real potential, so maybe there were redundancies built into their plan. We think you should look closely at H.W. Reese, the billionaire industrialist from Ohio. He could easily have been Manfred Gruber's partner in crime—his dates are right and so's his marriage. His unsavory sons, Heinrich and Werner, run his empire now and his grandson is a senator with presidential aspirations, but, unfortunately, he's not the only candidate with creds like that. So I leave what we've got on him and his progeny in your fine hands to prove or disprove, along with the others."

The room erupted into speech, everybody talking at once, everybody asking rapid-fire questions. Georgia laughed out loud. "Hold your horses, everybody! Seems like I need to turn this discussion back to Fitz, who knows how to handle unruly crowds. I'm just the messenger."

"This is un-fucking-believable!" Matrix exploded. "Wait till you hear what Finn and Manny have to say. With this added intel it gives us our next move!"

"It's not just us who did it, guys," Finn interjected. "It's Annie's whole team who swiped the AI tech so we could use it to find missing links. Manny … tell them what this gives us. It's so dope!"

Manny shook his head, the expression on his oddly mismatched face one of undisguised delight.

"We came here tonight to tell you the fine news that not only have we been able to positively identify, through this state-of-the-art technology, Ghisella Wallenberg as *both* the Magdalena and the elder daughter of Baron von Zechandorff, but to say we believe we can use the same technology to pursue the identity of the family that received Hitler's seed! I'll leave it to Annie and her genius squad to explain how this can happen. Now, after Georgia's input, we have a short list of suspects, which makes the job easier by far!"

Mimi broke in as gracefully as she did everything else.

She began, "There's a world-class geneticist from India doing a year in the lab at my hospital, sharing ideas and tech with our guys. It occurred to me, he might be willing to work with us on a separate project if we offered to pay for his time. I'd be happy to pay him if he'll do it, and I don't see any conflicts of interest, but maybe Rory can vet that question for us?" She looked to Rory, who nodded affirmatively.

"I'm thinking he could help in several ways if he's game," Mimi continued. "First, to tell us the odds on tracking genetic markers through three generations; second, if we're able to narrow down a pool of suspects and can get their DNA by hook or by crook, he could help us know for sure if it's the bloodline!

"I've gotten to know him because of a paper I wrote on Down syndrome that segues into his field of expertise, and he's been generous with his knowledge and time. If you all think it's worthwhile, I'll ask him if he's willing to engage in a privately funded project." She looked around expectantly.

"Wouldn't we need Hitler's DNA to compare it to? How on earth would we get any of that?" Matrix asked the question. "Anything that supposedly came from his corpse is probably really from his doppelganger, right?"

"True enough," Mimi said. "I know it's a longshot … but if we end up with more than one suspect it could be a tiebreaker. And my colleague has an amazing database we could use to see if anybody, *anywhere* has Hitler's DNA."

"Why not ask if he's game for moonlighting at least, without telling him exactly why," Fitz said. "I haven't given up hope of finding some long-lost Hitler relative, and that way if we need him and/or his genetic database, we're ahead of the game."

Annie's thin lips twitched into an almost-smile. Quite a lot was beginning to fall into place, so she spoke up.

"T-square has been deciphering the complex drawings in the encrypted journal and Lulu and I have been decrypting with more success than I anticipated when this began." She made the announcement without undue fuss but it was apparent that whatever she had to say was important. "Bridget and Matrix created an AI algorithm that teaches AI to create better AI, pitting machine against machine if you will. Really advanced work.

"The math and schematics in Ghisella's clothing supplied the final key to our Rosetta stone!"

"Inasmuch as the science and mathematics is probably beyond the comprehension of most physicists, never mind laypeople, let me and T give you the Reader's Digest version—and I ask you to accept my word that from a physicist's point of view, this is not only earth-shattering intel, but it is very dangerous intel."

She looked around at the watching faces and made sure they were paying attention.

"Let's call it New Physics, stolen and unshared for three generations—or rather, kept from the *common man*, but assuredly shared years ago, only with those who could make billions from it by claiming ownership. Or use it to rule the world…" She let that sink in.

"The existence of this knowledge unmasks a multinational conspiracy of lies to the American people—indeed, to humanity as a whole—while putting into the hands of the military industrial giants and certain bankers and corporate interests, and of course, the powers behind the throne that really pull the strings of all of the above, a highly competent way to damn near control everything on earth. It also confirms an alarmingly vast amount of what, up to now, has been consigned to the fringe of conspiracy theorists."

"S'cuse me, Annie," T piped up. "I just got one thing I really want to give a shout out to before everybody's brain implodes with what we've got to tell them. With everything else going on, it's easy to pass over this fact without applause, but what Mrs. W pulled off here is frackin' unbelievable. I mean, like she was a *homeschooled* physicist—just think about that for a minute!

"She had no formal training except her dad's tutoring, yet she managed to put down on paper info that's so far beyond what science *thinks* is cutting edge, and so detailed, most of it could knock the Nobel Committee on its ass!

"That's a freaking miracle in itself … and yeah, I know people could say she was just a glorified scribe, but holy fucking Jesus, she had to be six kinds of brilliant to get this stuff from her daddy, remember the details and put it down encrypted in invisible ink she cooked up in her kitchen! I mean, like it defies nature that *anyone* could do that!" The admiration on his face and in his voice spoke volumes.

"And then she protected it for seventy-five years. And finally gave her life for it!" Bridget added. "Kudos for that as well, don't forget."

Annie nodded approval at her troop. "What Ghisella Wallenberg has given us is a new "off the books" physics. As radical a breakthrough as superstring theory was in its day, and based on a hyper-dimensional unified-field theory of electromagnetism and gravitation that relies on five-dimensional cylindrical geometry to achieve unification and control time-space itself. This has Tesla written all over it, puts Einstein in the shade, and it wasn't even supposed to *exist* in 1940. In fact, it's only in the past five years of this whole new millennium that physicists have even postulated that it *could* exist!

"What this material proves is that stealth tech, antigravity tech, V-3 rockets that could have decimated the east coast of America, and a helluva lot else including an atomic bomb and the refined plutonium it needed—all *this* was in Hitler's hands and only a few months from operational when the war ended. Hell, it was probably all operational in the Neuschwabenland airbase that Admiral Byrd documented finding before our own government shut him up!

"We've ink- and paper-dated the book, the journal and the fabric, so no one can say it's a current forgery. And what's in it is enough to blow the lid off both science and politics. These journals are quite simply, *priceless*. And deadly. So we all must think long and hard about what to do with them now. If we have these *and* can somehow find the Protocol itself, I think we've got a slam dunk about why Ghisella was killed and why we're all in danger. Probably a whole lot else, too. But the question is, *if* we blow the lid off, how long will any of us stay alive?"

Dec stood up slowly after the murmuring voices had stilled. "Not easy to follow that act, to be sure," he said, as disturbed by Annie's words as were the rest of the listeners. "So, let's save our discussion until everybody's cards are on the table and we know exactly what we've got among us to bargain with." He took a deep breath.

"Meantime, I'm afraid my contribution is rather meager compared to what we've just heard, but my people in Europe have found Dieter Streger. He's living in a villa in Villefranche-sur-Mer. He has agreed to talk to me about his memories of the Steiners, whom he admired, loved and saved—first rescuing the professor from the Nazis in 1935 and later rescuing Ghisella from imminent death at the hands of the Stasi. He says his memory hasn't been impaired by age, but he admonished me to see him quickly, because one never knows at ninety-six when the Grim Reaper has you on his receivables schedule.

"I've made arrangements to leave tomorrow. I'm hoping Maeve will go with me, if she's up to traveling. Streger may know more than he thinks he does and she's adept at intuiting things beyond the ordinary." He looked to her for a response.

"I'd kill to meet someone who actually *knew* Ghisella," she said, "but I don't want to leave while my family's in danger. Dad, what do you think?"

Fitz weighed the question before answering.

"We have Dec's security men on the job and Cochrane has a black-and-white drive-by scheduled every few hours. After the attacks, everyone in this room is on high alert and Mimi's security company is so chagrined at having their state-of-the-art system breached, they've kicked in extra surveillance for her and for Finn. I'm here with Rory and we're both armed to the teeth. Georgia has a cop fan club, to say nothing of her own personal arsenal. I'd say you can go if you're up to it, luv."

Maeve nodded slowly, deciding. "Then let's talk about the attacks and get everything out on the table. They—whoever *they* are—obviously could have killed us if they'd wanted to. So my bet is they just intended to scare the bejesus out of Fitz to shake loose what he knows."

"And they did a fine job of that, lass, let me tell you," Fitz said. "Let's give the devil his due. I'd walk away from this whole bloody mess right this minute if I thought that would keep you all safe. I'm just not sure it would do that, as the blaggards obviously know we're onto them."

"So we've got a helluva lot more to talk about tonight," she pursued, "like where do we want to go from here? Does anybody want out, and is that even possible now? What's our risk level? For that matter, what are we willing to tell the police … the more we tell them, the more liable we are to get slammed for obstructing an investigation. The less we tell them, the less we can rely on their help."

"Let's go around the room and hear from everybody," Dec added in his CEO voice. "Questions, fears, ideas, you name it. Now's the time."

"Okay then," Georgia said as she stood up. "That's gonna need rocket fuel, not tea, by my reckonin'. Fitz, darlin', where do you keep the John Jameson and The Bushmill's? Irish coffee or a stiff whiskey on the rocks is more in keepin' with what we all got to say to each other here tonight. Who's with me on this point of order?"

"Hard liquor doesn't really fix anything," Bridget said prissily.

"True enough, darlin'," Georgia quipped as she headed for the bar. "But neither does milk."

There were no other dissenters.

91

"Let me get this straight, Lieutenant Cochrane," Maeve said, trying not to laugh. "You want *me* to do *your* horoscope?"

He nodded an emphatic yes. He had arrived unannounced at her door and taken her by surprise.

"You are so far down on my list of probable clients—maybe just above Mike Pence—that you're going to have to convince me you're not pulling my leg."

He grinned back at her, and she thought he should smile more often.

"Yeah, yeah, I know," he said. "But you just don't look like a crackpot to me and I try to keep an open mind about weird stuff, ya know, so I figured the best way to find out if you're just a bullshit artist is to get my chart done."

She burst out laughing, liking him for his honesty, at least.

"Okay," she said, composing herself, "I'll need your date, place and time of birth."

He relaxed. "How much do you charge? Remember I'm a cop, not a billionaire."

"Worry not, Lieutenant, this is on the house—"

"I can't accept gifts—" he began.

"Quite right," she said, "but this is for *my* edification, not *yours*. I want to see what makes you tick and if you can be trusted."

He blinked, then nodded and wrote down the info she'd asked for.

Maeve took the paper, typed some things into her laptop, then scrutinized the chart that came up on the screen.

"Give me a day or two, Detective. Now *I* need to do some detecting of my own."

92

Maeve pushed herself back from the table an hour later and started to laugh. She really had to pack for the trip, but Cochrane's request had been too wacky and intriguing to let slide, so she'd done the chart immediately. Wait till she told the others, especially Fitz.

As if the thought had made him materialize, she heard her father slam the front door and greet the dog. There was more spring in his step these days than there had been for a while. Being back on the job was the reason. He could feel them making progress, closing in on the truth, and that exhilarated him.

"I'm in the kitchen," she called out. "I have a bit of a surprise for you."

He shrugged out of his coat and hung it on the coatrack to leak snow onto the mat beneath.

"And what might that be?" He leaned over to hug her hello and she could feel the frost on his face.

"I've just done Lieutenant Cochrane's chart—at *his request* mind you—and he's not a bad guy! Just socially inept. Actually, he has a pretty big heart and a Cancer moon, but it's only the crochety Scorpio sun and critical Virgo ascendant anybody ever sees."

Maeve sat back and waved Cochrane's chart at him. "It's a revelation, Dad," she said with a grin. "He's a Scorpio with a heavy helping of Virgo, the heavenly critic, God help him and everyone around him. Apparently an excellent detective but a cosmic pain in the ass to anyone who doesn't see things his way or doesn't get *out* of his way while he does things his way! With Scorpio on the cusp of the third—the most acerbic mouth in the Zodiac, too—he's probably always pretty much on point with perps, always knowing where the weak spot is to plunge the knife in or to manipulate. Formidable in his line of work, don't you think? And with a Cancer moon, backed by a Taurean Mars, there's a romantic heart buried under all that take-no-prisoners skeptic's facade.

"But he's a decent guy underneath all that. A man of principle and ideals, spending his days in a world that is currently woefully lacking in both, so maybe we have to cut him a little slack." She finished her thoughts with satisfaction and waited to hear how her father would respond.

Having listened to her appraisal, Fitz chuckled. "So he's got the heart of a homebody, the disposition of a grizzly and the righteousness that will pursue you to the grave and beyond if you're an enemy?" Fitz hadn't been married to a mystic for half a century without learning a thing or two.

"In a nutshell," she agreed. "Probably makes him a damned good detective and a damned bad enemy. Dogged in the pursuit and all that. Like Javert in *Les Mis*."

"And just about as winsome," Fitz quipped. "So you liked him, eh?" he added with a chuckle. "I'll bear that in mind," he said, and she knew he would.

"He's trustworthy," she countered. "Tough-minded and good-hearted—not a bad combination. Thought you'd want to know."

"Indeed, I do," he said. "I've been doing some inquiring of my own about the man, and he comes out clean. Cranky but clean."

Maeve headed for the door to the hall.

"Are you really okay about my trip with Dec?" she asked.

"More than you know," he answered with a twinkle in his eyes. "I've grown to like the lad. And while no man short of the good Lord himself seems to me good enough for any of my girls, he comes closest of the ones I've met."

Maeve laughed, turned and hugged him, then headed for her bedroom to pack.

93

Maeve settled into the luxurious comfort of the camel-colored leather seat on the private plane, refused a proffered glass of champagne and asked for orange juice instead, which appeared as if by magic in the hands of the beautiful young flight attendant about thirty seconds later.

She smiled at Dec, who was seated across from her in the Gulfstream G650 he'd commandeered from his corporate air force for their flight to Dublin.

"How do you cope with all this luxury on a daily basis, my friend?" she asked. "Is it ever a burden?"

He laughed, a good-humored sound, and stretched his long limbs out across the ample space. "I think no one's ever asked me *that* before," he answered. "But the short answer is yes. Not because of the luxury itself—that's pretty much always a boon. But the guilt is sometimes a burden."

"Why guilt? Your money isn't ill-gotten, as far as I know."

He considered the question. "Not by me, it isn't, to be sure." The slight Irish brogue that persisted despite his British education always tickled her. She'd noticed before that it became more pronounced whenever he was in or near Ireland, as if he could safely let it breathe free there. "I work my tail off, give to good works and charities, try to be a decent man. But I inherited the wherewithal to do all that from my family, and they have as many reprobates in the closet as Georgia's does. A lot of our money came from railroads, and those poor sods who laid track were little more than slaves. And mining … which was fine for the owners, but not for the laborers underground who paid for feeding their families with black lung and indebtedness to the company store. And don't get me started on banking. My father and his cronies are thieves on the grandest scale. And they're absolutely untouchable, utterly above the law. So you might say most of the toys I own, the houses, planes, my island, the castle that won your heart the minute you stepped foot in it years ago … I owe much of it to their greed, avarice, cruelty, lawlessness, and lack of conscience."

He paused for a moment, considering. "Not all of it, of course. I've made my own way, built my own fortune, but I did it standing on the shoulders of my wicked forebears. So, how does one sort all *that* out? One doesn't." He smiled at her and she caught herself feeling touched by his candor—and by those eyes that crinkled at the corners in such a lovable way. But *who the hell owns an island?* was rattling around in there, too.

"The good news is that *sometimes* the guilt—which is, I'm afraid, only a part-time enterprise—abates, and just the joy of good fortune remains. Like now. I'm here with you, on a worthy mission, headed for a sun-drenched paradise and an old man with a story out of the history books … and I have all those old scallywags to thank for this rare opportunity. I assure you, Maeve, it would fuddle a Jesuit to sort it all out."

She couldn't help but laugh. "As I'm equally glad to be here with you, Dec, I suppose I'll have to be grateful to the family scallywags, too, no matter how much it pains my liberal heart."

"See what I mean about the moral GPS issue?" he chuckled.

"I do see. I'm afraid I may need to go to confession when I get back to New York. And it's been twenty years since I've ventured into a confessional."

He nodded in amusement. "Just see that you wait till you get home to do it, my girl … in case any other sins await you here, you might not want to get into a state of grace too early. I'm just suggesting most respectfully, mind you, that you might want to tuck another sin or two into that confession before you're through … one-stop shopping for repentance is an Irish institution, you might say. For all our religiosity, we're a lusty pagan country at heart."

That was part of what she loved about him, she thought as she settled back to enjoy the moment. The irreverence, the laughter, the untroubled view of the mostly untroubled universe he inhabited. It was tempting to just go along for the ride.

94

Cochrane had no illusions about the moral compass of the rich: it always pointed to True Greed. Actually, he had no illusions about anything much after eighteen years on the job. But from what he'd seen, when money was God and you had an obscene amount of it, you began to believe you ruled by divine right—and rulers don't ask permission, or worry about consequences, or even notice the people struggling below their lofty lives as anything other than service personnel. Useful, replaceable. It was just a fact of life, so it didn't bug him all that much, except when the overprivileged crossed the line into crime. Their everyday crimes on Wall Street or in DC were way above his pay grade or ability to affect, but when they ventured into New York City and his homicide division, it was a special pleasure to nail the smug bastards. And even though their high-priced lawyers—he thought of them alternately as pond scum or Satan's palace guard—could generally get them off the hook, every once in a while they could get nailed. He smiled just thinking about it.

Donovan's story was just nutty enough to be true. The old guy was smart, the daughters and granddaughter were good people as well as good-looking, and the story was so preposterous they were pretty much on their own where the law was concerned. It was an appealing combination.

And he was officially off the case, thus off the hook. If he colored a little outside the lines on his own time it was nobody's business but his own. It wasn't like he had a life.

Besides. He'd had an idea. Actually, a memory of something weird he'd heard about years ago, about somebody related to Hitler living in Manhattan. But where the hell had he heard it? He booted up his laptop and started to dig, then realized he knew somebody who could dig up the dead a lot better than he could.

95

"You are even more beautiful than I remembered, Millie," Cochrane said with a straight face to the aggressively homely, late-middle-aged Gorgon who had been working in the New York medical examiner's office since God's childhood. She had the personality of a sour pickle, the body of an immense pouter pigeon, and she ruled her departmental roost with all the subtlety of Attila. But she knew pretty much everything that had happened in New York City since the Nixon administration. If it had to do with death, what she didn't know, she could find out.

"True enough," she answered in a voice so deep it seemed to come from somewhere underneath her feet. "What do you want to wheedle out of me this time, Lieutenant?"

He pulled the box of chocolates out from behind his back with as much of a flourish as he was capable of, and handed them over.

"Good thing my girlish figure is untouched by time," she said drily, studying the box with an expert's eye.

"Why would Mother Nature mess with perfection?" he replied. He got a kick out of Millie. "It's just a bribe, kid," he said, matching her tone, "but there's more where that came from."

"What a surprise. But I gotta tell you, Cochrane, you don't get much for chocolates from CVS. Godiva maybe, CVS not so much." Her voice sounded as if she gargled with gravel, but he could see she was amused.

"What if I told you I'm on the trail of righting a great wrong? Would that help?"

"Nah," she said. "That's just your job description."

"True enough. But this one's a little off the books."

"I don't do off the books." Now she was interested.

"Me, too. This one's different."

Her over-furry eyebrow came up. "Don't tell me you've got a new girlfriend?"

"No way. My heart is yours."

That got her to crack a smile. "Okay. Out with it. I'll see if I can give you CVS-worth. What do you need?"

He told her, and after she'd blinked twice in surprise, she said, "Tomorrow. After six. If it's not at least Ghirardelli, don't bother to come back at all."

He laughed and she wondered why he never did that. He wasn't a looker, but he wasn't half bad when he smiled. But then again, maybe he didn't have much reason to smile since his divorce ten years ago.

Cops were a lousy bet for husbands, she knew, and he'd be a harder sell than most. But he was not such a bad guy. A pretty good cop, too. But all the finesse of a wrecking ball.

Not her problem, fortunately.

She made a note to find what he was looking for. It seemed a far cry from New York City and her bailiwick, but death's tendrils reached far and wide and Manhattan was, in her estimation, the hub of the universe. Sooner or later, everything landed there. If there was a New York connection, she'd find it.

PART IX

Going to the Source

**"How far that little
candle throws his beams!
So shines a good deed
in a naughty world."**

— Shakespeare, *The Merchant of Venice*

96

"Something tells me this trip is the catalyst for some kind of breakthrough to come to us, Maeve," Dec said cheerfully.

He'd been in high spirits ever since landing on Irish soil. Maeve had seen it the other times she'd been in Ireland with him, too. It was obvious that Dublin was home, even if he said he never intended to live there full-time again. They'd had dinner at a local pub—a rollicking good blend of hearty food, abundant drink and an earful of Irish music. The only time he hadn't seemed cheerful since arriving was when he spoke of seeing his father. He'd spent a couple of hours at his office after the plane landed, and she knew he intended to find out whatever he could from his father the following day before they flew to the south of France to see Streger.

"Have you checked the stars recently?" Dec asked as they reached the door of Maeve's room in his Dublin townhouse. "Don't we need a wee Jupiter aspect or some such to make good things happen?"

"Are you kidding?" she laughed. "Other than doing Cochrane's chart, I haven't even looked at my ephemeris since the attacks. I'm afraid we and the stars may be on our own for this trip."

"Then let's celebrate, just in case it turns out to be justified by heavenly decree." He was a little in his cups and looked at her expectantly as he put his hand on her doorknob.

"Not a chance, my friend," she laughed. "I *never* count chickens before hatching. It's bad joss."

"Then to hell with the chickens. Let's just celebrate each other tonight, Maeve. We're here alone. We have no idea what the rest of this trip will bring. But we know we're good together. We've been friends long enough. Don't we really need to be more than that now?"

He looked so handsome and boyish in his exuberance, egged on by countless pints and an evening full of fun and no responsibility. She wanted to say yes, *yes*, of course, we should be lovers! Of course, I'd love to feel your touch. Of course, I'd love to feel you inside me … She caught herself on that last thought. She'd be going down a dangerous road with *that* thought. And where would it lead them? She'd be just another notch on his night table. No longer the unattainable Maeve Donovan, just one more passing fancy to discard when somebody younger or lovelier or richer came along—and all those somebodies were probabilities in the life he led.

She was startled to realize how very empty that loss would make her feel. Loved madly, then left behind? She couldn't handle that a second time. And besides, she would miss his laughter and his intellect, his insights and the safety she always felt when they were together. The *God's in His heaven—all's right with the world* kind of safety she hadn't felt since her divorce.

"Did you just invent the need for this trip so you could seduce me?" She smiled as she said it.

"I do have to admit the thought crossed my mind."

She reached up and touched his face. "My very dear Declan," she began, trying to sound serious through a slight tipsiness from all the Guinness they'd consumed at the pub. "You have a queue of women lining up to get you into their beds, so you don't need me to join the crowd. And what if it didn't work for us? Our friendship would be ruined. I'd have no one to teach me billiards or fly me to castles. You'd have no one to tell you when to buy low and sell high …"

He was looking at her, amusement and confusion in his expression, trying to discern what this banter was covering up and what the truth was of her feelings toward him.

"And what if it *did* work?" he pressed. "What if we are the perfect fit of puzzle pieces? Think how happy we'd make Dougal."

She laughed at that. They both did, and it gave them a chance to escape the awkwardness. She reached up and kissed him lightly on the lips.

"Just to assuage your ego, I should tell you I *know* the loss is mine tonight," she said as she opened the door.

“And mine, my girl,” he murmured as he turned a bit ruefully to head down the hall to his own room. “More and more since we started on this lunatic quest, I’m thinking it might be my loss, too.”

97

"Declan, lad!" His father's booming greeting seemed genuinely delighted, and the older man rose from his imposing desk to underscore the fact. Rumor was Desmond Fairchild had, on occasion, greeted even heads of state pointedly *seated* behind the desk, if he didn't respect their point of view.

The elder Fairchild was a good-looking man, strong and sinewy in his seventies, tall as his son with a head of silver hair so abundant it seemed a gift of the fairies as much as of genetics. Light as his son was dark—his looks a legacy of his mother's clan—the man had grown a trifle portlier with the years but still maintained a formidable appearance. He didn't look nearly as ruthless as Declan knew him to be.

"Come sit with me," he said after embracing his son and standing back to look at him appraisingly. "All the time you've been spending in America doesn't seem to have harmed you much, from the look of you."

Dec acknowledged the compliment, knowing it suited them both to be an ocean away from each other. They ran the companies well enough together, but they did business differently, and it was hard for successful men and their sons to find a balance between mutual respect, mutual competitiveness, and a mutual desire to escape each other. An ocean helped.

The elder Fairchild motioned him to sit. "Out with it, then," he said. "Is this visit business or pleasure? The woman you've brought with you doesn't seem easy to categorize, or so I'm told."

Dec wasn't surprised his father knew Maeve was with him. The servants in both their households were old hands at passing along juicy gossip.

"She's a good friend of mine," Dec answered. "We're only here for a stopover, as it happens. On our way to France." His father's quizzically raised eyebrow invited more information but Dec changed the subject instead.

"I might need your help," he said, causing a second eyebrow to rise. "I'm researching some World War Two-era information I think you might be able to help me track down, if you're game. It has to do with our family's dealings with Hitler."

"We haven't often seen eye to eye about that part of history, Declan," his father replied, a chill in his voice. "I don't know that I care to revisit the question with you now. Rather after the fact, wouldn't you say?"

"I don't believe my questions would compromise your convictions, whatever they were or are. And I'm not questioning your motives either, Father, this far after the fact. I know your father knew Hitler and did business with the Reich and I suspect that in turn you continued associations with the heirs of the Reich, but I'd be hard-pressed to believe you would have sanctioned the atrocities he committed if you'd known about the suffering, so let's not beat that dead horse. I would, however, appreciate your best guess about some facts that have recently come into my possession. Or, if you have direct knowledge beyond a guess, I'd appreciate your candor."

Desmond Fairchild steepled his hands in front of his face, a gesture his son knew well. It meant tread lightly, but it didn't close the door entirely.

Dec decided to get it all out on the table at once. His father hated few things more than pussyfooting.

"Do you think Hitler died in Berlin?" he asked. "Do you think the Third Reich ended with the war or did a covert Fourth Reich supplant it? Do you think Hitler's bloodline still exists, waiting to someday reassert itself?"

Desmond unfolded his hands and sat back in his chair before responding.

"The Hitler death story was poppycock. The Russians have chapter and verse on the fabrication. The Fourth Reich is alive and well under so many banners and in so many disguises it will never be rooted out, so don't try, if that's your crusade. As to Hitler's bloodline … there were rumors of some kind of pact he made in the last year of the war to ensure his dynasty, or immortality, if you will. Seems he had all those geneticists of his working on his dream of perpetuating his supreme Aryan lineage or some such twaddle, but even if it's true, I see no way to ever find the recipient of his unsavory seed, so what does it matter?"

"And what if there were a way to prove any of this?" Dec continued.

"Any man who tried would be a fool. And soon a dead fool." His father said gravely, "I've never taken you for a fool, Declan. A bit too idealistic for my taste, yes. A fool, no."

Both men let the thought settle. Finally, Desmond spoke.

"And this woman?" he said. "How does she figure in?"

Declan shook his head. "As I said, she's just my cherished friend, has been so for years. Let's leave it at that for now."

"I'd like to meet her," his father said. "Dinner tonight, perhaps?"

Dec shook his head. "We're on our way to the south of France this afternoon, Father," he said. "A rain check would be good."

"Indeed." Desmond said, rising from his chair with the agility of a much younger man. "I'll look forward to that."

Dec took his leave. There was no doubt in his mind from his father's tone that he knew a great deal more about all three questions, but getting him to part with more than simple corroboration was unlikely. And besides, it was enough for now. He took out his cell to call Maeve to let her know he was on his way back. As he walked, he had a mental picture of their two fathers meeting, and a fleeting answer about which of the two was the richer man.

98

"Why the hell won't you leave this fucking obsession alone, Heinrich?" Werner's anger at his brother's relentless carping about the stupid dead woman was as virulent as his anger at himself for not having found her fucking dossier. Shit! Heinrich was like a dog with a bone. And such a vicious dog.

"And why do you persist in calling me Heinrich when the whole world calls me H?" Heinrich hissed the rebuke through clenched teeth.

"There is simply no place to go with this, *H*," Werner responded acidly, emphasizing the de-Germanized name his brother so preferred. "Let the old biddy go, and concentrate on the campaign. If the attacks on Donovan's nearest and dearest didn't shake anything loose, you're probably just barking up the wrong tree. The damned thing just doesn't exist!"

"Have you got operatives tracing her in Europe?" H demanded as if his brother hadn't spoken. "You do know this Maeve woman and Declan Fairchild are in Dublin together. And how the hell did she get her hooks into him?"

Werner knew the answer to that at least. "He's her client. Has been for years. They may be traveling together for some business of his. Or they may simply be fucking like rabbits! She's not bad looking."

"So you've left *that* undone, too, Werner? Did it not occur to you to have them followed? Perhaps I'd best see to all this myself."

"You can see to it yourself and then stick it up your ass, *H*. As this dossier of yours doesn't appear to exist, it won't hurt much! And who the hell do you think you are speaking to in such condescending terms? You're letting this whole business unhinge you. Give it a goddamned rest!"

Werner underlined the statement with the grand gesture of getting up and stalking theatrically toward the door.

"I'm not finished!" H sputtered after him.

"But I am!" Werner said as he slammed the door behind him and smiled. Now the ball was in his brother's court and good riddance.

Maybe he hadn't taken this seriously enough, pushed hard enough, given the job to the right man, but if Heinrich was right, what was the worst thing that could happen? A derailment for his son on the way to the Oval Office? And would that derailment be so bad? If Heinrich's son lost his bid for the presidency, his own sons were just as personable and rich, and a new race started every four years. Besides, it wouldn't hurt for Heinrich and his golden child to learn what second-best was all about for a change.

Werner found himself humming as he left the office for home. He'd call his son Jonathan when he got there. Maybe it was time to float the idea of his dabbling in politics in a more serious way. Now that the current president was in the White House, billionaires with political agendas were quite the rage in Washington.

99

The view of the Mediterranean from the portico of the old villa in Villefranche-sur-Mer was breathtaking. Turquoise water in a sheltered lagoon shimmered invitingly beneath white cliffs wreathed in the abundant flowers for which the Côte d'Azur was famed. Dec leaned on the elegant stonework railing and breathed in the beauty. "God really does great work when He puts His mind to it, doesn't He?" he said, meaning it.

"Don't be so quick to give Him all the credit," Maeve responded, equally awestruck and happily absorbing the welcome sunshine. "I think he just delegates the work to Mother Nature and she handles all the landscaping."

The ornately carved double doors behind them opened and they turned to see an ancient man in a wheelchair enter. He had a gold-headed walking stick laid across his lap, so perhaps he could walk in the best of times, but for now, he was rolled toward them by a pretty young woman in a nurse's uniform. She smiled and beckoned them toward an exquisite white wrought iron table and chairs as she said in charmingly accented English, "Herr Streger wishes you to join him if you would be so kind. Cook is preparing a light lunch and it will give him the greatest pleasure if you will dine with him."

"Welcome!" the old man interrupted in a remarkably clear and vibrant voice. He had quite obviously been unusually tall in younger years, and even in the chair he seemed for the most part unbowed by time. He offered his hand to each of them and clasped firmly. "Welcome to my home," he repeated. "I so seldom have visitors, I trust I've not totally forgotten how to be a good host."

He gestured them to be seated. "I must tell you your phone call took me by surprise. I was quite unprepared to imagine that the names you have invoked from the distant past would ever again be spoken at my table. I am therefore already in your debt for having given me the opportunity to reminisce and to speak of a story known to very, very few." His gaze strayed for just a nano-moment to some long-ago landscape they could not see.

"We're very grateful to you, Herr Streger, for seeing us," Declan began. "We've been on a rather quixotic quest to find some truths long buried and we believe you may hold the key to at least some of them."

The old man nodded, his expression one of great curiosity and interest. "May I ask you how my name came to you in the course of this gallant quest?"

"I regret I must be the one to give you this very sad news, Herr Streger," Maeve interceded gently. "You see, Ghisella von Zechandorff Wallenberg was my next-door neighbor in New York City for many years. Her recent death precipitated our quest for answers and it was from her that my father learned of your existence."

"I see. Then I'm afraid I must ask you how Ghisella died," he ventured, obviously concerned about the answer. "Not that death is a surprise at the ages both Ghisella and I have accumulated but …" he let the thought trail off.

"She was murdered." Maeve said the words quietly, gravely. "I'm so sorry to have to tell you this."

"So," he responded with emphatic regret. "The bastards found her at last. Mein Gott! After all these years, they finished the evil they'd started so long ago. It is unthinkable."

Neither Maeve nor Dec knew what to say to that. Streger took a moment, as if deciding something important, then said unexpectedly, "You will call me Dieter. And you will tell me all you know of her. And I will do the same. Never, never did I imagine I could tell this tale to a living soul. Not even my children know of it … know of her, my Magdalena. Herr Professor's so beautiful and brave young wife." His eyes brimmed and he wiped away the moisture with a hasty gesture.

"If I had been one week sooner at that cursed prison, I could have saved them both, you know? But I had to take such care, such pains, to save them at all, the red tape was nearly insurmountable and it slowed me down. My father, you see, controlled the purse strings until I was a man of thirty years, as he controlled so much of that world behind the Wall. He was a hard and pragmatic man who had sympathized with the Nazis and then had welcomed the Russians when they came into power, because in this way he was able to keep the family fortune from confiscation despite the changing of regimes.

"I hated him for it, yet, in a bizarre twist of fate, it was this pliable conscience of his that was the only reason I was able to accomplish what I did for Herr Professor and Frau Steiner. In the case of the professor in 1935, I was able to bribe the Gestapo to turn a blind eye to his escape to Poland, and in the case of Ghisella, I could intimidate even the Stasi with the power of my family name."

He looked at Declan, animated and curious.

"You said in our phone conversation that you believed her to be the phantom spy, Magdalena? We took such great pains to cover our tracks so no one could ever find her … how on earth did you learn this buried truth?"

"*That*, Herr Streger, is a very long story and a very strange one," Dec answered.

"I have all the time in the world, young man," the old aristocrat assured him, "or rather, I have whatever time is allowed one of my years, and I promise you your tale can be no stranger than my own. Do me the kindness of letting us share with each other the details of a great and noble story that will otherwise never be known at all."

Maeve laid a hand on Dec's arm. "He deserves to know everything, Dec," she said gravely. "Without him there would have been no story."

Dieter Streger smiled a thank-you to her for the acknowledgement of his pivotal role in the past. "Perhaps what I know will help you a good deal in your quest, my young friends. You see," his eyes sparkled as he said it, "I not only purchased her escape from the Hohenschönhausen, I bought her dossier from the Stasi. And sent her to America with a new identity."

Maeve and Declan stayed with Streger until the nurse came to say he must rest. They shared what they knew from the diary. He told them what he'd learned firsthand from the Steiners themselves and later from the Stasi records. They were as reluctant as he to have their conversation end.

100

The day at the villa had changed something between them, Maeve knew, as she sat across from Dec on the dining patio of the hotel he'd booked for them in Monaco. The air was intoxicating, the scents of flowers and the sea making it sensual and uninhibited by everyday reality. Perhaps the romantic setting was responsible, or the old-world courtliness of a man who had recounted for them not only a tale of war, but a great love story as well. The kind of love story she'd always dreamed of but never experienced, perhaps because such romance no longer existed in the world.

Maeve looked at Declan through the glow of breeze-flickered candlelight, marveling at the handsome face, the strong Anglo-Irish bones, the easy grace of his long-fingered hands when he punctuated his words with gestures. The dark, abundant hair the Black Irish were endowed with, now touched with gray at the temples and worn just a tad longer than a businessman should ... and then there were those eyes that wrinkled just enough at the corners to look experienced and understanding.

They were an oddly deep gray-blue, like the waters off the wild Dingle coast, she thought, and serious enough to suggest he'd looked at life and found it amazing but not without a price. She tried to drag her thoughts back to the conversation, realizing she was also trying not to want him so very much and wondering when that had changed for her—from friendship to something harder to define and harder to control.

Ghisella was to blame, she thought. The heightened sense of adventure, mystery, shared excitement, because of her story. The intensity of their conversations that were no longer merely playful and entertaining. She wished she could trust her intuition in this moment, but where men were concerned that hadn't worked out so well for her in the past. She'd been told by her grandmother long ago that in this lifetime a scrim of unknowing blocked her psychic gift when it came to love. Where men were concerned, she was as blind and vulnerable as the rest of humanity. She made a mental note not to have another glass of wine in this dangerously romantic milieu.

"You know we're not just friends anymore, Maeve," he said as if he'd read her thoughts. "All the time we've spent with Ghisella and the others, all the time we've spent together on this adventure of ours has opened a door that we can walk through if we choose to. You must feel it as intensely as I do."

"That's the problem, Dec. I do feel it and it scares me to death. Our friendship has meant so much to me ... more, in fact, than I really ever admitted to myself. The fact that we were just friends made it easy. It meant there needed to be no pretenses, no conscious seduction going on between us. We could be honest with each other, and vulnerable. I love knowing you that way, feeling I can say anything to you without worrying about judgment or how my hair and lipstick look! Our friendship has meant I could just be me, the essential me, none of the subterfuge of flirtation."

"Come now, darling Maeve," he said, his eyes suddenly merry in the candlelight. "We've been flirting with each other for years. Admit it."

She laughed a little. "I suppose we have, but it was a safe flirtation. It wasn't going to land us in hot water or in bed. So it had no agenda ..."

"And maybe no limits?" he offered.

"Just pure joy," she answered, putting her hand on his larger one that was resting on the table. "Just delight and laughter and friendship and truth." She took a deep breath. "You mean more to me than you know."

"Then why, in God's name, if we're already all that you say—and by the way, I couldn't have put it better myself—why can't we be even more? I *want* you, Maeve. I want to touch you and hold you and make love to you."

It took restraint not to simply go with it. Into his arms, into his world in which everything seemed always to turn out right. Unlike her world .... She sat back in her chair and tried to get a grip on herself, tried to know what she needed to say.

"Our lives are so very different, Dec. Yours is all glamour and money and private plane worldliness. Mine is all family and home and hearth. And there's my work, of course—work that I really get a kick out of and feel secure in. How could we ever blend the two without losing something precious or being resentful at the loss?" She was trying to say so much without knowing how.

"Your homes are magnificent, astounding really, but mine is warm and soft—filled with love and memories and family ties. Could our two worlds ever really mesh? Fitz would be the first to tell me to run off and be happy, but would I really leave him to face old age alone?"

Declan sat back, too, watching her closely, really listening. She could see in his eyes that he understood.

"We have so very much on our plates right now, Maeve," he said finally, carefully. "Perhaps we don't need to try to untie the Gordian knot tonight. We've at least opened our conundrum for discussion and maybe that's enough for now. We can leave brilliant solutions—and maybe even lovemaking—for another night." His eyes twinkled suddenly and his smile was knowing. "Especially as all my fine efforts to get you into my bed tonight seem to have failed so stunningly, and let me tell you that doesn't often happen."

That made her laugh out loud. "And *that* thought is not helping your case at all, my friend." She started to rise, but he caught her hand and brought it to his lips.

"This discussion isn't over, my girl," he said gently. "Not by a long shot." Then they both got up from the table and went out of the room, with his arm around her shoulders in a way that was both companionable and proprietary.

The gesture made her feel they'd backstroked to friendship. She couldn't decide if she was relieved or disappointed. Probably both.

When they got back to the hotel suite, Maeve took out the photocopies of the Streger passages in the journal, which she had brought with her to Europe in anticipation of meeting the man who had saved Ghisella's life. Needing something to take her mind off Dec, she unfolded the papers and reread them before going to bed.

Mrs. W's Journal

The Hohenschönhausen was the antechamber of Hell itself. We had been beaten on being taken prisoner, Gerhardt so severely I wasn't certain he was still alive when he was dragged past me as I was led to the dreaded interrogation complex. The cement buildings were windowless, inexorable and like a concrete homage to despair.

All in East Berlin had heard the stories and knew the probability of leaving this prison alive was very slim. Most captives, our informants had told us, prayed not for escape, as that was implausible, but for death. There lies in all of us, I think, the hope that we could withstand torture if faced with it—to save ourselves, our loved ones, our country—but we also carry the knowledge that every human has a breaking point and some things are simply beyond human endurance. Both thoughts were foremost in my trembling heart that day, knowing we were in the worst position of all because they had us both—they could use each one's suffering to coerce the other.

I was stripped and searched by a leering bitch who left no personal humiliation untested. Then garbed in an ill-fitting and dirty prison uniform and led to the office of a bureaucratic troll of a man, who, in the disinterested tone of an accountant, said my choices must be made now. Would I choose a hot or cold cell? he asked like a desk clerk at a cheap hotel. I knew from rumor that neither choice was bearable. Freezing brought almost immediate illness, sweltering brought extreme lethargy, torpor and despair. In neither could one sleep, even if the guards had not chosen to torment you with constant awakenings, intrusive light and disruptive sound. I chose heat, knowing the survival chance was marginally better there, and having suffered with weak lungs and bouts of pneumonia since childhood I was certain there would be no hope at all for me in the cold.

When the lethargic questioner rose from his desk and pulled his belt from the loops of his trousers, in my naiveté I expected to be beaten with it. Instead I was raped in the most perfunctory way, as if this horrific act of violation was no more than another box he must check off on a list of tasks to be completed to keep the files in order. Stupefied, injured, humiliated, I was pulled from his office by two brutish women and flung like a sack of laundry into a tiny, sweltering cell. There was a bed and a chair, nothing more, not even an ewer of water with which to wipe away the blood and semen from the rape.

Gerhardt was gone, and perhaps dead. My future was terrifying and most likely short. Probably in shock, my heart beating in my chest like the frantic wings of a captured bird, I sat down upon the wretched mattress and cried my heart out. So much for bravery, I thought, feeling shame and disgust at my own weakness. But I had so little left of myself with which to fight and never had I felt so alone.

It was at that moment I heard the first of my husband's screams of anguish, the sound of which has never left me. As the days wore on, he was frequently tortured where I could hear his cries. The agony he endured both weakened me and strengthened my resolve. I didn't know whether to rejoice that he was alive or pray for the surcease of pain that death could bring to him.

Maeve had to put down the journal, reach for a tissue and take a minute or two to regain control of herself before reading on. Even though she'd read it all before, this passage was very hard on the heart.

She dried her eyes, finally, and picked up the journal again. There were only a few pages left to read, but she felt she owed it to Ghisella to see her through to the end of this passage. It was, after all, the end not only of an era for this extraordinary woman; it was the moment when the Ghisella von Zechandorff she was born to be was left behind forever.

Mrs. W's Journal

The most brutal part of the Hohenschönhausen, where most atrocities were carried out, was called the U-boat. When the wall fell and this place of unspeakable horrors was destroyed, much of the evidence of its tortures went with it. But for those who were ever imprisoned there, nothing in this world or the next could obliterate the indelible memory of the U-boat and the despair it embodied.

In this underground hell, long corridors stained with mold and rust housed rows of cells beyond endurance. Tiny blackened cells, some so small one could neither sit nor lie, most lined with dense rubber. Scholars have said the psychological torture of sleep deprivation, hunger, unbearable temperatures and being told your spouse or children had been similarly imprisoned were the worst of what happened there, as this was a Stasi testing ground for psychological methods to break prisoners in the field. But if you were a prisoner, already weakened by the unendurable, what you feared most was the Chinese water torture chamber, from which few emerged alive and none emerged sane.

After weeks of the "softening up" of prisoners by all the techniques I have catalogued here and, in the case of the women, the addition of repeated rapes, the most recalcitrant prisoners were subjected to this nightmare device.

One terrible morning, the guards gleefully taunted me with the fact that Gerhardt had been taken to this blackened cell of doom, where he had been chained in freezing temperatures into a device that would drip ice water onto his head until he broke or died. After a time, they said he would feel as though a hole was being drilled into his head and he would go insane.

My beloved husband died there three days later.

Gerhardt had not betrayed the identities and whereabouts of his comrades, they told me, and he had refused to implicate me in his crimes, so I would be the next to be taken to the chamber.

Indeed, when I was dragged from my cell on that final day, emaciated, broken in spirit, in the depths of mourning for my Gerhardt and nearly catatonic, I no longer cared if I lived or died—I only hoped my weakness meant the end would come swiftly.

But I did not die.

As I was dragged along by the guards, it dawned on me that I was being pulled away from the water pit, not toward it.

We climbed the stairs that led to the tiger cages of the exercise yard—outdoor cages in which prisoners were left in rain and snow to perish of exposure—and we continued to the office of the commandant.

Confused and half mad with fear and grief, I was confronted not only by the commandant himself but by Dieter Streger, the old student of Gerhardt's who had been his friend before the war. In this man's eyes I saw shock and profound compassion as he took measure of my unspeakable condition.

He did not address the commandant with deference, as all others did, but rather with the kind of authority that is passed on by noble birth and the knowledge of true power. He gave succinct instructions.

"Herr Professor Steiner's body will be remanded with all respect and dignity to my men," he ordered. "Frau Steiner will accompany me to my automobile immediately so that medical attention can be afforded her. She will be taken to a place of my choosing for recovery.

"Is this perfectly clear, Comrade?" he added, obviously expecting an affirmative answer.

"It will be as you wish, Comrade Steiner," the man replied and I wondered how much money had changed hands to accomplish this miracle.

Dieter turned to me and quite gently helped me rise from the chair into which I had been flung by the guards.

"You are safe now, Frau Steiner," he whispered to me as he lifted me with strength and kindness, to as near a standing position as I could manage.

"We will be traveling to my home," he informed the silent commandant. "All appropriate papers have been secured and all documents signed. We will <u>not</u> be followed nor will my guest be harassed in any way." His voice was harsh and

brooked no equivocation. "Is this perfectly clear?"

The commandant nodded curtly.

"Do you wish my men to carry you, Frau Steiner?" he asked as we exited the office door, but I shook my head no, the small triumph of walking upright the only defiance left to me. I grasped the arm he extended, and we made our way out of the compound to the waiting limousine. I saw that an ambulance had been procured and followed us through the gates.

"You have my most heartfelt condolences, Frau Steiner," he said gravely when we had cleared the barbed wire and the gates of hell. "Herr Professor was an extraordinary man whom I admired more than any other I have met in all my years at university. A true giant intellectually and morally. I cannot tell you how deeply I regret what has befallen you both. I came as quickly as I could after hearing of your incarceration, but these damnable Soviets have entangled their machinations in such red tape it took me the devil's own time to secure your release. Had I been but a few days earlier ..." his voice faltered and I saw how distressed he was that he had not been able to save Gerhardt. He told me he had secured my husband's body so that I could say goodbye.

I had no strength to speak but I laid my hand upon his and turned my face away so I would not see his tears and he would not see mine.

101

After crying her way through the journal entries, made all the more poignant by their conversation with Dieter, Maeve hit the pillow drained of all but sorrow and exhaustion. She'd loved the marvelous old man at the villa, loved his story, loved his courage in bucking a tyrannical father to follow his own conscience, loved the puzzle pieces he had added to the extraordinary jigsaw they were constructing.

She sneezed twice because the immense feather bed she was snuggled in tickled her nose as it enveloped her, then in minutes, she was fast asleep.

The vision began for her in a dream. The most powerful ones always did—the first half of them, at least. The dream would begin to show her a story, then she'd suddenly be wide awake, sitting straight up in bed, watching the second half of the vision as if it were playing on a giant screen in front of her.

In this night's vision, she and Declan were in a country landscape she didn't recognize. It was heavily treed, a forest really, and beyond it lay a great river and the partially rebuilt ruin of a castle that overlooked both river and woods. She was seeing it in two time frames that overlapped each other, so it took a few moments for her to understand that the scene was *now* and some other *then*, superimposed on each other and therefore blurring the current images that were unfolding in the darkened hotel room. She struggled to sort it all out, the *then* and the *now* intersecting seamlessly but confusingly.

Maeve could make out several small outbuildings on the castle grounds in the *then* that no longer seemed to exist in the *now*. She could see great battlements and vast gardens long decimated by time and war. There was a hedge maze, a monastic herb garden, a folly. There were stables and a slaughterhouse and the great house itself, which had obviously been badly damaged, then rebuilt to a new architect's specifications, so that old rooms and hallways and underground passageways had been replaced or rerouted, yet both past and future passages were still contained in some molecular suspended animation.

Was it possible that all time existed at the same time in a given space, as Master Ling had once told her, with each era existing on differing frequencies so they didn't collide? She hadn't believed him then, but now …

Maeve forced herself to memorize all she could of the place before it faded. It was essential to learn all she could because once a vision fled she had no way to call it back. She looked for landmarks, signage, *anything* that would tell her where the vision originated. Germany, Austria, Poland? Somewhere else entirely? Then there was a flash of light, followed by another and another, then total darkness and a final flash, obliterating her view and plunging her back into real time in a warm bed in a chilly hotel room.

The vision ended abruptly as they always did, and she found herself staring at a wall in the darkness with further sleep highly unlikely.

102

"Can that magic carpet of yours make it to Poland?" she asked Dec at breakfast. She'd nearly awakened him in the middle of the night to tell him of her vision, but had decided that was playing with fire in her current off-balance state of mind and the growing attraction between them. "I think that's where I spent last night." She recounted the dream and its aftermath and he accepted her account with only a nod of the head.

"My flying carpet is, as ever, at your disposal," he answered, "but might I ask where in Poland we're going? Your vision seems to have shown you a *castle*, but it didn't tell you why or even where to find it—or did I miss that part of the narrative?"

She poured a cup of strong coffee, savoring its much-needed wake-up aroma as she sat down. "This gift of mine isn't like cosmic GPS, you know," she responded with a regretful sigh. "I wish it was that simple and came with instructions. Best I can figure it, my subconscious, or my good fairy or whoever it is who gives me visions, knows more than I do about what I need to know on a given day. Just clues, mind you. Never the whole story. So, after my vision last night, I got out the laptop and tried to find the castle I'd been shown. I figured it was probably Ghisella's childhood sanctuary, but I couldn't remember its long Polish name so it was no easy feat to track down, as that stretch of the River Queis is littered with the remains of more castles and great manor houses than you could shake a stick at, and most of what's on the internet about the area is in Polish or German. I didn't want to wake up Fitz or Rory in New York to tell me the name of the place shown in Mrs. W's book."

"I'll bet Finn could have told you in a heartbeat," Dec said, "and she stays up all night as any sensible twenty-two-year-old should."

"Why didn't I think of that?" Maeve looked momentarily miffed. "But anyway, I think I found the place online, and I'll ask Finn today to scan us some scenes from that coffee-table book of Ghisella's to see if it triggers anything. Most everything I found on the computer was in Polish, and we'll need a translator for the book, too, but what if that's where she hid the Protocol?"

"*If* she hid it," he reminded her," and *if* she kept it and *if* that's what she wanted us to find. And assuming affirmative answers to all of the above, exactly how many acres will we be ploughing through on today's mission?" His expression was both quizzical and good natured.

"Not more than five hundred I think, plus a forest," she said, nibbling on a piece of crisp bacon, looking deep in thought. "But this is no time to get fainthearted on me, Dec. You're the one who said we're on the verge of a big find."

He touched his napkin to the corner of his mouth to hide a grin. "So I did. And as you know, I'm seldom wrong about anything."

She tossed a roll at him, which he caught so effortlessly she couldn't help but laugh.

"I'll fuel up my carpet and if you'll tell me exactly where to tell the Blue Jin we're headed, we'll file a flight plan. How does an hour suit you?"

"I'm beginning to see there really are perks to having all the money in the world."

"Does this mean I don't need the Whistling Gypsy's minstrel harp to win your heart, as I'd thought I might?" The Irish lilt in his voice was as mischievous as the words.

"You won my heart years ago," she called over her shoulder as she left to pack. "It's the rest of me that doesn't know what to do about you." Then she was out the door and gone and he was left wondering how on earth to interpret what she'd just said.

103

"Poland, you say?" H Reese felt a genuine surge of excitement. "No one goes to Poland on a lark." He dismissed the underling who'd brought him the news. His target must know something important. At least *his* operative knew how to get things done. *Maybe* the damned thing wasn't kept in New York after all! Of course, if Werner had paid more attention to business when he sent that inept asset to get the information out of the old bat, they wouldn't have had to go to all these lengths to get what he wanted.

But no harm done, really. Once the Protocol was in his hands, the whole unsavory business would be over with once and for all. There was probably no way on earth for there to be any corroborating evidence, with the old woman dead. He just wished his father could be here to see it all unfolding just as it had been planned with der Führer himself—and to see that he had bested his brother in this as in so many other things over the years would be the frosting on the cake. Three generations it had taken to bring about Endsieg. But now it was nearly a fait accompli, and soon he could relax in the knowledge that he himself had been the one to eliminate the last threat to the final triumph of the Reich.

104

The plane touched down on a private airfield as close to the castle's rural location as was feasible to accommodate the Gulfstream. Maeve could see a Mercedes with darkened windows idling on the tarmac as she left the aircraft—Dec had borrowed the two men inside it from his Berlin office, which was just a few hours away, he explained, and he knew both men by name.

He gave instructions to the pilots about when to return for them, then briefed the driver and the man whom he introduced as both guide and interpreter. The drive would take an hour or more, they said, and arrangements had been made for full access to the castle grounds. The current owners didn't live there, and only the groundskeepers and a local farmer couple who tended to the property's needs were in part-time residence. The groundskeeper kept to himself and the couple would not be at the castle today.

The countryside was spectacular. It was easy to see why this stretch of Lower Silesia had been a prize jewel through centuries of varied rule: annexed by the kingdom of Bohemia, then the Hapsburg monarchy, then the king of Prussia before becoming part of the German empire and finally settling back into being part of Poland, as it first had been in medieval times. Maeve stared out the car window, breathing in the atmosphere of the place, absorbing the multilayered emotions of the passing landscape and trying to sort them. For centuries, the bucolic scene she was passing through had been the site of revelry and excess, and also a hotbed of bloodshed, anguish and war. She could feel its confusions in every cell. Layer upon layer of unresolved energies were trapped here in the aether of this ancient land that had endured so much, yet kept rising from its own ashes. The guidebook had proudly proclaimed that one of the great castles along this stretch was now being used by Disney as a faux Hogwarts for

Harry Potter weekends, but the feel of the whole area was more tortured than entertaining.

But they were on the right track now. She'd known it since the dream-vision, and all her psychic senses had been on high alert ever since they'd entered Polish airspace. She felt as if she'd been here before, lived here before. Psychic transference of some kind, she knew, as the only knowledge she had of this part of the world had come from Ghisella's diary and the internet, yet the landscape felt as comfortable to her now as if the memories of the place were her own. That was sometimes the way of it with important visions—they sucked her in on some cellular level and wouldn't relent until she'd done whatever it was the vision had been sent to accomplish.

Maeve had said little since they'd landed and she felt Dec's eyes on her as they drove in silence, but she'd told him she couldn't respond or converse and still keep her concentration where it needed to be, and he had acquiesced. She kept replaying Streger's words in her mind.

"Where did you and Ghisella bury Gerhardt's body?" she'd asked him in an early morning phone call before leaving Monaco.

"*We* did not bury him and there was no body," he'd answered, surprising her. "Ghisella had him cremated and she took his ashes with her to inter them somewhere on the estate that had been her grandmother's. I wanted to go with her on this journey, needless to say, but she told me she must do this alone. Her final goodbye to the man she loved was too intimate to be shared even with me." He'd sighed, remembering.

"I recall feeling somewhat miffed at the rebuff under the circumstances—I confess I thought myself her savior—but a part of me was touched by the poignancy of their love, so I simply made arrangements to get her there. You see, she had never had the means to secure closure about the loss of her entire family. No bodies to bury, no prayers to be offered at a graveside. Gerhardt's ashes stood proxy for them all, I believe. All the loved ones, all she'd lost. Such things are too profound to demand explanation."

Maeve had thanked him and asked one more question before hanging up the phone. "In what did she carry his ashes?"

"Odd that you should ask me that," he'd responded. "You see, I offered her an urn—a beautiful antique porcelain—as a repository, but she refused it. A box, she said, an airtight metal box large enough to contain her husband's ashes, was what she required. Something about not wanting anyone ever to be able to disturb its precious contents: I didn't press her about it. I simply obliged and off she went in her sad, determined way."

So their needle in the haystack was a sealed metal box that must have been about a foot square. Maeve had been glad to hear it. It was far easier to dowse psychically for metal than for ceramic.

Now all she had to do was get there and hope her good angel or her mother or Ghisella would send her the kind of directions she'd need to find what they sought. Despite Dec's misgivings, she no longer had any doubt whatsoever about what, besides Gerhardt, was in that box.

105

Rory's enforced inactivity had been driving her up the wall since the attack. The hairline fracture and torn meniscus she'd sustained when the ceiling fell meant six weeks on crutches or in a wheelchair. She couldn't be on the jobsite and she'd have to rely on the new project manager she'd hired so as not to lose the crew to other jobs while her leg mended. The woman seemed competent enough and able to handle the job—and, she had to admit, she was beautiful to boot and seemed like she'd be fun to work with—but none of that quelled Rory's agitation at being housebound.

She'd volunteered to use the downtime to research whatever leads Finn and Manny's photos, Georgia's documents and Itzak's pursuit of Ghisella's wartime associations in Germany could provide. There were so many cooks in the broth now, it was time for somebody to organize everyone *and* their intel into one intelligible whole. And she was just the girl for the job.

Rory knew she was a superb researcher and she got a kick out of computer-driven detective work. One of her first degrees had been in computer science, so she wasn't in the least intimidated by the Babushkas. Besides, she had an old pal from law school who'd ditched her law career same as Rory and had become a research librarian in the New York Public Library, so if push came to shove, she could call on Mandy for rarefied resources. *God bless computers,* she thought, and helpful friends, too, as she began cross-referencing the list of possible Paperclipped Nazis whose age, fortunes, inclinations, networks, progeny, net worth and/or areas of expertise could dovetail with the kind of secrets they now knew Ghisella had been hiding. They had plenty of data at their disposal, but maybe not in a form they needed to winnow out the "major monsters" as Finn called them. These sons of bitches were in here somewhere, she told herself, and by God, she was going to find them.

The BSI had narrowed them down to a handful of potential Johann Grusses. Georgia's picks and several likely matches from Manny's and Finn's research had been added to the prime suspects. Each had vast fortunes, each had sons and some had grandsons, with a moneyed hand in politics, *which really made you think twice about the state of the nation,* Rory thought wryly as she catalogued their varied power bases in Washington. None had any discernible scruples. Sadly for the country, that kind of self-serving political corruption expanded the field rather than narrowing it.

Okay, she thought, entering the dates, places, and the probability data Matrix had supplied into a spreadsheet so she could cross-reference that information with every characteristic she could think of that identifies an individual and makes him or her utterly unique. By her reckoning, there was a lot more to identity than facial and body specifics, important as they were. There were emotional proclivities, natural gifts, academic and business successes and a million other small and large social as well as physical details that went into making each individual unique and recognizable.

Rory frowned in concentration at the complexity of the list she was compiling. Identity was a combo platter of people's physicality and their emotional responses and moral compass, but it was also dependent on their time in history, whether they were in a war zone or were protected by money and politics, and about a thousand other variables she needed to catalog. *If* the Babushkas could use their astounding tech skills to somehow correlate the answers to all these nuances with the rest of the data they were recording, surely they could nail the bad guys.

"We're onto something, Kuma. We can *do* this!" she said enthusiastically to the dog who was curled up at her feet. He wagged his tail and roo'd his complete agreement.

"Great way to go, Rory!" T said when she handed him her compilation. He was trying to head off the erudite geeky explanation he knew Bridget was about to launch at Rory in answer to her question about what kinds of identifying surveillance already existed and how to access them.

"It's not just facial rec anymore, it's bodies and movement and emotions and DNA and anything else anybody can scan to make money," he said. "So your intuition about what we need to suss them out is right on. This list you've made goes a long way toward helping us create an algorithm that will help sort the field."

"Biometrics is *big* business and bigger to come," Bridget interjected. "Everybody's trying to cash in on the surveillance boom. Casinos use expression software to spot addicts and card counters, retailers want to know if you smile or frown when you see purple merch so salesgirls can show you only the purple thing you smiled at on the way in. Dating sites match people who have similar facial and body features or personal tells, hotels and restaurants greet you by name, to make you feel like a VIP. Law enforcement is trying to create a central registry with everybody's retinas, eyeball shapes, voices, walking styles, DNA, all recorded and categorized—not just criminals, mind you. *Everybody!*"

"Like how much freedom do you think we'll have left after all *that?*" Matrix interrupted. "We already live in a surveillance state. Now there's 3D imaging from the thirty million cameras on our streets, skin texture analysis that's accurate from scanned images, and worst of all, you don't have to give your permission to *anybody* for them to scan whatever part of you they fucking well please! And don't even get me started on what Facebook and Google sell to 'interested parties,' or how your devices can be turned against you by the alphabet soup federal agencies."

"After an interested party has your age, gender, ethnicity, emotions, sentiments, movement, stature, face, body, and genetic profile, just how much privacy you think we got left, girl?" T asked to finish off Matrix's diatribe.

Rory looked both disgusted and excited. "That's exactly what I thought!" she said. "It's all bad for humanity and freedom, but it's potentially great for our current needs so let's suck it up and *use* it to our advantage. If we can latch onto all *that* data about our suspects and then your genius quant squad takes all the individuating items on *my* list—like dates, money trails, politics, geography, etc.—we'll have an electronic tracking system that can pop out our perps, yes?"

"Yeah sure, easy for you to say!" Matrix responded. "All *we* have to do is *create* algorithms that can do all that! They don't exactly all exist yet, you know—or if they do, they're at the NSA. No sweat."

But Rory was psyched and not to be deterred. She tapped her list and said, "Sounds like there's no time to lose then, right? I know how you brainiacs love a challenge. I'll bet you a hundred bucks you can do it."

Matrix gave her the finger and Bridget glowered but said, "Okay, sweet talker, hand it over. We'll see what we can do."

106

Poland, Milewicz Castle Access Road

The two operatives in the black minivan had their instructions. Follow and surveil. Don't get spotted and take no action at all unless it appears the targets have already procured some unidentified object they seem anxious to protect. The orders had come from the top with enough caveats to make them understand failure was not an option. In their line of work, it seldom was, so no big deal.

This looked to be a fairly easy day. Mostly surveillance, maybe an easy takedown. Hit and run. Neither of the subjects looked dangerous nor did the bios they'd been supplied with suggest otherwise. The male subject was big and in good physical shape from frequent time spent with his personal trainer. He'd been in the military but primarily in intelligence, not combat. The female studied martial arts in Chinatown, but she was most likely a dilettante who used it as a workout tool like yoga or the qigong that was all the rage. Neither of the subjects appeared to be armed.

An easy day, maybe, but it never paid to be careless. They and their follow car took turns falling in behind the Mercedes so they wouldn't be spotted by anyone but a trained professional, which neither subject was. Once they reached the estate, the follow car would leave them to their task unless backup was requested, which wasn't likely.

107

The Milewicz castle was a marvel from another age. Even without the ruined castle walls that overwhelmed a portion of the facade and made the immense manor house appear to have blossomed organically from the leftover energies of the mighty stone fortress that had once protected this land, the sight was formidable. Crenellated battlements gave way to round towers and medieval loggias. Turrets marked the four corners of the edifice like plump sentinels and a mighty portcullis still yawned its ancient jaws beyond what appeared to once have been a moat. Beyond the castle walls was a mansion worthy of a fever dream.

Both Maeve and Dec were mesmerized by the sheer majesty of the structure and the view it commanded of the winding river below, the forest on its southern border and the majesty of the mighty cliffs it was perched atop. Cliffs that must have afforded its defenders a mountaintop advantage in every battle for nearly a thousand years.

"I'm not sure my castle holds a candle to Ghisella's," Dec quipped, taking in the dramatic grandeur of the place.

"Don't tell me you have castle-envy!" Maeve answered with a laugh. "Now that's a rarefied malady." She was feeling slightly less disoriented now, as if her body and mind had settled into a familiar landscape. But then she added, "Though I do have to admit this one has a palpable might even in its decay, hasn't it? What must it have been in its glory days when Ghisella was a child?"

Dec offered her his hand as they made their way along the uneven and rock-strewn path leading to the ancient portcullis that had once guarded the fortress entrance from invaders. It occurred to him that if their mission hadn't been so serious today, they both would have thoroughly enjoyed this mighty portal to the past and all its promise of a day's adventure.

The interior of the great house was a massive reliquary of unfathomable wealth and privilege, now frozen by time as inexorably as Pompeii had been captured by volcanic ash. Even in its decay, it seemed a fairy tale interrupted. A tribute to a time when a hundred servants were none too many to run a household that lit five hundred candles a night and laid fires in dozens of rooms each wintry evening.

Cobwebs and worse covered the shrouded antiques. Spiders spun their silvery webs from ancestral paintings to ancient Persian rugs and stranded bibelots. Light filtered tentatively into rooms that had once rung with careless laughter, then sobered under the tread of marching feet, and finally had been forgotten in the dust of time. In current times, only the oil- or cyber-rich could afford the upkeep on a place this vast.

"Hers must have been a dazzling childhood," Dec voiced the thought in both their minds. "My own boyhood home was lavish, but nothing like this magnificence."

Maeve thought of her own cozy childhood and wondered where a child of such excessive privilege would find most comfort in this gilded mausoleum.

"Let's try the nursery, the bedrooms and the kitchens first," she said with no particular conviction beyond common sense. "Children in Ghisella's era spent more time with servants than with family, so maybe she had a favorite nook or cranny she would remember in a time of need."

"That'll keep us busy enough," he said as he contemplated the immensity of the house and the number of cubbyholes it would provide to any child with the imagination of a newt for hiding-places.

"And we need to find the chapel," she added, remembering what Finn had told her. "Finn said Mrs. W spoke of the chapel as a place where she could hide out from grownups whenever that was prudent."

Three hours of fruitless searching later they broke for lunch, having realized the task they'd set themselves was hopeless without considerably more help.

The hotel in which they'd booked rooms so they could spend the night if their search ran late had packed a picnic basket for them and one for their driver and guide. Dec gave the men leave to take a half-hour break and then looked for a likely spot outdoors for their own lunch, as the gloomy cold and atmosphere of abandonment in the mansion was beginning to feel bone-deep and oppressive.

"With no one living in the house," Dec said, scanning the grounds for a comfortable place to sit, "I suppose the barest property maintenance is all that makes economic sense, but it's a pity, isn't it? These formal gardens look as if they could have rivalled Versailles." Now they were choked with sturdy vines that were only partially tended and the plants had either died or run riot over the elegant stonework perimeters. He led Maeve beyond the immediate periphery of the house and garden, seeking a spot where sunlight might have warmed a patch of ground enough for comfort. Finally finding a gazebo that offered a break from the rising wind they spread out the cloth and food, then settled in to eat.

Maeve was in midsentence about the surrounding beauty when it suddenly began to morph radically in her sight. The psychic shift was so unexpected, she lost her equilibrium and had to grip Dec's hand for support as her visual field changed to a nearly liquid state, the molecules of the landscape all in sudden uncontrollable motion. Images began imposing themselves on the scene, just as they had done in her earlier dream-vision, so she tried to make sense of whatever it was her instincts were attempting to tell her while fighting the nausea of disorientation. She couldn't let any detail of this escape her, she knew—whatever it had to tell might only come once.

"It isn't *in* the house!" she whispered, willing herself to stand up and sound coherent. "I think Ghisella knew the house itself would be vulnerable to future destruction so she couldn't trust it. She'd seen what war could do even to mighty structures, so she needed someplace more protected for her secret treasure … something like a cemetery or a catacomb."

"But our guide said the old cemetery and burial grounds were totally laid waste in the war," Dec reminded her. "The surviving tombstones were dragged away or sent to museums and the place was never again used by the family. We'll never find Gerhardt's grave if that's what you're thinking, luv."

She nodded and struggled to speak coherently although she was feeling bilocated in dual worlds now, and something completely beyond her control was compelling her to move. It wouldn't have surprised her if she suddenly began to babble in Polish. "Would you be willing to forego that sandwich to follow a hunch I can't explain?" she managed to say through the gathering visionary haze.

"I would, if a bit reluctantly," he answered, laying down his half-eaten sandwich with sincere regret. But he could see she was in the grip of something. "I just wish your inspiration had waited a quarter hour more before asserting itself. Where are we going?"

Maeve stood up, suddenly energized as a hound on the scent. "The cemetery was over there," she pointed to an overgrown area at the edge of the forest to the southwest. "But it was connected to the chapel and to the great house by tunnels, and I'm almost certain what we're seeking lies underground in a crypt of some kind. A burial chamber, maybe nearer the old dungeons? If the way into such a place hasn't been destroyed or permanently blocked, I think that's where we'll find Ghisella's box. I don't know why I didn't think to look for a way into it from the dungeon when we were in the house. It would make sense that they'd need a way to bury prisoners …" She let the grisly thought hang.

"We couldn't get out of that dungeon fast enough," he reminded her, "and we didn't find *any* evidence of a chapel in the house."

"Because it wasn't *inside* the house! It must have been a separate building that no longer exists but I think I might know where it was …"

Her eyes tracked the landscape in all directions, straining to bring into focus what she'd seen in her visions, trying to bring the *then* and the *now* into more coherent focus.

"I think it's one of the small buildings from my dream-vision, the ones that kept fading in and out so I couldn't be certain what they were. It might not be accessible from the house any longer but maybe there's an entrance of some kind from the cemetery? If we find it, maybe we can find a way into the vault."

The odds of finding an entrance to a demolished chapel and an underground crypt, after decades of war, destruction and neglect, seemed slim to none to him but he could see Maeve was not to be deterred.

"Let me get the men from the car to bring what tools we have and we'll see what we can find, Maeve. There's no cell service here—probably no cell tower for miles, so I can't just call them, I'll have to go find them, but it shouldn't take long. Show me where you believe the old cemetery was and we'll give it a go."

She watched him head out, scooping up his half-sandwich and eating as he went. The urgency was growing inside her, escalating from one minute to the next, so she turned toward the woods and started moving rapidly.

A large fallen tree limb, crumbled pieces of marble from the base of a demolished tombstone, a lone granite angel wing and a severed head of what must have once been a cherub were all that was left of what had been the family burial ground. An ornate iron gate with a family crest marked the entrance to hallowed ground but the fence that had once surrounded the place lay in fragments, buried in the haphazard debris of the forest that was encroaching to reclaim its own.

Dec and the men returned and began to clear away the mountain of leaves and downed limbs, having no idea what they were looking for. No remnants of a foundation or other evidence of a chapel or mausoleum offered an obvious entrance, and nature was winning back what had been taken from it, but Maeve was adamant.

Finally, after more than an hour of hard labor, the cleared foliage and debris revealed a large iron plate with a pull-ring in its center buried deep in the ground. It promised an entry to something, but it was obvious to Maeve that none of the men shared her excitement about finding out what might lie within. The late afternoon winter sun was sinking fast and the wind had turned bitter as they worked.

"We should get back to the plane, Maeve, before night falls, if we can," Dec said sensibly. "Finding anything at all in a darkened underground tunnel without serious lights and excavation equipment being brought in is a grisly prospect at best, a useless labor at worst. We can radio for reinforcements once we get back to the plane, and return in the morning with proper help and equipment, but it's far too dangerous to attempt anything further in the dark."

"No, Dec. Please!" Her voice was pleading, urgent and thoroughly unlike her. "If we leave, I'll lose the vision that's drawing me in. Something will go *very* wrong—we'll lose the advantage somehow, I just don't know how. If the Protocol is here, and I know in my gut it is, we can't leave without it."

"Bloody hell, Maeve, that makes no sense! It's too dangerous to stay overnight. The house will be freezing by now, it was cold as a witch's tit before the wind picked up. We're too far away to chance getting to the plane once solid darkness falls. The roads are unmarked and we're in territory we don't know well enough to risk traveling after nightfall. The only thing that makes sense is to head back while there's still a bit of daylight and begin again at dawn. I promise you I'll get you back here first thing in the morning with proper help."

"I *need* you to listen to me, Dec!" she shouted over the wind. "We and your men might be able to open the hatch if we pool all our strength together. If we can open it, we'll at least know if there's anything down there at all! It may be a dead end or just a hopeless maze of roots and debris, but I swear to you it's important that we get in there *now*!"

Dec sighed, defeated by the desperation in her voice. He signaled the men to bring what tools they had to try to pry up the iron hatch. Best-case scenario, he thought, trying very hard not to be angry at her unreasonableness, is that the damned thing wouldn't budge an inch or it would turn out to cover nothing more than a fancified toolshed.

The watchers in the woods had been told only to surveil unless it appeared their quarries had discovered whatever it was they sought. They could see by the recent spurt of activity that soon action could be required of them, so they checked their weapons and their night vision goggles. These yahoos seemed to intend to go underground if they could get that old hatch opened. They'd be easy prey down below if the hatch opened to a tunnel or room of some kind, but there could be a problem making sure they'd actually found whatever it was they'd come after before killing them.

The team leader decided to watch a while longer before signaling what should come next. The old hatch had probably rusted shut fifty years ago and wouldn't open without power tools, anyway. Odds were they'd give up for the night and leave.

108

When it finally creaked open on ancient hinges, the hatch made a terrible moaning sound as if its ghosts were protesting an unacceptable disturbance of their desolate resting place.

Freezing, mold-choked air rose from steps that had been carved into the same granite from which the old citadel had been constructed. Dark was falling fast now and the pit below the stairs was singularly uninviting and dank. Maeve started down the steps like one possessed but Dec caught her arm to hold her back. It wasn't like her to be so unreasonable and God only knew what was in that pit.

"Please listen to reason, Maeve," he said urgently, but she pulled away with sudden ferocity that startled him. "This isn't safe … you've got to listen to me!"

"It's here!" she said, as if that made sense of everything. "We're so close we can't stop now."

"If you're right and it's been here in this damp, freezing hellhole for half a century, another twelve hours can't matter! It may have disintegrated by now, and surely there are rats and all manner of vermin down there in that stinking pit and we're miles from medical help if anyone should get hurt…"

But she was already at the bottom of the steps so, cursing under his breath, he followed her, wishing every step of the way that he didn't have to, but unwilling to let her go alone.

Bollocks! She could be stubborn as hell. Who knew?

He stationed his men at the top of the stairs for safety's sake. God forbid that hatch slammed shut in the now-insistent wind, they'd be buried alive and without cell service they had no way to contact the men in the plane for help.

Both Maeve and Dec had only the lights on their cell phones to inch their way forward through what appeared to be a winding catacomb. The tunnel was long and confusing—it felt far from the surface, the air stagnant and filled with mold spores that made breathing a chore. The floor was hard-packed dirt, the walls earth and granite, both weeping with mold, moisture and all manner of organic tangles that seemed filled with chittering creatures.

"There's a chamber carved out of rock somewhere dead ahead," Maeve said excitedly. "It's full of burial niches and funeral regalia. That's where the box is but it's hidden in a gilded chest from another age. I can see it clearly now! I think it wants to be found, Dec, and something is leading me to find it." He didn't answer her. What was there to say?

Chirping, skittering creatures scurried past their feet and something slithered out of the way as they moved, but an arched doorway was now visible ahead of them. Iron bands on the old oak door that guarded the entryway would have made it impenetrable had the door not been jammed ajar by a pile of tumbled rocks.

Outside the door, a torch sat in a web-encrusted holder on the rock outcropping. Dec took a gold lighter from his pocket. His father had given it to him on his sixteenth birthday, telling him a gentleman always knew how to properly enjoy a good cigar. He almost laughed to imagine what his arrogant father would say about its current purpose. He swept the ominous spiderwebs away with the sleeve of his jacket and attempted to light the pitch that coated the torch head. When a sickly flame finally caught, he breathed a little easier, wondering how they could breathe at all in this godawful crypt meant only for the dead. He held it out for Maeve, who was already pushing her way inside the cavernous room that was just as she'd said it would be, a vast underground cathedral with burial niches studding the stone walls.

Caskets and urns filled most of the niches, but bones were visible where caskets had been damaged or simply succumbed to time. Jewel-encrusted chests stood beneath the openings and gilded weaponry was piled around them, seemingly ready for the dead to take up arms. Without conscious thought Maeve blessed herself with the sign of the cross and turned toward Dec.

"We have to find it and then we have to get out of here as fast as we can," she said, agitated but seemingly snapped out of the weird trance state that had propelled her through the tunnel. "Something is coming to kill us."

"Just the news I was hoping for," he said drily. "Are they ghosts or humans?" He was only half joking.

"Human and armed," she replied. "We were followed. They know why we're here." Her voice seemed her own again and that comforted him slightly, despite the warning in the words.

"My men won't let them get to us in here, Maeve—they both have sidearms. I didn't want to alarm you but just in case—"

"We need to find Gerhardt's box and some kind of weapons that are still usable," she interrupted so urgently he didn't question her further. She'd been right about all this so far.

The interior of the chamber was eerie as hell but splendid in its own ghostly way. Weapons from other decades or centuries glittered as the torch's light reached them. Broadswords and rapiers, épées and sabers, knives in gilded scabbards, daggers in jeweled sheaths. A king's ransom in antique armory awaiting the touch of long-dead hands. Dec picked up several blades and tested their weight and feel in his grip before choosing a saber and an épée, just in case. Laying them near the entrance door, he turned his attention to the casks, as Maeve chose a knife from the pile and shoved a jeweled push-dagger into her pocket.

They rooted through the chests hastily; some opened easily, some had to be pried loose, but halfway through the dozen or more casks that were filled with the artifacts of the dead, they found a metal container, nearly a foot square with a locked clasp and the Streger name engraved on it.

"If we could get this open we could leave the ashes behind where they belong," Dec said, hefting it. "I don't like disturbing the dead."

"I'll pick the lock," she answered, searching the ground for a pin that might be used as a tool and smiling a little at his dumbfounded expression. "My dad was a cop, Dec. He worried about kidnappers and taught Rory and me how to pick locks in case we ever got trapped and had to escape. God bless his foresight."

She fiddled skillfully with the lock for a moment, then yanked open the metal box and stared. Inside was a large, embroidered velvet pouch, presumably filled with Gerhardt's ashes. Beneath it was what appeared to be a waterproof envelope. She knew before opening it that this was the Endsieg Protocol.

Maeve handed the envelope to Dec, left the ashes intact, then replaced the box where they'd found it. Dec shoved the Protocol inside his shirt and they headed back toward the door to the winding tunnel just as muffled gunshots and the sounds of a scuffle somewhere far above them stopped them in their tracks.

Dec picked up the two weapons he'd chosen, putting the épée through his belt and hefting the weight of the old saber. Maeve wished she had a butterfly knife like the ones she'd trained with at the dojo, but what they had would have to do.

"You do know most people advise you not to take a knife to a gunfight?" Dec whispered as they reached the door. They heard the scurrying sounds of vermin in the tunnel and knew someone was moving toward them. Dec swore softly. These were not his men. His men would be calling out to them by now, but there were only stealthy steps disturbing the silence. Both his men must be out of commission for anyone to have gotten into this catacomb, and that was very bad news. The men in the plane were ex-military, but the two in the car were not. Either they'd been surprised or outgunned. Neither boded well.

"I'll kill the torch!" Maeve whispered, dousing the flame in the dirt. Dec nodded. Dark would be their friend in uneven combat and the tunnel was long and winding enough that it would take a minute or two for the intruders to get to them.

"The only advantages we have are that they don't know exactly where we are and that we're armed," he whispered.

"Without the torch, it's black as the hammers of hell down here," she whispered back. "At least we know the lay of the land."

Any edge counts in battle, he thought, *including confidence in your plan.* "We *must* surprise them as they enter, Maeve," he whispered urgently. "If it's only one or two, we stand a chance, but only at the entrance."

Maeve's heart was pounding so hard in her chest she thought it must be audible outside her body. Soundlessly, she and Dec positioned themselves on either side of the entry door, which was still ajar, and tried to judge timing by the approaching sounds. Their inadequate weapons and their wits would have to be enough, and there would be only one chance to surprise their pursuers.

Maeve forced herself to remember Master Ling's instructions. *Play the fight in your mind first. Let your training take over, so muscle memory prevails. Remember to control your breath. Make the decision <u>now</u>, that you will disable your opponent or kill him without hesitation, if there's no other choice to stay alive. If your opponent is bigger, better trained or better armed, dim mak may be your only way to leave the battle alive.* She only knew two dim mak moves, but both were deadly.

She willed her breathing to calm and listened to soft footfalls nearly on top of them now. As no beam of light radiated ahead of the steps, they must be using goggles to navigate the tunnel. Such goggles had flaws as well as virtues.

Good.

They screwed up your vision once they were off. Especially if a sudden light was turned on you.

Maeve checked her cell phone in case she could use the flashlight app to blind them momentarily, if the goggles were dislodged, then decided the knife in her hand was the better bet.

The first man came through the door weapon-first, but a ferocious slash of Dec's saber knocked it from his grip. So much blood sprayed Maeve thought he might have taken the man's hand off, but couldn't be certain in the pitch dark. The startled second man's shot went wild, but he rallied instantly and barreled into the chamber firing as he moved. Maeve slashed at him viciously from the side as he passed her and the unexpected impact of the big curved blade and the woman behind it sent him sprawling, his weapon flying from his grip as she landed on him. She could hear Dec in hand-to-hand with the first attacker but had to concentrate everything she had on the man who had rebounded and was now on top of her, outweighing her by fifty pounds.

There are no rescuers. Master Ling had said that a hundred times or maybe a thousand. *You rescue yourself or you die.* The man's goggles had wrenched loose as he fell but there was no way to get to her cell light now. His weight was crushing her and his hands were grasping for her throat, no way to get to her other weapons even though her right hand was free. Desperate to breathe, Maeve flattened two fingers and drove them knifelike into the man's right eye. He roared with pain as blood and viscous fluid spurted from the wound and he loosened his grip on her throat just enough so she could free her other hand and grab his earlobe. She wrenched it down and outward with all her strength, causing so fierce a nerve pain that he reared his head back instinctively, trying to shake her hand loose, but in doing so he exposed his Adam's apple.

She struck with another ferocious knife-hand blow, powered by absolute desperation and the need to breathe. This time he crumpled sideways and rolled off her just enough so she could scramble to her left and make a grab for the weapon he'd dropped when he fell. Sensing the move, her enraged opponent flew over her to get there first, but Maeve's jackknifed legs caught him full in the solar plexus and the satisfying crack of ribs not only lifted him and flung him into the wall, but it gave her the heart to keep fighting.

You have not the upper body strength of a man, Lulu Ling had taught her, *but the power of your hips and your legs can put an opponent through a wall.* How many years had Lulu and Master Ling drilled her in Wing Chun, a kung fu style created five hundred years ago by a young Buddhist nun as a woman's fighting form? A form meant for fighting close to the body, where a man's longer arms and legs and superior weight could not put a female fighter at an impossible disadvantage. She saw the man's knife clear leather as he rose to come in for the kill, but she had the gun in her hand now, and he was the one with the knife in a gunfight. The sound of the head shot reverberated in the echoing burial chamber and the man dropped before the sound had died away.

Breathing so hard she thought her lungs or heart would burst, she turned her head to see Dec, alive and breathing hard, too, kneeling over his downed and bleeding opponent, who was either dead or unconscious. She saw that the man's right hand had not been severed by the first saber strike but was badly damaged, and the blood loss from such a wound must have weakened him severely.

"You're alright?" she managed to gasp and he nodded.

"Amazing what fifteen years of competitive fencing can accomplish," he said, panting. "That, and a bit of luck. If there'd been a third man we'd be dead now." He stood up none too steadily and reached out a hand to pull her up from the dirt of the floor, too, just as the sounds of voices calling their names echoed down the tunnel. One of the pilots, sidearm in hand, rushed the door; the other was carrying a lantern that illuminated the scene.

"Everything under control here, sir?" the captain asked, seeing the two men down and noting the bloody knife and saber as well as the assault weapon on the ground beside them.

Dec nodded affirmatively. "How the devil did you know we needed help?"

"We got worried when you didn't return by dark and we couldn't raise anyone on the radio. I'm afraid we have casualties above, sir. The driver and interpreter are both alive but one's lost a lot of blood from a gunshot, the other's badly beaten and unresponsive. We brought satellite with us and we've radioed for help, but there may be trouble with the local authorities about all this—so if you've got some kind of pull, this might be a good time to use it."

"Bloody good idea," Dec said. "I'll borrow your phone for that if you don't mind, Captain, and as odds are we'll not be getting out of here tonight, we'll need to get back to the hotel as soon as the authorities are done with us. Can you handle that, too? And good work using your initiative to come after us. I won't forget."

"Thank you, sir. Just doing my job."

"And very well indeed. Now let's get us all out of this crypt and leave the dead to rest in whatever peace they can find here."

He reached for Maeve's arm. "I told you we were good together," he said, and she had almost enough energy left to smile in agreement, but it hardly seemed appropriate under the circumstances.

109

"Okay, kid, here's the scoop," Millie said, munching on the new chocolates that Cochrane had brought her. "I had fun tracking it and I asked Doc just to be sure there wasn't any new intel not in the database. I told him a friend was writing a book." Millie and the chief medical examiner of New York went back a long way.

Cochrane perched on her desk and she raised a disapproving eyebrow but went on. "Der Fucking Führer's suicide was most likely rigged: even the FBI now agrees. I checked. Looks like the intelligence community knew he'd skedaddled to Argentina on a U-boat and knew all about the big scam while it was happening, but it was better propaganda if he was dead, so dead he was declared, even though all the evidence pointed in a different direction. So, the DNA that people *think* is his from the bunker, the shallow grave and the clothes on the corpse, plus a piece of skull somebody stashed in a museum, is most likely all bogus."

Seeing his disappointment, she continued hastily. "*But* there's been a pile of new activity about all this in the forensics world ever since 2009, when an anthropologist from the University of Connecticut was allowed to take DNA samples from the bone fragments found in the supposed grave outside the so-called suicide bunker. He proved it was a female skull, so not our boy—so the FBI had to release its formerly redacted appraisal of the story! By the way, Stalin said it was a hoax from the get-go and so did General Patton, so there you have it.

"Anyway, after all that, a Belgian journalist named Jean-Paul Mulders teamed up with a Hitler historian named Marc Vermeeran to collect saliva samples from known living Hitler relatives in Europe, and would you believe a great nephew of his was found living right here in Gotham. What they found was that all the samples were from one haplogroup called E 1b1b that's rare in Western Europeans but common among North Africans, and present in eighteen to twenty percent of Ashkenazi Jews and eight point six to thirty percent of Sephardic Jews." She looked triumphant, then added, "A haplogroup shows genetic origin, in case you're not up on your forensic science."

"So you're telling me the son of a bitch who killed six million Jews was really a Jew?" Cochrane looked suitably appalled.

"Looks probable, but hard to pin down and cloaked in mystery and scandal besides." She said it with exaggerated relish and popped another chocolate. "Some say his father, Alois, was born to an unwed woman named Maria Schicklgruber, impregnated by Leopold Frankenburger, a Jew. She later married a guy named Johann Georg Hiedler—later spelled Hitler—and little boy Adolf took that name. There's also a story on the internet, so who knows about *that* provenance—but it says that Alois's biological father was also the grandfather of Hitler's mother Klara Pözl, so there's a possibility of incest in the ancestry, too. We all know there were bats in the belfry, so hell, why not a little incest in the DNA chain. I'm just saying…" Millie looked so smug, Cochrane realized there had to be more to come.

"But that's *not* the big news here, I'm sensing from that cat-that-ate-the-canary look on your beautiful face?" He raised a questioning eyebrow. "Gimme a hint, here …. Is it worth Godiva?"

"It's worth Willy Wonka's whole freaking factory," she said, deadpan, but he could tell she was dying to spill the beans.

"You might have to take an IOU on that one … or maybe a field trip to Dylan's Candy Store?"

"You are a sweet talker, Cochrane," she chortled from some subterranean place where she kept her laughter tucked away for special occasions.

"What would you say if I told you I'd turned up three bona fide Hitler relatives living on Long Island?"

Cochrane craned forward in his chair. "No way!"

"Way, dahling," she responded, handing him a file folder with official-looking photocopies and a bunch of old newspaper clips.

"There were three brothers, sons of Alois Hitler, Jr., who was Hitler's half brother on his father's side. It's all in the file. They lived in Patchogue, hiding in plain sight in front of God and everybody, for decades.

"There are more cousins in Europe, but you might hit pay dirt right here in Long Island. I've got death dates on some of them, but their progeny live, so you just need a genetics guy to tell you how viable DNA evidence is after it's been diluted for several generations."

"You're a miracle worker, Millie!" he said, meaning it. "And I owe you for this one."

"Do I ever get to know what this is about?" she asked, seeing his genuine excitement. "The doc and I will be interested because of the New York connection."

"I'll check out this intel and let you know as soon as I can, Mil; you have my word on it!" And on that he and the notepad he'd been writing on were gone, leaving her both laughing and wondering why in hell Hitler was on the radar of an NYPD detective *now*.

Elated by the news, Cochrane left Millie, pondering his next move. He surprised himself by wanting to hand Fitz *something* that would make a difference in the case. Was it just one-upmanship and the desire to say, "See what I found that you didn't?" Or was it that he'd genuinely gotten a kick out of the old guy and his Don Quixote–style *Mission: Impossible*?

Cochrane laughed a little at his own introspection. He suddenly knew exactly what he wanted to say to Fitz, so he took out his cell and dialed.

"Say, Donovan," he opened when Fitz answered the phone, "Just how well do you know the commissioner?"

"And good day to you as well, Lieutenant," Fitz said amiably in reply, "and in answer to your question, he's not exactly a hearty of mine, but

I've known him both well and long. Is there a reason you're wondering about my acquaintanceship?" He didn't sound annoyed by the question, just amused.

"We gotta thin the herd, as your Texas Ranger would say. We got too many unsavorys running around loose, and it occurred to me that *one* of them put the arm on the commish to squash the investigation. If we could get Tarantino to spit out a name, it might tilt the board in one direction or another."

"And Donovan," Cochrane relished the news he was about to deliver. "I may have found you some genuine Hitler DNA that could clinch the ID if you come up with anything to compare it to. I'll keep you in the loop."

Fitz chuckled. "A lovely thought *that,* Lieutenant. And now I suppose I can see why some of the guys like you," he echoed Cochrane's words, mischief in his voice. "I'll see what I can do and get back to you."

110

Rory, Manny, Finn and Matrix spread out the collective charts, photos and dossiers on the long table in Manny's loft and he turned on the overhead light. A large computer screen showed photo comparisons sent over by Annie, and Rory's spreadsheet dominated the table's center. The intel from their varied sources had led them to this moment of reckoning. Before this afternoon was over they planned to know where Hitler's seed had taken root or die in the attempt. Looking at the over privileged faces of the contenders, now all displayed on the monitor, it wasn't hard to believe that any one of them could be the Hitler spawn. They'd narrowed the field down to three potential families, each with maddeningly similar histories, money and political ambitions. But what came across most in the photos was the self-satisfied arrogance on all the faces they were staring at.

"*Masters of the Universe*," Manny murmured with disdain.

"*The Devil Wears Prada*," Matrix pronounced.

"They *are* well groomed for monsters," Finn deadpanned. "You gotta give 'em that." Everybody laughed.

The whiteboard was littered with bits and pieces of three generations of three famous families and every bit of data they'd collected from dozens of sources. The Babushkas had produced algorithms able to hit all the individuating characteristics on Rory's master list and more. They'd assessed everything from physical and emotional characteristics, to provable whereabouts from the end of the war till now, to propensities for neurosis or psychosis in any of the male lines, to political pretensions, and a host of other variables too multitudinous to name. It was a magnificent piece of techno-detecting far beyond what any police department, probably including the FBI and Homeland could have duplicated, but the final answer still would have to be a choice made on gut instinct, or as Rory called it, "the grace of God and a fast outfield."

Rory had made a master plan of characteristics and information she believed could pin the tail on the Nazi, and Annie's troop had found a way to vet reams of variables and information. Fortunes had been traced, businesses catalogued, affiliations to Germany logged, then state-of-the-art facial and body language recognition had been employed to cross-reference characteristics of the Hitler Inner Circle to the next two generations of the "American success story" progeny they'd been able to track down.

The last of the data had been inputted and the assemblage waited now, feeling like contestants on *Jeopardy* anticipating the clue that would win the jackpot. Finally, pages of code stopped flashing over the screen at lightning speed and Matrix said, "And the winner is …" then stopped short, shouted, *"Yes!"* then pronounced, "The Reese clan, the progeny of Johann Gruss, born September 3, 1900 in Dusseldorf, reborn as H.W. Reese in 1945, by the artificial insemination of his file with bogus creds formulated by our very own OSS and the addition of an American-heiress wife. In 1946, said wife gave birth to twin boys, Heinrich and Werner, but by then Gruss had magically turned into Reese and vast sums of blood money had magically turned into a flourishing international business empire attributed to hard work, smarts and governmental connections.

"The terrible twosome—let's call them Tweedledum and Tweedledee Reese—went on to make a great fortune greater still, and to become model citizens who gave to the right charities, supported the right causes and fathered the right children, one of them currently a senator from New York on the fast-track for a presidential nomination!"

"How certain can we be of this ID without DNA?" Finn asked the question on all minds.

"Exactly 96.356 percent," Bridget answered. "Best we can do at this point. DNA would cinch it but if that's not possible, this is the best we can hope for. But the numbers are pretty conclusive anyway. And the fact that Johann was so easily assimilated into the US because of his having an American wife and a ready-made American fortune would probably have meant he didn't need to get a new face, so we have quite a few bits of genetic and biometric data that add up. A couple of his grandkids are dead ringers for Johann, by the way. It's the nose.

"Number Two choice on our hit parade is the Shlossburg dynasty out of Pittsburgh, and Number Three the Linzer crowd out of New York and Philadelphia. One has a pharmaceutical fortune, the other made its ill-gotten gains from pesticides and genetically altered food crops, and they're all crooks. Unfortunately, all three families have the right creds to take the crown."

Finn broke in. "Call it gut feel or an artist's eye, but my money's on Reese. Tyler buys art at the gallery and I've seen him up close and personal there and at one of Mimi's functions, and there's just something about him that raises my smarm-alarm. But it makes me nervous that all three of these families have the creds and the chops for this, so let's keep going. I think Grand has an idea up his sleeve, in case we need a tiebreaker."

111

"Sorry to tell you this, Mim," Finn said solemnly over a glass of wine in Mimi's living room that evening. "If the needle lands on the Reeses you may have to take one for the team to get Tyler's DNA." Mimi was so prim about sex, it made Finn merry just to suggest it.

Mimi looked indignant. "Not *that* one, I won't! He's a great dancer and a miserable human. I found that out at the party. It galls me that if we'd only known *then* what we know *now*, we could have gotten his saliva that night from the catering staff."

"Not to worry, Mim," Finn responded. "I can probably get him to spit at us if I key his new Ferrari."

That caught Mimi in mid-sip and she nearly choked with laughter. "Even *that* would be preferable to my having to go on a date with him. Besides, now that we know we may be able to get a definitive sample of Hitler's DNA from his Long Island relatives, we may be closing in on the real thing—but we're not quite there yet. My genetics colleague agreed with Cochrane's ME friend, although he said he heard on the grapevine there could be a genuine Hitler body in Argentina, so he's looking into that for me, too. So for now, I'm saved!"

"I think we'll nail it tomorrow, Mim," Finn said. "We're all meeting at Annie's to see where the last of the AI input lands us. She says she has created some sort of AI gizmo that's programming another AI gizmo, so they're competing and making each other smarter! Really cool and utterly incomprehensible to us mere mortals. Also a little scary, but in this case, useful. Want to be there for that moment of truth? We still don't know what Grand has up his sleeve."

Mimi shook her head no. "You'll have to text me. I'm in the NICU all day tomorrow and I wouldn't miss that for the world. I think the baby I've been babbling to you about will get into her mommy and daddy's arms for the first time and I want to see that happen." She beamed at the idea and Finn grinned. Mimi was such a truly good person despite having all the money in the world. It just showed how you should never make generalizations.

"Excellent," Finn declared. "We'll be unveiling the sins of the past and you'll be beaming at a hope for the future. Very balanced. Master Ling would be proud."

Mimi's happy expression clouded over.

"Do you really think we can pull this off, Finn? I mean, let's say you figure it all out tomorrow, does your Grand really know what to do next—like what to do about all we now *know*?"

Finn got up from the fluffy sofa and stretched the kinks out of her long body. She really should get home, now that everybody was so worried about everybody else and probably with good reason.

"One step at a time and by the seat of our pants," she said. "That's how we've done this from the get-go. We never exactly *knew* what we were doing, Mim. Why stop now?"

When they got to the door Finn said, "Don't forget to set the alarm—you know how well that works!"

"I'm thinking of getting a big dog. Kuma has inspired me." Mimi said musingly. "That's probably a more secure system, don't you think?"

"Absolutely!" Finn laughed. "Not only would he bark an alarm, he would corner the perp and eat him if necessary."

Mimi giggled. "So glad you said *that*! It reminds me I've been dying to tell you the great tidbit I found out from my geneticist about Hitler, but I kept forgetting."

"What'd he tell you?"

Mimi grinned. "It seems Hitler had only one testicle: he claimed the other had been blown off in the First World War. But rumor has it that the truth is the other was eaten by a dog when he was a boy. So when he got into power, he tried to wipe out the whole breed that had de-balled him!

They're called Bouvier des Flandres and they weigh a hundred fifty to two hundred pounds. He declared *all* Bouviers had to die and they were added to his list of undesirables. He practically wiped out the entire species, but a few escaped and now they're highly prized. So as a gesture of support for so discriminating an animal, I thought I'd get one of them … or maybe two. I mean, it's a big house, right?"

Finn laughed and hugged her friend and Mimi closed the door after her, thinking maybe a two-hundred-pound dog would be a really good idea. Ever since the break-in she'd felt skittish in her own home, and she didn't like the feeling one bit. Besides, the Bouvier story would make great cocktail party fodder.

PART X

Endgame

"Never send to know for
whom the bell tolls;
it tolls for thee."

— John Donne

112

It was well past midnight before the Polish police let Maeve and Dec go. They'd answered an inordinate number of questions over and over, had called in heavy-hitter help from both the American and British Embassies—facilitated by Dec's father's coterie of friends in high places—and they'd made use of Dec's corporate law firm in Berlin.

They made it back to the hotel in such bedraggled, mud-caked condition they provoked disgruntled stares in the hotel lobby as they passed through, but were just too whipped to care.

Dec walked Maeve to her door, neither saying a single word in the elevator or the lushly carpeted hallway. They were all talked out and the exhaustion that had come after the adrenalin of the fight in the crypt had left them both utterly depleted.

"I'll not trust this to the hotel safe," Dec said, patting his pocket as they reached her room. She nodded understanding, overwhelmed by all that had happened. Finding the Endsieg Protocol, nearly dying to protect it, and killing a man was just too much to process. What was there to say about such a day or its implications for the future safety of her family?

Numb with fatigue, Maeve fumbled as she attempted to use her key card and her hand was trembling as she tried to turn the gilded doorknob. Dec covered her hand with his larger one. "Do you want me to stay with you tonight?" he asked quietly. "It's been a terrible day and—"

"I'm okay." She cut him off in a voice that belied the statement. "I just need a hot bath and maybe a glass of wine before I can calm down enough to think about all that's happened. It's all too much to wrap my head around isn't it, Dec? I killed a man…" she looked up at him and there were tears in her eyes. Her expression was not triumph at survival and at having fulfilled their quest, it was an amalgam of sorrow, guilt, confusion and exhaustion.

He pulled her close for a moment, feeling the beat of her heart, breathing the warmth of her skin, wanting so much more, then he let her go. "You had no choice at all, Maeve. You must know that, we could both be dead now if you hadn't pulled that trigger. There simply was no other choice you could have made in that moment." He saw her nod, but knew she was far from okay with what she'd been forced to do.

"I'm going to secure extra help from my men. You don't have to worry about anything … not for tonight, at least. I'll be right next door and my men will be on guard with a convoy at their beck and call, if need be. My father has called in all but the United Nations and SEAL Team Six by now. I promise you'll be safe."

She nodded. There was so much she wanted to say to him; she just couldn't right now, couldn't sort it out or know what any of it meant, couldn't find the words. She nodded, then let herself into the lavish room, turned the thumb latch and engaged the chain. She stood for a long moment, back against the door, then on unsteady legs crossed to the bathroom. She stripped to her skin, uncharacteristically dropping a trail of clothes on the floor as she headed toward the tub. Then, naked and feeling terribly alone, she turned on the taps in the tub, poured in half a bottle of something that smelled of lavender, but instead of getting in, she sat down on the porcelain side of it and cried her heart out. She wasn't even quite sure why.

Less than an hour later the doorbell rang and she answered it in the soft cotton robe she'd found in the bathroom closet.

Dec stood in the doorway, his large body filling most of the frame. "I want to come in," he said simply. "Don't say no, Maeve. Please just don't say no."

113

Maeve stepped back from the door wordlessly and Dec walked into her room, then turned to face her, an expression she couldn't name on his face.

"Why have you never wanted me to make love to you, Maeve? No witty rejoinders, no obfuscations, no lies, please. I need to know." The question was so unexpected and out of sync with this awful day … but there was something so earnest in his voice that it made her want to tell him the truth.

"I think I've never *not* wanted you to make love to me, Dec," she answered simply.

"Then why have you always said no to me? I want so damned much to be here for you, Maeve, but I never know if I'm doing more harm than good by trying. What am I missing here? Please, help me understand."

Maeve drew in a long, deep breath and let it out, slow as a sigh. "I'm afraid." She said it simply, too weary for anything but small truths. "I'm afraid to trust my own instincts where men are concerned. Mostly I'm afraid if I ever let myself feel the things I want to feel about you, it will destroy our friendship and …" she hesitated, "and I'm afraid that would break my heart."

He resisted the urge to just take her into his arms and overwhelm her with his wanting; that wouldn't do at all. It would be unworthy, too cliché, and she was far too vulnerable for him to take advantage.

Besides, what she was saying to him was really a question, as well as a statement, wasn't it? What are your intentions? it asked. Where are we going? What do you want of me? Am I to be just another passing fancy? If I give myself to you, body and soul, what are you willing to give in return? A question that had been a long time coming. He needed answers to those questions as much as she did, and she was far too precious to him to be trifled with. He must be very, very careful about whatever words came next.

"I need to stay with you tonight," he said finally. "I need to know you're safe." And as he said the words, he somehow knew the answers to the questions she hadn't asked.

She nodded. "I'm very tired, Dec," she said, barely able to get the words out.

"I know, Maeve," he answered. "I'm not that far behind you. Lie down, luv, and I'll watch while you sleep. At least as long as I can keep my own eyes open."

He led her to the bed and covered her with a quilt. Then he nestled himself in beside her, fully clothed, put his arms around her, and kept his promise.

Maeve woke up in Dec's arms and it took her a minute to remember exactly what had happened. And what had *not* happened. She glanced down and saw that the robe she'd slept in had fallen open sometime in the night and his large hand was resting proprietarily on her breast, but she was sure they hadn't made love. That must have been a really difficult choice for him, she thought, not sure if she should be chagrined or amused. It would have been so easy for him to have crashed through the last of her defenses last night, considering all that had happened to them and between them in the previous twenty-four hours. But instead, he hadn't tried. He'd taken her at her word, and that meant a great deal to her.

Or did it simply mean that in the end, he, too, had decided not to lay their friendship on the line?

Dec was waking up, too. She felt his even breathing change, felt a subtle movement brush her nipple as he tried to move his hand to more neutral ground before she woke up. His touch sent a ripple of urgent desire all the way to her core. She felt him hesitate for a moment, then turn to wrap his arms around her in earnest. He buried his face in her hair and said very softly, his lips next to her ear, "I am going to make love to you, if you'll have me, Maeve Donovan, I promise you that. Not here, not now, not because of all that's happened to us in the past few days, but just because I love you."

And she heard in his voice that it was true.

114

FitzHugh Donovan waited in the lobby at 1 Police Plaza for his audience with the commissioner. Francis Tarantino wasn't quite an old friend, but they'd known each other since boyhood and he'd been an ally for the years when Fitz had been on the job. He'd even tried to convince Fitz not to take early retirement, and had shaken hands with him on Fitz's last day on the force, looked him in the eye and said, "If you ever need a friend or a favor and it's in my power to oblige, you have my word on it."

Fitz had never asked until today. But Cochrane was right about this. Knowing who had put the fix in might be the tiebreaker.

The pretty young brunette who was the commissioner's personal assistant came to retrieve him from the lobby. She looked just a bit older than Finn, but Fitz assumed she'd been on the job at least five years to have been tapped by the PC for this responsibility. She'd be an ambitious young officer with superb shooting skills as well as administrative ones, and she'd be smart as a whip, loyal to a fault. He admired all those creds and thanked her when she let him into the commissioner's sanctum sanctorum.

Tarantino rose from behind his big desk and came forward to grip Fitz's hand in a well-practiced shake. Everyone knew the next step after NYPD police commissioner was politics.

"Long time, Fitz," he said. "What brings you here after—what is it now—ten or twelve years?"

"Eleven years, eight months and ten days," Fitz responded with a short laugh. "But who's counting?"

Frank Tarantino chuckled and motioned him to the tufted leather sofa. "Must be something important, then," he said. "I don't imagine you just dropped by to say hello after a decade."

"No, indeed. I'd not waste your time on a less-than-worthy cause." He leaned forward. "I need to know who put pressure on you to put the squeeze on the chief about dropping the murder of my neighbor."

Tarantino leaned back and contemplated Fitz's intent. "I'm sorry to say that information isn't readily available."

Fitz cocked an eyebrow. "And why is that, Frank?" he asked.

"You might say it was a favor asked by a friend who was afraid his privacy would be breached by an investigation that would come to nothing anyway. I looked into it and couldn't see any point at all in wasting city resources."

"Did your 'looking into it' go so far as to see the attempts on my daughters' and granddaughter's lives, by any chance? I've not known you to be the kind of man, Frank, who'd turn a blind eye to attempted murder." He let the thought hang.

Tarantino sat up straighter. "Certainly not!" he said. "Aren't you being a bit dramatic about this, Fitz? An accident in an old house doesn't have any connection to a subway incident or the attempted kidnapping of an heiress .... This is Manhattan. Things happen here."

Fitz's face made it clear he wasn't buying the dodge.

"Cut the bullcrap, Frank. We've known each other too long and too well for blarney to sit well between us. I'm not asking you to reopen the investigation: in fact, I'd put the arm on you to keep it closed tight as a prelate's purse if it came to that. I'm just asking you to tell me who put the fix in."

"Now hold on a minute, Fitz, let's be perfectly clear. There was no fix put in. That's patently ridiculous. It was just a bit of gentle pressure."

"Alright, then. Man-to-man, and it never leaves this room, mind you, who applied the gentle pressure to see that the case was closed? You'll not be wanting to take the death of one of my children to your grave with you over some gentle pressure, would you now?"

Tarantino sat back and Fitz could see the calculation going on behind his eyes. How much would he lose if he told the truth? How much could he trust Fitz if he did so? He remembered Fitz's daughters as children who had gone to Sacred Heart with his own kids.

"I can't be certain," he said finally. "My pressure came from the mayor, but this is his last term so he's collecting friends for his foray into national politics. Word is, several very heavy hitters in the RNC are pressuring him to run for the senate. That kind of race takes big bucks, and as far as I know he doesn't have that kind of money himself."

"Give me three names," Fitz said sharply, cutting off the political ramble, "and this conversation never happened. We've narrowed the field to the likeliest blackguards and your names could be the clincher, so I'm calling in that favor you promised me eleven years, eight months and ten days ago."

Commissioner Tarantino snorted a response, and, unwilling to commit anything to paper, he spoke three names aloud.

"Bingo!" Fitz said as the door closed behind him. One of the names was the right one. As soon as he hit the street, he dug his cell out of his pocket and dialed.

115

The BSI was somber as Fitz drew the shades on the windows and Finn hung the "Sorry to close early. Book Club tonight." sign on the door.

Each to his or her accustomed place now, Fitz thought as they settled themselves in without the usual banter. How far they'd come on this unexpected detour on the road of life, in little more than a month, and all with the best intentions. But then everybody knew the road to hell was paved with such as that. He drew a deep breath and looked at the worried faces around him.

The air was thick with nervous energy, anxiety and an odd disappointment, all in equal measure. They'd done what they'd set out to do, but from the look of things there was little joy in that. They'd unearthed the truth about Mrs. W and in the course of it they'd opened Pandora's box; having glimpsed the demons inside, what they now knew was almost too big and too evil to contemplate. Worse yet, it was far too big to fix.

They'd put themselves in real peril. The New York attacks and the Poland episode had made it clear they could be reached and could be killed if they didn't back off. Their only insurance policy was that nobody knew for certain if they'd found the Protocol in Europe, only that they knew it existed and had gone in search of it, and nobody knew for certain that they had the corroborating diaries. But those incidents had set the price for continuing to poke the bear.

So, what now? he thought, plumbing the depths of his own culpability in reaching this moment, as a saying of his mother's came into his head. "What's the point of being Irish," she'd told him, "if you don't know the world will break your heart." A case could be made that he'd had a right to place himself in danger for a just cause, but he'd inspired others to follow him into jeopardy, and his conscience balked at that. Nothing mattered as much now as keeping everyone from harm.

How do we put the lid back on Pandora's box, he wondered, looking at the serious faces, *so they all don't have to spend the rest of their lives looking over their shoulders? That* question was foremost on everybody's mind and it was up to him to provide the answer.

Fitz surveyed the circle. The people he loved most in the world were in this room, and with them were others he cared about deeply. All were here because he hadn't been able to let go of the mystery of the Old Lady's death, so whatever happened to each and every one of them was his responsibility. It weighed heavy on his heart.

He cleared his throat and all eyes were on him, so he forced his expression to soften into a somewhat rueful smile.

"We've got a mighty dilemma on our hands, now, haven't we?" he began. "No need to belabor the dangers we're up against. I doubt there's anyone here who's been thinking of anything else but the possible—no, probable—consequences of what we've dug up. That said, I believe we need to take inventory of all that's happened on this investigation—all we've unearthed and concluded from the evidence—all some of us have endured ..." he looked at the worried, intelligent faces with affection and admiration. They'd followed his lead into battle and now they looked to him to give them a viable battle plan. That was only fair. He just hoped he was up to the task.

"We need to be all on the same page before we decide which page we turn next," he said, looking around to see that all heads were nodding assent, "or whether we decide to close this book entirely. So, I think it's best if we take a bit of an inventory." He said this in a voice used to cutting to the core of things. "Here's what we know thus far."

"We know the identities of the two bastards who most likely ordered Mrs. W's death and the attacks on many of us in this room. But we don't have enough evidence to stand up in a court of law to prosecute them, and we don't know who else they represent in a cabal that's far bigger and deadlier than we knew when we began.

"We know these crimes and attempted crimes were meant to cover up other, far larger and more heinous crimes that go back to the war and before, but it's apparent now that engaging an enemy so big and so ruthless is well beyond our capability.

"We've surmised they meant to intimidate, not kill, us, but as several of the attacks could easily have been lethal, we can't be at all certain of our assumption.

"We know how powerful these forces we've uncovered are, not just the two brothers who spearheaded this operation but the vast cabal behind them. Not only has this cabal successfully covered up their long-ago and current crimes, but they've secured a damned good foothold on covertly ruling the world while they were at it. At the start of this, I don't think any of us could have imagined the magnitude of the enemy. In this particular game of thrones, I'm afraid they are practiced hands at it and we are naught but skilled amateurs.

"We know that a number of governments, religions, and powerful individuals have been complicit in allowing terrible truths to be perpetrated on the world and hidden from it. And we know our adversaries are both ruthless and conscienceless, so the odds against us are monumental.

"We also know an epic secret. Hitler's faked death, the continuance of Nazi power and the bloody bloodline. It's a secret the world deserves to know too, but we can tell them this secret only at great risk to ourselves—definite risk of ridicule and personal discredit, probable risk of death.

"We've learned that a nefarious cabal of evil power brokers is poised to put one of Hitler's bloodline into the Oval Office and we feel powerless to stop it. But even as I say it aloud, even knowing all that we know, I realize how mad and preposterous this statement would sound to most of the world.

"We also know our little army hasn't a prayer of righting all the terrible wrongs we've unearthed. At best, we can only—perhaps—increase awareness." He paused and Dec leaned forward to interrupt.

"But Fitz," he said, obviously moved by the older man's emotional recounting. "Surely, we mustn't forget we've also pulled off a magnificent piece of detective work here. Ghisella would be proud of us, I believe. We're more than a bit like her Resistance."

"Yeah!" Matrix said drily, "and we all know how well that worked out for her."

Fitz nodded at the exchange. "Indeed, you're both right. Small we may be, but we've managed a formidable feat … and a dangerous one. But cold comfort that gives us, knowing the reality of the dangers we face because of what we know."

He smiled a little at Dec. "So we're here tonight to say all that's on our minds and in our hearts, at least to one another. I believe we deserve to vent our spleens and then open the floor to everyone's best brilliance on how we proceed.

"And, perhaps, we might even take a moment to pat ourselves on the head for a job well and truly done, either way," Annie added.

"What if," Maeve asked suddenly, startling everyone out of their silent depression, "we start by pooling our best *what ifs*? And see where that takes us?"

"What the fuck does *that* even mean?" Bridget exploded the uncharacteristic expletive so forcefully that every head whipped in her direction.

"Shit and hallelujah!" Matrix yelled like a cheerleader, both fists pumped toward the ceiling. "I *knew* you could curse! I'm so proud of you!"

Bridget glared at her and spoke again. "What I mean is, we know a *lot* of valuable things, not just one big secret! Maybe we don't have to walk away from all of it … maybe there's a covert way to spread the truth."

"Right on, Bridge!" T agreed. "We got proof about thefts and lies and corruption in math, science, physics, the military, aerospace—where ideas came from and how they were sold to the highest bidder. We know who made the big bucks out of those lies and thefts. We know things about politics and famous fortunes and families … even if we back off the murder and the bloodline, we got a lot of intel the Babushkas can get out there into the world of science and whistle-blowers. It's not as easy to keep secrets now as it was in Ghisella's day."

"That's exactly what I mean by *what ifs*!" Maeve agreed eagerly. "Maybe we have more leverage than we think. Maybe everybody here is thinking about *what if* we could do just *this* one part of it? Bridget and T are right: maybe we don't have to do it all. If we think about a few things we *could* accomplish, maybe we'll feel better, and if the bad guys see we've backed off the bloodline issue, maybe they'll back off their threats."

"No chance of that, Miz D.," T cut in. "Hate to burst your bubble, but gangs don't work that way. They win by fear and force, so they don't ever let loose ends stay loose. They got the manpower to kill off loose ends, so that's just what they do." He looked around to make sure everybody got it. "'Cabal' is just a fancy word for gang. Gang go against gang, there's always blood."

"Unless you can broker a standoff of some kind," Dec mused. "Maybe barter the bloodline info for our safety … maybe say we'll leave the documents and the whole story with a major law firm and the New York or London *Times*, instructed to make it public if anything happens to any of us…"

Rory hadn't said a word all evening, but suddenly she thumped her cast on the floor, trying to stand up. "I have a crazy idea!" she blurted. "What if we have our own cabal?"

Confused looks all around the room greeted that. "I'm talking a *counter*-cabal of equal power and equal money and an equal amount of passion to checkmate these bastards who are so sure they're above the law."

"Where the fuck we gonna find *that* cabal, girl?" Matrix asked.

"Is there even such a cabal in existence?" Finn asked. "Like a secret White Hat Society nobody told me about? Or a Superheroes Club?"

Rory shook her head vehemently. "Not that I know of, but I think we might be able to *make one happen*." She turned to Itzak.

"How many Jewish billionaires do you know who have serious ties to the Holocaust?"

He blinked, thought a moment, then realized where she was going.

"Far more than a few," he answered. "There are dozens of great Jewish dynasties in New York alone with such ties."

"Exactly my point!" she said. "Think about it. Real estate, publishing, cosmetics, banking, theatre, you name it! My bet is, they all lost loved ones to the Nazis. Grandparents, great-grandparents, family fortunes, artwork, treasures, *whatever.* Surely they've been raised on all the horror stories … the cruelty, the losses, the tragedies. Surely they don't want Hitler's spawn in the White House any more than we do. What if we could talk them into helping us stage a détente?"

"Why should they?" asked Bridget. "They've already got it all, why risk it for us?"

"Not for us!" Rory said. "That's the whole point. For their own sense of honor and family. For history. For justice. For a great front-page story or a bestseller or a movie. Who cares why they buy in as long as they do!"

"My dad might help us," Matrix murmured, startling the room further.

"You won't even tell us who he is!" Bridget snarked. "Why would you be willing to let him out of the closet now? And how could he help us?"

"I never wanted to tell you for my own good reasons!" Matrix snapped back, "but he might help anyway with something as hinky as this. He's got big balls and the cash to go with them."

"I could ask my father, too," Bridget responded, her old prim self again. "I'm just not sure he actually knows any Jews." The laughter at that ingenuous statement burst the tension bubble in the room.

"Maybe they don't all have to be Jewish," Dec mused, intrigued by Rory's idea. "If a cause seems challenging enough, some very powerful people might be willing to pit power against power just for the gamesmanship of it. I know at least a few I could approach. No, I don't think they all have to be Jewish. I'm not. Most of the people in this room are not."

"I like it in principle," Annie said judiciously, "but it's treacherous terrain to navigate. If we ask the wrong power players and they alert the other side prematurely, the plan fizzles or triggers immediate payback."

"But if we pick the *right* ones and they'll play ball with us," Rory countered, "we might be able to broker a détente at the very least. Power usually wins because those with less haven't the resources to fight back. But power against *power*? Money against money? That becomes a test of testosterone, doesn't it?"

"A gorgeous, bold idea it is, Rory my girl!" Fitz said, squeezing Rory's shoulder. "I say we each make a list of possible people to approach. They'd have to be people we can speak to face-to-face, without underlings in the loop."

"We are gonna need so much more coffee, boys and girls!" Georgia announced, already on her way out the door. "An army moves on its stomach and there's a good chance we're not ready to leave the battlefield just yet." *And if that ain't a fact, God's a possum,* she murmured to herself as she headed for the kitchen. It wasn't that she thought food could make a difference. It was just that this was the only thing she could do right this minute to bring comfort to a roomful of very worried friends.

116

Twenty-four hours later the BSI all sat anxious and twitchy, lists in hand. Everyone had struggled hard to vet their own list of possible candidates for the counter-cabal. Each had narrowed their list and brought one or more candidates' names and bios to the meeting so they could collectively assess the possibilities and the liabilities, before approaching anyone at all. The notion of creating a counter-cabal had sounded so plausible when Rory suggested it, but if they let the cat out of the bag to just one wrong person …

Dec scanned the composite list he'd been handed and breathed a little easier. These were damned good names. Powerful names.

"I'd suggest we begin by going around the room, person by person, so everyone can make a case for his or her own candidates and hear the thinking of anyone who has an objection," Fitz began. "Many heads are better than one here, and one wrong choice loses a dangerous game. Agreed?" Murmurs and nods of approval met his suggestion. "Let's vet the list but leave questions about procedure till the end."

He started to sit down again, then said, "Before we begin, I'd like to suggest we blackball any clerics on the list. I see Father Zander's name here. He's the cardinal's second-in-command and I know him well. I like him, but I don't trust him to have any interests at heart but those of the Church, and as many of you know, Pius XII was a Nazi sympathizer and Ratzinger, who became Pope Benedict, was a member of the Hitler Youth."

"Scratch the whole bloody lot of them!" Annie said definitively. "The Church was an evil empire before anybody else thought of it …" Everyone laughed.

"My nominee is Estelle Sorenson," she continued. "She's the widow of a billionaire industrialist and uses her money to support women's and children's causes. I know her well. Her mother was an Army nurse who cared for and fell in love with a wounded GI in 1945. They lived a great life together until he died a few years later, when my friend Estelle was just a year old. Her mother later married a man who made a huge fortune in fertilizer, but Estelle says her mom never forgot her first love: the injuries he suffered in a German POW camp later caused his death. I trust her. She may not choose to help us, but she sure as hell won't betray us."

Fitz looked around the room for objections, and finding none gave the nod to Matrix, who was seated next to Annie. The girl looked troubled, not her usual cocky self. Sensing her hesitation, he asked, "Would you rather be called on a bit later, Matrix?"

"No!" she snapped the word out. "I can handle it now." She ran her fingers through her multicolored, multi-spiked hair and took a deep breath.

"Here's the thing," she said. "I already asked my dad to help and he already said yes. But he's like my secret, ya know?" No one in the room had ever before seen Matrix look vulnerable, so there was a small uncomfortable shuffling among the onlookers as they attempted, however subconsciously, to give the girl some space. Annie broke the awkward silence.

"No reason why he can't remain your secret, M," she said emphatically. "Whether he helps us or not. No one here would ever reveal his identity." She looked around the room for dissenters and found none. "I already know who he is and no one will ever hear it from me."

Matrix looked up and her eyes circled the faces in the room.

"He's A.D.," she said. "I'm his illegitimate kid." There was both pride and pain in the revelation.

A collective intake of breath followed. A.D. was an icon. Aging star of the rock group *Apocalypse,* who, like Mick Jagger and Steven Tyler, had miraculously survived from the '60s to now. Brilliant, intellectual, a born showman, A.D. initially trained as a barrister in Britain. Wealthy banking family, superb education. Filthy rich, great musician, credited with understanding the music masses and being able to continually evolve with their tastes. Flamboyant marriages, one to royalty, he was always a shock when met personally because people expected a wired rocker but found instead a brilliant, probing wit and a social conscience. But why, then, had he not acknowledged Matrix? Or had that been her own idea? The room was soundless.

"Here's the deal," she said, sensing the question. "He was born after the war, of course, I mean he's only seventy now. But he's the son of a woman who survived the camps and then married a wealthy Englishman. My grandmother gave him visceral knowledge of all she lost to Hitler and the Nazis, so I was pretty sure he'd support our cause and I was right. He's in if you want him in. He pretty much knows everybody who's important on the planet, and has more money than you could even believe." Seeing both amazement and confusion on the faces around her, she burst out, "If you're wondering why I'm a secret, it's because I hate his life! And his other children hate *me*. So I stay away. But he loves me and he knows I'm smart."

Maeve heard such pain and pathos in the childlike word—*smart* hardly described a 190 I.Q. like Matrix's—she reached a hand to pat the girl's leg, but Matrix pulled away from her touch self-consciously.

"It's complicated!" she said to end the explanation. "But he's in. Nobody has to know why."

Fitz signaled Rory with a glance and she took the floor to end the awkwardness.

"I'm suggesting Arthur Aronowicz, real estate magnate extraordinaire, but there is one caveat. Artie's an old client of mine who owns acres of the most expensive real estate in Manhattan, and he's actually a pretty good guy ..." she hesitated.

"And your caveat?" Fitz prompted.

Rory calculated how to succinctly express her reservation. "Artie's a friend and I think we could trust him, but he's head of a dynasty of real estate piranhas with holdings all over the tristate area as well as all over the globe. I don't trust the kids, primarily because I don't know them well enough individually, but also his son Teddy has political aspirations, and our story could be a bargaining chip for him with the politicos.

"But Aronowicz pulls the strings of a fistful of politicians in NY and Washington and he's known for his charm, wit and also his ruthlessness in negotiating, so his skills might be useful to us. His ties to the Holocaust are through his mother, who lost her whole family to Hitler's machinations. I've actually seen him tear up at the mention of how much he loved her and how much she suffered in the war. So I guess you'd say Artie's a definite maybe."

"Let's keep him on the list for the moment, shall we?" Fitz said. "Until we see how many probables we have to choose from, we should only delete those whom someone here has a genuine reason to mistrust."

Itzak leaned forward in his chair and spoke. "I wish to suggest an old friend and a long-time contributor to the Wiesenthal Center's work," he said.

"Jason Malosian is the son of Isaac Malosian, who was a legendary name in art circles in the twentieth century. Jason is, as I'm sure many of you know, art dealer to the wealthiest collectors in the world. He grew up hearing stories of his own father's pivotal place in the pre-war art scenes of Paris, London, Vienna, Berlin, so it was inevitable that he would follow in his father's footsteps. The original Malosian Galleries' clients in Europe included potentates, prelates and princes as well as the simply seriously rich, but all was lost to the Nazi storm troopers, who confiscated everything and exterminated both the dealers and the cognoscenti who had decorated their homes and estates with the work of masters, old and new.

"An entire generation of Jason's family perished, but his father somehow survived, penniless and bereft of all but his knowledge, his client list and his love for art. He began again after the war, and, as they say, the rest is history.

"Jason's commitment to Nazi-hunting is unquestionable, as is his integrity. I have known the man for more than half a century.

"I also intended to suggest Rabbi Shindberg, who has a different kind of power to wield, not based on money but on philosophy and a well-heeled congregation, but if Annie's concern about clerics includes Jewish ones, I'll replace him with someone else."

"Give me twenty-four hours and I'll get back to you on that," Annie said, holding her ground. "Organized religion has killed more people on this planet than the bubonic plague, so I don't trust any of them," Annie said. "But I trust you so I'll check him out."

Fitz saw that all but a few in the group were making notes on their lists. He turned to Maeve, who nodded and spoke up.

"I have two on my list," she began. "The easy one is Albert Lowenstein. Newspaper and magazine magnate. Al's very rich, *very* influential, very much the New York power player. He's been my client for years, and while he'd probably not admit it publicly, he's a big believer in astrology." Everyone in the room smiled, as many of them felt the same ambivalence about Maeve's belief in the stars.

"Al has a charming, low-key demeanor," she continued, "but wields enormous clout in media and politics. I've been doing his family charts for years, so I know his character well and that of his closest relatives. I also know his beloved mother's own mother died at the hands of the Gestapo. She surrendered herself to them in order to remain with her husband when he was arrested, but they were separated anyway and both died in separate camps. It's quite a love story actually, but all that aside, Al bears no love for Nazis.

"My second candidate is not so easy to praise or vouch for. Marietta Frangellica—who was born Miriam Rosenberg by the way—is the business brain behind her brother's spectacular fashion-design business. As I'm sure you know, they began with fashion, then branched into cosmetics, interiors, architecture and anything else that bears the stamp of unmitigated luxury. Her speed dial holds the most prominent names on earth from Milan to Moscow. Women, it seems, tell their high-end couturiers secrets they wouldn't even tell their hairdressers. She knows everybody's most intimate business. Which is both good and bad for us, I think. She knows everybody's vulnerabilities, but I can't be certain what she trades for all this knowledge, so she should probably go on the maybe list.

"I've been doing her family's charts for years, as she gives them all gifts of my charts on their birthdays, so I know her family, too. And I know she gives huge amounts of money to Israel in memoriam for her mother's and father's relatives who died in the Holocaust."

"So we have one more good bet and one more maybe," Fitz said as he passed the floor to Georgia.

"My Uncle Hutch is in," she said simply. "He'll help us any way we need him to. You all don't know him, but he's one mean son of a bitch in a fight, takes no prisoners and has more money than God. He's been running with the big dogs a long, long time."

"I wish I could say the same for my father," Bridget said primly. "About the participating part, that is, but after careful consideration and an analysis of the preliminary conversations I initiated with him as reconnaissance for our mission, I couldn't find anything that would make me feel certain he'd cooperate.

"I don't believe he'd betray us, but my analysis suggests he has no Jewish ties or particular sympathies, so it would be a foolish move to try to recruit him." She paused. "I'm sad this is the case and wish it were not. I might add that my extraterrestrial friends advised me not to ask him. But I do have some money I could access in my trust if that would help." She looked embarrassed but determined.

"No need for that, Bridge, money is not the issue here," Fitz said hastily, "but thank you, nonetheless. That's a sweet and generous offer."

"You've helped in many other ways, child," Itzak put in, feeling sorry for the girl. "We will find our counter-cabal, and for safety's sake, it would be best if everyone we recruit has skin in the game, as you Americans say … some genuine emotional connection to our cause." He smiled at her benevolently.

Finn spoke up, obviously wanting to relieve Bridget's distress. "Mimi and I have a possibility you could maybe consider, even though it might be better if somebody else contacts her rather than us, because she thinks of us as kids and might not take us seriously." She looked around to see if all understood.

"Leila Landrue was a friend of Mrs. W's, so I know her a little." That revelation took everybody but the other Donovans by surprise. The woman was a cosmetics legend with a business worth billions. "I met her at one of Mrs. W's tea parties. I'd just turned thirteen and was interested in makeup and fashion, so for my birthday surprise, Mrs. W asked Mrs. Landrue to come and tell me about makeup." She glanced at Mimi. "And I invited Mimi to come, too. When I told Mimi about it, she said Mrs. Landrue and her husband were social acquaintances of her grandparents'."

Mimi chimed in, "Which is how we know that a cosmetics queen, now in her nineties, is closely connected to the Holocaust. According to my grandfather, it seems Leila completely reinvented her past, so no one would know she was a child who lost her entire family in the camps and walked across Europe to get to America after the liberation. She was forced to sell her thirteen-year-old body in order to survive, but she finally connected with a man who helped her get started in the cosmetics and beauty world in Paris.

"After she got to America, she married the husband with whom she founded the cosmetic empire that now bears her name. My grandfather didn't really approve of her, but was an early investor in her business because he thought her husband was a genius accountant and she was a great saleswoman. He said it was a superb investment."

"Anyway," Finn finished, "we think she might have possibilities and I'm sure she'd bring her son who inherited the business, and if you can believe anything you read in the fashion magazines, he's a very nice man."

"I agree," said Itzak enthusiastically. "Her family gives a great deal of money to Jewish charities and causes. Her sons and her grandchildren contribute large sums to the Center."

"Good. Then we have another definite maybe," Fitz said with a smile, "and I can add one or two more to our list."

"My maybe is Senator John Weiss of Connecticut. He's a respected doctor of law who once told me over a couple of Irish whiskeys that he had a much-loved father who was a young lawyer and soldier in WWII, present at the liberation of Birkenau. On Liberation Day it seems his father made a promise to some famous legal scholar who'd been incarcerated there and was already dying when John's dad identified him in the camp.

"John told me this scholar, whose work he had admired in school, asked his father to promise to never forget what he'd seen in that hell on earth, and to do whatever he could to bear witness whenever possible. John said that as a tribute to his father, he had always done everything in his power to support Jewish causes.

"He might be one to approach, although with him being so long in the political game, I just can't be certain who his political bedfellows are or whether he'd be willing to engage in controversy of any kind."

He adjusted his perpetually displaced eyeglasses and said, "I have no such qualms about the Mandelbaum movie family and any number of their relatives. Theatre and banking seemed like the only categories we hadn't covered, and I couldn't think of a single banker or Wall Street guy I'd trust with a gold watch, never mind a secret of this stature, so I thought adding a theatrical dynasty might be just the ticket. You can probably take your pick among the Mandelbaum crowd. Movie stars, theatre owners, movie producers, playwrights, they've got them all in abundance; and the founder of their little theatrical dynasty died in

Auschwitz and her oldest daughter in Treblinka.

"Several of them have been my friends for decades. I expect one or more of them would step up, but if I had my druthers I'd pick one of the women. They're a force of nature, like a cadre of Jewish Amazons."

He thought a minute then said, "And then there's the oft-married Ava Bradshaw Chapin Eden Diementopolous, etc., etc.—too many names, I'm afraid, for even an old friend to remember. She's a philanthropist now with all the money from all those marriages *and* her own stellar theatrical career. She does a considerable amount of good in the world. She might even be coaxed into bringing along a few of her exes, as they've all stayed friends."

"And how exactly do you know all this, Dad?" Rory asked, trying not to laugh. "Have you been reading the grocery store tabloids instead of Mrs. W's journal?"

Fitz hesitated a moment, then said, "Well now," adjusting his glasses again. "That's a tale for another day, isn't it? But here's the short of it: everyone assumes she married for money, which she did in part as she'd been born poor—little Annie Brady, when I knew her in the neighborhood—and she had to make her way into a wider world than the Bronx by varied means, not all of them respectable. But I'd put good money on the fact that she loved each husband in turn. Annie manipulated men, not the other way around, a rarity in Hollywood in the old days, and every one of her husbands was mad about her, as I know, because I've been in the company of most of them on occasion. Wit, beauty and sex is a heady cocktail, not soon forgotten by any man.

"For now, let's just add her to the list, shall we, and I'll give her a call. Annie's not one to betray a friend's secrets. She has too many of her own."

Bridget looked up from her tablet. "Lovely!" she pronounced. "By my preliminary calculation, we have ten good bets so far, eleven including Declan, and four maybes, plus a pile of theatrical extras." She smiled at

Fitz. "We're a bit light on men, so we might want to add a couple."

"My father is willing, but only as an understudy," Dec said. "If we can't get enough others to commit, he'll reluctantly come along. But Antonio Ferrara of the international publishing family said 'yes.' I had a sense he thinks it will give him the inside track on a blockbuster bestseller, but perhaps that could work to our advantage."

"That helps even up the genders," Bridget approved. "So, if we agree that six heavy hitters could make our counter-cabal potent enough, that means four definites could say no and we'd still have potential for understudies. That gives us a comfortable margin to pull this off."

Fitz suppressed a smile at her quant exuberance and said, "Let's finish whatever questions we each may have, make a best-guess selection and form a plan of engagement."

"Let's put a timeline to this, too," Rory added, "and decide precisely how much to tell these people and how to present the facts. They're going to ask hard questions about our evidence and where it came from, but some of *that* we just can't tell them."

"We'll also need to give them risk assessments," Bridget cautioned.

"And they'll probably want to know who else has said 'yes,'" Maeve added, "so maybe it should be a two-step program. First, we float a hypothetical to each person on the list, then if they seem willing to go further, we swear them to secrecy and say we'll get back to them with data and details. *Then* we can make the final presentation to them when they're all together, show them the evidence, answer their questions and see if all these very powerful players are really willing to lay it on the line for strangers."

"And we don't leave *anything* with *anybody*," Rory added. "No paper, no emails, *nada*."

"Manny and I can do a video or PowerPoint to show them all they need to see," Finn suggested.

"Good idea," Maeve agreed. "And maybe there's more ammo we

can give them for whatever showdown we or they come up with."

"Like what?" Annie asked.

"Like *what* if this has the juice to be turned into a global news story, a book, a movie, a documentary? The people on our list have the creds to make all that happen, and the other side will know that. I realize all we're really trying to do here is stay safe and get a little justice for Ghisella, but what if letting it all hang out would pull their teeth? Wouldn't *outing* their secret publicly make us safer than just threatening them with what we've learned?"

"The bloodline is all they care about," Dec said. "Maybe we keep that as our hole card, so they have a real reason not to just kill us all now."

"A sobering thought, *that.*" Fitz replied. "Let's sleep on it."

Several hours later, Fitz watched the room clear of the BSI conspirators one by one or two by two and replayed the possibilities in his mind. How much would the people on this list really be willing to risk to keep Hitler's bloodline out of the White House? Lawsuits? Death threats? Business reprisals? Would the victims' families and friends have as much passion for justice as the perpetrators had for keeping their evil plan a secret? *It's easy to sleep on another man's wound* ran through his head. How much sleep would the people on this list be willing to lose over such a very old wound?

117

The people seated around the immense mahogany table in Dec's dining room could boast the net worth of a small nation—or maybe not so small, Fitz thought, as he watched them watch each other with obvious calculation and a certain wary interest.

They all knew why they were here, each having passed the preliminary meeting in which the hypothetical had been dangled. Now he saw them assessing each other in the knowledge that this was a unique gathering of extraordinary peers and must not be taken lightly.

Most of them knew each other, at least casually. Those who were outliers, like Hutch Walker, were known by name and reputation. Not all were friends, but all thoroughly understood the magnitude of wealth and power that was assembled here.

A.D.'s entrance had been the evening's highlight so far. They all owned the world, but he looked like it.

They'd met for drinks in the library first, so all the air-kissing and handshaking and surprised hellos were over with by now and with that, a certain gravitas had descended on the group. Until Desdemona Drake swooped into the room like a galleon in full sail. She'd been added to the list by Fitz as an afterthought. She'd been called the Empress of Broadway by *Variety*. Her endless blond hair streamed like gossamer threads tipped with platinum teardrops, her wolf-trimmed cloak looked borrowed from the *Game of Thrones* set. As she let it slide negligently to the floor—to be spirited away by fairies, Fitz assumed, amused by the spectacle—she rose to her full five-feet-eleven stature, then assessed the gathering for the most important person there to hug first. She surprised the well-heeled crowd by sailing directly toward Fitz.

"FitzHugh darling," she gushed as she planted a kiss on each cheek. "Where do I sign up?"

"You've already given me your word, luv," he said with a twinkle. "That's more than enough for any man."

"What just happened?" T whispered to Finn, obviously startled by the star-power.

"Grand saved her bacon years ago when he was a detective and she was accused of a murder she didn't commit. I think they've been friends ever since." She counted heads on the list of expected guests and said, "Only a few more to fill the dance card, unless one of them comes equipped with an unexpected plus-one."

As if on cue, the door opened a second time and Marietta Frangellica walked in, accompanied by an immense ebony-skinned sports star whose face was known to everyone at the table, and probably everyone on earth who hadn't been in a coma for the past ten years. Trailing behind the two was Sidney, Marietta's son and heir.

Last to arrive was Ava Bradshaw. Strikingly beautiful and statuesque in old age, she made as dignified an entrance as Desdemona Drake's had been flamboyant. Both great old dames, Fitz thought, with very different temperaments. Ava was flanked by four of her ex-husbands. Scooter Chapin, scion of the Boston Brahmin banking fortune, Charles Eden, courtly British collector of great horses, houses and art, and a true admirer of great women, Demitri Diementopolous, reclusive Greek shipping tycoon, and Isaac Shapiro, her long-retired Hollywood agent. As she greeted Fitz, she whispered something into his ear that made him laugh out loud.

Maeve reached over to lay a hand on her father's sleeve.

"What did she just say that made you laugh like that, Dad?"

Fitz chuckled. "She said the Dalai Lama was on board with us if we wanted him. Seems she gave him a call. She's a corker, that one. I told her I'd let her know if we needed him for backup."

"That's it then," Fitz announced, after greeting all the newcomers and giving them time to find a place at the table. "All present and accounted for."

Dec stood and the murmur of voices quieted expectantly. "I may be your host this evening, ladies and gentlemen, but I am not the originator of the quest that has brought you here. Very shortly, I shall turn over the floor to others whose courage and expertise have forged the links in the chain of evidence that has bound us to each other, and to the task we'll present to you tonight in hopes that you'll join us in bringing it to fruition.

"I know you would not have come had you not been intrigued by the proposition already sketched out for you by someone you trust. Some of your fellow guests, you should know, have already wholeheartedly pledged themselves to our cause. The rest of you presumably need to be further convinced of its worthiness, its veracity and its plausibility. All of you deserve to be shown all the evidence we have at our disposal. After you've seen the material we've prepared, we'd like to invite each of you to add to our plan your own thoughts on the best way to achieve our goal. You should, however, be reminded that you've already pledged absolute silence about anything said here tonight and about the identities of all at this table."

Handling this rarefied gaggle of titans is akin to wrangling cats at a crossroad, Fitz thought, watching the canny, privileged faces, each one paying close attention now.

"It all began for us only a little more than a month ago," Dec continued, "when a ninety-six-year-old woman asked FitzHugh Donovan, retired NYPD chief of police and her next-door neighbor, for help. She was murdered two hours later, before he had time to render that help.

"Several of you here know Fitz . For those who don't, you should be assured he is one of the most highly decorated officers in the history of the NYPD. For your information, we also have among our small cadre of investigators a Nobel Science prize nominee, two Rhodes scholars, a renowned legal brain, the foremost forensic archivist from the Wiesenthal Center, a young doctor, two lawyers, an astrophysicist, a theoretical physicist, multiple math prodigies and a mystic. A group as diverse as that on your side of the table, I might add.

"Now, we have a lot of ground to cover, so I'd like to relinquish the floor to Chief Donovan, who'll take you on the first leg of a remarkable journey."

Fitz thanked Dec and rose to his feet. He took the time to deliberately look each person at the table in the eye, taking their measure before he spoke.

"*The only thing necessary for the triumph of evil,*" Fitz began, "*is for good men to do nothing.* Edmund Burke said that, and I'm sure we'd all agree with the man. The trouble with doing *something,* however, is that it usually demands a risk or a sacrifice, and that's hard to swallow for most of us."

There was a soft shuffling of bodies as people moved into sharper listening positions. There was in Donovan's gravitas something that commanded attention and respect.

"Ghisella von Zechandorff Gruber Steiner Wallenberg, once known as the Magdalena, lived a hero's life. Others here will provide chapter and verse on that, so you can get to know her as we did in the course of our investigation. And she died a hero's death, a little more than a month ago, right here in New York City, because she possessed a terrible secret. A secret she believed would deny the Third Reich their final victory."

A murmuring arose around the table, and Fitz held up a hand to quiet it. "Yes, yes, I know, we all think of the Reich as ancient history now, but before this evening ends you may have reason to reconsider that assumption.

"But there's more here for you to know than political science, ladies and gentlemen. It's been said we live in a post-truth world now and, God help us, that may be true enough. But if so, it's a world with terrible parallels to the Weimar Republic and Hitler's game plan, and to the creeping infringements on freedom and humanity that culminated in the tragedies of World War Two. The free press vilified, the Constitution trashed, freedom abridged in the name of safety, surveillance everywhere, scapegoats chosen as a minority to hate, women treated as broodmares." He let the thought reverberate in the quiet room.

"*They came for the socialists and I did not speak out because I was not a socialist.* We all know the famed Niemöller poem, don't we, now?" The seriousness of Fitz's voice pinned them as he recited.

Then they came for the trade unionists
And I did not speak out
Because I was not a trade unionist
Then they came for the Jews
And I did not speak out
Because I was not a Jew
Then they came for me
And there was no one left
To speak out for me

"I believe we're in just such a perilous time again, and not by accident. The data we'll present to you tonight suggests it's been a long time coming because the foe is patient as well as cunning, and they are willing to play the long game.

"We'll show you a document signed by Adolf Hitler himself that promises to put one of his own bloodline in the Oval Office, no matter how many generations it takes. Long game indeed, and a chilling prospect. Closer to fruition than you might imagine.

"You could argue that this bloodline is naught but a symbol, yet symbols can be powerful catalysts. The flag is a symbol, yet millions have died for it. The cross is a symbol, the swastika, too—think about their weight in history. All it takes to change the face of the world it seems, is a symbol powerful enough to raise an army to do its work."

A murmuring rose and this time he waited for it to quiet. He had their attention now.

"The presidency of the United States is not merely a symbol. It's an extraordinary power base. One that can facilitate a deadly agenda that has been lying in wait to destroy our democracy and all it stands for, for three-quarters of a century.

"Can they fulfill their mad, evil plan? We think they might. Will it matter?

We don't know. Can we stop it and throw a monkey wrench into the works of their well-oiled evil machinery? We're going to open that very question to your collective brilliance, once you've seen the evidence we've assembled."

He surveyed the table. "You are all *powerful* women and men," he said. "So you know *exactly* what power and great wealth can do to tip the balance in this world, be it for good or ill. You know that those who have what you have, are by and large above any laws but God's. So tonight, you might say we are petitioning you on God's behalf," he smiled as he said it. "And on that of humanity, freedom and truth.

"Without you, those who killed Ghisella Wallenberg and who wish to bring about a seventy-five-year-old dream of the triumph of tyranny, will most likely fulfill what Hitler called the Endsieg Protocol: the Final Victory. Without you, the people on our side of the table, who risked so much to uncover the truth, may soon be silenced or killed. This has already been attempted on more than one occasion.

"Our plan is a simple one. We wish to pit our own cabal of power players against theirs, in a kind of Mutual Assured Destruction. Not a war, you understand, but a sufficient threat to keep war from happening. We intend to throw down the gauntlet and make it known to the other side that Hitler's secret is a secret no longer, for a diary that tells the whole story is in our hands, and the Endsieg Protocol document itself, signed by the Führer, is already in the possession of those with power equal to their own. In short, the people at this table.

"In this room alone is the talent and power to create a bestselling book, a worldwide whistle-blowing news story, a movie, a TV documentary, a scientific exposé of monumental proportion. *If* you so choose. In this room alone is the power to derail a political juggernaut headed for the Oval Office. In this room is the power to stop the Fourth Reich's Final Victory—maybe not forever, but for a period of time long enough to make them realize there is a resistance movement as determined and powerful as they are.

"We are not fools, ladies and gentlemen. We don't expect to *win* in some spectacular Hollywood ending," Fitz tipped his head toward Harriet Mandelbaum. "Real life doesn't work like cinema, more's the pity. But perhaps we can slow them down for a bit, maybe even long enough so that we and others of like mind can figure out just what the next steps in preserving our freedom must be.

"Michell Obama reminded us that courage can be contagious, and hope can take on a life of its own. In the kind of future the Endsieg Protocol wants to give us, neither courage nor hope will have the chance of a snowball in hell. So tonight, I'll leave you with a line from the diary of a once-famous, now-forgotten hero, who is known to us as Ghisella Wallenberg, but was once known to history as the Magdalena, hero of the Polish Resistance, courier and spy. In her diary she tells us she learned something incalculably important in the most powerful resistance movement of World War II: 'Sometimes,' she wrote, 'the removal of one critical stone from a mighty dam can cause a flood that cannot be contained.' Tonight, we ask you to help us move that stone."

He looked the room over, letting his wise eyes rest a moment on each at the table. Then he spoke again.

"I'll take no more of your time. We have history, science and political skullduggery for you to vet before you can make an informed decision, so I'll next be handing the floor over to a man who has lived the horror our enemies represent, one who can speak eloquently about those whom we hope to keep from fulfilling their mission. It is my great pleasure to introduce you to Itzak Mendelsohn of the Wiesenthal Center."

As Fitz sat down and Itzak rose, Harriet's son Simon leaned toward his mother and whispered, "If that guy doesn't have an agent, we should nail him for a speaking tour…" She silenced him with a raised eyebrow. "I'm just saying…" he trailed off as Itzak began his part of the presentation. After him, it would be up to Annie and the Babushkas to explain the science.

118

Annie surveyed her overprivileged audience before she began to speak. Itzak had introduced her by citing her extraordinary scientific credentials, but it was the gravitas of her demeanor that had quieted the room.

"The first thing you need to accept, before we attempt to explain the significance of the secrets Ghisella von Zechandorff Wallenberg left in our care, is this: What you think you know about history is a tiny fraction of the truth. What you think you know about science is even less than that. What you've been told is 'cutting-edge science' is actually generations behind what's already going on at DARPA, the NSA and other experimental laboratories all over the planet.

"You are too sophisticated an audience *not* to already know that the government we see has its strings pulled by the government we can't see. The Council of 13, the Order, the Illuminati, the Committee of 300, the Club of Rome and many other names have been ascribed by conspiracy theorists to those who rule our lives, our governments and our perceptions of reality through careful disinformation and news that is vetted before it gets to us. Whatever we choose to call them, these are the puppet masters. They are very, *very* dangerous, and they are the ones we are pitting ourselves against."

She looked around at her rapt audience, waiting for that to sink in. "What we're about to tell you is scientifically astonishing. Our opinion about its validity is unprovable by ordinary means, because it has been protected by layers and decades of obfuscation, redacted or deleted documents, top-secret compartmentalization and all the other covert means that world manipulators at the highest level have at their disposal. So I'm afraid you must take our collective scientific credentials as validation for the fact that we are not wasting your time here.

"We believe the documents we've assembled as a result of Ghisella's secret will expose decades of political subterfuge, assassinations of those in high places who sought to reveal pieces of this toxic puzzle, and many other nefarious projects that would turn your stomachs. Her information was well worth killing for and I assure you, it has been killed for at many turns in the road.

"Here's the crux of the story we wish to tell you: We believe the Nazis invented a new science, a new physics. One that could open interstellar space to our exploration, interplanetary mining to those who could reach and control the planets first: to the Powers That Be at the very top of the food chain, men and women whose fortunes have increased exponentially because of a tech they've controlled since WWII that propelled them into almost godlike superiority on this planet, and beyond that, into control of interstellar space.

"Ask yourselves this: What if the moon and Mars have already been colonized and exploited for the benefit of certain interests? What if medical steps toward immortality are much further along than our medical science has led us to believe? What if the knowledge is withheld from the common man so that only the chosen survive Armageddon? What if we are pawns in a long game being played by master gamers?"

She paused again, took a deep breath and continued.

"*What if* the secret science Ghisella protected for a lifetime has already primed the playing field and the agenda is nearly fulfilled? What if all they need do—let's call them the Fourth Reich—is to put only one more puzzle piece in place to make their mad dreams come true? And that piece is Hitler's spawn in the White House?"

There was disturbed murmuring among the listeners, then anticipatory, nervous silence.

"What difference would it make, you might ask? And I would answer you that the presidency in the hands of a despot has immense power! He can decimate the news media with threats and repudiation. He can silence critics and dissidents, even jail them. He can militarize the police. He can declare martial law. He can curtail rights and imprison unjustly: we are already without habeas corpus, and for the first time in our history, a man or woman can be whisked off the street, taken to a black site, tortured or killed, all without benefit of a lawyer or the rule of law itself. Such an unscrupulous president could change laws by presidential order, especially if he controls the Congress and the judiciary. He can start a war to distract us and fill the pockets of his special-interest friends. With the help of an obedient Congress he can reinstitute the draft to provide cannon fodder for an unjust war and can sell this idea to a nation already frightened into false nationalism. He can create a war to control space itself.

"In truth, the list of potential damage is such that America, and with it the world, might never recover either civilization or democracy in the wake of such an onslaught … and the noble experiment of our Founding Fathers that has allowed the greatest steps forward for humanity since the Magna Carta could be consigned to the dustbin of history.

"Ghisella and her father saw the handwriting on the wall. We do, too. That's why we're risking so much and asking your extraordinary help.

"My protégés Matrix, Bridget, Lulu and T-square will show you certain diagrams and schematics that you most likely won't understand; indeed, there are physicists in major universities who might not fully understand them, but we hope to convey to you the level of scholarship and research that have been lavished on verifying the validity of the work that has been left in our keeping by Mrs. Wallenberg.

"If any of you have a working knowledge of physics, please feel free to ask your questions of these extraordinary young people. And I caution you not to let their youth unnerve you. Among them there are multiple doctorates from Cambridge, Oxford, Harvard, Yale, Stanford and MIT.

"The only possible way to fight such power is with power they will respect. We're not such fools that we think we can stop them forever, but if we can stop them for now … maybe we can give the world a fighting chance."

Annie searched the faces arrayed in front of her and decided it was going to be a long, long night.

119

The wrangling lasted much of the night. The younger members of the BSI marveled at the stamina of those in the room who were in their eighties and nineties. It said a lot about both genetics and the strength generated by passion. Fitz marveled at the remarkable presentation his people had created to showcase the evidence they'd amassed.

"It's a great story, well told," Artie Aronowicz said, rising to applaud after the multimedia presentation had ended. "Bravo! Should be a movie! But I gotta tell you, I still fail to see why any one of us should take the risk of this thing getting out of hand. Let's say you're right about the scope of the power we'd be up against—the ruthlessness of those we'd be putting on notice—do you have any idea how much we'd stand to lose? Well, it's a hell of a lot. Who knows how many of our clients are part of this whole cabal-thing you want us to buck? Do you think the kind of people who can afford the hundred-million-dollar apartments I sell are *ever* saints? No way! And frankly, I don't give a rat's ass how evil they are if they plunk down their cash on the barrel. Why should I risk my own business by antagonizing the bad guys? My clients are probably *all* bad guys!"

He looked around the table at the disapproving frowns he'd provoked, then tried to backpedal a little. "I gotta say, guys, I'm in the middle of the road on this whole proposition. It's just too big an ask with no upside for us!" When no one spoke up to agree, he added a petulant coda. "Come on now, am I the only one here with the balls to say this out loud?"

"Down where I come from," Hutch's whiskey voice interrupted, "we don't think it takes balls to chicken out of a fight. In fact, we pretty much think just the opposite. We got a saying in Texas: 'ain't nothin' in the middle of the road but yellow stripes and dead armadillos.'" He smiled benevolently as he said it. "Far as I can see, this little troop here is just asking us for some help to make it a *fair* fight. Big kids against big kids."

"Damned straight!" Harriet Mandelbaum agreed in her deeply Brooklyn-tinged voice. "My brass ovaries couldn't agree more. They're in the game and so am I."

Chagrined, Artie snapped back at her, "I didn't say I wasn't *in,* Harriet, I'm just the voice of reason here, pointing out I see no advantage for us whatsoever."

"So you'll do it as a mitzvah, not for personal gain. You've got too much money already, Artie." She turned to Fitz. "Put us both down as yesses. I'll talk him around."

And so it went, back and forth, smart, shrewd, self-serving and selfless, all fighting for the floor. *Not a naïf among them,* Maeve thought, watching and feeling the roiling emotions of every player in her own empathic gut. They questioned the journal, the photography, the history, the science. They questioned why the police couldn't handle it. They questioned motives and credentials ad nauseum. *Just as they should,* she thought, admiring the lot of them for being there at all.

"Why the hell should I believe some geek with one blue eyebrow when she talks physics?" Sidney Frangellica asked pointedly.

"Because she has a doctorate in theoretical physics from Oxford," Annie snapped.

"And because she's my daughter," A.D. added with quiet authority that seemed to settle that matter, but didn't stop Sidney.

"And why the hell should any of us give a flying fuck what happens to the rest of these people?" he said truculently. "I mean nothing personal here, but we don't even know them, for Christ's sake. They're *nothing* to us."

"And that's just what the Nazis said about *us*, isn't it, Sidney? Isn't that why they could stuff us into ovens with a clear conscience?" Leila Landrue said in a voice that halted the rising babble. Then she turned to her son Lawrence, who now ran the family business. "Tell them we're in,

Larry dear, and give them whatever they need. I'm going home to bed." She was, after all, ninety-five. And so it went, deep into the night.

Before morning they had eleven yesses, two I'll-think-about-its, one definite no, and a relatively cohesive plan.

120

It was agreed that one of the counter-cabal should be chosen as spokesperson. Lawrence Landrue was a dignified sixty-five-year-old who looked a good deal younger. Fit, golf-tanned, confident of his place in the world, the good-looking heir to a vast skin-care fortune, he'd never lacked for anything, but unlike many sons of the rich, he had always approached his good fortune in having chosen the right parents with both gratitude and a practical eye. He'd been given a great deal by fate and the lucky sperm club, he reasoned, and had no problem working hard to make it a great deal more. He'd also been given the wherewithal for that. He was smart—smarter, indeed, than his parents—but all the family skills were complimentary parts of the magic that was the family business. Salesmanship, marketing genius, accounting, work ethic, creative diligence. But of all the family members, his charm was the most natural. The most believable, and that had served him well.

Of the eleven billionaires who had not only signed on but were willing to be the face of the confrontation, he also had the least explosive temper and the best control, so after the ballots and a lot of wrangling for position, he was chosen as presenter of the plan to the other side. He'd impressed them by saying he felt the confrontation could be kept decorous in tone, as the opposition would recognize the assembled power, whether their counter-cabal all attended, or their names were simply presented on a list. The names were impressive enough to make the enemy believe this might be just the front line of a far larger and even more formidable force.

"I feel as if I've just been elected Pope," he quipped when his role had been decided. "Send up the white smoke."

"Hold on there, young fella! Not so fast." Hutch Walker, who'd been silent as he watched and listened much of the night, spoke up.

"That's all fine and dandy as far as it goes, but it puts us only halfway to where we need to go. You'll do fine for Pope, son—you got the smarts and the strut for it—but we're still missing one important thing for our little confrontation, and that's a bully. Everybody at this table knows the velvet glove ain't worth a damn without an iron hand in it.

"So when we lay it out to these two peckerwoods who are just the messengers to the bigger kids, you can be as subtle as a high-priced whore about what's goin' down here—that's just good sense and good manners—but we gotta let 'em know if they don't comply with our demands we'll come down on 'em like God Almighty Hisself has sent us to clean up Babylon!

"Now, I'm the best bully at this table, far as I can see, so I'm electing myself to do that job. Larry here can sweet talk 'em and I'll scare the crap out of 'em. How's that double whammy sound to y'all?" The tired table broke out in spontaneous applause.

All that was left was to hammer out the details. "Cain't let 'em think this is a negotiation," Hutch said as he began to list the demands he'd penned as the night progressed. "They gotta know from the get-go we got their king in check. Get 'em by the balls, their hearts and minds will follow.

"I made a list," he said with a nod to Lawrence.

1. The Resistance has the Endsieg Protocol *and* scientifically dated journals authenticating it.
2. We intend to make the Protocol and diary public, in a book-and-movie deal that's already been made, so the story's gonna be right out there in front of God and everybody, come hell or high water.
3. With the secret no longer a secret, anyone who chooses to follow the same trail to the truth we did is free to do so, but the current investigators are passin' the torch.

4. Senator Reese will withdraw from the primary race for unspecified personal reasons.

5. Those who already know the truth will not be harmed. Documents have been placed in appropriate legal and media hands so if anyone on our side is hurt, the rest of our evidence will be made public.

6. The concession we'll make to the other side to get this deal made, is that the names of those who carry the Hitler bloodline will not be revealed unless the terms of our agreement are not met, in which case all bets are off.

"I think that'll settle their hash for the moment, don't you, Larry?" he said, not expecting to be shouted down. "To paraphrase old Stephen Vincent Benét, 'If a New Yorker and a Texan ain't a match for the devil, we might as well give the country back to the Indians.'"

Larry Landrue knew a good deal when he heard one, so he said, "I believe the confrontation will be relatively cordial, Hutch. They'll see the people on our side of the table as the possible tip of an iceberg as big as their own. They'll admit nothing without lawyers present anyway, and simply retire to their corners to assess their options."

It didn't take long after that to make arrangements.

As he was leaving, Lawrence smiled at Maeve. "I assume, Ms. Donovan, you will let us know the most auspicious timing for our meeting with the opposition?" he said. "My mother told me she's heard splendid things about your astrological prognostications from several of her friends, and she believes in having everything, including the stars, on our side for such an important moment."

Maeve smiled acknowledgement of the compliment and handed him an astrological chart. "I'm delighted to hear that," she said. "Please give my regards to your mother and tell her March 3 is the day our Resistance should make its stand."

As she passed by Hutch Walker on her way out, Harriet Mandelbaum said, “Consider me your understudy for best bully in the room, kid. Just in case you get struck by an asteroid or some such before the third.”

“I’ve no doubt you’d be up to the job, Miz Mandelbaum,” he said with an admiring chuckle. “If y’all are ever in Texas, we should compare our techniques.” She winked at him and headed for the door.

121

The announcement was all over the news. The charismatic young senator from New York was withdrawing his hat from the ring of primary hopefuls. The needs of his New York constituents took precedence over his own personal needs and ambitions, he said. His family preferred that his children be older before they were placed in the presidential limelight. He was not withdrawing forever, he assured the news media. Just for now.

Fitz turned off Chris Matthews, who was doing a splendid job of trying to figure out the truth of what the hell was going on, and turned to face Maeve, who was dressed for a date with Declan.

"Well, luv, we haven't quite saved the world," he said with a regretful note in his voice. "Just our wee corner of it, and maybe the Lincoln bedroom for a while."

"But we've saved *us*," she answered, "and those we care about. No mean feat, Dad. And we've been faithful to Ghisella, don't forget that. Her story will be told now and we can leave it to others to follow the same bloodline trail we did if they care enough."

"So you think we won by not totally losing, eh?" He chuckled at her pragmatic—or was it just optimistic? take on life.

"I think we won by stopping them for now and letting them know that neither the White House nor Final Victory will be theirs without a helluva fight, because the good guys aren't out of the game and the bad guys have been outflanked for now. No war is won with a single battle, Dad. You've told me that yourself." She smiled at him.

"We stayed alive, unraveled a monumental cold case, stopped a probable takeover, saved a historic document from never seeing the light of day and alerted the world that old and pernicious evil still needs to be held at bay. Not too shabby."

"When you put it like *that* ..." he said, his expression softened by the realism that comes with age. "It doesn't sound too bad, does it?"

"Ghisella's headstone is ready, by the way," Maeve added. "We can have our little memorial service for her now. I thought maybe this weekend would be good." The doorbell rang and he saw not the sheer joy he'd expected, but rather an expression that said she wasn't looking forward to seeing Dec tonight.

"Trouble in paradise?" he asked, not wanting to pry, just to show concern and offer an ear or a shoulder if either would help.

"A little," she said, "but I'll figure it out." She leaned down to kiss him on the cheek before leaving in the car Dec had sent for her.

122

Dougal opened the door to Maeve, delight in his eyes and smile. He'd hoped for years that Declan would come to his senses and realize the opportunity for real love that was right within his reach if he'd just get his blinders off and his arse in gear. But happiness dimmed the minute he saw Maeve's troubled face, and so he hurried her inside to the library he knew she loved, and went to alert Dec to her arrival in person rather than by intercom.

"Something's up with the lass," he said conspiratorially. "I think you'd best tread gently on her heart tonight, lad, if I may be bold enough to give you some advice."

Dec, just having dressed, was slipping into his shoes. He'd felt uncharacteristically happy all afternoon and had even found himself whistling earlier in the day, an unheard-of event that seemed to have been called forth by his anticipation of the evening's pleasures. He frowned a little at the unexpected report, thanked Dougal and headed to the library. On seeing her standing with her face to the fire, not the door, he knew Dougal was right.

Maeve turned when she heard Dec enter the room and he walked to where she stood, then wrapped his arms around her. "Out with it," he said, his voice a little playful and more than a little worried.

"I can't let myself be in love with you," she blurted.

"And why the devil not?" he inquired, genuinely baffled. "And besides, you already *are* in love with me, if memory serves, and I with you, so what the hell happened between when I left you this morning and this minute to have you in such a dither?" He held her out at arm's length, not just so he could see her face but because he had a sudden fear she could slip away. She looked stricken, he thought, by something she truly feared. What could it be that couldn't be fixed?

"Do you love me, Maeve?" he asked, looking for solid ground.

"I do," she answered without hesitation, "and that's the problem, don't you see? We live such different lives, Dec, how can they ever be made to mesh? And how long will it be before you miss the Kellogg's Variety Pack of beautiful young women you're always seen with? How long before the novelty wears off or we have a fight, and you look to greener fields? Newer thrills, someone who loves living in the limelight and being on Page Six with you?"

He stared at her, not knowing whether to laugh or cry. It wasn't an unreasonable fear. Men in his position changed partners as often as they changed their Gucci loafers. But that really wasn't the life he'd ever wanted for himself. He'd wanted love and family and he'd had that for a time, so he knew the difference.

He took a deep breath. "What else?" he prompted. "I need to hear it all. That's only fair, Maeve."

"Okay," she agreed, trying to arrange her thoughts logically. "I love my home. I love living there with Fitz and Finn and Rory whenever she can get there to visit. It's my sanctuary. *They are* my sanctuary. I was so shattered after my divorce, on such unsteady ground, as if so much of what I'd loved and hoped and dreamed had been pulled out from under me …" *There's that stricken look again,* he thought. *Now we're getting to the truth of it.*

"If that kind of nova-ing of my life were to happen to me again, I honestly don't think I could live through it—at least not whole. I struggled so hard to make a good life for Finn and me. Tried to make sense of what had happened. Tried to forgive myself for marrying someone so feckless and robbing Finn of the great father she deserved. How could I have believed in such a con man and put our lives and hearts in his hands? Believed he loved us as he lied about absolutely everything beyond hello?

"How could I ever trust another man? I used to ask myself that every time I went out on a date." She was biting her lower lip, trying to keep the real truth from being spoken, he thought. The most painful truth. Finally, she blurted in a sort of anguished whisper, "But the real question was how could I ever trust *myself* again. Trust my own judgment. Trust myself to make the right choice to love someone …"

"Ah, Maeve," he said as gently as she'd ever heard him say anything. "There it is, then, the heart of it." He pulled her down beside him on the sofa, and he wanted more than anything to just reach out and fold her into his arms and soothe away such fears and such raw pain, even after so many years. But he didn't do that.

If he was to make a stand, he thought, *he had to do it right.*

"I've listened to you, my Maeve, and now you must listen to me. You see, I've given this love of ours every bit as much thinking as you have, whether you believe that or not. And to tell you the truth, I've asked myself some of the same questions. But here's the truth of it, my girl.

"I loved my wife. I loved my unborn child, and had I been given the chance by capricious fate, I would have loved them forever. I'm not a philanderer by nature and it's naught but the truth that they took a part of my heart with them to the grave. The rest of it, I think I all but shut down. It was as if being open to love again would have been a betrayal of Eileen and the baby we called Liam.

"And so yes, I have dated a great many women, some of them interesting, some strategically advantageous, some merely beautiful or available in a moment of true loneliness …" He stopped, breathed, and began again.

"And then there was you, Maeve. My friend. My confidante. Someone who demanded nothing but friendship and gave me something I didn't even know I was seeking that maybe has no name—or hadn't, until I read Ghisella's journal and remembered it was the truest kind of love. You gave me respite, understanding, hope, and you were right about the safety of our flirtation. It was just enough to assuage the great need in me that I couldn't acknowledge, the need for someone to love truly and be loved by. A safe place to lay bare our souls and tell the truth, just as Ghisella and Gerhardt did.

"Dougal knew better all the while, it seems. He tells me he knew we loved each other years ago, but worried we'd never be smart enough to actually let ourselves *fall* in love.

"And then, through the bizarre grace of Ghisella's life and death, we experienced each other in the trenches. That's when I knew, you see. I knew so viscerally that if anything happened to you, I would be undone … bereft in the way I'd been when my well-planned life fell to ruin the first time. Perhaps you knew the same.

"I think Dougal's right. We've been in love for some time, but were too afraid to admit it even to ourselves because it meant we'd have to make life-altering decisions, and we might get mortally wounded again. But in the end, Maeve, the heart wants what the heart wants.

"As to all the rest of your worries, we can handle them, luv. Living arrangements are flexible, love of family's a given. We would never abandon Fitz or Finn or Rory just because we love each other. Did you know that Finn and I have been on the case for a while, to get you to think of me as more than just a pal? I think I've even got Fitz on my side after all that's happened to us."

He stopped for breath, then stood up, only to kneel down in front of her so he could see her face and she his. He brushed back the hair that had fallen forward on her cheek and brushed away her tears.

"So here's my commitment to you, Maeve Donovan," he said very solemnly, "and I hope you know it's my blanket answer to all the objections you've raised and any more you may think of in the next sixty years or so.

"I love you. If you'll let me, I'll love you forever. I give you my solemn word that I value truth and honor and fidelity as you do. You can trust me with your life and all you hold dear and I will never, as long as God gives me life and breath, betray that trust."

They held onto each other for a very long time after that before they climbed the stairs to his room without touching the oysters that Dougal had thoughtfully left out for them on the dining room table.

They talked long into the night, remembering all the things they wanted to remember. Finally, they undressed and Dec handed her a shirt of his to wear because she'd brought nothing with her and had not intended to stay the night. He knew enough to let her choose the timing, the rhythm of what would happen next—indeed, if it might happen at all—tonight. He felt as if too sudden a move might make her fly like a startled bird, and wondered at the fool of a man she'd been married to who had wounded her so very deeply.

It was late when they found their way to his bed and he reached for her, still not altogether certain she wouldn't flee.

But instead, she let his fingers trail gently down her cheek to her throat to her breast. He touched her nipple and felt it respond, felt her arch and stretch her long body as if expanding out of an invisible confinement. A butterfly from the chrysalis. He sensed a deliberate letting go, as if having made her decision, she was peeling away a protective cloak and letting it fall wherever it might.

He knew in that odd, intuitive moment that she had decided to love him back, and the knowledge made him feel giddy as a schoolboy. But he wasn't a schoolboy, and that was why he could feel the subtle change in her—could feel it in her touch, so light and delicate as her fingers sought him, as he sought her. See it in her half-shut eyes, feel it in her altered breathing and in the trust he sensed in the openness of her movements beside him.

Her breasts were full beneath his hands. He touched his lips to each breast tentatively, exploring possibilities, then, feeling the response, he touched her in all the ways he knew. Testing limits, circling, kissing, touching all the while, trailing his other hand down her taut body to where they both wanted him to be. Loving the wetness of her, moving his intuitive fingers inside her as she tightened against them, pulsing around them, wanting so much more. Opening herself to so much more.

Her hands were exploring him, too, but he whispered *let me do it all, just this once, luv, let me give you everything I've longed to give. Let me make you feel everything a woman can with a man who truly loves her.*

There was a moment of hesitation as she absorbed the authenticity of the words, then she lay back, opening herself to him and his touch, his lips, his thrusting, stroking intimacy that blotted out the world and worries and fears and foolishness for a while. Letting in such waves of pleasure that it made her gasp and ask for more.

She wanted him deeper, deeper inside her. Wanted to be subsumed by his entry and his love. She felt him in every cell as the waves broke over both of them and they were lost in the torrent that's older than time and sweeter than all the rest of life combined.

"I love you, Maeve," he said when he could speak again and she could feel both joy and urgency in his voice. "I finally know how very much I love you."

She smiled at him and he smiled back, the lazy smile of utter satiety. "I love you, too, Dec," she said, "and if I'm ever able to move my limbs again, I'll show you just how much."

His smile was knowing. "I thought you just did," he said.

Epilogue

"All will be okay in the end.
If it is not okay, it is not yet the end."
— Proverb

123

The headstone was a simple one. Far simpler than the ornate angels and gargoyle-guarded mausoleums that marked the ancient cemetery all around them. It read

Ghisella Magdalena von Zechandorff Steiner Wallenberg
1922 – 2017
Endsieg

Fitz smiled with satisfaction at the two small triumphs that perhaps no future person looking at this stone would ever understand, but he and his little band of stalwarts understood. He had included Ghisella's maiden name, of which she was so justly proud, and left out Manfred Gruber's name, which she despised. And he had added the name she'd earned in battle as well as what she had achieved with the help of those who stood with her now in this cemetery.

Endsieg. Final victory.

"Is there a prayer you'd like to say, Dad?" Rory asked quietly as she took his arm in hers.

"There is," he answered, his voice a little huskier than usual. "I'm told it was inspired by the Kaddish and written by two poet-rabbis." He took a piece of paper from his pocket and unfolded it.

"You think then that she was Jewish after all?" Itzak asked, surprised, moving in a little closer.

"I have no evidence of that, my friend," Fitz replied, "but she died to bear witness to Hitler's lunacy that had its beginnings in his hatred for the Jews. And the one man she truly loved was a Jew. So somehow, I think she would like this to be our farewell—for her and all she loved and lost."

He put his reading glasses on his nose firmly, as much to hide the moisture in his eyes as to read, and he began to recite the prayer.

"At the rising of the sun and at its going down,
We remember them

He thought how very true that was of all the lost ones ...

At the beginning of the year and when it ends,
We remember them.

When we are weary and in need of strength,
We remember them.

When we are lost and sick at heart,
We remember them.

When we have joy we crave to share,
We remember them.

When we have decisions that are difficult to make,
We remember them.

When we have achievements that are based on theirs,
We remember them.

For as long as we live, they too will live;
for they are now a part of us,
As we remember them."

She was no longer just the Old Lady next door.

He knew her now as he had not known her in life. Through her story, she had become his friend. And strangely, having never really known her in life, he would now miss her in death, and he would remember her. If the Mandelbaums made the film of her life as they said they would, perhaps she'd be remembered by many. Fitz shook his head at the paradox that is life, and Maeve, sensing his mood, took his hand in hers.

Finn raised her camera and snapped a photo of the group as they stood in various modes of silent reverie around the grave. Grand, Mom, AR, T, Mimi, Georgia, Itzak, Annie and the Babushkas, Declan, even Lieutenant Cochrane was there—every one of them had played a part in the Endsieg. What a funny little army they comprised. She could see the beginnings of the documentary in her mind's eye as she surveyed the faces she'd just captured in her images, and smiled just a little.

Grand had been right after all. Once in a while, Goliath doesn't stand a chance.

Acknowledgements

Nobody writes a book alone, as the process of bringing a story to life is far more arduous and consuming than most of the world dreams.

I've been particularly blessed by the presence in my life of a few stalwart allies on the path who make all the difference in my life and work. For them no thanks could possibly be enough.

Conny Cash, my beloved sister, who has played a pivotal role in every book I've ever written ... who never gives up on me or my work and without whose loving help and counsel I could never have seen my writing dreams come true.

Dakota Cash, my beloved daughter, who makes me laugh in the clinches, and always, always assumes that together we can find a way to make all things go right.

Diana Zitnay, whose skills in manuscript typing and in keeping track of all the complexities of my stories, are nothing short of miraculous and who's equally amazing good humor encourages me all the way to the finish line.

Megan Zitnay, who through this and several other books kept my office running like clockwork, made me smile when needed and made it possible to actually find things in the ever-expanding research files!

Beverly Guarascio, who arrived in my life many years ago as a faithful reader and has remained ever since as a cherished friend.

The Donovans and
The Bleecker Street Irregulars
return in:

A Murder on Mott Street

by Cathy Cash Spellman

A Murder on Mott Street

1

"Another OD?" the weary Assistant M.E. for Manhattan asked as yet another gurney was wheeled in. It had been an unusually busy Saturday night at the busiest Morgue on the East Coast.

"Yeah, maybe, but not just any old OD," the man responded conspiratorially. "You listen to electro jazz?"

The M.E. looked up enquiringly. "What's that got to do with the price of fish?"

"Your OD is #3 on the charts, my man! Or should I say *was*? He's *Jonny Wu,* a real hot ticket, on the VIP list at every club in town. Platinum sales, awesome lifestyle, dead at 24 from a massive heart attack caused by too much of some unnamed illegal substance, unless you find anything else that coulda sent him early to the Pearly Gates."

"No shit? 24? That sucks," the young ME pointed to a slot in the queue of gurneys. "Does the press know?"

The EMT shook his head. "Nobody knows yet but us chickens, the unies at the scene and Detective Cochrane from the 6th.

"Okay," the M.E. said. "I'll call the boss and roust him from some disease dinner he's at. It's a fundraiser for one of his wife's charities, so he'll probably give me a promotion for having helped him escape."

The EMT started to leave, then turned. "Say, Doc, take a look at this guy's awesome ink and tell me what you think. It's mostly Chinese or some other kind of Asian. Real Bruce Lee stuff and there's a bruise under his arm like nothing I ever seen."

"Thanks, Freddie. I'll look at both. Just try to keep this on the downlow until I get the Boss into the act, will you? You know how testy he gets about leaks before he's figured out what's what. He'll want to make a statement to the press and all."

"Sure thing, doc," Freddie said, over his shoulder and waved as he headed out.

Dr. Matt Malone opened the body bag and sighed at the waste. The guy was fucking gorgeous – almost too perfect to be human. Eurasian of some sort and really tall, so maybe a Chinese/Japanese/American mix? Handsome as fuck, rich, successful, an international celeb. What was it that would make a guy like this throw away all that for a recreational high? Just too much fame and money too soon, maybe? It was easy to feel immortal at 24. Even easier to be stupid. He unzipped the bag further and did a cursory check of the dead man's arms. Clean as a whistle, not a needle mark in sight. Of course there were other places to shoot up, but still…

The ink was spectacular. Work of pure genius. Not just tats but wild Asian landscapes like those Hiroshige woodcuts at the Met. At least a quarter of the kid's body was covered with exquisite scenes of some mythic Asian world.

Intrigued, Malone moved the guy's arms to get a better look at how the artwork wrapped around to the back. Then he saw the bruise. In the armpit – how the hell do you get that badly bruised there? – it was shaped like a star. Okay. So maybe this was not your run of the mill Saturday night OD.

He heard the door open behind him and turned. The beautiful young blonde doctor named Mimi something-or-other was standing, staring at the man on the gurney with her mouth open and her hand covering it as if to hold back a scream.

"Oh my God!" she blurted sounding stricken. "Tell me that isn't Johnny Wu!"

Weird, he thought. She was rumored to be some high falutin' socialite when she wasn't doctoring. Otherwise two thirds of the guys in the building would have tried to nail her by now. And socialites weren't usually awed by stars. They fucked them, maybe, but they weren't awed.

Her unusual China-blue eyes were shiny with tears when she looked up at him. "That's Jonny isn't it?" she whispered. "He's a really good friend of my *best* friend… and her family. I went to his 24th birthday party three weeks ago. What on earth happened to him? He was in perfect physical shape – I mean absolutely perfect. He was a great martial artist and took amazing care of his body. Didn't even drink…" A single tear escaped her efforts to hold it back and she swiped at it, embarrassed by this undoctor-like show of grief, then spoke again.

"He was unbelievably talented," she said quickly, as if trying to take the curse off having shown too much emotion. "He just signed a recording contract that would have made him independent for life. And he was such a good guy…" She tried to get hold of herself with some obvious effort. "He shared all his good luck with family, friends, the neighborhood…"

"You come down here for something, doc?" Matt prompted trying to help her out.

Mimi took a deep breath and collected herself.

"I've got some personal effects from Mrs. Morrissey," she said, trying for her best doctor voice and laying a box on the desk. "Her daughter will want them. She's a very sweet kid and really devastated. Would you see that she gets her mother's things, please?"

"I thought you just did babies, Doc," he said surprised.

"I do," she answered and her blonde waves bounced as she shook her head. God, she really was a looker as well as being rich, he thought. Some people get all the goodies.

"Mrs. Morrissey's daughter has a baby in my NICU, so I got to know the family…"

"Would you let me know what you find out about Jonny at autopsy, Matt, please. My friend will be hit pretty hard by this."

"Sure thing. Are you on night shift? This one's going to be top priority so check with me in a couple of hours."

Mimi took her phone out of her pocket as she left the morgue, and dialed Finn Donovan.

"Oh, my dear, dear Finn," she said softly, the minute her friend answered. "I have some pretty awful news that I don't want to have to tell you, but I think you'd rather hear it from me than on the news." She heard the quick intake of breath on the other end and realized she should have let her friend know it wasn't family she was calling about. She'd never known a family as close as Finn's.

"It's Jonny," she said quickly. "Something terrible has happened to Jonny Wu..."